one of the
decades. A Comp
she has been awarde
Literature, Spain's Pr
Catalunya Award and th
Lifetime's Distinguished
other international awards.  es in north London.

By the same author

NOVELS

The Grass is Singing
The Golden Notebook
Briefing for a Descent into Hell
The Summer Before the Dark
Memoirs of a Survivor
Diary of a Good Neighbour
If the Old Could . . .
The Good Terrorist
The Fifth Child
Playing the Game
    (illustrated by Charlie Adlard)
Love, Again
Mara and Dann
The Fifth Child
Ben, in the World
The Sweetest Dream
The Story of General Dann and Mara's
    Daughter, Griot and the Snow Dog
The Cleft

'Canopus in Argos: Archives' series
Re: Colonised Planet 5, Shikasta
The Marriages Between Zones
    Three, Four, and Five
The Sirian Experiments
The Making of the Representative for
    Planet 8
Documents Relating to the Sentimental
    Agents in the Volyen Empire

'Children of Violence' novel-sequence
Martha Quest
A Proper Marriage
A Ripple from the Storm
Landlocked
The Four-Gated City

OPERAS

The Marriages Between Zones Three,
    Four and Five (Music by Philip Glass)
The Making of the representative for
    Planet 8 (Music by Philip Glass)

SHORT STORIES

Five
The Habit of Loving
A Man and Two Women
The Story of a Non-Marrying Man
    and Other Stories
Winter in July
The Black Madonna
This Was the Old Chief's Country
    (Collected African Stories, Vol. 1)
The Sun Between Their Feet
    (Collected African Stories, Vol. 2)
To Room Nineteen
    (Collected Stories, Vol. 1)
The Temptation of Jack Orkney
    (Collected Stories, Vol. 2)
London Observed
The Old Age of El Magnifico
Particularly Cats
Rufus the Survivor
On Cats
The Grandmothers

POETRY

Fourteen Poems

DRAMA

Each His Own Wilderness
Play with a Tiger
The Singing Door

NON-FICTION

In Pursuit of the English
Going Home
A Small Personal Voice
Prisons We Choose to Live Inside
The Wind Blows Away Our Words
African Laughter
Time Bites

AUTOBIOGRAPHY

Under My Skin: Volume 1
Walking in the Shade: Volume 2

Doris Lessing

A Proper Marriage

Book Two of the
'Children of Violence' series

Flamingo
An Imprint of HarperCollins*Publishers*

Flamingo
An imprint of HarperCollins*Publishers*
77–85 Fulham Palace Road,
Hammersmith, London W6 8JB

Flamingo is a registered trade mark of
HarperCollins Publishers Limited

www.**fire**and**water**.com

A Flamingo Modern Classic 2002

Previously published in paperback by
Grafton 1966, Paladin 1990 and Flamingo 1993

First published in Great Britain by
Michael Joseph 1954

Copyright © Doris Lessing 1954

Photograph of Doris Lessing © Chris Saunders 2002

ISBN 978-0-586-08999-6

Set in Melior

A Proper Marriage

Part One

'You shouldn't make jokes,' Alice said, *'if it makes you so unhappy.'*

LEWIS CARROLL

Chapter One

It was half past four in the afternoon.

Two young women were loitering down the pavement in the shade of the sunblinds that screened the shop windows. The grey canvas of the blinds was thick, yet the sun, apparently checked, filled the long arcade with a yellow glare. It was impossible to look outwards towards the sun-filled street, and unpleasant to look in towards the mingling reflections in the window glass. They walked, therefore, with lowered gaze as if concerned about their feet. Their faces were strained and tired. One was talking indefatigably, the other unresponsive, and – it was clear – not so much from listlessness as from a stubborn opposition. There was something about the couple which suggested guardian and ward.

At last one exclaimed, with irritated cheerfulness, 'Matty, if you don't get a move on, we'll be late for the doctor.'

'But, Stella, you've just said we had half an hour to fill in,' said Martha as promptly as if she had been waiting for just this point of fact to arise, so that she might argue it out to its conclusions. Stella glanced sharply at her, but before she could speak Martha continued, deepening the humorous protest, because the resentment was so strong, 'It was you who seemed to think I couldn't get through another day of married life without seeing the doctor, not me. Why you had to fix an appointment for this afternoon I can't think.' She laughed, to soften the complaint.

'It's not easy to get an appointment right away with Dr Stern. You're lucky I could arrange it for you.'

But Martha refused to be grateful. She raised her eyebrows, appeared about to argue – and shrugged irritably.

Stella gave Martha another sharp look, tightened her lips with calculated forbearance, then exclaimed, 'That's a pretty dress there. We might as well window-shop, to fill in the time.' She went to the window; Martha lagged behind.

Stella tried to arrange herself in a position where she might see through the glass surface of reflections: a stretch of yellow-grained canvas, a grey pillar, swimming patches of breaking colour that followed each other across the window after the passers-by. The dresses displayed inside, however, remained invisible, and Stella fell to enjoying her own reflection. At once her look of shrewd good nature vanished. Her image confronted her as a dark beauty, slenderly round, immobilized by a voluptuous hauteur. Complete. Or, at least, complete until the arrival of the sexual partner her attitude implied; when she would turn on him slow, waking eyes, appear indignant, and walk away – not without throwing him a long, ambiguous look over her shoulder. From Stella one expected these pure unmixed responses. But from her own image she had glanced towards Martha's; at once she became animated by a reformer's zeal.

From the glass Martha was looking back anxiously, as if she did not like what she saw but was determined to face it honestly. Planted on sturdy brown legs was a plump schoolgirl's body. Heavy masses of lightish hair surrounded a broad pale face. The dark eyes were stubbornly worried, the mouth set.

'What I can't understand,' said Martha, with that defensive humour which meant she was prepared to criticize herself, even accept criticism from others, provided it was not followed by advice – 'what I can't understand is why I'm thin as a bone one month and as fat as a pig the next. You say you've got dresses you wore when you were sixteen. Well, this is the last of mine I can get on.' She laughed unhappily, trying to smooth down crumpled blue linen over her hips.

'The trouble with you is you're tired,' announced Stella. 'After all, we've none of us slept for weeks.' This sophisticated achievement put new vigour into her. She turned on Martha with determination. 'You should take yourself in hand, that's all it is. That hair style doesn't suit you – if you can call it a hair style. If you had it cut properly, it might curl. Have you ever had it cut properly – ?'

'But Stella,' Martha broke in, with a wail of laughter, 'it needs washing, it's untidy, it's . . .'

She clutched her hair with both hands and moved back a step as Stella moved to lay her hands on it in order to show how it should be arranged. So violent and desperate was her defence that Stella stopped, and exclaimed with an exasperated laugh, 'Well, if you don't want me to show you!'

In Martha's mind was the picture of how she had indubitably been, not more than three months ago, that picture which had been described, not only by herself but by others, as a slim blonde. Looking incredulously towards her reflection, she saw that fat schoolgirl, and shut her eyes in despair. She opened them at once as she felt Stella's hand on her arm. She shook it off.

'You must take yourself in hand. I'll take you to have your hair cut now.'

'No,' said Martha vigorously.

Checked, Stella turned back towards her own reflection. And again it arranged itself obediently. Between the languidly enticing beauty who was Stella before her glass and the energetic housewife who longed to take Martha in hand there was no connection; they were not even sisters.

Martha, sardonically watching Stella in her frozen pose, thought that she would not recognize herself if she caught a glimpse of herself walking down a street, or – a phrase which she saw no reason not to use, even to his face – managing her husband.

Stella saw her look, turning abruptly, and said with annoyance that they would go that moment to the hairdresser.

'There isn't time,' appealed Martha desperately.

'Nonsense,' said Stella. She took Martha's hand in her own, and began tugging her along the pavement: an attractive matron whose sensuality of face and body had vanished entirely under the pressure of the greater pleasures of good management.

Martha pulled herself free again, and said, 'I don't want to have my hair cut.' Then, as a final appeal: 'I'll miss my appointment with Dr Stern.'

'You can have an appointment with Dr Stern any time. I can always fix it.' Stella, preoccupied, frowned at Martha, and commanded, 'Just wait for me here, I'll go and tell Mrs Kent you're a friend of mine, she'll do it as a favour.' With this she hastened over the street and vanished into a door under the sign 'Chez Paris. Coiffeuse'.

Martha remained at the street's edge, telling herself she would hurry after Stella and put her foot down. A familiar lassitude overcame her, and she remained where she was, wishing that Stella would leave her alone and return to her own life – if she had one at all. But this spiteful final jab was rather as if she were sticking a pin into her own image, for whose fault was it, if not her own, that she had spent most of the last month with Stella, that the four of them had even gone off together on what was virtually a honeymoon for four? 'After all, I don't even like her,' muttered Martha obstinately, thus committing herself to the acknowledgment, always imminent the moment she was left alone, that she didn't like any of the things she had become obliged to like by the fact of marrying. The communal exaltation, like a sort of drunkenness, vanished the moment she was alone, leaving her limp with exhaustion. But she had not been alone for five minutes since her marriage.

Feeling her back stung by the sun, she moved into the shade of a pillar to wait. She was looking along the pavement backed by low buildings. Half a mile away, at the end of the street, a glint of waving burnished grass showed the vlei. The urban scene, solid and compact in the main streets, tended to dissolve the moment one moved into the side streets. The small colonial town was at a crossroads in its growth: half a modern city, half a pioneers' achievement; a large block of flats might stand next to a shanty of wood and corrugated iron, and most streets petered out suddenly in a waste of scrub and grass.

Outside a sprawling shed that was a showroom for agricultural implements lounged a group of farmers in their khaki; past them came a city man in smooth grey flannel. Martha's eyes followed this man, the only moving object in the heat-stilled street. She was deep in worried introspection. Into this grey lake plopped the thought, I know that man, don't I? It was enough to restore a little sight to her eyes, and she watched him coming towards her, while with another part of her mind she was thinking, When Stella comes out I shall tell her I won't have my hair cut – as if this act of defiance would in itself be a protest against her whole situation.

The man was tall, rather heavy; the grey flannel which encased him was like a firm outer skin to his assurance. His large elderly face had the authority of a commanding nose, jowled cheeks, strong hazel eyes deep under thick black brows. It was that English face which, with various small deviations, has been looking down so long from the walls and countless picture galleries of country houses. Handsome it was, but more – every feature, every curve, had an impressive finality, an absolute rightness, as if the atoms which composed it had never had a moment's hesitation in falling where they did.

Martha thought: here is another person who is *complete* – finished in his way as Stella is in hers. Whereas she herself was formless, graceless, and unpredictable, a mere lump of clay. She rejected even the sight of him, and returned to her own preoccupations.

Mr Maynard was also preoccupied, whether pleasantly or not could be deduced only by a certain sarcastic twist of the lips. He noticed a girl standing listlessly by a pillar, and was about to walk past her, when he slowed his pace: he ought to know her. Then he remembered that less than a week before he had married her to her husband. She was looking through him; and at once he was annoyed that she should not remember such an important figure at what was surely an important occasion. This annoyance was succeeded by a more sincere pressure: she, if anyone could, would be able to tell him where his son Binkie was.

He stood firmly before her, blocking her preoccupied stare, and said, 'Good afternoon, Mrs Knowell.'

Martha glanced hastily sideways to see whom he was addressing, then blushed. She looked closely at him, and then exclaimed, 'Oh – Mr Maynard!'

'And how,' inquired Mr Maynard, cutting short this mutual embarrassment, 'do you find the married state?'

She considered this seriously, then said, 'Well, I've only been married five days.'

'A very sensible attitude.'

She looked at him and waited. He was struck by her tiredness, and the unhappy set of her mouth. That critical look, however, checked in him the instinct to instruct. He was not a magistrate and the descendant of magistrates and landowners for nothing. He found himself searching for the right tone.

She saved him the trouble by asking, 'Has Binkie come home yet?'

'I thought you would be able to tell me.'

'The last we saw of him was when he left the Falls at two last night. He said he was going to swim across the Falls if it was the last thing he did. It probably would be, too,' she added dispassionately.

Mr Maynard winced. 'He was drunk, I suppose?'

'Not *drunk*.' This, it seemed, she found crude. But she added, 'No more than usual.'

Mr Maynard looked sharply at her, saw this was not criticism but information willingly given, and said, 'I suppose the fact that the river is full of crocodiles wouldn't deter him?'

'Oh, I'm sure he wouldn't really do it,' she said quickly, on a maternal note. 'They rushed off in a horde saying they would. Three years ago they say one of them tried to jump across to that little island – you know the one, when the river is low – and he went over the edge. We reminded them about it just as they left. Besides, Binkie's far too sensible.'

'Binkie's *sensible*?' exclaimed Mr Maynard, very bitterly.

Martha, feeling that she was included in the bitterness, moved slightly away with 'Well, I'm not responsible for Binkie.'

He hesitated, then again moved in front of her. 'Young

woman, it would interest me very much to know why you think Binkie is sensible. He drinks like a fish. He never does any work if he can help it. He is continually either giving it a bang or tearing the place to pieces.' He heavily isolated these last phrases, and handed them to her, as it were, like a challenge.

After a pause for reflection Martha observed, 'He always knows what he's doing.' This comment, it appeared, was enough.

'You amaze me. You really do amaze me, you know.' He waited for more.

Martha offered him a sudden friendly smile, and said, 'I shouldn't worry. In twenty years' time he'll be a magistrate, too, I shouldn't wonder.' She laughed, as if this in itself was funny.

'My youth was not misspent. We neither gave it a bang nor tore the place to pieces.'

Martha's eyebrows at once went up. 'Really? I understood that you did – judging from novels, at least. Though of course in England you'd call it something else probably, you people.'

'Who is "you people"?' he asked, annoyed.

Martha looked at him as if suspecting a deliberate dishonesty, and then remarked, blushing because she had to put it into words, 'Why, the upper classes, of course, who else?'

Ironically stiff, he remarked, 'My son Binkie also uses the phrase "you people" – and in the same way.'

'For all that, he'll end up by being a magistrate.' And Martha laughed with real enjoyment and looked straight at him, expecting him to share it.

He did not laugh. He was hurt. 'You are exempt from this law?'

The shaft went home at once. She lost her shell of confidence, her face contracted, she looked at him from a haze of anxiety before turning away from him. He had no idea why this should be so.

He was contrite. Then he said apologetically, 'Well, thank you. I daresay Binkie will turn up at midnight again. I don't know why he imagines he can miss three days at the office without even ringing up to apologize – his chief rang me this morning.' He heard his own voice becoming so bitter that he hastened to restore his balance by sarcasm. 'Don't imagine I am inquiring on my own account. As far as I am concerned, I decided long ago it would be no loss to society if Binkie did fall prey to the crocodiles. But my wife will have a sick headache until he returns.'

Under the impression that he had ended the interview on a note which must leave him whole in her eyes, he was about to turn away with a 'Good afternoon', when he saw her offering him a look of such ironic pity that he stopped.

She smiled and he found himself returning her smile. 'Well, Mr Maynard,' she remarked in precisely his own tone of cool self-punishing sarcasm. 'If Binkie has learned to ignore sick headaches, then it must be because he knows he'd be doing someone out of a pleasure if he did not.' But this logical sentence crumbled, and she added awkwardly, 'I mean, everyone knows about sick headaches . . . Besides – they're so old-fashioned,' she went on angrily. And then: 'Not that everything doesn't just go on, even when one might think they had no right to exist any longer.'

Ignoring the last part of this, he seized upon the first with an ironical 'Well, well!' His relations with his wife had been conducted on this principle, but he would have considered it unchivalrous to do more than talk blandly about 'the female element' when with his male friends. Yet here was a representative of this same element who seemed to feel no disloyalty in putting what he had imagined to be a male viewpoint. It occurred to him, first, that he was out of touch with the young; secondly, a note had been struck which he instinctively responded to with gallantry.

Instilling gallantry into his voice, and a gleam of ironic complicity into his eyes, he moved nearer and said, 'You interest me enormously.'

At once she frowned, and even moved away. He dropped the tone; but held it in reserve for a later occasion.

Then he lowered his voice like a conspirator, and inquired expanding his eyes with a look of vast inquiry, 'Tell me, Mrs Knowell, is it the fashion now for young people to take their

16

honeymoons in crowds? In my young days a honeymoon was an opportunity to be alone.'

'You know quite well we did our best to get away without Binkie and the gang,' said Martha resentfully.

'I was referring to the other couple, the Mathews.'

For a moment it was touch and go whether she would repudiate them; but another loyalty was touched, for she laughed and asserted that they had all had a marvellous time and it was absolutely gorgeous.

Mr Maynard watched her, then raised his heavy brows and said drily, 'So it would appear.'

He had expected her to succumb in confusion to this pressure; instead she suddenly chuckled, and met his eyes appreciatively. He said quickly, 'Our generation has not made such a success of things that we can expect you to follow our example.' This seemed to him the extreme of magnanimity, but she smiled sceptically and said, 'Thanks.'

There was another pause. Martha was thinking that his eighteenth-century flavour had, after all, its own piquancy – not fifty yards away the farmers still lounged and argued prices and the weather and the labour question, while almost at their elbow arched the great marble doors of the cinema.

But surely Stella should be returning by now? And all this talk of generations had a stale, dead ring. Martha reacted violently against Mr Maynard, particularly because of that moment when he had invited her to flirt a little. She thought confusedly that there was always a point when men seemed to press a button, as it were, and one was expected to turn into something else for their amusement. This 'turning into something else' had landed her where she was now: married, signed and sealed away from what she was convinced she was. Besides – and here her emotions reached conviction – he was so old! She wished now, belatedly, that she had snubbed him for daring to think that she might have even exchanged a glance with him.

He was inquiring, in a voice which engaged her attention, 'I wonder if I might take this opportunity to inquire whether "the kids" – or, if you prefer it, "the gang" – behaved so badly that I may expect a bill for damages.'

This was, underneath the severity, an appeal. Martha at once replied with compassion, 'Oh, don't worry, I'm sure it will be all right.'

He retreated from the pity into gruffness, remarking, 'I live in terror that one day Binkie'll behave in such a way that I'll have no alternative but to resign – not that you would see any misfortune in that,' he added.

Martha conceded that she was sure he was a marvellous magistrate; she sounded irritable. Then, as he did not move, she began to speak, giving him the information he was obviously waiting for, in the manner of one who was prepared to turn the knife in the wound if he absolutely insisted. 'Binkie and the gang caught up with us that night about twelve. We shook up one of the hotels and made them open the bar . . .'

'Illegal,' he commented.

'Well, of course. We – I mean the four of us – sneaked out while the gang were "giving it stick"' – here she offered him an ironic smile, which he unwillingly returned – 'and we drove all night till we reached the hotel. The gang came after us about eight in the morning. Luckily the hotel wasn't full and there was room for everyone. The gang didn't behave so badly, considering everything. The manager got very angry on the last day because Binkie – you remember those baboons that come up to the hotel for food? Well, Binkie and the gang caught one of the baboons and made it drunk and brought it on to the veranda. Well, it got out of control and started rampaging. But they caught it in the end, so that was all right. The baboon was sick,' she added flatly, her mouth twisting. 'Binkie and the baboon were dancing on the lawn. It was rather funny.'

'Very funny.'

'It was – very. However,' she pointed out coldly, 'since the gang have been tearing the place to pieces for years, and no one has got hurt, they can't be so crazy as they make out.'

'Except for young Mandolis, who went over the edge of the Falls three years ago.'

She shrugged. An allowable percentage of casualties, apparently. Then she added, in a different voice, hard and impatient, 'There's going to be a war, anyway.'

'Since this will be my second world war, I have the advantage of knowing that those follies we commit under the excuse of wartime are not cancelled out when it's over. On the contrary.'

Again he had made a remark at random which went home. Mr Maynard, whose relations with his fellow human beings were based on the need that they should in some way defer to him, found that this young woman, who until now had clearly recognized no such obligation, was all at once transformed into a mendicant. She had come close to him, and was clutching at his sleeve. Her eyes were full of tears. 'Mr Maynard,' she said desperately, 'Mr Maynard . . .' But he was never to know what help she was asking of him. Afterwards he reflected that she was probably about to ask him if he could divorce her as rapidly and informally as he had married her, and was irrationally wounded because it was in his capacity as a magistrate that she was demanding help.

A loud and cheerful voice sounded beside them. 'Why, Mr Maynard,' exclaimed Stella, grasping his hands and thus taking Martha's place in front of him. 'Why, Mr Maynard, how lovely to see you.'

'How do you do?' inquired Mr Maynard formally; in his manner was that irritation shown by a man who finds a woman attractive when he does not like her. He moved away, smiling urbanely at Martha. 'I shall leave you in the hands of your matron – matron of honour?' With this he nodded and left them. He was thinking irritably, Wanting it both ways . . . and then: Am I supposed to supply the part of priest and confessor as well? She should have got married in church. Nevertheless, he was left with the feeling of a debt undischarged, and he glanced back to see the two young women crossing the street, and apparently engaged in violent argument.

'But I've just made the appointment,' said Stella angrily.

'And she's had to cancel someone else. You can't change your mind now.'

'I'm not going to have my hair cut,' said Martha calmly. 'I never said I would. *You* said so.' It was perfectly easy to resist now; it had been impossible ten minutes ago. She gave a glance over her shoulder at the firm and stable back of Mr Maynard, who was just turning the corner.

'She's a very good hairdresser, Matty – just out from England. Besides,' added Stella virtuously, 'you look awful, Matty, and it's your duty to your husband to look nice.'

But at this Martha laughed wholeheartedly.

'What's funny?' asked Stella suspiciously. But she knew that this amusement, which she never understood, was Martha's immunity to her, and she said crossly, 'Oh, very well, I'll cancel it again.'

She went into Chez Paris; and in half a minute they were continuing on their way.

'We'll be late for the doctor,' said Stella reproachfully, but Martha said, 'We are ten minutes early.'

The doctor's rooms were in a low white building across the street. Looking upwards, they saw a series of windows shuttered against the sun, green against the glare of white.

'Dr Stern's got the nicest waiting room in town, it's all modern,' said Stella devotedly.

'Oh, come on,' Martha said, and went indoors without looking back.

On the first floor was a passage full of doors, all marked 'Private'. Stella knocked on one of these. It opened almost at once to show a woman in a white dress, who held its edge firmly, as if against possible assault. She looked annoyed; then, seeing Stella, she said with nervous amiability, 'It's lovely to see you, dear, but really I'm busy.'

'This is Matty,' said Stella. 'You know, the naughty girl who married Douggie behind everyone's back.'

The young woman smiled at Martha in a friendly but harassed way and came out into the passage, shutting the door behind her. She pulled a half-smoked cigarette from her deep white pocket, lit it, and puffed as if she were starved for smoke. 'I really shouldn't, but the doctor'll manage,' she said, drawing deep breaths of smoke. She was a thin girl, with lank wisps of thin black hair, and pale worried blue eyes. Her body was flat and bony in the white glazed dress, which was a uniform, but no more than a distant cousin of the stiff garments designed by elderly women to disguise the charms of young ones. 'My Willie knows your Douggie – they've been boys together for years,' she said with tired indulgence.

Martha was by now not to be surprised at either the information or the tone, although she had never heard of Willie.

'My God, but I'm dead,' went on Alice. 'Dr Stern is my pet lamb, but he works himself to death, and he never notices when anyone else does. I was supposed to leave an hour ago.'

'Listen,' said Stella quickly, 'that's easy, then. Just slip Matty quickly in for her appointment, then we'll all go and have a drink.'

'Oh, but I can't dear,' said Alice feebly; but Stella gave her a firm little push towards the door; so that she nodded and said, 'All right, then, there's lots waiting from before you, but I'll manage it.' She slipped the crushed end of cigarette back into her pocket, and went into the room marked 'Private'.

Martha followed Stella into the waiting room. It was full. About fifteen or twenty women, with a sprinkling of children, were jealously eyeing the door into the consulting room. Martha edged herself into a seat, feeling guilty that she was about to take priority. Stella, however, stood openly waiting, with the look of one for whom the ordinary rules did not apply.

Almost at once the consulting-room door opened, and a bland voice bade a lady goodbye; she came out blushing with pleasure and giving challenging looks to those who still waited.

'Come on,' said Stella loudly, 'now it's us.'

She pushed Martha forward, as Alice looked around into the waiting room, and said in the kindly nervous voice

21

which was her characteristic, 'Yes, dear – it's you, Mrs Knowell.'

Stella went beside Martha to the door; but there Alice held out one barring hand, with a professional look, and pulled Martha forward with the other. The door shut behind Martha, excluding Stella.

This was a large, quiet room, with a white screen in one corner which was bathed in greenish light from the shutters over the window. An enormous desk filled half the outer wall, and behind it sat Dr Stern, his back to the light. Over an efficient white coat a smooth pale heavy-lidded face lifted for a moment, the pale cool eyes flicked assessingly over Martha, and dropped again as he said, 'Please sit down.'

Martha sat, and wondered how she should start: she did not really want any advice. She looked at the top of Dr Stern's head, which was bent towards her as he flicked quickly through some papers. He had a mat of thick black crinkling hair; his neck was white, thin – very young. She saw him suddenly as a young man, and was upset. Then he said, 'If you'll excuse me for one moment . . .' and glanced up again, before continuing to leaf through the papers. The upwards look was so impersonal that her anxiety vanished. She yawned. A weight of tiredness settled on her, with the cool silence of the room. A patch of yellow sunlight slanted through the slats of the blind on to the desk. Her eye was caught by it, held. She yawned again. She heard his voice: 'Allow me to congratulate you on carrying off young Knowell – I've known him quite a time.' He sounded quietly paternal; and she was reminded again that he was probably no older than Douglas, who had agreed enthusiastically to Stella's insistence that Martha should see the doctor at once: 'Yes, Dr Stern's just the ticket – yes, you go along, Matty, and get to know him, he'll show you the ropes.'

Yet, since Martha knew the ropes, there was nothing to say. Her eyes still fixed by the yellow patch of light, she let herself slide deeper into the comfortable chair, and Dr Stern inquired, 'Sleepy?'

'Haven't had much sleep,' she agreed, without moving.

Dr Stern looked at her again and noticed that she, in her

turn, was unhappily regarding Alice, who was folding something white behind the white screen.

'It's all right, Mrs Burrell, just go next door for a moment. I'll call you.' Alice went out, with a kind, reassuring smile at Martha. 'And leave the door open,' said Dr Stern, for Martha's benefit, which she did not appreciate: she would have preferred it shut.

And now Dr Stern, whose handling of the situation had been by no means as casual as it appeared, gave a swift downwards glance at his watch. Martha noticed it, and sat herself up.

'Well, Mrs Knowell,' he began smoothly, and, after a short silence, went on to deliver a lecture designed for the instruction of brides. He spoke slowly, as if afraid of forgetting some of it from sheer familiarity. When he had finished, Martha said obstinately that according to authority so and so another method was preferable. He gave her a quick look, which meant that this was a greater degree of sophistication than he was used to; almost he switched to the tone he used with married women of longer standing. But he hesitated. Martha's words might be matter-of-fact, but her face was anxious, and she was gripping her hands together in her lap.

He went off at a tangent to describe a conference on birth control he had attended in London, and concluded with a slightly risky joke. Martha laughed. He added two or three more jokes, until she was laughing naturally, and returned to the subject by a side road of 'A patient of mine who . . .' Now he proceeded to recommend the method she had herself suggested, and with as much warmth as if he had never recommended another. His calm, rather tired, remote voice was extremely soothing; Martha was no longer anxious; but for good measure he concluded with a little speech which, if analysed, meant nothing but that everything was all right, one should not worry, one should take things easy. These phrases having repeated themselves often enough he went on to remark gently that some women seemed to imagine birth control was a sort of magic; if they bought what was necessary and left it lying in a corner of a drawer, nothing more was needed. To this attitude of mind, he said, was due a number of births every year which would astound the public. He laughed so that she might, and looked inquiringly at her. She did laugh, but a shadow of worry crossed her face. He saw it, and made a mental note. There was a silence. This time his glance at his watch was involuntary: the waiting room was full of women all of whom must be assured, for various reasons, that everything was all right, there was nothing to worry about, of course one did not sleep when one was worried, of course everyone was worried at times – of course, of course, of course.

Again Martha saw the glance and rose. He rose with her and took her to the door.

'And how's your husband keeping?' he asked.

'Fine, thanks,' said Martha automatically; then it struck her as more than politeness and she looked inquiringly.

'His stomach behaving itself?'

'Oh, we've both got digestions like an ostrich,' she said with a laugh, thinking of the amount they had drunk and eaten in the last few weeks. Then she said quickly, 'There's surely nothing wrong with his stomach?' Her voice was full of the arrogance of perfect health. She heard it herself. 'What's the matter with him?' she repeated. The solicitude in her voice rang false.

'I believe I've been indiscreet,' said Dr Stern. 'But he is silly not to tell you. Ask him.' And now he smiled, and held out his hand, saying that if she wanted help, if she just wanted to drop in for a chat, she must give him a ring. Martha wrung the hand, and left his room with the same look of soft, grateful pleasure that the previous patient had worn.

The other women watched her critically; they found that confused, self-confessing smile ridiculous. Then, as Stella rose to join her, they lost interest and turned their eyes back to the closed door.

'Well, was he nice, did you like him?' asked Stella urgently; and Martha said reticently that he was very nice.

Nothing more, it seemed, was forthcoming; and Stella urged, laughing, 'Did you learn anything new?' And it occurred to Martha for the first time that she had not. Her sense of being supported, being understood, was so strong that she stopped in the passage, motionless, with the shock of the discovery that in fact Dr Stern had said nothing at all, and in due course Douglas would be sent a bill for half a guinea – for what?

Stella tugged at her arm, so that she was set in motion again; and Martha remarked irritably that Dr Stern was something of an old woman, 'sitting all wrapped up behind his desk like a parcel in white tissue paper, being tactful to a blushing bride.'

At once Stella laughed and said that she never took the slightest notice of what he said, either; as for herself and her husband, they had used such and such a method for three years, and she distinctly remembered Dr Stern telling them it was useless.

'Well,' asked Martha ungratefully, 'what did you send me for, then?'

'Oh!' Stella was shocked and aggrieved. 'But he's so nice, and so up to date with everything, you know.'

'He can't be much older than you are,' remarked Martha, in that same rather resentful voice. She was astounded that Stella was deeply shocked – at least, there could be no other explanation for her withdrawal into offended dignity. 'If you don't want a really scientific doctor then . . .' Belatedly, Martha thanked her for the service; but they had reached the door marked 'Private', where they must wait for Alice; and Stella forgot her annoyance in the business of wriggling the door handle silently to show Alice they were there.

. On the other side of the door, Alice was holding the handle so that it should not rattle, and watching Dr Stern to catch the right moment for announcing the next patient. Usually, having accompanied a patient to the door, he went straight back to his desk. This time, having shed his calm paternal manner over Martha's farewells, he went to the window and looked down at the street through the slats in the shutter. He looked tired, even exasperated. Alice expected him to complain again about being a woman's doctor. 'I can't understand why I get this reputation,' he would grumble. 'Nine-tenths of my practice are women. And women with nothing wrong with them.'

But he did not say it. Alice smiled as she saw him adjust the shutter so that the patch of sun, which was now on the extreme edge of the desk, should return to the empty space of polished wood nearer the middle. He turned and caught the smile, but preferred not to notice it. He frowned slightly and remarked that in three months' time Mrs Knowell would be back in this room crying her eyes out and asking him to do an abortion – he knew the type.

Alice did not smile; she disliked him in this mood. Her eyes were cold. She noted that his tired body had straightened, his face was alert and purposeful.

He seated himself and said, 'Make a card out for Mrs Knowell tomorrow.' He almost added, laughing, 'And book her a room in the nursing home.' But he remembered in time that one did not make this sort of joke with Mrs Burrell, who was sentimental; his previous nurse had been better company. All the same, he automatically made certain calculations. January or February, he thought. He even made a note on his pad; there was a complacent look on his face.

'That will do, Mrs Burrell. Thank you for staying over your time – you mustn't let me overwork you.' He smiled at her; the smile had a weary charm.

Alice did not respond. Her criticism of him formed itself in the thought, he has to have his own way over everything. And then the final blow: Heaven preserve me from being married to *him*, I wouldn't have him as a gift.

'Who's next?' he asked briskly.

'Mrs Black,' said Alice, going to the other door to call her in.

'She ought to be starting her next baby soon,' he remarked.

'Have a heart,' she said indignantly. 'The other's only six months old.'

'Get them over young,' he said. 'That's the best way.' He added, 'You ought to be starting a family yourself.'

Alice paused with her hand on the knob of the door, and said irritably, 'The way you go on! If I catch you with less than five when *you* get married . . .'

He looked sharply at her; he had only just understood she was really annoyed; he wished again that he might have a nurse with whom he did not have to choose his words. But she was speaking:

'You Jews have got such a strong feeling for family, it makes me sick!'

He seemed to stiffen and retreat a little; then he laughed and said, 'There's surely every reason why we should?'

She looked at him vaguely, then dismissed history with 'I don't see why everybody shouldn't leave everybody else alone.'

'Neither do I, Mrs Burrell, neither do I.' This was savage.

'You're the sort of man who'd choose a wife because she had a good pelvis,' she said.

'There are worse ways of choosing one,' he teased her.

'Oh, Lord!'

'Let's have Mrs Black. Okay – shoot.'

Alice opened the door and called, 'Mrs Black, please.' She shut the door after the smiling Mrs Black, who was already seating herself; and, as she crossed the room on her way out, heard his voice, calmly professional: 'Well, Mrs Black, and what can I do for you?'

She joined Martha and Stella, saying, 'Wait, I must tell the other nurse . . .'

She came back almost at once, pulling out the frayed cigarette stub from her pocket and lighting it. Then she began tugging and pushing at the wisps of black hair that were supposed to make a jaunty frame for her face, but were falling in lank witch locks. 'Oh, damn everything,' she muttered crossly, pulling a comb through her hair with both hands, while the cigarette hung on her lip. Finally she gave a series of ineffective little pats at her dress, and said again, in a violent querulous voice, 'Oh, damn *everything*. I'm going to give up this job. I'm sick to death of Dr Stern. I'm just fed up.'

Martha and Stella, momentarily united in understanding, exchanged a small humorous smile, and kept up a running flow of vaguely practical remarks until they had reached the hot pavement. They glanced cautiously towards Alice: she had apparently recovered. Stella immediately dropped the female chivalry with which women protect each other in such moments, and said jealously, 'I wouldn't have thought Dr Stern would be so hard to work for.'

'Oh, no, he's not,' agreed Alice at once, and without the proprietary air that Stella would have resented. 'Anyway, I'm really going to give it up. I didn't train as a nurse to do this sort of thing. I might as well be a hotel receptionist.'

'You're mad to work when you're married,' said Stella. 'I've given notice to my boss. Of course, we're quite broke, but it's too much, looking after a husband then slaving oneself to death in an office.'

Alice and Martha in their turn exchanged an amused smile, while Stella touched it up a little: 'Men have no idea, they think housework and cooking get done by miracles.'

'Why, haven't you got a boy, dear?' inquired Alice vaguely, and then broke into Stella's reply with 'Do you like Dr Stern, Matty? If not, I shan't bother to make out a card for you.'

'One doctor's as good as another,' said Martha ungraciously. 'Anyway, I'm never ill.'

'Oh, but he's very good,' exclaimed Alice, at once on the defensive. 'He's really wonderful with babies.'

'But I'm not going to have a baby, not for years.'

'Oh, I don't blame you,' agreed Alice at once. 'I always tell Willie that life's too much one damned thing after another to have babies as well.'

'What do you do?' inquired Martha, direct.

Alice laughed, on the comfortable note which Martha found so reassuring. 'Oh, we don't bother much, really. Luckily, all I have to do is to jump off the edge of a table.'

They were at a turning. 'I think I'll just go home, dear, if you don't mind,' said Alice. 'Willie might come home early, and I won't bother about a drink.'

'Oh, no,' protested Stella at once. 'We'll all run along to Matty's place. You can ring Willie and tell him to come along.'

And now Martha once again found herself protesting that of course they must all come to her flat; an extraordinary desperation seized her at the idea of being alone; although even as she protested another anxious voice was demanding urgently that she should pull herself free from this compulsion.

'Oh, well,' agreed Alice good-naturedly, 'I'll come and drink to your getting married.'

Martha was silent. Now she had gained her point she had to brace herself to face another period of time with both Stella and Alice. She thought, Let's get it over quickly, and then . . . And then would come a reckoning with herself; she had the feeling of someone caught in a whirlpool.

The three women drifted inertly down the hot street, shading their eyes with their hands. Alice yawned and remarked in her preoccupied voice, 'But I get so tired, perhaps I'm pregnant? Surely I'm not? Oh, Lord, maybe that's it!'

'Well, jump off a table, then!' said Stella with her jolly crude laugh.

'It's all very well, dear, but this worrying all the time just gets me down. Sometimes I think I'll have a baby and be done with it. That'd be nine months' peace and quiet at least.'

'What's the good of working for a doctor if he can't do something?' suggested Stella, with a look at Martha which said she should be collecting information that might turn out to be useful.

Alice looked annoyed; but Stella prodded, 'I've heard he helps people sometimes.'

Alice drew professional discretion over her face and remarked, 'They say that about all the doctors.'

'Oh, come off it,' said Stella, annoyed.

'If Dr Stern did all the abortions he was asked to do, he'd never have time for anything else. There's never a day passes without at least one or two crying their eyes out and asking him.'

'What do they do?' asked Martha, unwillingly fascinated.

'Oh, if they're strong-minded, they just go off to Beira or Johannesburg. But most of us just get used to it,' said Alice, laughing nervously, and unconsciously pressing her hands around her pelvis.

Stella, with her high yell of laughter, began to tell a story about the last time she got pregnant. 'There I was, after my second glass of neat gin, rolling on the sofa and groaning, everything just started nicely, and in came the woman from next door. She was simply furious. She said she'd report me to the police. Silly old cow. She can't have kids herself, so she wants everyone else to have them for her. I told her to go and boil her head, and of course she didn't do anything. She just wanted to upset me and make me unhappy.' At the last words Stella allowed her face and voice to go limp with self-pity.

'The police?' inquired Martha blankly.

'It's illegal,' explained Alice tolerantly. 'If you start a baby, then it's illegal not to have it. Didn't you know?'

'Do you mean to say that a woman's not entitled to decide whether she's going to have a baby or not?' demanded Martha, flaring at once into animated indignation.

This violence amused both Stella and Alice, who now, in their turn, exchanged that small tolerant smile.

'Oh, well,' said Alice indulgently, 'don't waste any breath on that. Everyone knows that more kids get frustrated than ever get born, and half the women who have them didn't want to have them, but if the Government wants to make silly laws, let them get on with it, that's what I say, I suppose they've got nothing better to do. Don't worry, dear. If you get yourself in a fix just give me a ring and I'll help you out, you don't want to lose sleep over the Government, there are better things to think about.'

Stella said with quick jealousy, 'I've already told Matty, I'm just around the corner, and God knows I've got enough experience, even though I'm not a nurse.'

Surprised, Alice relinquished the struggle for the soul of Martha – she had not understood there was one.

'Well, that's all right, then, isn't it?' she agreed easily.

They had now reached the flats. They were a large block, starkly white in the sunlight. The pavement was so heated that its substance gave stickily under their feet; and its bright

grey shone up a myriad tiny oily rainbows. A single tree
stood at the entrance; and on this soft green patch their eyes
rested, in relief from the staring white, the glistening grey,
the hard, brilliant blue of the sky. Under the tree stood a
native woman. She held a small child by one hand and a
slightly larger one by the other, and there was a new baby
folded in a loop of cloth on her back. The older children
held the stuff of her skirt from behind. Martha stopped and
looked at her. This woman summed up her uncomfortable
thoughts and presented the problem in its crudest form.
This easy, comfortable black woman seemed extraordinarily
attractive, compared with the hard gay anxiety of Stella and
Alice. Martha felt her as something simple, accepting —
whole. Then she understood that she was in the process of
romanticizing poverty; and repeated firmly to herself that
the child mortality for the colony was one of the highest in
the world. All the same . . .

Alice and Stella, finding themselves alone in the hall,
came back and saw Martha staring at the tree. There was
nothing else to look at.

'It's all very well for us,' remarked Martha with a half-
defiant laugh, seeing that she was being observed. 'We're all
right, but how about her?'

Alice looked blank; but Stella, after a spasm of annoyance
had contracted her face, broke into a loud laugh. To Alice
she said boisterously, 'Matty is a proper little Bolshie, did
you know? Why, we had to drag her away from the Reds
before she was married, she gets all hot and bothered about
our black brothers.' She laughed again, insistently, but Alice
apparently found no need to do the same.

'Come along, dear,' she said kindly to Martha. 'Let's have
a drink and get it over with, if you don't mind.'

Martha obediently joined them. But Stella could not leave
it. She said brightly, 'It's different for them. They're not
civilized, having babies is easy for them, everyone knows
that.'

They were climbing the wide staircase. Alice remarked
indifferently, 'Dr Stern has a clinic for native women. Every

Sunday morning. I tell him he's so keen on everybody having babies that he can't even give Sunday a rest.'

Stella involuntarily stopped. 'Dr Stern treats kaffirs?' she asked, horrified. It appeared that he was in imminent danger of losing a patient.

'He's very goodhearted,' said Alice vaguely. The words restored her own approval of Dr Stern. 'He only charges them sixpence, or something like that.' She continued to drag herself up the staircase, ahead of the others.

Stella was silent. Her face expressed a variety of emotions, doubt being the strongest. Then Dr Stern effected in her that small revolution in thinking which crosses a gulf to phil-anthropy. She remarked, still dubiously, 'Well, of course, we should be kind to them.'

Martha, three steps below her, laughed outright. Alice looked at her in surprise, Stella with anger.

'Well, if everyone was like you, they'd get out of hand,' Stella said sourly. 'It's all very well, but everyone knows they are nothing but animals, and it doesn't hurt them to have babies, and . . .' She added doubtfully, 'Dr Stern is always modern.'

'He's making a study about it,' said Alice. She was waiting for them on the landing. 'It's not true they are different from us. They're just the same, Dr Stern says.'

Stella was deeply shocked and disturbed; she burst into her loud vulgar laughter. 'Don't make me laugh.'

'But it's scientific,' said Alice vaguely.

'Oh, doctors!' suggested Stella, in precisely the same indulgent tone Alice had previously used for 'the Government'.

Martha, arrived beside them on the landing, said bitterly, 'It seems even Dr Stern is only interested in writing papers about them.'

Alice was offended. 'Well, so long as they get help, I don't suppose they mind, do you? And he's very kind. How many doctors can you think of would work as hard as he does all the week and every night and then spend all Sunday morning helping kaffir women with their babies? And for as good as nothing, too.'

'Well, sixpence is the same for them as ten shillings would be for us,' protested Martha.

Alice was really angry now. 'It's not the same for Dr Stern.'

'Whose fault is that?' demanded Martha hotly.

Stella cut the knot by opening the door. 'Oh, let's have a drink,' she said impatiently. 'Don't take any notice of Matty. Douggie'll put some sense into her head. You can't be a Red if you're married to a civil servant.'

They went inside. Martha was acutely depressed at the finality of what Stella had said. She began to take out glasses and syphons, until Stella took them impatiently out of her hands. She sat down, and let Stella arrange things as she wished; with the feeling she had done this many times before.

Alice was unobservant and relaxed in a deep chair, puffing out clouds of smoke until she was surrounded by blue haze. 'For crying out loud, but I'm tired,' she murmured; and, without moving the rest of her body, she held out her hand to take the glass Stella put into it.

The room was rather small, but neat; it was dressed with striped modern curtains, light rugs, cheerful strident cushions. Stella's taste, as Martha observed to herself bitterly, although telling herself again that it was her own fault. Well, she'd be gone soon, and then . . .

She took the glass Stella handed her, and let herself go loose, as Alice was doing.

Stella, accompanied apparently by two corpses, remained upright and energetic in her chair, and proceeded to entertain Alice with an amusing account of 'their' honeymoon.

'. . . And you should have seen Matty, coping with the lads as if she were an old hand at the game. No wedding night for poor Matty, we were driving all night, and we had two breakdowns at that – the funniest thing you ever saw. We got to the hotel at two in the morning, and then all the boys arrived, and it wasn't until that night we all decided it was really time that Matty had a wedding night, so we escorted them to their room, playing the Wedding March on the mouth-organs, and the last we saw of Matty was her taking off Douggie's shoes and putting him into bed.' She laughed, and Martha joined her. But Alice, who had not opened her eyes, remarked soothingly that Douggie was a hell of a lad, but Matty needn't worry, these wild lads made wonderful husbands, look at Willie, he'd been one of the worst, and now butter wouldn't melt in his mouth.

The thought of her husband made her sit up, and say in a determined voice that she really must go; Willie was a pet lamb, he never worried about anything – but all the same, she wasn't going to start setting a bad example. She struggled out of her chair, drained her glass, and nervously pressed Martha's hand. 'Sorry, dear, but I really must – I'll see you soon, I expect, my Willie and your Douglas being such friends. And now I really . . .' She smiled hastily at Stella, waved vaguely, and hurried out. They could hear her running down the stairs on her high heels.

'Alice is just an old fusser,' said Stella, settling herself comfortably. 'If Willie isn't tied to her apron string she can't sit still.' Martha said nothing. 'That's no way to keep a man. They don't like it. You should manage them without them knowing it.'

Martha observed irritably that Stella and Alice talked about husbands as if they were a sort of wild animal to be tamed.

Stella looked at her, and then remarked in an admonishing way that Martha was very young, but she'd soon learn that the way to keep a lad like Douggie was to give him plenty of rope to hang himself.

Irritation was thick in the air, like the tobacco smoke that now made a heavy bluish film between them. Martha was praying, I wish she'd go.

Stella made a few more remarks, which were received in silence. Then she looked angrily across and said that if she were Matty she'd have a good sleep and then take life easy.

She rose, and stood for a moment looking at the mirror inside the flap of her handbag. Everything was in order. She shut the handbag, and gazed around the little room; she adjusted a cushion, then turned her gaze towards Martha, who was sprawling gracelessly in her chair.

Martha looked back, acknowledging the discouragement

that filled her at the sight of this woman. Stella must have gained this perfect assurance with her maturity at the age of – what? There were photographs of her at fifteen, showing her no less complete than she was now.

It appeared that the moment for parting had at last arrived. Martha struggled up. And now Martha was filled with guilt. For Stella's face showed a genuine concern for her; and Martha reminded herself that Stella was nothing if not kind and obliging – for what was kindness, if not this willingness to devote oneself utterly to another person's life? Martha was too tired even to instil irony into it. She kissed Stella clumsily on one of her smooth tinted cheeks, and thanked her. Stella brightened, blushed a little, and said that any time Matty wanted anything she had only to . . . At last she left, smiling, blowing a kiss from the door, in precisely that pose of competent grace which most depressed Martha.

The moment she was alone, Martha rummaged for a pair of scissors and went with determination to the bathroom. There she knelt on the edge of the gleaming and slippery bath, and in an acutely precarious position leaned up to look into the shaving mirror. It was too high for her. There was a large mirror at a suitable height next door, but for some reason this was the one she must use. Nothing in her reflection pleased her. She was entirely clumsy, clodhopping, graceless. Worse than this, she was filled with uncomfortable memories of how she had looked at various stages of her nineteen years – for she might be determined to forget how she had *felt* in her previous incarnations, but she could not forget how she had looked. Her present image had more in common with her reflection at fifteen, a broad and sturdy schoolgirlishness, than it had with herself of only six months ago.

Her dissatisfaction culminated as she put the scissors to the heavy masses of light dryish hair that fell on her shoulders. She remembered briefly that Stella had laid stress on her hair being *properly* cut; but the mere idea of submitting herself to the intentions of anybody else must be repulsed. Steadily, her teeth set to contain a prickling feverish haste, she cut around her hair in a straight line. Then she fingered the heavy unresponsive mass, and began snipping at the ends. Finally she lifted individual pieces and cut off slabs of hair from underneath, so that it might not be so thick. From the way the ends curved up, she could see that Stella might be right – her hair would curl. At last she plunged her head into water and soaped it hard, rubbing it roughly dry afterwards, in a prayerful hope that these attentions might produce yet another transformation into a different person. Then she swept up the cushions of hair from the floor and went into the bedroom. It was after six, and night had fallen. She switched on the light, to illuminate the cheerful room whose commonplace efficiency depressed her; and stood in front of the other mirror trying to shape the sodden mass of hair into waves. She thought her appearance worse than before. Giving it up in despair, she switched off the light again and went to the window. She was thinking with rueful humour that now she was undeniably longing for Douglas to come so that he might reassure her; whereas for most of the last week she had been struggling with waves of powerful dislike of him that she was too well educated in matters psychological not to know were natural to a newly married woman. Or, to put this more precisely, she had gone through all the handbooks with which she was now plentifully equipped, seized on phrases and sentences which seemed to fit her case, and promptly extended them to cover the whole of womankind. There was nothing more paradoxical about her situation than that, while she insisted on being unique, individual, and altogether apart from any other person, she could be comforted in such matters only by remarks like 'Everybody feels this' or 'It is natural to feel that'.

She leaned against the sill, and tried to feel that she was alone and able to think clearly, a condition she had been longing for, it seemed for weeks. But her limbs were seething with irritation; she could not stand still. She fetched a chair and sat down, trying to relax. Behind her, the two small and shallow rooms were dark, holding their scraps of furniture in a thinned shadow, which was crossed continually by shifting beams of light from the street. Under her, the thin floor crept and reverberated to footsteps behind the walls.

Above her, feet tapped beyond the ceiling. She found herself listening intently to these sounds, trying to isolate them, to make them harmless. She shut her mind to them, and looked outwards.

The small, ramshackle colonial town had become absorbed in luminous dark. A looming pile of flats was like a cliff rising from the sea, and the turn of a roof like a large elbow half blocking the stars. Below this aerial scene of moon, sky, roofs and the tops of trees, the streets below ran low and indistinct, with lights of cars nosing slow along them among the isolated yellow spaces which were street lamps. Whiffs of petrol-laden dust and staled scent from flowers in the park a hundred yards away drifted down past her towards the back of the building, where it would mingle with the heavier, composted smell: the smell which comes rich and heavy out of the undertown, the life of African servants, cramped, teeming, noisy with laughter and music. Singing came now from the native quarters at the back; and this small lively music flowed across the dark to join the more concentrated bustle of noise that came from a waste lot opposite. The fun fair had come to town; and over the straggling dusty grass, showing yellow in the harsh composite glare from a hundred beating lights, rose swings and roundabouts and the great glittering wheel. Once a year this fair visited the city on its round of the little towns of southern Africa, and spilled its lights and churning music for a few hours nightly into the dark.

The great wheel was revolving slowly, a chain of lights that mingled with the lamps of Orion and the Cross. Martha laid her wet and uncomfortable head against the wall, and looked at the wheel steadily, finding in its turning the beginnings of peace. Slowly she quietened, and it seemed possible that she might recover a sense of herself as a person she might, if only potentially, respect. It was really all quite simple, she assured herself. That this marriage was a foolish mistake must certainly be obvious to Douglas himself; for if humility can be used to describe such an emotion, Martha was genuinely humble in thinking of him and herself as involved in an isolated act of insanity which a simple decision would reverse. His personality and hers had nothing to do with it. The whole graceless affair had nothing to do with what she really felt or – surely? – what he felt, either.

The dragging compulsion which had begun to operate when they met, which had made it impossible for her to say no at any stage of the process, seemed broken. It would be easy, she thought, to tell Douglas when he entered the room that they must part at once; he must agree. For since he shared her view that the actual ceremony was no more than a necessary bit of ritual to placate society, it followed he would view a divorce in the same light.

Thus Martha – while her eyes hypnotically followed the circling of the great wheel. But at the back of her mind was an uncomfortable memory. It was of Stella roaring with laughter as she told the story, while her husband laughed with her, of how she had, the day after their wedding, run back to her mother, because she had decided she didn't want to be married at all, and most particularly not to Andrew; after some months of marriage, it seemed that Stella found this mood nothing but a joke. The fact that what she was feeling now might be nothing but what everybody felt filled Martha with exhaustion. She remained clinging to the sill, while tiredness flowed into her, an extreme of fatigue, like the long high note on the violin that holds a tension while the ground swell of melody gathers strength beneath it. Her limbs were so heavy she could hardly prevent herself from sliding off the chair; while her mind, like a bright space above a dark building, was snapping with activity. The small, clear picture of Stella laughing at her own story was succeeded by another: she saw Binkie, large, fat, heavy, grotesquely dancing with the baboon on the lawn outside the hotel; she saw herself laughing at the scene, arm in arm with Douglas. Finally, she saw a small yellow flower on the very edge of the Falls, drenched with spray and tugging at its roots like a flag in a gale, but returning to its own perfect starred shape whenever the wind veered. She could not remember having actually seen this flower. It was frightening that she could not – yet there was something consoling about it, too. She tried again and again to place the moment she had seen it; her mind went dark with the effort, as if a switch had been turned down. Then she heard, with a movement of slow, swelling sadness, the music from the amusement park. And now she understood that she was looking back at the hectic elation of those four days with regret – nostalgia was invading her together with the rhythm of the false cheap music. Yet the truth was she had disliked every moment of the time. She jerked herself fully awake; *that* lie she had no intention of tolerating. She stood up, and told herself with a bleak and jaunty common sense that she needed a good night's sleep.

The outer door crashed open; the light crashed on. A cheerful young man came towards her, whirled her up in his arms, and began squeezing her, saying, 'Well, Matty, here we are in our own place at last, and about time, too!' With this he gave her a large affectionate kiss on the cheek, and set her down, and stood rubbing his hands with satisfaction. Then it seemed that something struck him; doubt displaced the large grin, and he said, 'But, Matty, what've you done to yourself?'

Turning away quickly, Martha said, 'I've cut off my hair. Don't look at it now, it'll be all right in the morning.'

Taking her at her word, he said, 'Oh, all right, changed your hair style, eh?' And he rubbed his hands again, with pleasure: she could see he took it as a compliment to himself that she should. 'Sorry I was late, but I ran into some of the boys and I couldn't get away. Had to celebrate.' His proprietary look half annoyed her; but she could feel the beginning of fatal pleasure. From the way he looked at her and rubbed his hands, she knew that he had again been congratulated on his acquisition; and while she puzzled over the knowledge that this could have nothing to do with *herself*, she could not help feeling less heavy and unattractive.

'They think I'm a helluva lucky . . .' he announced; and at the thought of the scenes in the bar with the boys, a reflection of his proud and embarrassed grin appeared on his face. He swooped over to her, ground her tightly to him, and announced, 'And so-so I am.'

Then, still holding her, but loosening his grip because his mind was on them and not on her, he began telling her some of the things they had said, in a comradely way, sharing the pleasure with her. At first she said, half anxiously, half pleased, 'And what else?' 'And what did they say then?' Until suddenly she jerked away from him, angry and red, and said, 'I don't think that's funny, that's disgusting.'

The very image of an offended prude, she turned her back on him; while, half shamefaced, half sniggering, he looked at her and said at last, 'Oh, come off it, Matty, don't put on an act.'

Martha undressed in silence, flinging crumpled blue dress, knickers, petticoat, in all directions. She stood naked. In the mood she was in, it had nothing to do with coquetry.

To Douglas, however, this was not apparent. He found the naked and angry girl an argument for forgiveness. Flinging off his own clothes, he bounced on to the bed, and moved over to give her room. Still frowning, she moved chastely in beside him; for the fact that they were annoyed with each other made the act of getting naked into bed on a level with sitting beside him at breakfast. She was irritated to discover that he did not understand this. She was on the point of turning over away from him, when the instinct to please turned her towards him. Love had brought her here, to lie beside this young man; love was the key to every good; love lay like a mirage through the golden gates of sex. If this was not true, then nothing was true, and the beliefs of a whole generation were illusory. They made love. She was too tired to persuade herself that she felt anything at all. Her head was by now swimming with exhaustion.

'God, but I'm tired, Matty,' he announced, rolling off her. He yawned and said with satisfaction, 'How many hours have we slept during the last fortnight?'

She did not reply. Loyalty towards love was forcing her to pretend that she was not disappointed, and that she did not – at that moment she was sick with repulsion – find him repulsive. But already that image of a lover that a woman is offered by society, and carries with her so long, had divorced itself from Douglas, like the painted picture of a stencil floating off paper in water. Because that image remained intact and unhurt, it was possible to be good-natured. It is that image which keeps so many marriages peaceable and friendly.

She listened, smiling maternally, while he calculated aloud how many hours they had slept. It took him several minutes: he was nothing if not efficient.

'Do you realize we couldn't have slept more than about three hours a night during the last six weeks?' he inquired proudly.

'Awful, isn't it?' she agreed, in the same tone.

After a pause: 'It's been lovely, hasn't it, Matty?'

She agreed with enthusiasm that it had. At the same time she glanced incredulously at him to assure herself that he must be joking. But he was grinning in the half-dark. She simply could not comprehend that his satisfaction, his pleasure, was fed less by her than by what other people found in their marriage.

Her silence dismayed him. He gripped her arm, pressed it, and urged, 'Really, everyone's been awfully good to us, haven't they, Matty? Haven't they? They've given us a hell of a start?'

Again she enthusiastically agreed. He lay alert now, feeling her worry and preoccupation. Then he suddenly inquired, 'Did you see the doctor? What did he say?'

'Oh, nothing much,' she said, sleepy and bad-tempered. 'He doesn't seem to know more than we do, only he does the big-medicine-man act awfully well.'

But Douglas could not agree with this. 'He's very good, Matty – very good indeed.'

Her motherliness was warmed by his anxiety, and she at once assured him that he had been very kind and she had liked him enormously.

'That's all right, then. You'll be all right with him.' A pause. 'Well, what did he recommend? Those effells are a pain in the neck, only for bachelors.' He laughed proudly.

'He made a joke about them.'

'What did he say?' She told him. 'He's a helluva lad, Dr Stern, isn't he, Matty? Isn't he?'

She hesitated. Besides, she did not want to think now about the machinery of birth control, which suddenly appeared to her distasteful. But since from the beginning it had been a matter of pride to be efficient, gay and matter-of-fact, she could not say that she detested the jellies and bits of rubber which from now on would accompany what Dr Stern had referred to as her love life as if it were something separate from life itself; she could not now say what for the moment was true: that she wished she were like that native woman, who was expected to have a baby every year. She wished at the very least that it should not all be made into a joke. She wanted to cry her eyes out; nothing could be more unreasonable.

Suddenly Douglas observed, 'We've just done it without anything. I suppose that's a bit silly, eh, Matty?'

'Oh, it'll be all right,' she said hastily, unwilling to move. She felt it would be 'all right' because since the 'act of love' had been what Dr Stern described as unsatisfactory, she felt it had not occurred at all. She was unaffected, and therefore it would be unfair, if not unnatural, that a child might result from it.

'Because you'd better get out of bed and go to the bathroom,' he suggested uneasily.

'Judging from the book of words,' she said, with a dry anger that astounded even herself, 'those little dragons of yours go wriggling along at such a rate it would be too late by now.'

'Well, maybe it would be better than nothing,' he urged.

'Oh, I'm too tired to move,' she said irritably. 'Besides,' she added firmly, 'I'm not going to have a baby for years. It would be idiotic, with a war coming.'

'Well, Matty . . .' But he was at a loss for words in the face of this irrationality. 'At any rate,' he announced firmly, 'we mustn't take any more chances at all. Actually we're being helluva fools. It's not the first time.'

'Oh, it'll be all right,' she agreed amenably, quite comfortable in the conviction, luckily shared by so many women who have not been pregnant, that conception, like death, was something remarkable which could occur to other people, but not to her.

'Did you tell Dr Stern about your periods?' he persisted.

'What about them?' she asked irritably, disengaging herself from his arm and lying parallel to him, not touching him.

'Well, you did say they were a bit irregular.'

'Oh, do stop fussing,' she cried, tormented. 'According to the book of words thousands of women have irregular periods before they have a baby and it doesn't mean a thing.'

'But, Matty, do be reasonable,' he implored.

She was silent. Even more did she want to weep. But this would have meant abandoning herself to him, and to explanations of what she could not explain herself – a feeling of being caged and trapped. Until two weeks ago, her body had been free and her own, something to be taken for granted. She would have scorned to fuss about, or even to notice, a period that was heavy or one that chose not to come at all. And now this precious privacy, this independence, so lately won from her mother's furtive questioning, was being threatened by an impertinent stranger.

'Matty,' he said again, 'don't you think you're being unreasonable?'

'I'm so tired I could scream,' she muttered defiantly.

Silence. Music from the waste lot came throbbing into the room. The big wheel, glittering with the white lights, revolved steadily, Like a damned wedding ring, she thought crossly, abandoning herself to anger, since she was not free to cry.

'I do hope you'll be in a better humour in the morning,' said Douglas coldly, after a pause.

Her mind began producing wounding remarks with the efficiency of a slot machine. She was quite dismayed at the virulence of some of the things that came to her tongue. She cautiously turned her head and saw his face showing in the steady flicker of lights. He looked young – a boy, merely; with a boy's sternness. She asked, in a different tone, 'Dr Stern said something about your stomach.'

His head turned quickly. Guardedly he said, 'What did he tell you,?'

'Nothing – only mentioned it. Why didn't you tell me?'

'Oh – I don't know.'

The pride that concealed a weakness appealed to her. She reached out her hand and laid it on his arm above the elbow. It stiffened, then responded.

'I've an ulcer – nothing much. I just go on the tack when I feel it.'

She could not help a pang of repulsion from the idea of an ulcer; then another of pity. 'I thought you had to have a special diet for ulcers?'

'Oh – don't fuss.' He added, contrite, 'I lay off fats when it starts up.'

'You're very young to have an ulcer,' she remarked at last. Then, thinking this sounded like a criticism, she tightened her fingers about the thick warm flesh. It was slack. He was asleep, and breathing deeply.

Chapter Two

When Martha woke, she knew she had slept badly. Several times she had half roused, with the urgent knowledge that she ought to be attending to something; and this anxiety seemed to be of the same quality as that suggested by the great dragging circle of lights, which continued to flicker through her sleep like a warning. The ceiling of the small bedroom spun with light until after midnight, when the wheel was stilled; then bars of yellow light lay deep over the ceiling, over the bed, across Douglas's face, from a room opposite, where a man must be lying awake reading, or a woman keeping vigil with a sick child.

At six she was fully awake. The sky outside was chilly white-gold haze; winter was coming. She leaned on her elbow to look out at the wheel; in this small colourless light it rested motionless, insignificant, and the machinery of the fun fair beneath it seemed tawdry and even pathetic. It no longer had the power to move her; and the fact that it had so disturbed her sleeping was absurd. But Martha had been born – or so it seemed – with the knowledge that the hours of sleep were long and busy, and of the same texture as the hours of waking. She entered sleep cautiously, like an enemy country. She knew, too, however, that for most it was a sudden dropping of a dark curtain, and regarded this other family of mankind with a simple envy, the result of her upbringing so far away from the centres of sophistication, where she would have learned to use the word 'neurotic' as a label that would make any further thought on the subject unnecessary, or as a kind of badge guaranteeing a superior sensibility. She was in that primitive condition where she was able to pay healthy respect to – Douglas, for instance.

She looked at him now with a rather wistful curiosity. He lay on his back, easily outstretched among the sheets and blankets. He was handsome when he slept. His face was open and rather flushed. An outflung arm, as if it had just fallen loose from the act of throwing something, lay in a calm, beautiful line from waist to shoulder. The upper part of his body emerging from the clothes, was solid, compact, the flesh clear and healthy; a light sprinkling of freckles over white, bright skin. He looked stern and dignified, sealed away from her in his sleep, and restored to the authority of good sense. Martha's respect for him was now deep and genuine. She thought, with a simplicity which was authorized and confirmed by the dignity of his face, I shall say we must stop being married; he won't mind.

When he woke, everything would be explained and settled.

Waiting for him to wake, she sat up and looked out. The town, no less than the fun fair, looked small and mean after the hazy splendours of the night. The two big blocks of flats opposite rose white and solid, but rain had streaked their sides into dinginess. Their windows were dead and asleep. Beyond them, half a dozen business houses, their surfaces clean with paint, glossy with money; and beyond these again, the tin-roofed shanties of the Coloured town, which marked the confines of order; for on two sides of this organized centre stretched the locations, or straggling slums where the Africans were. From a single small window she could overlook at least three worlds of life, quite separate, apparently self-contained, apparently linked by nothing but hate . . . But these familiar ideas, sprung in her mind by the simple act of looking through a window, were too much of a burden this morning. First Douglas should wake, and then it would be time to look out of the window. She might suggest to him, for instance, that he should at once throw up his job, and they should go and 'live among the people'.

She sprang out of bed, but noiselessly, and went next door to the living room. There, as she expected, lay a small heap of letters where Douglas had flung them down the night before. She carried them back to bed with her. Most were of that sort which people write to those getting married, in order that they may say with pride, 'We have had so and so many letters of congratulation.' At least, Martha could not yet see letters of politeness in any other way. She therefore tossed them aside, and took up one from her brother, now at the University of Cape Town. It was a good-humoured letter, full of determinedly humorous tolerance; their relations were always harmonious; in order that two people may quarrel they must have something in common to quarrel over.

The next, also from the university, was from Joss Cohen. She opened it with the most vivid delight; she even held it unopened for a moment, to delay the pleasure of reading it. What she expected from it was – but what did she *not* expect from Joss Cohen! At last she opened it. Four lines.

Dear Matty,
   Your brother mentioned that you got married last week. I must admit this was something of a surprise. However, please accept my congratulations. I hope your marriage will be happy and prosperous.

Yours,
Joss

She put it down slowly, flushing with hurt anger. It was that word 'prosperous' which stung her. Then she reread it, trying to revive him as he really was, since these colourless lines could have no power to evoke him. She admitted at last that she felt abandoned because he had not thought her worth even the trouble of a sarcastic phrase. Very well, then: she dropped the letter into the pile of purely formal ones.

The third was from Marnie Van Rensberg, on blue paper with a pink rose in one corner.

Dear Matty,
   Mom told me your news this morning. She heard it from your Mom at the station when she went in to get the mail. I am so happy Matty now we are both married. I hope you will be very happy. I am going to have a baby in January. The doctor says February, they think they know everything. I hope it will be a boy because Dirk

wants a boy. I don't mind what it is, but for my sake I hope it's a girl really, but who would be a woman in this world. Ha. Ha.

Affectionately, your old pal,
Marnie

The fourth was from Solly Cohen, and from the moment Martha opened it she knew she would find in it everything Joss had refused.

Well, well, Martha Quest. I'm not surprised, you are a born marrier, and I always told Joss so when he insisted something might be done with you. I hear high civil service prospects, pension, and no doubt a big house in the suburbs. If not yet, it will come, it will come. Well, well, you'll have to be a good girl now, no naughty ideas about the colour bar – no ideas of any kind, for that matter. If there is one thing you can't afford, dear Matty, in the station of life into which you've chosen to marry, god help you, it is ideas.

Well, as you will see from the address, I'm not in Cape Town any more. The higher education, being nothing but sh —, is not for me, though Joss is apparently prepared to go through with it. I'm making an effort towards communal life in the Coloured quarters of our great metropolis, a small light in a naughty world. All the boorjoys are very shocked, of course. I shall naturally not be allowed to have visitors of your sort, but if at any time you feel like dropping a line from your exalted world of tea parties, sundowners and sound incomes, I shall be pleased to read it.

Yours,
Solly

(I am not supposed to have letters unless the whole group approves, but I shall explain that a certain amount is due to you as a victim of the system.)

At first Martha allowed herself to feel angry and hurt, but almost at once she laughed, with the insight of fellow feeling. She read it again, isolated the word 'god', with a small g, and then the word 'boorjoys'. That's what you are doing it for, she thought maliciously. At once Joss seemed infinitely better than his brother; Solly was nothing but a child beside him. But at the same time she was thinking of this communal household as a refuge for herself. She had decided she would go there at once, that very morning, and ask if she might join them. She yearned towards it – a life of simplicity, conversation and ideals. And in the Coloured quarters, too . . . she was about to leap out of bed to pack a suitcase which would be the most final of arguments against being married, when she saw there was another letter lying among the folds of the bedclothes. It was from her mother.

My dear Girl,
   I do hope you enjoyed your honeymoon, and are not too tired after it. I am just writing to say that we have finally decided to sell the farm, we have had a good offer and shall settle in town. Somewhere near you, so that I can help you now that you are married and . . . (Here a line was carefully scratched out, but Martha made out the word 'baby', and went cold with anger.) At any rate, perhaps I can be of use.
                              No more now, affectionately,
                                                  Mother

This letter affected Martha like a strong drug. She threw herself on Douglas.

'What's the matter?' he jerked out, as he woke. He looked at her closely, and at once sat up. He yawned a little, warm and easy with sleep, then he smiled and put his arm around her.

'Douglas,' she announced furiously, 'do you know, I've had a letter from my mother, and do you know, they're moving into town after me, just in order to run my life for me, that's all it is, and – '

'Hold your horses,' he demanded. He absorbed this information, and said at last, 'Well, Matty, they were bound to move in sometime, what of it?'

She froze inwardly; and after a pause, moved away again. He moved after her, and began patting her shoulders rhythmically: he was calm, matter-of-fact, sensible.

'Now look here,' he went on. 'I know you have a thing about this, but you seem to think fate's got it in for you specially or something of the sort. All girls quarrel with their mothers, and mothers interfere – you should have seen my sister and my mother before Anne went to England. They were just like a couple of cats. Of course your mother's a bit of a Tartar. Just don't take any notice. And in any case' –

there he laughed good-temperedly – 'you'll be just as bad at her age,' he teased her.

These sensible remarks struck her as the extreme of brutality; but no sooner had she felt a rush of emotional indignation than a sincere emotion took hold of her. What Douglas had said, phrase after phrase, struck straight at her deepest and most private terrors. For if she remained in the colony when she had wanted to leave it, got married when she wanted to be free and adventurous, always did the contrary to what she wanted most, it followed that there was no reason why at fifty she should not be just such another woman as Mrs Quest, narrow, conventional, intolerant, insensitive. She was cold and trembling with fear. She had no words to express this sense of appalling fatality which menaced everyone, her mother as well as herself. She wriggled off the bed, away from his warm and consoling hand, and went to the window. Outside, the sunlight was now warm and yellow, everything was activity.

'Look,' she said flatly, 'it's like this. Ever since I can remember, they've been on that farm, stuck in poverty like flies on flypaper. All the time, daydreams about all kinds of romantic escapes – for years I believed it all. And now suddenly everything becomes perfectly simple, and don't you see, it was all for nothing. That's the point – it was all for nothing.'

She heard her voice rising dramatically, and stopped, irritated with herself.

Douglas was watching her. There was a look in his eyes which struck her. She looked down at herself. She was wearing a thin nightgown. She saw that he was finding her attractive in this mood. She was completely furious. With a gesture of contempt she picked up a dressing gown and covered herself. Then she said flatly, 'I can see I am being ridiculous.' Then, since he looked hurt and shamefaced, she began hurriedly, in an impulse to share it with him, 'The whole point is this: if it wasn't the sweepstakes, it was a gold mine or a legacy. In the meantime, nothing but the most senseless poverty – '

But again she heard that dramatic note in her voice, and

stopped short. *That* was not what she felt! She was unable to say what she meant in a way that sounded true. Silence – and she was filling with helpless exhaustion. Suddenly she thought, It's all so boring. She felt obscurely that the whole thing was old-fashioned. The time for dramatic revolts against parent was past; it all had a stale air. How ridiculous Solly was, with his communal settlements, and throwing up university – for what? *It had all been done and said already*. She had no idea what was the origin of this appalling feeling of flatness, staleness and futility.

'Oh, well,' she began at last, in a cheerful hard voice, 'it all doesn't matter. Nothing one does makes any difference, and by the time we're middle-aged we'll be as stupid and reactionary as our parents – and so it all goes on, one might as well get used to it!'

'Now Matty!' protested Douglas, helplessly, 'what on earth do you expect me to do about it? I'll stand by you, of course, if that's what you want.' He saw her face, which wore an unconscious look of pure hopeless fear, and decided it was enough. He got out of bed, and came to her. 'Now, don't worry, I shall look after you, everything's all right.'

At this Martha clung to him. 'I'm sorry,' she said brightly and falsely. 'I'm an awful fool.'

He kissed her, patted her here and there in an affectionate and brotherly way, and then said, 'For God's sake, I shall be late for the office. You should have woken me before.' He went whistling into the bathroom, and began shaving.

She went back to bed, propped a hand mirror on a ridge of blanket, and tried to brush her hair into shape. She did not want to be noticed, and each time Douglas came in to fetch something she hastily turned away. But when he at last came in fully dressed, he remarked, 'Your hair doesn't do too badly like that.' He was now in very good spirits. He announced, rubbing his hands, that he must not be late. There would be some sort of show at the office for him – this was the first day he would be at work since his marriage. As he picked up some papers, and gave his usual efficient glance around to see what he might have forgotten, he remarked, 'And don't forget the sundowner party tonight at the Brodeshaws.'

Martha said quickly, 'Douglas . . .'

He stopped on his way out. 'I'm awfully late.'

'Douglas, why can't we go to England – or somewhere?' she inquired resentfully. 'After all, you said . . .'

But he cut in quickly, 'There's going to be a war, and we can't take chances now.'

The newspaper was lying over the bedclothes – one glance at the headlines was enough. But she persisted. 'But it would be much better there than here if the war comes – at least we would be really in it.'

'Now look, Matty, I really am late.' He went out, hastily.

For some time she remained where she was, surrounded by the lanky sheets of newsprint, by scraps of letter, by the hand mirror, the brush, a tangle of the new white wedding linen. The headlines on the newspaper filled her with nothing but the profoundest cynicism. Then she saw a small book lying open on the bed, and pulled it towards her. She saw it was Douglas's engagement book, and left it; for it was certainly her strongest principle that a wife who looked at her husband's letters or pockets was the blackest sort of traitor to decency. But the little book still lay open, at arm's length. It was, after all, only an engagement book; and these engagements would concern herself. Compromising with her principles by not actually touching it, she moved closer and read the entries for the next two weeks. There was not a day free of sundowner parties, dances, lunches. Most of the names she did not know. The little book, lying beside the crumpled newspaper with its frightening black headlines, provided the strongest comment on her situation. She saw Solly's letter, with its emphatic scrawl of an address, foundering among billows of sheet. Her anxiety focused itself sharply with: I've got to get out of it all. She got up, and dressed rapidly. Her clothes were all crushed from packing; there was nothing to wear but the blue linen from yesterday. But what she looked like, she assured herself, would be quite irrelevant to Solly, who was now monastic and high-minded in his communal settlement. In a few minutes she had left the untidy flat behind, and was in the street.

And no sooner had she turned the corner which shut out the flats, than it seemed as if not only they but her marriage did not exist – so strong was her feeling of being free. She was regarding her marriage, the life she was committed to, with a final, horrified dislike. Everything about it seemed false and ridiculous, and that Matty who apparently was making such a success of it had nothing to do with herself, Martha, now walking at leisure down this street on a cool fine morning. It was only a short walk to the Coloured quarters, and she went slowly, loitering along the pavements under the trees, picking off leaves from the hedges, pulling at the long grass which forced itself up wherever there was a gap in the pavement.

What puzzled her most was that she *was* a success. The last few weeks, confused, hectic, hilarious, had one thread running through it: the delight of other people in this marriage. How many had not embraced her, and with the warmest emotion! Everyone was happy about it – and why? For – and this was surely the core of the matter? – how could they be so happy, so welcoming, when they didn't know her? She, Martha, was not involved in it at all; and so in her heart she was convicting them of insincerity. They could not possibly mean it, she concluded at last, dismissing all these friends and acquaintances, the circle into which she was marrying. The whole thing was a gigantic social deception. From the moment she had said she would marry Douglas, a matter which concerned – and on this point she was determined – no one but their own two selves, some sort of machinery had been set in motion which was bound to involve more and more people. Martha could feel nothing but amazed despair at the thought of the number of people who were so happy on their account.

And now she began walking as quickly as she could, as if running away from something tangible. She was already, in mind, with Solly, who would most certainly help her, rescue her; she did not quite know what he would do, but the truth of her relations with the Cohen boys, difficult, sometimes, but at least based on what they really thought and felt, could not possibly betray her now.

The street he had chosen to live in was in the most squalid part of town. She could not help smiling sourly as the poverty deepened around her: nothing less than the worst would do for Solly! Once these houses had been built for the new settlers. They were small and unpretentious, simple shells of brick covered with corrugated iron. Now each house held half a dozen families. Each was like a little town, miserable ragged children everywhere, washing hanging across doorways, gutters running filthy water. Between two such concentrated slums was a small house high on its foundations, in the centre of a fenced patch of garden. There were no other gardens in the street, only untidy earth, littered with tins, bits of cloth, trodden grass. Here, inside the new fence, was rich dark earth, with neat rows of bright green vegetables. The gate was new, painted white, and on it was a large board which said 'Utopia'. Martha laughed again: that touch of self-derision was certainly Solly's, she thought.

She was opening the gate when she heard a voice. A youth with a watering can emerged from a small shed and demanded what she wanted.

'I've come to see Solly Cohen,' she said, with a touch of defiance, for she had not, until now, remembered those other members of the community who might forbid her.

He was very young, Jewish, and every inch of him an intellectual, though it appeared he wanted to look like a peasant. After a pause, he nodded reluctantly, and turned away.

Martha went on up the path. There was a smell of hot sun on hot earth, the smell of evaporating water. Small bunches of brilliant green lettuce studded the dark earth, drops of water hung glistening in their leaves. They had just been watered; she could hear the deep soft drinking sound of water being sucked into dry soil. She walked slowly, for the pleasure of hearing it. She remembered how on the farm, after a storm, the tiny mealie plants held in their centres a single round, perfect drop of glittering water . . . But she was being observed, and by someone who resented her being there. She hurriedly climbed the steps. Whatever squalor had been here was cleaned away. The veranda, a small patch of dark-red cement between low grey walls, was polished and gleaming. The front door was newly painted a bright, strong blue. New paint, and cleanliness, and the windows were sparkling! She opened the blue door and found herself in the living room. It was empty. It was not a large room, but looked so because it had so little in it. The red cement floor had a piece of striped purple-and-yellow matting on it. There were half a dozen low wooden chairs, painted yellow. The walls had books all round them. That was all. To find this room in this street . . . But at this moment, a door was pushed open and Solly entered. His face showed blank surprise; then he hastily adjusted his expression.

'What are you doing here?' he asked unwillingly.

Martha sat down without being asked. 'Do you mind my coming to see you?' she asked. It sounded rather aggressive.

He could only reply that he did not. He sat down himself, with the air of one being polite against his will. Martha looked to see how he might have changed. Since she had seen him last, he had been to the university, quarrelled with his family, made a trip to England, *almost* got to Spain, had a love affair, returned, thrown up university for good. None of this showed on his face. He was exactly as he had been, tall, very thin, with a loose knobbly look about his movements. His face was sharp-featured and bony, with the look of the young intellectual Jew: lively and critical, but with an additional sarcastic hostility about him. His clothes were different, however. He wore very short dark-blue shorts and a rusty-brown shirt, falling loose. He was tanned a dark brown.

'I like the name you've chosen for your communal settlement,' said Martha, ready to laugh with him.

'We didn't choose it. It was the name before.'

'Oh!' Then: 'Do you mean the Coloured people called it Utopia?' she asked, dismayed and touched.

'That's right. Stoo-pid, isn't it?'

She saw he was jeering at her, and came back with 'I thought you had the grace to laugh at yourselves, at least.'

But he was not prepared to be provoked. In any case Martha blurted out, 'Can I come and live here, too?'

He looked at her, first grinning, then grave. 'Well, well,' he commented at last. Then, cautiously: 'I thought you'd just got married?'

'I have. But I want . . .' But it was impossible to make explanations. 'I shouldn't have got married, anyway. I would like to come and live here. Why shouldn't I?' she demanded like a child.

Here Solly, who had been preparing some gestures of amazement or amusement, simply shrugged.

'But you can't do that,' he said reproachfully at last.

Martha was indignant. 'Why did you write me that letter, then?' she asked naïvely.

'But, Matty . . .' Here he relapsed into his old manner. He was going to be simple and natural. 'But, Matty, you can't go getting married one week and throwing it up the next.' He was looking at her inquiringly; his face showed an intelligent comprehension – but not kindness.

Martha's spirits were sinking lower and lower. She saw she had been extremely foolish. However, she continued lamely, 'You mean, *everyone* feels like this, it's like measles, one just has to go through with it?'

'Having never been married myself . . .' he began portentously, but dropped the manner at once. 'What did you get married for?'

'I have no idea,' said Martha ruefully.

'Anyway, you can't live here,' he announced at last. 'For one thing, there aren't any women.'

Martha felt herself blushing, and was furious. For the first time it occurred to her that Solly might be taking this as a personal interest in himself. It was intolerable! She exclaimed belligerently, 'You keep out women?'

At once Solly recovered his jaunty manner. 'We did ask some girls. Unfortunately none of you can be torn away from your bright lights and your clothes. I suppose you understand that here everything is in common – books, money, everything. And we don't smoke and we don't drink.'

'And you are all celibate?' she inquired sarcastically.

'Naturally.' Then he added, 'But marriage is allowed.'

But now she laughed scornfully. 'Anyone'd see that married couples would wreck it.'

'Luckily we are none of us intending to get married, so that's all right.' She was sitting upright in her chair, eyes bright with anger, face flushed – he deliberately lounging in his, with an appearance of conscious ease. 'And you're not Jewish either,' he said. He sounded embarrassed.

This was something she had not thought of; and she saw at once it was unpardonable of her. She flushed deeper; her face was burning steadily, so that she would have liked to hide it. She wanted to say something like 'So now *you're* being exclusive,' but an awkward guilt stopped her. 'Well, that's certainly final,' she said, trying to sound light and casual. And then, seeing that he was still a little embarrassed, she went on: 'How many of you?'

'Four, at the moment. We are modelling ourselves on the settlements in Israel.'

'Israel?'

'Palestine to you,' and he could not help a sudden savage grin.

'But what will you do when the war starts?' she asked awkwardly.

'When the old men have finished their diplomatic fiddling and we can see what they're up to, we'll decide. I shall be a conscientious objector if they turn the war against the Soviet Union, and I shall fight if it's against Hitler.'

She felt very small beside this enviable clarity of mind. 'How nice to have everything so tidily planned, how nice to be so sure about everything.' She tried to jeer at him, but it sounded thin.

'There's nothing to stop you,' he said.

She got up, and with a familiar gesture turned to look at the bookshelves. She had only the time to see the names of books she had not heard of, authors that were new, when he said, trying to make a joke of it, 'No, Matty, you can't borrow books here. It's a joint library.'

'I wasn't going to.' She moved towards the door. 'Well, I'll go back home, then.'

But now he was obviously contrite. 'You don't have to run away. We won't eat you.'

After hesitation, she returned to her chair. They were now warm with friendship for each other. They were both remembering how often they had sat thus, in a small room filled with books, at the station; outside, the ox waggons rolled heavily through clouds of red dust, and the farmers in their loose working khaki hurried from store to garage, from garage to post office, with their letters and groceries; outside, the black people swarmed around the door of the store, fingering their bits of money and talking excitedly about the bargains they would make. Martha looked out of the window: a mass of dirty little houses, swarms of brown-skinned, poverty-ridden children; but under the window a Jewish youth was hoeing a patch of potatoes.

'You have no servants?'

'Of course not.'

'Well, I don't see what you're going to achieve by it,' she said doubtfully. 'Except, of course, you'll have a lovely time yourselves.' Her tone suggested that this was an aim she was prepared to approve of; but his black eyes watched her sarcastically as from an inner truth she could not be expected to see.

Silence, and the hoe rose and fell in the soft earth outside, with a thud, thud, thud. Someone turned a tap on somewhere close inside the house; the water rushed loudly, then it was cut off – silence again.

'You study all day, you discipline yourselves, you work hard?' Martha attempted again.

'That's right.'

'You might just as well be – up in the white town. Why do you have to come and live here?'

'We have contacts with the local people,' he said defensively; it seemed this was a weak point.

'You could have classes for them?' she said excitedly.

But at this he laughed heavily. 'That's right, so we could. As for you, you'll be dishing out charity to the poor from your lofty position in the civil service, inside five years.'

She shrugged this off impatiently, untouched by the gibe.

'What sort of — contacts?' She used the stiff, impersonal word with difficulty, trying to make it into a picture: Solly and his friends, talking, in this room, with some of the poor Coloured people she could see out of the window.

'Actually,' he announced briskly, 'the Coloured community are a waste of time. In their position halfway between the blacks and the white Herrenvolk, they are bound to be unstable, they are petty bourgeois to the core, all of them.'

He was jettisoning them all! Martha, very shocked, said feebly, 'They are human beings, after all.'

'So they are,' he said with his brisk jeer, his black eyes snapping scorn. 'So they are. We are all human beings, and everyone is as good as everyone else, all born equal in the sight of God.'

'Well, you brought in God, I didn't. What's God got to do with it?'

They were now as awkward with hostility as they had been a few moments before with friendship.

'Anyway, there are a few hundred Coloureds, and several million Africans — what's the point of it?'

'We'd have lived in the location, but it's against the law. So we chose the next best thing.'

'Rubbish, you only came to live here because people'd be shocked, that's all.'

He tapped the long bony fingers on the arm of his chair and yawned. It was not for some seconds that she realized the yawn was deliberate. At once she got up and said, 'I'll go. I've got things to do.'

'Your housewifely duties?' he asked sarcastically.

She stood behind her chair, looking regretfully at this pleasant room, the books, feeling the atmosphere of dedicated freedom, feeling herself an exile. But she felt something else too: a deep pity for him. He seemed all at once very young and absurd.

'Well,' she said flatly, 'when the war comes, that'll be the end of it. But it'll be nice while it lasts.'

He regarded her in silence, apparently considering whether she was worth the trouble he might decide to take.

Then he said, 'Now, listen, Matty, I shall now give you a short lecture on the international situation.' He grinned savagely, and she smiled back gratefully. She noted at the same time, half consciously, that he, unlike his brother, could take nothing seriously. That was how she felt it: the jaunty self-consciousness, the invisible quotation marks around his phrases, the drawled 'situ-a-tion', gave her a strong feeling of disbelief.

She stood, however, behind her chair and listened. He spoke for some ten minutes, as if he were delivering a lecture, but in the harsh, flat language of controlled cynicism, which chimed in very well with what she felt herself. And although the picture he presented of what was happening in Europe was cold, simple and logical, that harshness and cynicism could only feed her own. So that when he had finished she said drily, 'Well, whichever way it goes, there'll be a war, won't there?'

'Well?'

She shrugged, avoiding the hard aggressiveness of that black stare.

He began to jeer again. 'Yes, poor Matty, life is hard, life isn't easy. People get killed, the cows get into the rose garden, violence keeps popping up its ugly head.'

She remarked irrelevantly, 'My father was in the last war. He talks about it.'

He stared. 'Well?' Then, in a flat, angry voice, quite different from any she had heard from him − for the first time carrying the conviction of deep personal feeling: 'And the Jews are in the concentration camps. Who cares? Do you? If the British Government wanted, they could stop it all in a month − if they wanted. As for you,' and here he mimicked her doubting, hesitant voice, 'all you say is, Don't let's have any nastiness, please let everything be comfortable.'

She was now so confused by all this hostility − for it was clear that she had become for him the enemy he hated most − that she could only say, 'Well, Solly . . .' and tailed off into silence.

He was now waiting for her to go. She asked, 'What do you hear from Joss?'

'We don't write.'

She went towards the door.

'He's joined the Communist Party,' she heard.

'Well, I thought he was a Communist anyway.'

'He's joined it, that's quite different from talking.'

There was such spite in his voice that she turned and inquired, 'Why, do you mind him joining?' Then she saw it was directed against herself. He picked up a newspaper from beside him and handed it to her. It was a thin, limp paper. She looked at it dubiously. It was called *The Watchdog*. The headlines, large and strident, assaulted her mind. She heard him laugh, and saw that she was holding the thing as if it might explode in her face. She smiled ruefully.

'Nasty crude paper,' he said. 'You don't want to be seen with it. What would your friends say? Let alone your nice husband.'

Since she did not feel at all identified with her husband or his circle, she let this pass. She looked down again at the paper. The exclamatory style, the hectoring language, affected her uncomfortably, as if her whole system had been injected by some powerful irritating substance that it must throw off. But she looked at it steadily and saw that what it was saying was no more than Solly's just-concluded lecture on the international situation.

He summed up her thought by saying, 'It's all right if you hear it all said in nice intellectual language in a nice comfortable room, but it's quite different like that, isn't it?'

She laid it down on a chair and looked at him. She needed to wound him as he was wounding her. She asked, 'Why don't you join the Communist Party, then?' He simply maintained his steady grin; she realized that he must have joined it, otherwise he would not look so satirical. After a moment, she tried another tack: 'Who's paying for this house and this quiet intellectual existence?' He reddened; and she persisted, 'Your four fathers, no doubt. So your share of it comes from the profits made out of the kaffir store in the district. I don't see that you are any better than I am, if it comes to that.' He was waiting for a chance to get in at her, but she went on hastily, delighted with her advantage: 'So I'll leave you to your *independence*, until the bull gets into this rose garden.'

She quickly shut the door behind her, and walked rapidly down the garden. All vegetables, of course, she thought, trying to be spiteful, but on the verge of tears. No flowers for the high-minded, naturally! While she had been inside, the earth around the little green clumps of lettuce had dried. Small granules of grey earth lay evenly over the base of wet dark richness. The youth was steadily hoeing potatoes at the far end of the garden. He did not lift his head as she came past. Then she heard her name called: Solly stood on the veranda.

'Matty – would you like to come to a meeting here tonight?'

She hesitated, then called back sardonically, 'Unfortunately I have a sundowner party – ' But she was unable to finish. Solly was doubled up in a pantomime of laughter.

She turned her back on him and walked away under the trees that shaded the pavement. It was some minutes before she was able to smile at herself and at him, her regret at having to leave was so strong. She felt forsaken; and nothing but the memory of Solly's savage farewell laughter prevented her from hurrying back and saying that of course she would come to the meeting. When she reached the flat, she occupied herself with altering a dress to fit her for the sundowner party that night, and with an ironical consciousness of how Solly would see this proceeding. But there was something much stronger, a feeling of Well, then, I'll show him! The showing him consisted in making the dress and herself as attractive as she knew how. It was not until she realized this that she remembered the moment when she had felt he might be thinking that she had come to him as a man, and not as a person in that romantic thing, a communal settlement. She burned with embarrassment; she could not forgive him. Now, looking back at the meeting, she could see the thing in no other way; everything they had said was permeated with this other emotion; to it she attributed his aggressiveness and that sarcastic stare. She was hating him quite vividly. In a short while, the memory of that interview had become quite unbearable; and she was putting stitches into the fabric of her dress with strong stabs of the needle, while she muttered incoherently, Idiot! Conceited idiot! And even: Can't they ever see us differently?

When Douglas returned that afternoon, he was welcomed by an extremely cheerful young woman, who proceeded to amuse him with a satirical account of how she had rushed down to see Solly – all intelligent in blue trousers and sunburn – and how she had wanted to join the settlement. Because, as everyone knows, we girls go through these moments of not wanting to be married.

'And me too,' confessed Douglas, apologetically, kissing her with a rueful laugh. This mutual confession delighted them. They were back together in the warmest affection, which almost at once led to the bed – there was half an hour to fill in, as he pointed out. The half-hour was hilarious. In a mood of tearing gaiety, they experimented with a couple of new positions sanctioned by the book, and were freshly delighted with their efficiency. Then, seeing the time, six o'clock, that hour sacred to sundowner parties, they hastened off the bed and got dressed. They drove off to the party with the look of competent unconcern that they had both already learned to wear in public.

Colonel Brodeshaw's house was in the part of the town which had been the most fashionable before the new suburbs began to spread. There were several avenues of big sprawling shady houses in big gardens – these were the nearest approach to an individual architecture the colony had achieved. They had been built for comfort, for the climate, by people with money and enough self-confidence not to need the extra boost of that kind of smart house which was now being built. They were the natural expression, in fact, of the type of English person whose families have been in the habit of administering this part or that of the British Empire, accustomed to making themselves comfortable in a difficult climate. Comfort was their keynote. The servants' quarters, built in a row along the end of the back garden, and reminiscent of stables, were vast – not because these people intended to make their servants comfortable, but because they meant to have plenty of servants. The rooms were large and cool, the verandas enormous; whatever these houses might look like from outside, sprawling, shapeless, often shabby, they were a delight to live in.

The young Knowells drove through several avenues filled with such houses, and were able to feel a pleasant regret for the past. They murmured that it was a pity people did not build like that these days. They parked the car with a dozen others in the ditch outside a flaring hibiscus hedge, and walked up a narrow drive that was like a green tunnel. Through gaps in the foliage, hoses could be seen playing on a smooth green lawn, and beyond that the garden was bounded by a warm red-brick wall draped with morning glory, a vivid sky blue which was beginning – the sun was setting – to show edges of white. Soon it would be as if scraps of limp dirty-white linen hung among the green. A few steps further, and the front veranda was in sight, a garden inside a garden, for it was filled with painted tubs of flowering plants, and festooned with golden shower. People too, of course; but the veranda was as big as a large room, and able to absorb large numbers of people among the columns of brick and tubs of flowers.

From outside, Martha caught a glimpse of faces she knew, and felt a stab of disappointment: she could not rid herself of the belief that being married would introduce her to something new and exciting. She could see Donovan, and Ruth Manners; and was looking for others, when Douglas remarked, 'Mr Player is going to be here, I believe.' He tried to sound casual, but could not prevent a note of pleased deference.

Martha was looking for Mr Player, when they arrived at the top of the steps and were met by Colonel Brodeshaw and Mrs Brodeshaw. The Colonel was a tall, thin, bent man, with a small dark moustache and mahogany skin, so much the colonel in manner and appearance that it must save Martha the effort of looking for further individuality. His wife was competently dispensing hospitality in a black-and-white flowered dress, a colonel's lady, clipped, brisk and smiling.

Martha had not taken two steps before she was absorbed into the warm embrace of Mrs Talbot, and welcomed with a warm but timid smile by Mrs Talbot's daughter. Martha knew that of all the people who were being made happy by this marriage, Mrs Talbot was perhaps the happiest. She had received no less than three charming notes from her in the last week, welcoming her into – what? And now she was putting her arm around Martha's shoulders, turning her away from other groups on the veranda, and leading her to a chair beside her own. Over her shoulder she smiled and murmured to Douglas, 'You really must allow me to deprive you of Matty for just a few minutes.' And Douglas, smiling and touched, seemed prepared to wait.

Mrs Talbot was, above all, a lady of charm. In each movement, each tone of her voice, was this suggestion of deferential murmuring grace; and as she seated herself beside Martha she did so with a hurried, almost apologetic movement of her hindquarters, as if even this personal necessity was something deplorable because it detracted from the wholehearted attention she was determined to bestow upon Martha. Both she and her daughter then leaned towards her, smiling with warm friendship, and proceeded to tell her how happy they were that Douggie was married at last, how wonderful, how suitable, how . . . As one woman arrived at the end of a breathless phrase, searching for the superlatives that could not express what she felt, the other took it up; and it was a duet of self-immolation towards Martha.

Martha seated, smiling a little awkwardly, looked from one to the other, trying to see them, for she felt herself in danger of being smothered by this perfumed attack. She was able at last to see Mrs Talbot as a tall, fair-haired woman, slight, pliant, with a smooth oval face tinted uniformly pink, like a fine breathing enamel. Everything, hair, face, dress, was so smoothly perfect, so exquisitely created, that one felt impelled to look at the daughter to find the raw materials from which this work of art had been begun. Elaine was like her mother, a slight graceful creature, but the oval face, the large grey eyes, showed signs of strain and ill-health. The skin was pale, flawed; there were faint blue shadows under the eyes. Martha looked from one to the other, noting the looks of affectionate reassurance that continually passed between them, and thought only that for a girl of eighteen to be so close to her mother must in itself be perverse. She felt herself menaced by it. But since there was no need for her to say anything but 'Thank you' and 'How very kind of you', she allowed her attention to pass to that other problem which was so much her preoccupation. For the spiritual hangers-on which every marriage attracts must certainly expect to suggest the question, What is it they themselves have found, or lack, in marriage? Since Mrs Talbot and her daughter could not be delighted that it was *Martha* who had married Douglas – they did not know her, as Martha reminded herself – it must be the idea of marriage that fed this delight? Martha tried to form some sort of image of Mr Talbot, and it was only then that she realized that she did not even know whether there was one. She had heard a great deal about Mrs Talbot during the past weeks, but it was always 'Mrs Talbot and Elaine', 'Elaine and Mrs Talbot' – that was how the world spoke of the Talbot family. Together they enveloped Martha in caressing affection, and together they rose, after a long, smiling, intimate look at her which – even in this small matter of agreeing that it was time to release Martha – overflowed into a glance of understanding between them. The young Knowells were invited to spend the evening very soon with Mrs Talbot and Elaine, and (for of course he was so happy about the marriage, too) Mr Talbot – if he wasn't out ('He always has so much to do'); and the two women withdrew into chairs further away, where they proceeded to allow their reservoirs of charm to overflow on to Douglas.

Martha was therefore left alone for a moment, looking down the great veranda, which was like a room with three walls of green leaves. The last rays of sunlight fell through the leaves, patterning the faces of the guests. Perhaps forty people were sitting, with glasses in their hands, in this green-dappled glow. Martha could see Donovan poised on the edge of his chair, addressing Ruth Manners. 'But, my dear, it was the funniest thing you ever saw,' she heard his light voice say, before he let it drop and leaned forward to continue the sentence in a lower key; it was a bit of gossip: the discreetly malicious smile on Ruth's face showed it. Beside Ruth sat a young man whom Martha had not seen before. She immediately recognized him as being fresh from England, because of his pink-faced, cautious look of one on trial. From the way he and Ruth smiled at each other, it was clear they were a couple.

Far down the veranda, in a well of green shadow, Mr Maynard was surveying the guests with his look of sardonic but controlled contempt. Beside him was that formidable lady his wife, who in a high, firm, commanding voice was saying the last word about something she felt strongly: 'And so I said to her, "It is quite out of the question!"' She turned to look at her husband, commanding agreement; but Mr Maynard continued to gaze in front of him, lightly flipping his fingers against the glass he held. The clink, clink, clink, came travelling softly down among the voices and laughter, like irritation made audible; and Martha looked at this black-browed energetic woman, and remembered, with a strong feeling of incongruity, that sick headaches were her weapon of choice. She was convicting Mrs Maynard of having no sense of period, when she saw Mr Anderson, sitting not far from his son, a small dapper man radiating bad temper because it was necessary to be here at all and to make conversation. He was making it, Martha saw with surprise, to Mrs Anderson, who sat near him. The fact that Mr Anderson could be persuaded to leave his solitude reminded Martha that this was an important sundowner party, and she searched for Mr Player. Remembering a brief glimpse of a large, red-faced man, she searched in vain – he could not have arrived.

The chair beside her was still empty. Donovan rose from his place and joined her, remarking gaily, 'Well, Matty, so here you are nicely settled at last.' This reference to her marriage she let pass; she was looking to see if there was anything in his face which might suggest that he remembered the ugliness of their last meeting. But it seemed not. He proceeded to entertain her with a scandalous story about their hostess. To which Martha replied that the moment he left her he would undoubtedly make a spitefully funny story about her marriage. He giggled gracefully and said that he had been dining out on stories about her for the last week. 'Really, Matty, why do you waste such an occasion for being on show? Now, look at Ruth, she's got herself engaged, and she's having a nice engagement party, and we'll all give her expensive presents, and everything's so satisfactory for her and her friends.'

'On the other hand, there won't be any funny stories about her wedding,' she pointed out. 'You can't have it both ways.'

'True,' he conceded, 'true.'

He was looking among the guests to see if there might be someone to inspire an anecdote, when Martha inquired, 'What's Ruth's young man like?'

'On the way up. Secretary to the secretary of Mr Player. Money, family, everything.' Then with his usual gay spite: 'One could hardly expect less of Ruth, after all, considering what's been done for her.'

'Yes, but what's he like?' inquired Martha naïvely, looking at the neat little English face, all the features correctly in place, the small fair moustache, the sober clothes that succeeded in suggesting only what the limbs and body must be like underneath – correct, controlled, adequate.

Donovan grinned pleasantly; then he said in a soft lowered voice which for the first time allowed that they did, after all, know each other quite well, 'Really, Matty, you'll never learn! Surely that's enough!'

Here she laughed with him, in genuine appreciation of that wit which, however, he was determined should never be more than socially agreeable. But he went on, with the astounding frankness with which he said what he really felt: 'Anyway, Matty, if a girl marries a man with money and so on, what more can she want?' He sounded really aggrieved. She let out a snort of laughter; saw him flush, and then he rose gracefully. 'Well, Matty, I shall now leave you.' His smile was cold; their eyes met unpleasantly; then he sailed, in a way which was reminiscent of his mother, across the veranda to another empty chair.

Martha's glass was refilled for her. She was becoming depressed as the alcohol took effect. She was disappointed that there was anyone here that she knew; and looked back to her first weeks in town, when the people she met seemed like glorious and disconnected phenomena, meteors and rockets that went shooting across her vision, only to disappear. But certainly not tamely connected in social circles. That Donovan, Ruth, even Mr Maynard, should be brought to this veranda on this evening by a mysterious connection gave her a feeling of oppression. She could feel the nets tightening around her. She thought that she might spend the rest of her life on this veranda, or others like it, populated by faces she knew only too well. It was at this point, and for the first time, that she found herself thinking, The war will break it up, it won't survive the war. Then she was sincerely dismayed and ashamed. She said it must be her own fault that she could see no face, hear no voice, which could make her happy at the idea of being here.

Half a dozen chairs away, Mrs Talbot and Elaine were discussing with a third lady a new method of cutting sandwiches, and, Martha noted, with precisely the same allowance of deferential charm that they had given her marriage. Opposite them, two ladies were arguing – what else? the iniquities of their servants. Mrs Maynard, at the other end of the veranda, and at the top of her confident voice, was discussing hers. Mr Maynard, from the depths of his resigned boredom, took up the theme with a slow, deliberate account of a case he had judged that morning. A native youth had stolen some clothes from his employer; the question before him, the magistrate, had been: Should the sentence be prison or an official beating? He told his story with a calm objectivity that sounded brutal. But Martha, as she watched that heavy and handsome face, saw the full, authoritative eyes move slightly from one face to another, saw suddenly that he was using this audience, which, after all, was not so arbitrarily associated, as a sort of sounding board.

Everyone was listening now, waiting to jump into the discussion with their own opinions; for certainly this was a subject, *the* subject, on which they were all equipped to speak. But Mr Maynard was not yet ready to throw the ball out for play. Having concluded with the bare facts of the case, he turned to a similarly large and authoritative gentleman in a neighbouring chair, and remarked, 'It is a question, of course, of whether a sentence should be regarded as a punishment or a deterrent. Until that is decided – and they certainly haven't decided it even in England – I can hardly be expected to have any opinions?'

The half-dozen people who had been leaning forward, mouths half open, ready to say what they thought, were taken aback by the depths of intellectuality into which they were expected to plunge. They waited. One lady muttered, 'Nonsense, they should all be whipped!' But she turned her eyes, with the rest, towards the gentleman appealed to.

He appeared to be thinking it over. He sat easily in his chair, an impressive figure, his body and face presenting a series of wide smooth surfaces. His corpulence was smoothly controlled by marvellous suiting, the fat pink areas of cheek and chin seemed scarcely interrupted by the thin pink mouth, the small eyes. When he lifted his eyes, however, in a preliminary circling glance before speaking, it was as if the bulk of ordinary flesh, commonplace cheeks, took an unimportant position behind the cold and deliberate stare. Those eyes were not to be forgotten. It was as if the whole personality of this man struggled to disguise itself behind the appearance of a man of business who was devoted to good, but good-natured, living – struggled and failed, for the calculating, clever eyes betrayed him. He said in a casual voice that in his opinion the whole legal system as affecting the Africans was ridiculously out of date and should be radically overhauled.

One could hear the small suppressed gasp of dismay from his listeners. But Mr Maynard kept his full prompting eyes fixed on the cold grey ones, and merely nodded; whether in agreement or not, he intended to convey, was quite unimportant, for it was his task to administer the law and not to change it. Martha was expecting an outburst from these people; she had not spent the greater part of her nineteen years listening to talk about the native problem for nothing. She was astounded that they remained silent.

It was Mrs Maynard who spoke for them; it was the politeness of her disagreement that told Martha that this fat pig of a man must be Mr Player. She could not easily believe it; a man cannot become a legend without certain penalties, and it seemed to her altogether too simple that people so inevitably become like the caricatures that their worst enemies make of them; besides, it was hard to connect the groomed pink face with that large hot red one she had once caught a glimpse of on a racecourse. Mrs Maynard was announcing firmly that it was obvious the natives were better served by being whipped than being sent to prison, for they didn't mind prison, it was no disgrace to them. They were nothing but children, after all. At this a dozen ladies angrily flung out their agreement. Martha listened with tired familiarity – this was something one could always be sure of. One after another, it was stated in varying ways that the natives should be kept in their place – and then Martha lost a few remarks, because she was considering something she had just realized. Two familiar words had not been used: *nigger* and *kaffir*; either this was an evolution in opinion or this circle of people were different and less brutal than those she had been used to.

There was a silence in progress when Martha became attentive again. Then the second camp made itself heard. It was Mrs Talbot who said, with a breathless air of defiance, that the poor things shouldn't be whipped, everyone should be kind to everyone else. Her daughter murmured agreement, and was rewarded by a glance of grateful affection from her mother, who was flushed by her own daring. For while 'poor things' was certainly not a new note, the suggestion that poor things and children should not be whipped for their own good, was.

At this point, the young man from England, the secretary of the secretary, gave it as his opinion, with a quick and rather nervous glance towards Mr Player, that public opinion in the colony was behind the times. The silence that followed was a delicate snub to the newcomer because of the burden of problems that they all carried. Ruth remarked in a detached voice that progressive people thought that whipping only made people worse. The word 'progressive' was allowed to pass; she was very young, and had been educated largely in England. Then Douglas stoutly averred, with the slight stammer which Martha was only just beginning to see could be a delicate compliment to superiors, that what was needed in the colony was good housing and good feeding, and the colony could never move forward while the bulk of the population was so backward. A silence again, during which Martha looked with grateful affection towards him; and everyone looked towards Mr Player.

The great man nodded affably towards Douglas, and said, 'I quite agree.' Again he allowed a pause for considered thought, and that slow, circling grey stare. Then he began to speak; and Martha heard with amazement the liberal point of view expressed by this pillar of reaction, this man who was a symbol of 'the Company'. It was a shock to everything she had believed possible. And now many people who had been silent came in. Martha looked from face to face and tried to see what connected the champions of progress. At first she failed. Then she saw that mostly they were 'business' as opposed to 'civil service'. The talk went on, and it was not until she had heard the phrases 'greater efficiency', 'waste of labour', etc., etc., often enough, that she understood.

What she had understood was finally crystallized by Mr Player's summing up. He said that the whites were ruining their own interests; if the blacks (Martha noted that his use of the emotional word was calculated) were not to revolt, they must be fed and housed; and he, Mr Player, blamed above all the Editors of the *Zambesia News*, for persistently feeding the public with nonsense. For the last ten years, said Mr Player, ignorance had been pandered to by a policy that could only be described as monstrously stupid; any expression of a desire for improvement on the part of the natives was immediately described as impertinence, or sedition, or even worse. We were, after all, living in the twentieth century, concluded Mr Player, while he directed his grey stare towards a man halfway down the veranda.

Following the searchlight of that stare, Martha saw at the end of it an uncomfortable, flushed gentleman angrily clutching at a glass of whisky. Since it was obvious that Mr Player did nothing casually, it followed that this gentleman must be connected with the press. As soon as Mr Player had finished, he remarked aggressively that the press was not concerned with fostering the interests of any particular section of the population. His look at Mr Player was pure defiance.

Mr Player stared back. Then he said that it was in no one's interest that the blacks (this time the word was a small concession to the press) should be ill-fed and ill-housed into a condition where they weren't fit for work. He paused and, having narrowed his eyes for a final stab, said, 'For instance, I hear that on the Canteloupe Mine a policy of proper feeding and housing is gaining quite remarkable results.' He elaborated this policy for some time. It occurred to Martha belatedly that this same mine was almost certain to be connected with the Company, and that Mr Player himself had originated this enlightened policy. Mr Player redirected his stare towards him, and remarked, 'Some people might wonder why something that is after all an experiment is not considered newsworthy by a paper which claims to represent everybody?'

The victim grew redder, resisted for a moment, then said clumsily, 'Well, of course, we are always ready to print genuine news.'

At once Mr Player removed his gaze and elaborated his theme in a different key for a while, then passed to another. He did not look towards the *News* again. They all listened in silence – the Service, business, two members of Parliament, the press – while Mr Player continued to express views which ninety per cent of the white population would consider dangerous and advanced. Obstinate, even ironical faces seemed to suggest that it was all very well for Mr Player, who did not have to answer to this same ninety per cent, but only to investors overseas. One felt that no slighter provocation than this could have provoked them even to think of these investors, particularly as such thoughts were likely to be followed by others – such as, that the Company indirectly owned a large part of the *News* and most of the businesses who used its advertising space.

A telephone rang inside the long room which could be glimpsed through the open French windows. A native servant emerged, anonymous in his white ducks and red fez, to say Mr Player was wanted on the telephone. The secretary of the secretary made a movement towards rising; and subsided as Mr Player rose with a sharp look at him. He sat stiffly beside Ruth, discomfited. There was a long silence, while they listened to the voice inside. Then Mrs Brodeshaw remarked with a smile that Mr Player had a horse running in a race in England. There was a burst of relieved, admiring laughter.

Martha was looking at Mr Maynard, who did not laugh, but appeared bored and indulgent. Her persistent, speculative stare had its effect, for he got heavily to his feet and came down towards her. He sat down, saying, 'If you young women will change your hair styles every day, what can you expect?'

'I cut it,' said Martha awkwardly – everyone had watched him coming to join her. Then Mrs Brodeshaw mentioned her roses, and conversation began again.

'Did Binkie come back?'

'He returned last night,' said Mr Maynard. A glance at him showed his face momentarily clenched; a second, blandly indifferent. 'His mother is a different woman as a result,' he remarked; but at this point Mr Player returned. Everyone looked expectantly prepared to triumph or commiserate over the horse in England, but Mr Player sat down, and leaned over to murmur something to the young secretary. He was pink with importance.

Mr Maynard watched the scene, holding his glass between two loosely cupped hands, and said, 'That is a very pretty young man.'

'Oh, very!' she agreed scornfully.

'Have you noticed that the type of immigrant is changing?

The era of the younger sons is passing. A pity – I am a firm believer in younger sons. Now we have what the younger sons, such as myself, for instance, left England to escape from.' The idea of Mr Maynard as a younger son made Martha laugh; and he gave her a quizzical look. 'Now, in the old days – but you wouldn't remember that.' He glanced at her and sighed. Martha felt she was being dismissed. He did not continue. Instead he asked, in a casual but intimate voice that referred to yesterday's encounter, 'Well, what do you make of it all?' He glanced around the long veranda and then at her.

Martha blurted out at once, 'Awful. It's all awful!'

He gave her another glance and remarked, 'So I thought. I have been looking at you and thinking that if you must feel so strongly you'd better learn to hide it. If I may give you advice from the height of my – what? fifty-six years.'

'Why should I hide it?' she demanded.

'Well, well,' he commented. 'But it won't do, you know!'

'You didn't even know it was me, you didn't recognize me,' she accused him.

'I have noticed,' he swerved off again, 'that at your age women are really most extraordinarily unstable in looks. It's not till you're thirty or so that you stay the same six months together. I remember my wife . . .' He stopped frowning.

There was a conversation developing at the bottom of the veranda. Martha heard the words 'the war', and sat up.

'Mr Player must naturally be concerned with the international situation,' remarked Mr Maynard. 'A man who controls half the minerals in the central plateau can hardly be expected to remain unmoved at the prospect of peace being maintained.'

Martha digested this; what he was saying had, to her, the power to blast everyone in this house off into a limbo of contempt. It was more difficult for her to understand that for him it was enough to say it. She could find nothing polite enough to express what she felt. He looked at her again, and it disconcerted her because he saw so clearly what she would have liked to say.

'My dear Mrs Knowell, if I may advise you – ' But again

he checked himself, and said, 'Why should I? You'll do as you like, anyway.'

'What advice?' she asked, genuinely.

But now he fidgeted his large and powerful dark-clad limbs in his chair, and said with the gruffness which was his retreat, 'Let's leave it at this: that I'm profoundly grateful I'm nearly sixty.' He paused and added scathingly, 'I can leave it all safely in the hands of Binkie.'

'There are other people,' she remarked awkwardly; she was thinking of Joss and Solly. Suddenly it occurred to her that there was an extraordinary resemblance between this dignified man and the rebel in the settlement in the Coloured quarters. Of course! It was their savage and destructive ways of speaking.

But now he remarked, 'I daresay one attaches too much importance to one's own children.' He sounded tired and grim. She was immediately sorry for him. She was trying to find words to express it, when he nodded down towards the end of the veranda to direct her attention there.

Colonel Brodeshaw was speaking. '. . . a difficult problem,' she heard. 'If we conscript the blacks, the question of arming them arises. It'll come up before the House in due course . . .' Once again, this gathering was being used as a sounding board. This time there was no doubt, no cleavage of opinion, no need even for discussion. From one end of the veranda to the other, there was a murmur of 'Obviously not. Out of the question.' It was so quickly disposed of that Colonel Brodeshaw had the look of an orator on a platform who has been shouted at to sit down in the middle of a speech. He murmured, 'Well, it'll not be settled as easily as all that.' People looked towards Mr Player; it appeared he had no views on the matter. Mrs Maynard announced finally, 'If they learn to use arms, they can use them on us. In any case, this business of sending black troops overseas is extremely shortsighted. They are treated as equals in Britain, even by the women.' There was no need to say more.

Mr Maynard remarked, 'One of the advantages of living in a society like this, though I don't expect you'll appreciate it yet, is that things can be said. Now, in Britain it would take a very stupid person to talk in such a tone. In the colonies there is an admirable frankness which makes politics child's play in comparison.'

'It's revolting,' she said angrily.

'Well,' he said, flipping his forefinger against his glass again, 'well, when this colony has reached the stage where a gathering like this talks about uplifting the masses of the people, you'll find that politics will be much more complicated than they are now.'

'Mr Player has just been talking about it.'

'But with what engaging truth, with what disarming frankness. Enlightened self-interest – it has taken us long enough to reach it. Why, only a year ago, I remember, the suggestion by dieticians that Africans were not conveniently equipped by nature to subsist healthily on mealie meal and nothing else was treated as the voice of revolution itself. We advance, we advance! Now, in my youth, my "class" – as you so refreshingly have no inhibitions in putting it – were for the most part outspokenly engaged in putting the working classes in their place. But when I paid a visit to England last year, how different things were! The working classes were undoubtedly just where they used to be, but everyone of my "class" seemed concerned only to prove not only that they were entitled to a good life, but that they had already achieved it. Further, it was almost impossible to hold a conversation with my friends and relations, because their speech was full of gaps, pauses, and circumlocutions where words used to be. With what relief did I return to this country, where a spade is still called a spade and I can use the vocabulary that I was taught to use during my admirable education. I can no longer say, 'The kaffirs are getting out of hand', that is true. But I can say, 'The blacks need firm treatment.' That's something. I am grateful for it.'

Martha did not know what to say. She could not make out from this succession of smooth and savage sentences which side he was on. As she put it, with a straightforwardness which she imagined he would commend, 'If you think it's terrible, then why do you . . . ?'

'But I didn't say I thought it was terrible. On the contrary, if there's one thing my generation has learned it is that the more things change, the more they remain the same.'

Martha reached out her hand to take his glass. 'You're going to break it,' she warned. He had in fact broken it – there was a mess of wet glass in his hand. He glanced at it, with raised brows, then reached for a handkerchief. Martha was looking around to see if the incident had been noticed. But everyone was listening to Mrs Brodeshaw, who was explaining how she was forming a women's organization in preparation for the war.

A servant came forward to remove the bits of glass.

'We old men,' Mr Maynard said apologetically, 'are full of unaccountable emotions.'

'I know,' said Martha at once. 'You're like my father – what upset you was the 1914 war, wasn't it?'

He looked exceedingly uncomfortable, but assented.

'You really seemed to think it was going to change things, didn't you?'

'We did attach a certain importance to it at the time.'

She heard her name called. Donovan was grinning at her with a gay spite which warned her. 'You don't agree, Matty dear, do you?' he was calling down the veranda.

'I wasn't listening.'

Mrs Talbot came out with apologetic charm, 'Donovan was telling us that you were a pacifist. I don't blame you, dear, war is so utterly dreadful.' She broke off with a confused look around her.

'But I'm not a pacifist,' said Martha stubbornly.

Mr Maynard broke in quickly with 'All my generation were pacifists – until 1914.'

There was a burst of relieved laughter. Donovan looked at Martha; she looked back angrily. He turned back to Ruth with a gay shrug.

Martha saw that Mr Maynard had been protecting her. She said in a low voice, 'I don't see why one shouldn't say what one thinks.'

'Don't you? Oh, well, I'm sorry.'

This depth of irony succeeded in making her feel very young and inadequate. It was a snub to those *real* feelings she was convinced she must share with everybody, nothing less would do! After a moment she said, 'All the same, everyone here is planning for the war, and we don't know yet who the war is going to be fought against.'

She had spoken rather more loudly than she had meant; the gentleman from the press had heard her. He said irritably, 'You'd agree, I hope, that one must be prepared for a war?' This was the substance of the leader in that morning's *News*.

Mr Maynard answered for her, in a smooth voice, 'I daresay the younger generation, who will have the privilege of being killed, are entitled to know what for?' He had acquired another glass, and was engaged in flipping this one too with his fingernail. The journalist's look was caught by the gesture; he watched it for a moment; then some women sitting near asked him deferentially for his opinion on the international situation. He proceeded to give it. Martha listened to his string of platitudes for a few moments, then heard Mr Maynard again: 'Another of life's little disillusionments: you'll find the newspapermen are as stupid as they sound. One reads what they say, when young, with admiration for the accomplished cynicism they display; when one gets older one discovers they really mean what they write. A terrible blow it was to me, I remember. I had been thinking of becoming one myself. But I was prepared to be a knave, not a fool.'

He had meant her to laugh, but she was unable to. She wanted to protest. Fear of his contempt for her clumsiness kept her silent. She was prepared to be thought wrongheaded, but not naïve. He was using much more powerful weapons than she was to understand for a very long time.

'Come,' he said, 'let me fill up your glass.' It was her third, and she was beginning to be lifted away from herself.

'Tell me,' he inquired, having refilled his own, 'if it is not too indiscreet, that is: What decided you to get married at the age of – what is it? Seventeen?'

'Nineteen,' said Martha indignantly.

'I do apologize.'

She laughed. She hesitated a moment. She was feeling the

last three months as a bewildering chaos of emotion, through which she had been pulled, will-less, like a fish at the end of a string, with a sense of being used by something impersonal and irresistible. She hesitated on the verge of an appeal and a confession; an attempt, at the very least, to explain what it had been like. She glanced at him, and saw him lounging there beside her, very large, composed, armed by his heavy sarcastic good looks.

'If I may say so,' he remarked with a pleasantly pointed smile which was like a nudge to proceed, 'ninety-nine people out of a hundred haven't the remotest idea why they got married – in any case you are under the illusion that you are a special case.'

With this encouragement, she took a sip from her brandy and ginger beer and began. She was pleasantly surprised that her voice was no less cool, amused and destructive than his own. She noted, also, that words, phrases, were isolated in deprecating amusement – as Solly had used the language that morning. It was as if she were afraid of the power of language used nakedly. 'Well,' she began, 'not to get married when it is so clearly expected of us was rather more of an act of defiance than I was prepared to commit. Besides, you must know yourself, since you spend most of your time marrying us, that getting married is our first occupation – the international situation positively demands it. Who one marries is obviously of no importance at all. After all, if I'd married Binkie, for instance, I'm sure that everyone – with the exception of your wife, of course – would have been just as delighted . . .'

He laughed: 'Go on.'

'Though it would have been no less potentially disastrous than the marriage I'm committed to. Love,' she noted how she isolated the word, throwing it away, as it were, 'as you would be the first to admit, is merely a question of . . .' 'In short,' she concluded, after some minutes of light-hearted description of the more painful experiences of the last few weeks, 'I got married because there's going to be a war. Surely that's a good enough reason.' There was not even an undertone of dismay to be heard in her voice.

'Admirable,' he commented. Then: 'Entirely admirable. If I may give you some advice.'

'Oh, I do assure you that I've taken the point.'

He looked at her straight. 'And I assure *you* that you will find it much more tolerable this way.'

'I don't doubt it,' she said angrily.

He was on the point of making some further attempt, when she felt a hand on her arm. It was Douglas. He looked rather nervous, first because he was disturbing her conversation with Mr Maynard, secondly because she was looking so guilty. She felt very guilty. She jumped up quickly as he said, 'Matty, we should be going.'

Mr Maynard released her courteously, and returned to his chair beside his wife. They stood at the door shaking hands with Colonel Brodeshaw and his wife. Mrs Brodeshaw took the opportunity to ask, 'My dear, I wonder if you would like to help on the committee for organizing the ladies . . .' It took Martha by surprise, and Mrs Brodeshaw swiftly went on: 'Though of course, my dear, you don't want to be worried by all this sort of thing yet, do you? It's not fair, when you're just married. We'll leave you in peace for the time being,' she promised, smiling. Then she added, 'There's a suggestion of starting a committee to investigate the conditions of the Coloured – '

'I was down there this morning,' remarked Martha.

Mrs Brodeshaw looked startled, then said, 'Oh, yes, we know you are interested.'

Douglas came quickly in with 'Perhaps we can fix it later, when we're more settled.'

Again Mrs Brodeshaw retreated gracefully. They said goodbye. Douglas and Martha went to the car in silence. She saw he looked annoyed, and wondered why.

'You know, Matty, I think you might have been a bit more pleasant about it.'

'Charity?' said Martha angrily.

'It's not such a bad idea, you know.' He was referring to her being 'in' with the Brodeshaws.

'Charity,' she said finally. It dismayed her that he might

even consider it possible. Then she felt sorry for him – he looked utterly taken aback.

'But, Matty . . .'

She took his arm. She was now lifted on waves of alcohol: she was recklessly happy.

'Mr Maynard was having a long talk with you?' he inquired.

'Yes. Let's go and dance, Douglas.'

'The Club? What? With the gang?'

'The gang,' she mocked. 'We've put up with them for long enough, haven't we?'

'Let's have a night by ourselves.'

But by now she could not bear to go tamely back to the flat. There was something in the talk with Mr Maynard which had unsettled her, made her restless – she needed to dance. Besides, she was instinctively reluctant to go now, in this mood of disliking him, which she did unaccountably, to spend an evening with Douglas.

'Come on – come on,' she urged, tugging at him.

'All right, then, we'll go and beat up Stella and Andy – and let's get Willie and Alice. We'd better buy some brandy . . .'

She was hardly listening. She was wildly elated, she could feel that she was very attractive to him in this mood; it intoxicated her and deeply disturbed her that he should find her desirable when she was engaged in despising him. 'Come on, come on,' she called impatiently, and ran off down the path through the bushes to the car. He followed, running heavily behind her. It was dark now. The gateposts reflected a white gleam back to a large low white moon. The town had lost its ramshackle shallowness. A mile of roofs shone hard and white like plates of white salt, amid acres of softly glinting leaves. The road lay low and grey, with a yellow glimmer of light from the street lamps.

Chapter Three

'Well, Matty, and now you'll be free to get on with your own work.'

It was with these words that Douglas dropped his parting kiss on her cheek when he left for the office each morning, and with a look of pure satisfaction. The kindly, confident young man crossed the untidy bedroom towards the door, bouncing a little from the balls of his feet, smiling backwards at Martha, who was sitting in a tangle of crumpled and stained silk in a mess of bedclothes, and vanished whistling down the corridor. The gleam of proprietary satisfaction never failed to arouse in Martha a flush of strong resentment, which was as unfailingly quenched by a succeeding guilt. To account for the resentment, for above all it was essential to account for every contradictory emotion that assailed one, she had already formed a theory.

After Douglas had left, she kicked off the bedclothes, and allowed herself to fall backwards on the cooling sheets and pillows. She lay quiet. Opposite her, two neat squares of bright blue sky, in one of which was suspended the stilled black wheel of the fair; reflected sunlight quivered hot on the wall. From all around, from above, from below, the sound of voices, a broom swishing, a child crying. But here, in the heart of the building, two rooms, white, silent, empty. And, on the bed, Martha, uncomfortably fingering the silk of her nightdress, trying most conscientiously to relax into the knowledge of space and silence. At the same time she was thinking of Douglas, now already at his office; she could see the self-conscious look with which he allowed himself to be teased; every night he came back to share with her his pleasure in how the office had said this or that. And how she hated him for it! And it was her husband about whom she was feeling this resentment, this violent dislike.

Martha, ignoring the last few months in town before her marriage, because she could not bear to think about them, went back to that period when she was a girl on the farm. From this, several incidents had been selected by her need for a theory. There had been that young man who . . . and the other one . . . and that occasion when . . . After hours of determined concentration she would emerge with the phrase, 'Women hate men who take them for granted.' It would have done for a story in a magazine. But that impersonal 'woman' was a comfort — briefly, for no sooner had she reached it than she saw the image that the words conjured up: something sought, wooed, capricious, bestowing favours. No, there was something extremely distasteful about that capricious female; no sooner had Martha caught a glimpse of her than she must repudiate her entirely; she was certainly from the past! The suggestion of coyness was unbearable. Yet she and Douglas had achieved a brotherly friendliness almost immediately; and when he bounced cheerfully into bed, clutching her in a cheerful and companionable act of love that ignored the female which must be wooed, she undoubtedly loathed him from the bottom of her heart, an emotion which was as inevitably followed by a guilty affection. The situation was, as she jauntily and bleakly put it, unsatisfactory.

She therefore got out of bed and went into the living room, and knelt in front of the bookcase. Books. Words. There must surely be some pattern of words which would neatly and safely cage what she felt — isolate her emotions so that she could look at them from outside. For she was of that generation who, having found nothing in religion, had formed themselves by literature. And the books which spoke most directly were those which had come out of Western Europe during the past hundred years, and of those, the personal and self-confessing. And so she knelt in front of a bookcase, in driving need of the right arrangement of words; for it is a remarkable fact that she was left unmoved by criticisms of the sort of person she was by parents, relations, preachers, teachers, politicians and the people who write for the newspapers; whereas an unsympathetic description of a character similar to her own in a novel would send her into a condition of anxious soul-searching for days. Which suggests that it is of no use for artists to insist, with such nervous disinclination for responsibility, that their productions are only 'a divine play' or 'a reflection from the creative fires of irony', etc., etc. while the Marthas of this world read and search with the craving thought, What does this say about my life? It will not do at all – but it must be admitted that there always came a point where Martha turned from the novelists and tale tellers to that section of the bookcase which was full of books called *The Psychology of . . . , The Behaviour of . . . , A Guide to . . .* , with the half-formulated thought that the novelists had not caught up with life; for there was no doubt that the sort of things she or Stella or Alice talked about found no reflection in literature – or rather, it was the attitudes of mind they took for granted that did not appear there, from which she deduced that women in literature were still what men, or the men-women, wished they were. In this other part of the bookcase, however, were no such omissions; she found what she was thinking and feeling described with an admirable lack of ambiguity. And yet, after hours of search among the complexities and subtleties of character, she was likely to return to her bedroom profoundly comforted, with some such resounding and original remark as 'The young husband, therefore, must be careful to be specially understanding during the difficult weeks after marriage.' For, since Douglas, the young husband in question, so logically insisted on relying upon the common sense *she* insisted on, she must with some part of herself take his place by being understanding, compassionate, etc. Martha was able to preserve an equilibrium because of an observing and satirical eye focused upon her own behaviour from a superior vantage point that was of course in no way influenced by that behaviour. She achieved quite extraordinary degrees of self-forbearance by this device.

In the bedroom the bedclothes still lying dragged back,

clothes lay everywhere; the morning was slipping past and she was not dressed. And now this question of work confronted her. She had understood she was not alone in her position of a woman who disdained both housework and a 'job', but was vaguely expected by her husband – but only because of her own insistence on it – to be engaged in work of her own. Both Stella and Alice had claimed the state. Martha had heard their respective husbands speak to them in precisely the same tone of pride and satisfaction that Douglas used to her. Their wives were not as those of other men.

Feeling the distant pressure of this 'work', Martha dutifully went to the bathroom to equip herself to face it.

The bathroom was modern. A high window showed yet another angle of clear blue sky, together with the tops of the trees in the park. A large white bath filled with heavy greenish water where spangles of light quivered, white cabinets, white shelves – it was all a gleam of white enamel. Martha took off her nightdress, and was alone with her body. But it was not that calm and obedient body which had been so pleasant a companion. White it was, and solid and unmarked – but heavy, unresponsive; her flesh was uncomfortable on her bones. It burned and unaccountably swelled; it seemed to be pursuing ideas of its own. Inside the firm thick flesh a branch of bones which presumably remained unchanged: the thought was comforting. Martha looked down at her shape of flesh with the anxious thought that it was upon this that the marriage depended; for this, in fact, they – she and Douglas – had been allowed by society to shut themselves away in two high rooms with a bathroom attached. It was almost with the feeling of a rider who was wondering whether his horse would make the course that she regarded this body of hers, which was not only divided from her brain by the necessity of keeping open that cool and dispassionate eye, but separated into compartments of its own. Martha had after all been provided with a map of her flesh by 'the book', in which each area was marked by the name of a different physical sensation, so that her mind was anxiously aware, not only of a disconnected partner, a body, but of every part of it, which might or might not come up to scratch at any given occasion. There were moments when she felt she was strenuously held together by nothing more than an act of will. She was beginning to feel that this view of herself was an offence against what was deepest and most real in her. And again she thought of the simple women of the country, who might be women in peace, according to their instincts, without being made to think and disintegrate themselves into fragments. During those few weeks of her marriage Martha was always accompanied by that other, black woman, like an invisible sister simpler and wiser than herself; for no matter how much she reminded herself of statistics and progress, she envied her from the bottom of her heart. Without, of course having any intention of emulating her: loyalty to progress forbade it.

At that hour of the morning the sun fell in bright lances through the high window. Martha stood where they might fall on her flesh; her skin shone with a soft iridescence, the warmth kneaded together her unhappily disconnected selves, she began to dissolve into well-being. But first there was another ritual to be gone through. From the high cupboard she took down the cans and rubber tubes prescribed by Dr Stern and washed away the sweats of love in the rocking green water. Then she refilled the bath for what she thought of as her own bath. In this she wallowed, while the sunlight moved up over the sides of the bath and into the water, and she was whole and at peace again, floating in sunlight and water like a fish. She might have stayed there all morning, if there wasn't this question of work; so she got out too soon, and thought with vague anxiety that those areas of tenderness on breasts and belly were no more than was to be expected after such an intensive love life. The thought of pregnancy crossed her mind; and was instantly dismissed. She felt that it was hard enough to keep Martha Quest, now Knowell, afloat on a sea of chaos and sensation without being pregnant as well – no, it was all too difficult. But her dress was tight; she must eat less, she told herself. Then she made tea and ate bread and butter with satisfaction at the thought that she was depriving herself of a meal.

And now it was ten in the morning, and her day was her own. Her work was free to start when it would. Martha went to the other room, and arranged herself comfortably on the divan. Or rather, it was with the intention of comfort, for the divan was a high, hard mattress on a native-made bed covered with loosely woven brown linen. Comfortable it was not; but it suitably supported the rest of the room, and Martha chose it because one might sit there without surrendering to the boundaries of a chair.

Into this little box of a room had flowed so many different items of furniture – and then out again. Now two small jolly chairs were set at neat angles on a clean green rug. A new table of light wood, surrounded by four chairs of the same, filled the opposite corner. The curtains, of that material known as folk-weave, whose rough grain held pockets of yellow light, were of the same brown she sat on. It was safe to say that the furniture that had flowed in and out of this room with the restless owners of it was indistinguishable from what filled it now. This thought gave Martha an undefined and craving hollowness, a sort of hunger. Yet everything was so practical and satisfactory! She looked at this room, from chair to window, from table to cupboard, and her eyes rested on nothing, but moved onwards hastily to the next article, as if *this* might provide that quality she was searching for.

It was not her flat; it belonged to that group of people who had seen her married. Almost at once her thoughts floated away from this place she sat in, these white boxes in the heart of the building, and slowly she tested various other shells for living in, offered to her in books. There were, after all, not so many of them; and each went with a kind of life she must dismiss instantly and instinctively. For instance, there was her father's childhood in the English country cottage, honest simplicity with the bones of the house showing through lathe and plaster. Outside, a green and lush country – but tame, tamed; it would not do at all. Or – and this was a dip into the other stream that fed her blood – a tall narrow Victorian house, crammed with heavy dark furniture, buttoned and puffed and stuffed and padded, an atmosphere of things unsaid. If that country cottage could be acknowledged with a self-conscious smile, like a charmingly naïve relation, this narrow dark house could not be admitted too close, it was too dangerous. And that house which was being built now everywhere, in every country of the world, the modern house, cosmopolitan, capable of being lifted up from one continent and dumped down in any other without exciting remark – no, certainly not, it was not to be thought of. So there remained the flat in which she was in fact now sitting? But she was not here at all; she did not live in it; she was waiting to be moved on somewhere . . .

About eleven in the morning she roused herself. For she knew that since both Stella and Alice were as free for their own work as she was, either or both of them were likely to drop in. She therefore put the kettle on and made sandwiches, prepared to spend the rest of the morning gossiping or – as pleasantly – alone.

By now the stores would have delivered by native messenger the groceries, meat and vegetables she had ordered by telephone; putting away these things interrupted work for a few minutes. Preparing a light lunch for Douglas could not take longer than half an hour. In the long interval before lunch, Martha drifted once more in front of her mirror, with the air of one prepared to be surprised by what she saw there. And from this, as a natural consequence of a long and dissatisfied examination of herself, she collected scissors and needle and material, and in a few moments she was at the table with the sewing machine. And now her look of vagueness had vanished; for the first time since she had risen that morning, she was centred behind what her hands did. She had the gift of running up sundowner frocks, dance dresses, out of a remnant from the sales, even discarded curtains or old-fashioned clothes that her mother had kept. She could transform them without effort – apart from the long, dreamy meditations which might fill half a week; for when a woman claims with disarming modesty that she has run up this dress for ten shillings, the long process of manipulating the material around her image of herself, those hours of creation, are not taken into account. Very few women's time is money, even now. But while the clothes she made for after dark were always a success, it seemed her sureness of touch must desert her for the daytime. Her friends might exclaim loyally that her morning dress was absolutely wonderful, but it was only over the evening clothes that their voices held the authentic seal of envy. From which it follows?

The fact is that as soon as Douglas returned from the office for lunch, the day was already nearly at evening. For he returned finally at four; and after that, it was only a question of time before their eyes met on a query: at the Sports Club, everyone they knew would be delighted to see them, and afterwards there would be dancing there or at the hotels. It seemed as if the day was only a drab preliminary to the night, as if the pageant of sunset was meant only as a curtain-raiser to that moment when the lights sprung up along the streets, and with them a feeling of vitality and excitement. For in the hotels, the clubs and the halls, the orchestras struck up at eight and from every point in the town dance music was flowing like water from a concealed reservoir of nostalgia hidden below it. These were the nights of African winter, sharp, clear, cold, a high and luminous starlit dark lifting away from the low, warm glitter of city lights. In the white courts of the hotels, braziers offered a little futile heat to the cold dry air, and groups of young people formed and dissolved around them: there was no room for everyone inside, there was no room for all the people who needed, suddenly, to dance.

Night after night, they moved from the Club to the Plaza and on to McGrath's; and the self-contained parties that began the evening expected to dissolve into a great whole as midnight approached. By midnight they were dancing as if they formed one soul; they danced and sang, mindless, in a half-light, they were swallowed up in the sharp, exquisite knowledge of loss and impending change that came over the seas and continents from Europe; and underneath it all, a rising tide of excitement that was like a poison. Uniforms were appearing here and there, and the wearers carried themselves with self-effacing modesty, as if on a secret mission, but conscious that all eyes in the room were fixed on them. The rumours were beginning. This regiment was going to be called up, they were going to conscript the whole population; but the question of conscription was surely an irrelevance when every young man in the town was thinking only of the moment when he could put on a uniform – and that before it was decided what the war was to be fought about. They were all longing to be swallowed up in something bigger than themselves; they were, in fact, already swallowed up. And since each war, before it starts, has the look of the last one, it did not matter how often stern and important young men assured hushed audiences that the world could not survive a month of modern warfare, they would all be bombed to pieces by new and secret weapons; it was necessary only for the orchestra to play 'Tipperary' or 'Keep the Home Fires Burning' – which they did on every conceivable occasion – for the entire gathering to become transformed into a congregation of self-dedicated worshippers of what their parents chose to remember of 1914.

In between dances, groups formed to discuss what was happening in Europe – or rather to exchange the phrases they had read that morning in the *Zambesia News*. The fact that this newspaper was contradicting itself with the calmest of assurance from day to day did not matter in the least; there was going to be a war, and night after night youth danced and sang itself into a condition of preparation for it. Their days and work, their loves and love-making, were nothing but a preparation for that moment when hundreds of them stamped and shouted in great circles to the thudding drums, felt less as sound than as their own pulses; this was the culmination of the day, the real meaning of it, the moment of surrender.

Then the music stopped suddenly and disastrously, the managers came forward bowing with strained politeness, ignoring the pleas and imprecations about their hard-heartedness – and the masses of young people streamed out into the still, frost-bound air, under the glitter of the Cross. It was at this point that Martha and Douglas were reminded that they were married; for 'the gang' – those of them that remained unbound to the girls whose one preoccupation it was to get married to the doomed as quickly as possible – went off shouting and stamping to the fun fair, which they kept going until early morning. The young married couples departed to one of the flats; and it was then that it became apparent there was a certain difference of viewpoint between husbands and wives. Stella, Alice, Martha, might have been part of that single yearning heart only half an hour before, but now they tended to fall silent, and even exchanged tolerant glances as their respective young men held forth on their plans for joining up. For it is a strain on any marriage, which after all is likely to begin with the belief that it must provide satisfaction and happiness for at least a few years, when one of the partners show signs of such restlessness to 'rush off to the wars' – as the girls acidly put it – the moment a war, any war, offers itself.

By the time Martha and Douglas reached home, reached the small, brightly lit, untidy bedroom, still littered with their day clothes and filled with the loud, sad, bitter music from the fun fair – for the wheel was still dragging its glittering load of cars in its circle – by this time, their elation was flagging, and there was a feeling of anticlimax. Now, drenched and submerged by the music, which it was impossible to keep out even with shut windows, Martha crept closer to Douglas and demanded the assurance that he did not really want to leave her; just as Stella and Alice were doing in their bedrooms. Douglas, manfully clasping Martha to him, murmured reassurances and looked over her head at the glitter of the wheel. He had not known how intolerably boring and empty his life was until there was a chance of escaping from it; and the more fiercely he determined not to be left out of things, the more tightly he held Martha and consoled her. He was holding a warm, confiding bundle of female flesh, he wished only to love her and be proud of her – for, above all, his pride was fed by her anxious demands for his love; but it was all no use. For, just as he was playing a role which was surely inconsistent with what he thought – the young hero off to the wars for adventure – so she began to speak in the ancient female voice which he found utterly irritating. After a long silence, during which he hoped she might have gone to sleep so that he might dream of adventure without guilt, a small, obstinate, ugly voice remarked that there would be wars so long as men were such babies. At this point he would loosen his grip and lie stiff beside her, and begin to explain in an official tone that surely, Matty, she must see they must be prepared . . . But it was no use; that official tone carries no conviction any longer, not even to the people who use it. She sniggered derisively; and he felt foolish.

They rolled apart and lay without touching; even apologizing in an offhand, hasty way if they happened to touch by accident. Douglas soon fell asleep. Martha could not sleep while the wheel turned and churned out music. She was in a mood of angry self-contempt for being infected by that dangerous undertow of excitement. For she had caught herself daydreaming of being a nurse, and no less than a ministering angel. But, alas, alas, we know all about that ministering angel; we know what she comes to in the end; and Martha could only return to thoughts of her father. She considered the undoubted fact that while Mr Quest might expatiate about the inefficiency and corruption of the leaders of his war, about the waste of life, the uselessness of the thing, while he might push into Martha's hands books like *All Quiet on the Western Front* with an irascible command that she should read it and understand that *that* was war, while he might talk of that war with the bitter, savage consciousness of betrayal, yet there was always an undercurrent of burning regret. Then he had been alive. 'The comradeship,' he would exclaim, 'the comradeship! I've never experienced that since!' and then the terrible '*It was the only time in my life I was really happy.*'

When the wheel stilled at last Martha was able to sleep; and in the morning she was a different creature, easily able to withstand the insinuations of the ministering angel in the white coif, and prepared to look soberly at the alternatives – or rather at a single alternative, for the possibility of in fact settling down to a life of tea parties, sundowners, and in due course, children, was out of the question. She was trying to form the confusion of feelings that afflicted her to fit the sharp, clear view of life held by Solly and Joss – that was how she saw it. What she actually wanted, of course, was for some man to arrive in her life, simply take her by the hand, and lead her off into this new world. But it seemed he did not exist. And so she read the newspapers, and enjoyed the cynicism they produced in her. There was the *Zambesia News*, for instance, at that period in a state of such uneasy uncertainty. On the one hand it was reminding its readers about the atrocious nature of Hitler's Germany; on the other it seemed to be suffering from a certain reluctance to do so. Hard to forget that these same atrocities, concentration camps and so on, had been ignored by the *Zambesia News*, as by its betters, until it was impossible to ignore them; while even now, like those great exemplars overseas, it showed real indignation only over Hitler's capacity for absorbing other countries. Nor was she able to feel any less derisive when she read the great exemplars themselves, the newspapers from Home. As for that other, deeper knowledge, the pulse that really moved her, gained from her almost religious feeling for literature, a knowledge that amounted to a vision of mankind as nobility bound and betrayed – this was vanishing entirely beneath the pressure of enjoyable cynicism which was being fed by everything about her, and particularly by her own behaviour. For despite all her worried introspection, her determination to act rationally if only it was possible to find out what rational behaviour should be, the fact was that her sluggish days were nothing but a preparation for the first drink at sundown, which led to that grand emotional culmination at midnight when she joined the swinging circle of intoxicated dancers controlled by the thudding of the drums.

It was about six weeks after her marriage that all this confusion was shaken into a single current by the fact that she was violently sick one morning. Lethargy caused her to murmur consolingly that it must be the result of not sleeping enough – probably nothing but a hangover. But she succeeded in forgetting it.

Two days later, in Stella's flat, after a dance, it happened that Maisie was there. She was wearing a dress of white tulle, frilled and flounced like a baby's bassinette, and from it her plump shoulders, her lazy pretty face, emerged with a placid enjoyment of life which apparently had not been disturbed by the fact that she had become engaged to one of the young men who was training to be a pilot. She came to sit by Martha, murmuring vaguely, 'Well, Matty . . .' as if they saw each other every day. In fact they did, at dances but from across the room. She bent down to rip off a strip of dirty white from the bottom of her dress where it had been trodden on, rolled it up, and tossed it into the corner of the room; and sat looking speculatively at Martha, her fair face flushed and beaded with the heat. 'You look fine, you don't show yet,' she remarked good-naturedly, looking frankly at Martha's stomach.

'What do you mean?' asked Martha.

Maisie was startled. 'I'm sorry,' she apologized hastily. 'I thought . . .' Someone spoke to her, and she took the opportunity to get up and sit somewhere else. From time to time during the rest of the evening, she glanced towards Martha, but with the determination not to catch her eye. She left before Martha did, arm in arm with her pilot, including Martha with the rest of the room in a large, vague smile of farewell.

Afterwards Martha said indignantly to Douglas that it was the limit, people were saying she was pregnant. To which he replied a little awkwardly that some of the lads from the Club had suggested this was the case.

'Do you mean to say they think we got married because we *had* to?' she exclaimed, furious; for she felt this was an insult towards them as free beings able to do as they wished.

But he misunderstood her indignation, and said, laughing, 'After all, Matty, since most of the people who get married get married because they have to . . .'

She laughed, but she was very uneasy.

Again she forgot about it, until there was a letter from her mother, which immediately caught her attention because of its casual tone. At the end of it was an inquiry as to how she felt. Again she burned with indignation – there was a conspiracy against her!

For some days, there was no reason to think of it; then she got a charming letter from Mrs Talbot, which had the same hurried apologetic manner as her speech. She asked why Matty did not drop in to see her one morning, she would so like to have a proper talk.

The letters were always on thick white paper, in a fine-pointed black hand; they gave an impression of casual elegance which made Martha curious, for never had she known anyone whose letters were not utilitarian. The letters, like Mrs Talbot herself, spoke of an existence altogether remote from this colonial town. But what was this life which Mrs Talbot seemed so anxious Martha should share? And what was this proper talk?

'We have supper or spend the evening with them at least two or three times a week,' Martha pointed out to Douglas, quite bewildered.

'Oh, go and see her, Matty, she'll be pleased.'

Martha had discovered that Mrs Talbot was not, as one might infer from her appearance, about thirty-five, but over sixty; she was very rich, but in a way seemed to apologize for the unpleasant fact that there was such a thing as money in the world at all. During those evenings, she would take Douglas – apologizing first – into an inner room, and they would discuss investments and properties. 'There are no flies on Mrs Talbot,' he said appreciatively. And then, always: 'She's an absolute marvel, a wonder! Why, Matty, would you think she was a day over thirty. Isn't she terrific?'

'But Elaine . . .' pointed out Martha jealously.

'Oh, Elaine's all right, she's a nice kid,' said Douglas, dismissing her.

That Elaine should be thought of as a nice kid made Martha laugh – it was easier to tolerate the amazing Mrs Talbot. For at the bottom of an uneasy disapproval of that lady was Martha's physical arrogance – the pride of the very young. *She* was young and whole and comely; secretly she felt a fierce, shuddering repulsion for the old and unsightly. For a brief ten years – she was convinced that thirty was the end of youth and good looks – she was allowed by nature to be young and attractive. For Mrs Talbot to be beautiful at sixty was not fair.

'She *can't* be sixty,' she had protested hopefully. But she was.

Martha told Douglas that she didn't want to have a proper talk with Mrs Talbot; but on the morning after getting the letter she found herself disinclined for that 'work', and set off on impulse for Mrs Talbot's house. It was half past nine; the morning was well advanced for a society which began work at eight. Martha walked through the park and along the avenues: the house was one of the delightful houses of the older town. It was almost hidden from the street by trees and flowering bushes. The door opened immediately from the garden path, and not off a wide veranda. The house had an introspective, inward-turning look because of this discreet black door with its shining door knocker. Mrs Talbot's house, like herself, could not help suggesting the England one knew from novels. The door might be flanked on either side by poinsettias, ragged pointed scraps of scarlet silk fluttering on naked, shining silken stems, but one felt they were there only to suggest an ironical contrast.

Martha rang, and was admitted by a native servant, and shown into a small side room kept for just this purpose. She summoned her memories of what she had read, and then saw, as she had expected, a tray on a stand, littered with visiting cards. At this it occurred to her that the phrase 'dropping in' might have a different meaning to Mrs Talbot than it had for herself and her friends. Before she could recover herself, Mr Talbot came in. She had seen very little of him; he went to the Club in the evenings when his wife entertained. He was wearing a dark silk dressing gown, was tall and heavily built, with a dark, heavy face, and he came stooping forward with his hand outstretched, apologizing for his dressing gown. She was embarrassed because of her thoughts about him. She did not like him. She did not like the way he would come into his wife's drawing room, on his way out, a man paying forced tribute to women's amusements; besides, he suggested a spy – his look at Mrs Talbot always made her uncomfortable. Finally, he was an old man, and distasteful because he had a sardonic, intimate manner with her that made it impossible to dismiss him so easily. He was forcing her now to think of him as a man, and she stammered a little as she said she had come to see Mrs Talbot. He said very politely that he didn't think his wife was up yet, but that Martha might care to wait?

She said at once, no – of course not; she was only on a walk, and she would come up another time.

He held her eyes with his while he inquired if she would like to see Elaine.

Martha said yes, she would like to very much.

Mr Talbot stood aside for her to precede him out of the door, and she felt uncomfortable as she passed him, as if he might suddenly put out his hands and grasp her. In the passage, he indicated the drawing-room door, and apologized again for his dressing gown. Then he opened another door; Martha caught a glimpse of a large brown-leather chair, a pipe smoking on a small table, a litter of newspapers; he went inside, having held her eyes again in another direct glance.

She went into the drawing room, feeling its contrast with the brown masculine study he had gone into. It was large, low-ceilinged, rather dim. It was carpeted from wall to wall with a deep rosy, flowing softness that gave under her feet. It was full of furniture that Martha instinctively described as antiques. It was a charming room, it was like an Edwardian novel; and one could not be in it without thinking of the savage country outside. Martha kept looking out of the windows which were veiled in thin pale stuffs, as if to assure herself this was in fact Africa. It might have vanished, she felt, so strong was the power of this room to destroy other realities.

Elaine came forward, from a small sunny veranda enclosed by glass and filled with plants in such a way that it suggested a conservatory. Elaine was wearing a loose linen smock, and she was doing the flowers.

She asked Martha, with charming formality, if she would like to come to the sun porch, and Martha followed her.

There was a small grass chair, and Martha sat on it and watched Elaine fitting pink and mauve sweet peas into narrow silver vases like small fluted trumpets.

Elaine said that her mother was never up before eleven, and accompanied this remark by a small smile which did not invite shared amusement, but rather expressed an anxious desire that no one should find it remarkable. Elaine, standing by her trestle, with her copper jugs of water, her shears, her rows of sweet peas and roses, her heavy gauntlets, had the air of a fragile but devoted handmaid to her mother's way of life. Martha watched her and found herself feeling protective. This girl should be spared any unpleasantness which might occur outside the shining glass walls of the sun porch. Her fragility, her air of fatigue, the blue shadows under her eyes, removed her completely from any possibility of being treated by Martha as an equal. Martha found herself censoring her speech; in a few minutes they were making conversation about gardening. Then a bell shrilled from close by, and Elaine hastily excused herself, laid down her flowers, and went to a door which led to Mrs Talbot's bedroom.

In a few minutes she came back to say that her mother was awake and was delighted to hear that Martha had come to see her. If dear Matty did not mind being treated so informally – and here Elaine again offered a small anxious smile, as if acknowledging at least the possibility of amusement – would she like to come into the bedroom? Martha went to the door, expecting Elaine to come with her; but Elaine remained with her flowers, a pale effaced figure in her yellow smock, drenched in the sunlight that was concentrated through the blazing glass of the sun porch.

Martha's eyes were full of sunlight, and in this room it was nearly dark. She stood blinded just inside the door, and heard Mrs Talbot murmuring affectionate greetings from the shadows. She stumbled forward, sat on a chair that was pushed under her, and then saw that Mrs Talbot was up and in a dressing gown, a dim figure agitated by the delight this visit gave her, but even more agitated by apologies because she was not dressed.

'If I'd known you were coming, Matty darling . . . But I'm so terribly lazy, I simply can't get out of bed before twelve. It was so sweet of you to come so soon when I asked you – but we old women must be allowed our weaknesses . . .'

Martha was astounded by that 'old women'; but there was no suggestion of coyness in it. She tried to peer through the dark, for she was longing to see how Mrs Talbot must look before she had created herself for her public. All she could see was a slender figure in an insinuating rustle of silks, perched on the bed. Mrs Talbot lit a cigarette; almost at once the red spark was crushed out again; Martha saw that this flutter was due simply to a routine being upset.

'I rang up my hairdresser when I heard your voice, I told him not to come this morning. I'm sure it won't hurt me to show an inch or so of grey just for once. When you reach the age of going grey, Matty darling, don't be silly and dye your hair. It's an absolute martyrdom. If I had only known . . .'

Martha was now able to see better. Mrs Talbot's face came out of the shadow in a splash of white. It was some kind of a face mask. 'Shall I go out till you are dressed?' she suggested awkwardly.

But Mrs Talbot rose with a swirl of silk and said, 'If you don't mind it all, Matty, I'd adore you to stay.' There was a nervous gasp of laughter; she was peering forward to see Martha, to find out her reaction. It occurred to Martha that the apology, the deference, was quite sincere and not a pose, as she had assumed. Mrs Talbot's nervousness was that of a duchess who had survived the French Revolution and timidly continued to wear powdered curls in the privacy of her bedroom because she did not feel herself in the new fashions.

Martha saw the slight figure rise, go to the window, and tug at a cord. At once the room was shot with hazy yellow light. Mrs Talbot was wearing a shimmering grey garment with full flounced sleeves; she was covered in stark-white paste from collarbones to hairline, and from this mask her small eyes glimmered out through black holes. Her pale smooth hair was looped loosely on her neck; there was no sign of grey. She sat before a large dressing table and dabbed carefully at her face with tufts of cotton wool. The room was long, low, subdued, with shell-coloured curtains, dove-grey carpet, and furniture of light, gleaming wood which looked as if it had been embroidered; it had a look of chaste withdrawal from the world; and Mrs Talbot was a light, cool, uncommitted figure, even when she was poised thus on her stool, leaning forward into her mirror, her submissive charm momentarily lost in a focus of keen concentration. Her skin was emerging patchily from under the white paste, and she muttered, 'In a minute, Matty.'

Soon she rose and went to an old-fashioned washstand, where a graceful ewer stood in a shining rose-patterned basin. It was clear that taps running hot and cold would be too much of a modern note in this altar to the past. Mrs Talbot splashed water vigorously over her face, while the air was pervaded by the odour of violets. In the meantime Martha, still examining every detail of the room, had noticed the bed. It was very big – too big, she thought involuntarily, for Mrs Talbot. Then she saw it was a double bed, with two sets of pillows. She must readmit Mr Talbot, whom she had again forgotten. This bed, untidy and sprawling, gave Martha the most uncomfortable feeling of something unseemly: it was, she saw, because a man's pyjamas lay where they had been flung off, on the pillow. There were of maroon-striped silk, and strongly suggested the person of Mr Talbot, as did a jar of pipes on the bed table. So uncomfortable did this make Martha that she turned away from the bed, feeling her face hot. Mrs Talbot, however, returning from her ablutions, could not be aware of how Martha was feeling, for she carelessly rolled these pyjamas together and tucked them under the pillow, observing, 'Men are always so untidy.' Then she sat herself on the edge of the bed, with the air of one prepared to devote any amount of time to friendship.

And now they must talk. There would follow the proper talk. Martha saw the gleam of affection in Mrs Talbot's eyes and was asking herself, Does she really like me? If so, why? But Mrs Talbot was talking about Douglas: how he was such a dear boy, how he was always so clever and helpful, and with such a sense for these horrid, horrid financial things;

and then – impulsively – how lovely it was that he had married such a sweet girl. At this Martha involuntarily laughed; and was sorry when she saw the look of surprise on this delightful lady's face. She rose from her chair and began walking about the room, touching the curtains, which slipped like thick silken skin through her fingers, laying a curious finger on the wood of the dressing table, which had such a gleaming softness that it was strange it should oppose her flesh with the hardness of real wood. Mrs Talbot watched without moving. There was a small, shrewd smile on her lips.

'Are you shocked, Matty, at all this fuss?' she asked a little plaintively; and when Martha turned quickly to see what she could mean, she continued quickly, 'I know it all looks so awful until it's tidied up; Elaine is so sweet, she comes in and tidies everything for me, and then this is a lovely room, but I know it must look horrid now, with face creams and cotton wool everywhere. The trouble is . . .' Here she tailed off, with a helpless shrug which suggested that there was nothing she would like better than to relapse into the comfortable condition of being an old woman, if only she knew how. Martha involuntarily glanced at Mr Talbot's side of the bed and then blushed as she guiltily caught Mrs Talbot's eyes. But it was clear that this was one thing she could not understand in Martha; she looked puzzled.

After a short pause she said, 'I hope you'll be friends with Elaine, Matty. She's such a sweet thing, so sensitive, and she doesn't make friends easily. Sometimes I feel it is my fault – but we've always been so much together, and I don't know why it is, but . . .'

Now Martha's look was far more hostile than she had intended; and Mrs Talbot's thick white skin coloured evenly. She looked like an embarrassed young girl, in spite of the faint look of wear under her eyes. Martha could not imagine herself being friends with that gentle, flower-gathering maiden; she could not prevent a rather helpless but ironical smile, and she looked direct at Mrs Talbot as if accusing her of being wilfully obtuse.

Mrs Talbot cried out, 'But you're so artistic, Matty, and you would have so much in common.'

Martha saw tears in her eyes. 'But I'm not at all artistic,' she observed obstinately — though of course with a hidden feeling that she might prove to be yet, if given the chance!

'But all those books you read, and then anyone can see ...' Mrs Talbot was positively crying out against the fate that persisted in making Martha refuse to be artistic. 'And Elaine is so sweet, no one knows as well as I do how sweet she is and — but sometimes I wonder if she's strong enough to *manage* things the way all you clever young things do. You are all so sure of yourselves!'

Here Martha could not help another rueful smile, which checked Mrs Talbot. She was regarding Martha with extraordinary shrewdness. Martha, for her part, was waiting for the proper talk to begin; what was it that Mrs Talbot wanted to say to her?

Mrs Talbot sighed, gave the shadow of a shrug, and went back to her dressing table. Here she applied one cream after another, with steady method, and continued to talk, in between pauses for screwing up her mouth or stretching her eyelids smooth. 'I would so much like Elaine to get married. If she could only get properly married, and I needn't worry any more ... There is no greater happiness, Matty, none! She meets so few people, always my friends, and she is so shy. And you meet so many people, Matty, all you young people are so brave and enterprising.'

For the life of her Martha could not see Elaine with the wolves of the Club, with the boys, the kids and the fellows. 'I don't think Elaine would like the sort of men we meet,' observed Martha; and she caught another shrewd glance. She felt there were things she ought to be understanding, but she was quite lost.

'There's your Douglas,' said Mrs Talbot, a trifle reproachfully. 'He's such a nice boy.'

Surely, wondered Martha, Mrs Talbot could not have wanted Douglas for Elaine? The idea was preposterous — even brutal.

'So kind,' murmured Mrs Talbot, 'so helpful, so clever with everything.'

And now Martha was returned, simply by the incongruity of Douglas and Elaine, into her private nightmare. She could not meet a young man or woman without looking around anxiously for the father and mother; that was how they would end, there was no escape for them. She could not meet an elderly person without wondering what the unalterable influences had been that had created them just so. She could take no step, perform no action, no matter how apparently new and unforeseen, without the secret fear that in fact this new and arbitrary thing would turn out to be part of the inevitable process she was doomed to. She was, in short, in the grip of the great bourgeois monster, the nightmare *repetition*. It was like the obsession of the neurotic who must continuously be touching a certain object or muttering a certain formula of figures in order to be safe from the malevolent powers, like the person who cannot go to bed at night without returning a dozen times to see if the door is locked and the fire out. She was thinking now, But Mrs Talbot married Mr Talbot, then Elaine is bound to marry someone like Mr Talbot, there is no escaping it; then what connection is there between Douglas and Mr Talbot that I don't see?

But Mrs Talbot was talking, 'I'll show you something, Matty – I would like to show you, I don't everyone.'

Mrs Talbot was searching hurriedly through her drawers. She pulled out a large, leather-framed photograph. Martha came forward and took it, with a feeling that the nightmare was being confirmed. It was of a young man in uniform, a young man smiling direct out of the frame, with a young, sensitive, rueful look. 'Hardly anybody knows,' Mrs Talbot cried agitatedly, 'but we were engaged, he was killed in the war – the other war, you know – he was so sweet, you don't know. He was so nice.' Her lips quivered. She turned away her face and held out her hand for the photograph.

Martha handed it back and returned to her chair. She was thinking, Well, then, so Elaine must get engaged to *that* young man; is it conceivable that Mrs Talbot sees Douglas like that?

But more: her mother, Mrs Quest, had been engaged to such another charming young man. This boy, weak-faced and engaging, smiled up still from a small framed photograph on her mother's dressing table, a persistent reminder of that love which Mr Quest could scarcely resent, since the photograph was half submerged, in fact practically invisible, among a litter of things which referred to her life with him. Martha had even gone so far as to feel perturbed because this boy had not appeared in her own life; she had looked speculatively at Douglas with this thought — but no, weak and charming he was not, he could not take that role.

She sat silent in her chair, frowning; when Mrs Talbot looked at her, it was to see an apparently angry young woman, and one very remote from her. She hesitated, came forward, and kissed Martha warmly on her cheek. 'You must forgive me,' she said. 'We are a selfish lot, we old women — and you probably have troubles of your own. We forget . . .' Here she hesitated. Martha was looking through her, frowning. She continued guiltily: 'And to have children — that's the best of all, I wish I had a dozen, instead of just one. But Mr Talbot . . .' She glanced hastily at Martha and fell silent.

There was a very long silence. Martha was following the nightmare to its conclusion: Well then, so Elaine will find just such a charming young man, and there's a war conveniently at hand so that he can get killed, and then Elaine will marry another Mr Talbot, and for the rest of her life, just like all these old women, she'll keep a photograph of her real and great love in a drawer with her handkerchiefs.

'There's nothing nicer than children, and you look very well, Matty,' said Mrs Talbot suddenly.

Martha emerged from her dream remarking absently, 'I'm always well.' Then she heard what Mrs Talbot had said; it seemed to hang on the air waiting for her to hear it. She thought tolerantly, She's heard a rumour that I'm pregnant. She smiled at Mrs Talbot and remarked, 'I shan't have children for years yet — damn it, I'm only nineteen myself.'

Mrs Talbot suppressed an exclamation. She surveyed

Martha up and down, a rapid, skilled glance, and then, colouring, said, 'But, my dear, it's so nice to have your children when you're young. I wish I had. I was *old* when she was born. Of course, people say we are like sisters, but it makes a difference. Have them young, Matty – you won't regret it.' She leaned forward with an urgent affectionate smile and continued, after the slightest hesitation, 'You know, we old women get a sixth sense about these things. We know when a woman is pregnant, there's a look in the eyes.' She put a cool hand to Martha's cheek and turned her face to the light. Narrowing her eyes so that for a moment her lids showed creases of tired flesh, she looked at Martha with a deep impersonal glance and nodded involuntarily, dropping her hand.

Martha was angry and uncomfortable; Mrs Talbot at this moment seemed to her like an old woman: the utterly impersonal triumphant gleam of the aged female, the old witch, was coming from the ageless jewelled face.

'I can't be pregnant,' she announced. 'I don't want to have a baby yet.'

Mrs Talbot let out a small resigned sigh. She rose and said in a different voice, 'I think I shall have my bath, dear.'

'I'll go,' said Martha quickly.

'You and Douggie'll be coming to dinner tomorrow?'

'We're looking forward to it very much.'

Mrs Talbot was again the easy hostess; she came forward in a wave of grey silk and kissed Martha. 'You'll be so happy,' she murmured gently. 'So happy, I feel it.'

Martha emitted a short ungracious laugh. 'But, Mrs Talbot!' she protested – then stopped. She wanted to put right what she felt to be an impossibly false position; honesty demanded it of her. She was not what Mrs Talbot thought her; she had no intention of conforming to this perfumed silken bullying, as she most deeply felt it to be. She could not go on. The appeal in the beautiful eyes silenced her. She was almost ready to aver that she wanted nothing more than to be happy with the dear boy Douglas, for Mrs Talbot; to have a dozen children, for Mrs Talbot; to take morning tea with Elaine every day, and see her married to just such another as Douglas.

Mrs Talbot, arm lightly placed about her waist, gently pressed her to the door. She opened it with one hand, then gave Martha a small squeeze, and smiled straight into her eyes, with such knowledge, such ironical comprehension, that Martha could not bear it. She stiffened; and Mrs Talbot dropped her arm at once.

'Elaine, dear,' said Mrs Talbot apologetically past Martha to the sun porch, 'if you'd like to run my bath for me.'

Elaine was now painting the row of pink and mauve sweet peas in the fluted silver vases. 'Ah!' exclaimed Mrs Talbot delightedly, moving forward quickly to look at the water colour. She leaned over, kissing Elaine's hair. The girl moved slightly, then remained still under her mother's restraining arm. 'Isn't this lovely, Matty, isn't she gifted?'

Martha looked at the pretty water colour and said it was beautiful. Elaine's glance at her now held a real embarrassment; but she remained silent until her mother had gained her meed of admiration.

Then Mrs Talbot waved goodbye and returned to her bedroom; and Elaine rose, and said, 'Excuse me, Matty, I'll just do Mummy's bath – she likes me to do it, rather than the boy, you know.' Martha looked to see if there was any consciousness here of being exploited, but no: there was nothing but charming deference.

They said goodbye, and Martha, as she turned away, saw Elaine knocking at the door that led into Mrs Talbot's bedroom. 'Can I come in, Mummy?'

Martha walked away down the street, thinking of that last deep glance into her eyes. Nonsense, she thought; it's nothing but old women's nonsense, old wives' superstition. There seemed nothing anomalous in referring to the youthful Mrs Talbot thus at this moment. 'How can there be a look in my eyes?'

When she reached home, it was nearly lunchtime. The butcher's boy had left a parcel of meat. For some reason she was unable to touch it. The soggy, bloody mass turned her stomach – she was very sick. But this was nonsense, she told herself sternly. She forced herself to untie the wet parcel, take out the meat, and cook it. She watched Douglas eating it, while she made a great joke of her weakness. Douglas remarked with jocularity that she must be pregnant. She flew into a temper.

'All the same, Matty, it wouldn't do any harm just to drop along to old Stern, would it? We don't want kids just when the war's starting, do we?'

That afternoon, since Stella was not there to gain priority for her, she sat out her time of waiting with the other women; and in due course found herself with Dr Stern. He gave her instructions to undress. She undressed and waited. Dr Stern, whose exquisite tact had earned him the right to have his waiting room perpetually filled with women who depended on him, explored the more intimate parts of Martha's body with rubber-clothed fingers, and at the same time made conversation about the international situation. Finally he informed Martha that he did not think she was pregnant; she might set her mind at rest.

He than made the mistake of complimenting her on her build, which was of the best kind for easy child-bearing. Martha was stiff-lipped and resentful and did not respond. He quickly changed his tone, saying that she needn't think about such things yet; and suggested that there was no reason why she should be pregnant if she had been carrying out his instructions? The query dismayed Martha; but she had decided to remember that he had been definite about it.

When she had left, he remarked to his new nurse that it was just as well for the medical profession that laymen had such touching faith in them. The nurse laughed dutifully and summoned the next patient.

Martha walked home very quickly; she could not wait to tell Douglas that everything was all right.

Chapter Four

Officially pronounced not pregnant, Martha determined to use her freedom sensibly. But if there was a weight off her mind, her flesh remained uncomfortable. She might say that she would settle her future once and for all; but it was not so easy: she was feeling – but how did she feel? For no matter how many charts of her emotions and flesh she may be armed with, it is not so easy for a very young woman, newly married, to discriminate between this sensation and that. Her body, newly licensed for use by society, stimulated – as Dr Stern had so humorously and succinctly put it – three times a day after meals, was in any case a web of sensations. Buzzings, burnings, swarmings: she was like a hive. And as for her tendency to feel dizzy or queasy in the mornings – what could one expect if one slept so little, ate so erratically, and, it must be confessed, drank such a lot? That is, regarded statistically, she drank a lot. But not more than everybody else. Still, from six in the evening until four the next morning she was unlikely to be without a glass in her hand, or at least, without a glass standing somewhere near. Drunk, no; one did not get drunk. A person who drinks too much is he who drinks more than the people around him. Besides, she was persistently tipsy as much from excitement as from alcohol; for the wave of elation which rose as the sun went down was as much the expectation of another brilliant, festive dancing night where the braziers burned steadily into the dawn. So Martha shifted the load of worry about how uneasy and unpredictable she felt on to how she was behaving, which she would have been the first to describe as idiotic. But then, it would not last long: the very essence of those exciting weeks was nostalgia for something doomed.

The town was restless with rumour. The voice of authority, the *Zambesia News*, faithfully reflecting the doubts and confusions of the unfortunate British Government, left ordinary people with no resource but to besiege the men in the know with questions. Everyone had some such person to whom they repaired for information. The young Knowells, for instance, had Colonel Brodeshaw; everyone knew a minor member of Parliament or a big businessman. Whenever Douglas returned from the world of offices, bars and clubs, it was with some final and authoritative statement, such as that conscription was imminent, or that people wouldn't stand for it; or that the British Government was about to declare war on Hitler the next weekend, or that – and this was very persistent during those weeks of June and July – Hitler and the British Government would together attack Stalin, thus ridding the world of what was clearly its main enemy.

But alas for the glamour and glory of great public events, their first results, regardless of how one may see them afterwards, 'in perspective', as the phrase is, tend to show themselves in the most tawdry and insignificant ways. In this case, the business of collecting the latest news proved so fascinating that young husbands preferred the bars and clubs of the city to returning home for lunch with their wives.

These three young wives reacted to this state of affairs according to their respective temperaments. Alice, after three or four days of nervous speculation over her apologetic Willie, arranged that she would meet him every day at one o'clock, and go with him on his rounds; which meant, of course, that the specifically male establishments were now out of bounds. But it was not her fault, she remarked, with her vague good-natured giggle, if men were so silly as to exclude women. As for Stella, it was all at once made evident to everyone that she had a mother. A rich widow, she was living in the suburbs. Stella, like all these young women, had fought the good fight for independence, had routed her mother from her affairs as a question of principle, no less; but now, like the heroine of a music-hall joke, she rushed back to her. At five in the evening, when Andrew went home to find his wife so that they might start on the evening round of dancing and drinking, she was not there; he had to drive out to the suburbs, where he found these two antagonists drinking tea and treating him with a calculated coolness, a weapon taken from Stella's mother's armoury of weapons against men. But this time it did not work. After some days, Andrew remarked with calm Scotch common sense; 'Well, Stella, it's not a bad idea, your having lunch with your mother. It means you're not alone all day.' Stella was doomed to a life always much less dramatic than she felt it was entitled to be.

As for Martha, whose first fierce tenet in life was hatred for the tyranny of the family, naturally she was barred from these contemptible female ruses. It was she who, after Douglas had rung up twice at lunchtime to say that he was just running off with the boys for a drink, and did she mind if he was a little late, suggested that it would be more interesting for him if he did not come home at all. He was surprised and grateful that his wife set no bounds to his freedom. It was an additional reason to be proud of his acquisition. But later in the evening, when he came home, there was perhaps a slightly resentful look on his face, as Martha inquired where he had gone, and whom he had met – of course with the friendliest interest and without any suspicion of jealousy. She would then listen intently, making him retrace his conversations and arguments by the sheer force of her interest in them. It was almost as if she had been there in his place; almost as if *she* were putting the words into his mouth for future conversations. Tyranny, it seems, is not so easily legislated against.

Besides, Douglas, like all these other young men with wives, wore during these weeks a steady, if faint, look of guilt. It had become known that a dozen of the richer young men of the city had flown Home to England to offer their services to the Air Force. Douglas, Willie and Andrew, late at night, made reckless with alcohol, discussed hopelessly how they might do the same. But if it turned out there would be no war after all? They would be without jobs, without money; *they* were not the sons of rich fathers. But of course, if they had been free – if they had no responsibilities . . . Even alcohol, even the relaxed and intimate hour of four in the morning by the coffee stalls, could not release that thought into words. But the wives, listening with consciously sardonic patience, heard the sigh after lost freedom in every gap in the conversation.

'Men,' remarked Stella to Martha, with charged womanly scorn, 'are nothing but babies.'

Martha disliked her own most intimate voice in Stella's mouth. But she was wrestling with a degree of contempt for Douglas that dismayed her. She could not afford it. She pushed it away. These young men, so eagerly discussing the prospects of being in at the kill, seemed to her like lumpish schoolboys. She despised them quite passionately: the nightly-recurring sight of Douglas, Willie and Andrew behaving like small boys wistful after adventure made her seethe with impatient contempt.

To Stella she said angrily, 'If they knew they were going to fight for something, if they cared at all . . .'

To which Stella replied indignantly, after the briefest possible pause, switching course completely in a way which could hardly strike her as odd, since it was no more than the authorities did from day to day, 'But it's our duty to squash Communism.'

The Mathews' man in the know was an upper secretary in the establishment of Mr Player; fed from this source, Stella was a well of good reasons why Communism should be instantly suppressed. It had flickered into Martha's mind that Andrew had talked of getting a job in the Player offices. She instantly dismissed the suspicion. It was one of her more pleasant but less efficient characteristics that she was unable to believe in that degree of cynicism from anyone. For naturally she persisted in believing that people should be conscious of their motives. Someone has remarked that there is no such thing as a hypocrite. In order to believe that, one must have reached the age to understand how presistently one has not been a hypocrite oneself.

Martha devoted herself to explaining to Stella how intolerable it was that she as a Jewess should have a good word to say for Hitler; while Stella, torn between persistent suspicions that there might be something in the rumours that Hitler ill-treated Jews and her terror that Andrew might not conform to Mr Player's qualifications for a minor administrator, defended the Third Reich as an ally for Britain. That is, she continued to do so more or less consistently, interspersed with short periods when someone else's man in the know had supplied other authoritative information sufficiently persuasive.

It had reached the end of July. A second batch of young men left for England. It caused an extraordinary resentment. That there were no class distinctions of any sort in this society was an axiom; one was not envious of people who sent their children to university, or even – in extreme cases – to finishing schools in Europe; it was all a question of luck. But for some days now the young men who could not afford air fares, or to gamble with their jobs, spoke with a rancour which was quite new. Opinion seethed, and brought forth a scheme by which a sufficient number of young men should besiege their heads of department and employers to give them time off, so that they should be ready and trained for instant service when war started. This admirable scheme came to nothing, because the authorities in Britain had not yet made up their minds how the colonies were to be used. There was only one principle yet decided, and this was that the men from the colonies were clearly all officer material, because of lives spent in ordering the black population about. The phrase used was, 'They are accustomed to positions of authority.' It would be a waste for Douglas, Willie and Andrew to take the field as mere cannon fodder. But although the wave of determination disintegrated against various rocks of this nature, for at least a week the young men in question thought and spoke of little else. As a result, the women turned over various ideas of their own.

They were all sitting late one night in the Burrells' flat,

which it is unnecessary to describe, since it was identical with the Knowells' and the Mathews' flats, when Alice remarked, with a nervous laugh, that it was no good Willie's thinking of dashing off to the wars, because she thought she was pregnant.

Willie was sitting next to her as usual; he squeezed his large sunburnt hand on her shoulder, and laughed, giving her his affectionate protective look. 'It's all very well,' persisted Alice. 'Oh, well, to hell with everything.' And she reached for a cigarette.

No one took it seriously. But a week later, when the Burrells were rung up to join a party for dancing, Alice remarked in a calm way that she had no time for dancing for a couple of days, because she had to do something about this damned baby. Douglas, returning from the office, reported to Martha that he had met Willie in the bar and Willie said it was very serious, no laughing matter at all. Stella, all delighted animation, rang up to offer her services. But Alice, the trained nurse, was vaguely reassuring. She was quite all right, she said.

Stella was offended, and showed it by saying that it was stupid to get pregnant when – But this sentence flowed into 'And, in any case, she's only doing it to keep Willie from being called up.' Martha said indignantly that anyone would think Alice was doing it on purpose. To which Stella replied with her rich, shrewd laugh. Martha was annoyed because she was associated with a sex which chose such dishonest methods for getting its own way.

'I bet she's not really doing anything about getting rid of it,' said Stella virtuously. But one felt her energies were not really behind this indignation.

She and Martha were secure in a plan of their own. Martha had suggested they might go and take a course in Red Cross. It was on a day when the newspaper had warned them that an enemy (left undefined, like a blank in an official form to be filled in later as events decided) might sweep across Africa in a swastikaed or – the case might be – hammer-and-sickled horde. In this case, the black population, always ungrateful to the British colonists, would naturally side with the unscrupulous invaders, undermined as they were by sedition-mongers, agitators and Fabian influences from England. The prospect brightened the eyes of innumerable women; one should be prepared; and in due time Red Cross courses were announced.

'Matty and I are thinking of joining an ambulance unit,' said Stella demurely. 'After all, we won't have any responsibilities here if you go on active service, will we?'

Martha had dropped this suggestion in passing, just as she had tentatively suggested the Red Cross course, only to find it taken up and moulded by Stella. And the uneasy silence of their husbands contributed to their perseverance. At ten o'clock one morning, Martha and Stella were in their seats for the first of these lectures.

It was a large room filled with rows of school desks. They were crowded with about sixty women, who must be housewives or leisured daughters at this hour of the day. The lecturer was an elderly woman, fat, red-faced, with jolly little black eyes. Under the edges of her flowing coif showed flat scooplike curls of iron-grey hair, gummed against her cheeks; for, unlike the nuns whose garb this so much resembled, this woman was a female still – those curls proclaimed it. The masses of her flesh were tightly confined in glazed white, and supported on the large splayed feet which were the reward of her work.

This, then, was Sister Dorothy Dalraye, known for the last thirty years to her friends and colleagues, now numbering several thousands, as Doll. She introduced herself with the cheerful cry of 'Well, girls, since we're all going to be together for six weeks, you must call me Sister Doll!' And proceeded to a series of bright remarks, infusing into her animated black eyes a look of insinuating suggestiveness, so that her audience instinctively listened as if some doubtful joke was imminent. But no: it appeared her innuendoes referred to the coming war – or rather, the enemy who was as yet unnamed. Martha unravelled her ambiguities to mean that she, unlike Stella, hoped to fight Hitler and not Stalin; at last she made some references to 'the Hun' which settled the matter. That this was a memory from the last war was made clear when she called it, just as Mr Quest might do, 'the Great Unmentionable', but without his bitter note of betrayal. Sister Doll had fought alongside the boys during the Great Unmentionable, and on various fronts. She named them. She produced anecdote after anecdote, apparently at random. But Martha slowly realized that this was not at all as casual as it looked. This gathering of some sixty women had ceased to be individuals. They were being slowly welded together. They were listening in silence, and every face showed anticipation, as if they were being led, by the cheerful tallyhoing of Sister Doll, to view entrancing vistas of country. Sister Doll was adroitly, and with the confidence of one who had done it many times before, building up a picture of herself, and so of them, as a cheerfully modest, indefatigably devoted minister of mercy who took physical bravery for granted. But behind this picture, absolutely genuine, was another; and it was this that beckoned the audience: adventure. Sister Doll was promising them adventure. Once again Martha heard the mud, the squalor, the slaughter of the trenches recreated in the memory of someone who had been a victim of them – Sister Doll remarked in passing that she had 'lost' her boy at Passchendaele – as cleanly gallant and exciting.

She spoke for some twenty minutes, this jolly old campaigner; then, judging it was enough, she proceeded to talk about discipline. It was clear that this was by no means as popular as those inspiring reminiscences – perhaps because these women, being mostly married women with servants, had reached the position where they believed their task was to discipline others and not themselves. In this they resembled Sister Doll. At any rate, judging from the critical and sceptical look on their faces, they were reflecting that the discipline of the nursing profession, like its uniform, was more hierarchic than practical. They were minutely observing Sister Doll's uniform, with its white glaze, its ritual buckles and badges, and its romantic flowing white veil, with the common sense of disparaging housewives. They began to cough and shuffle like a theatre audience. Not a moment too soon Sister Doll prevented them from separating again into a collection of individuals, by turning to her main topic for that day, which was how to make a bed properly. Not, however, without remarking with a sort of regretful severity, looking at the wall in case she might be accused of singling anyone out, that some people said, though of course she wouldn't know if it were true or not, that the young people of today hadn't the sense of vocation of her generation. Martha had decided that she had no intention of devoting six weeks, although only a few hours a week were demanded of her, to the company of this elderly war horse who nevertheless continually suggested a happy hockey-playing schoolgirl. She therefore occupied her time in trying to decide what was the common denominator of this mass of women; for certainly there must be a special kind of woman who rushes, at the first sound of the bugle, to learn how to nurse 'the boys'. There was no doubt that this was how they were picturing themselves, and how Sister Doll was encouraging them to think; a white-garbed angel among wounded men was the image that filled their minds, despite this talk of a threatened civilian population. But she could only conclude that the difference between them and herself was that they were all taking down minute notes about the correct way to fold bedclothes.

She looked towards Stella, who was coiled seductively on the hard bench, head propped on slender hands, eyes fixed on Sister Doll. It was clear that she was not listening to a word. It looked as if she was deliberately trying to present the picture of a detached observer. She happened to be wearing a white linen dress, whose severity was designed to emphasize her slim curves; or perhaps it was that she had felt white to be more 'suitable' for a nursing course than any other colour. But her small, apricot-tinted face with its enormous lazy dark eyes, the soft slender body in its white, were the cruellest comment on the only other white figure in the room, fat and perspiring Sister Doll, half a dozen paces away. It appeared that Sister Doll felt it, or at least her inattention; for during those pauses while she was waiting for her class to take down sentences such as 'The greatest care must be taken to keep the patient's bed neat and tidy', she turned hot little eyes full of rather flustered reproach, on Stella, who was regarding her with indolent inquiry. Catching Martha's eye, Stella made a small movement of her own eyes towards the door. Martha frowned back. Stella gave a petulant shrug.

The moment Sister Doll dismissed her class, Stella took Martha's arm and hurried her out. Her first words were, 'Let's go and see Alice.'

'Really,' exclaimed Martha, her boredom and dissatisfaction exploding obliquely, 'what a waste of time — all this nonsense about making beds.'

'It's only just up the road.' Stella tugged at her arm.

'And we've paid all that money for the course.'

'Oh, well ... Anyway, I expect there won't be a war anyway.'

'Why not?' Martha stopped and looked at Stella, really wanting to know.

'Andrew says they won't start training them. Well, then, if there was going to be a war, they would train people like Douglas and Andrew, wouldn't they? He said so this morning. I thought they'd start playing soldiers any minute now.' Stella dismissed the thing, and said, 'Oh, come on, Matty, it's only just up the road.'

'But she doesn't know we're coming. She doesn't want to see us.'

'Nonsense,' said Stella with energy. The matter thus settled, they walked towards Alice's flat.

Stella knocked at the door in a manner that suggested discreet determination. Her eyes were alive with interest. There was a long silence.

'She's out,' said Martha hopefully. She knew that Alice, like herself, preferred to take the more intimate crises of life in private.

'Nonsense,' Stella said, and knocked again. A long silence. Stella changed the tempo of her knocking to a peremptory summons. 'She's only trying to get rid of us,' she remarked with her jolly laugh.

Alice opened the door sharply on that laugh. She was annoyed.

'It's us,' Stella said and walked blandly inside.

Alice was in a pale-pink taffeta dressing gown which had been bought for the fresh young woman she had been as a bride; now she was rather yellow and very thin, and her freckles seemed to have sprung up everywhere over the pale sallow skin. Her black hair hung dispiritedly on her shoulders.

'Well?' demanded Stella at once.

Alice regarded her from a distance, and remarked that she wasn't feeling at all well.

Stella, a little figure bristling with frustrated purpose, said, 'Oh, stop it, Alice.' then she frowned, decided to change tactics, and said diplomatically, 'Shall I make you a nice cup of tea?'

'Oh, do make it, dear. I'm really exhausted.' And Alice subsided backwards into a chair, and lay there extinguished.

The moment Stella had gone to the kitchen, Alice opened her eyes and looked at Martha as if to ask, 'Am I safe from you?'

Martha was equally limp in another chair. She inquired childishly, 'Is it true you only have to jump off a table?' She meant to sound competent, but in fact her face expressed nothing but distaste. 'Did you know I went to Dr Stern and he said I wasn't?' she went on.

'Did you, dear?' This was discretion itself; it was the trained nurse remembering her loyalties.

But it was not what Martha wanted. 'He said I was quite all right.'

A short silence. Then Alice remarked vaguely, 'You know, they don't know everything.'

Alarm flooded Martha; she shook it off. 'But he's supposed to be very good at – this sort of thing.'

To this Alice could only reply that he was, very. Then Stella came in with a tray. She set it down, and proceeded to cross-examine Alice while she poured the tea. Alice replied vaguely with that good humour which is rooted in indifference. Vague as a cloud, lazy as water, she lay with half-shut eyes and let fall stray remarks which had the effect of stinging Stella into a frenzy of exasperation. At the end of ten minutes' hard work Stella had succeeded in eliciting the positive information that Alice believed herself to be three months gone.

'Well, really!' Horror at this incompetence shook Stella. 'But three months!'

Clinical details followed, which Alice confirmed as if they could not possibly have any reference to herself. 'Well, dear, I really don't know,' she kept saying helplessly.

'But you *must* know,' exclaimed the exasperated Stella. 'One either has a period or one has not.'

'Oh, well – I never take any notice of mine, anyway.'

This caused Martha to remark with pride that she never did, either. For she and Alice belonged to the other family of women from Stella, who proceeded to detail, with gloomy satisfaction, how much she suffered during these times. Alice and Martha listened with tolerant disapproval.

Checked on this front, Stella brooded for a while on how to approach a more intimate one. Martha had more than once remarked with distaste to Douglas that if Stella were given a chance she would positively wallow in the details of the marriage bed. This chance was not given her. Women of the tradition to which Alice and Martha belonged are prepared to discuss menstruation or pregnancy in the frankest of detail, but it is taboo to discuss sex, notwithstanding the show of frankness the subject is surrounded with. It follows that they get their information about how other women react sexually from their men, a system which has its disadvantages. More than once had Stella been annoyed by reticences on the part of Martha and Alice which seemed to her the most appalling prudery; an insult, in fact, to their friendship. But she did not persist now; she returned to ask direct what steps Alice proposed to take. Alice said with a lazy laugh that she had done everything. Cross-examination produced the information that she had drunk gin and taken a hot bath. Even more shocked, Stella delivered a short and efficient lecture, which interested Martha extremely, but to which Alice listened indifferently, occasionally suppressing a genuine yawn. Stella then supplied the names of three wise women, two Coloured and one white, who would do the job for a moderate fee. To which Alice replied, with her first real emotion that day, that she had seen enough of girls ruined for life by these women ever to go near them herself.

'Well, then, how about Dr Stern?'

Alice said angrily, with the curtness of a schoolmistress, that if Stella wasn't careful she'd find herself in trouble, saying such things about honest doctors! Stella rose, red and angry, her tongue quivering with expert retaliations. Alice gave her a weary and apologetic smile, and said, 'Oh, sit down, Stella, I haven't the energy for a row.'

Stella sat. After a while she asked, in a deceptively sweet voice, on a note of modest interest, if perhaps Alice intended to have this baby after all?

Alice said good-naturedly, 'We all have to have them sometime, dear, don't we?' Here she laughed again, and it was with reckless pleasure; at the same time her look at Stella was challenging, triumphant, very amused.

Stella, after a shocked and accusing stare, turned away, with an effect of indifference, and elaborately changed the subject.

Leaving the flat, Stella remarked coldly that it was utterly irresponsible of Alice to have a baby when they were so hard up; then that it was criminal to have a baby when war was starting; finally, after a long pause, that as for herself she was too delicate to have a baby, she would probably die in childbirth. There was a speculative look on her face as she said this, which caused Martha to remark, amused, that it would be awfully inconsistent of Stella to have a baby herself, after what she had said. Stella reacted with an affronted 'It would be quite unfair to Andrew; I'd never do a thing like that.'

The two young women parted almost at once, without regret.

Martha walked slowly home, thinking about Alice. Her emotions were violent and mixed. She felt towards the pregnant woman, the abstraction, a strong repulsion which caused various images, all unpleasant, to rise into her mind one after another. From her childhood came a memory of lowered voices, distasteful intimacies, hidden sicknesses. It was above all frightening that all this furtive secrecy, which she and all her friends so firmly repudiated, was waiting there, strong as ever, all around her, as she knew: Alice, because she was pregnant, was delivered back into the hands of the old people – so Martha felt it. She felt caged, for Alice. She could feel the bonds around herself. She consciously shook them off and exulted in the thought that she was free. Free! And the half-shaded flat she had left, with the pale, sallow-looking woman in pink taffeta, seemed like a suffocating prison. But at the same time a deeper emotion was turning towards Alice, with an unconscious curiosity, warm, tender, protective. It was an emotion not far from envy. In six months, Alice would have a baby. Why, it was no time at all, she thought. But no sooner had she put it into words than she reacted back again with a shuddering impulse towards escape. She could see the scene: Alice, loose and misshapen, with an ugly wet-mouthed infant, feeding-bottles, napkins, smells.

Martha reached her flat, removed her clothes and anxiously examined every inch of her body. Unmarked, whole, perfect – smooth solid flesh; there was not a stain on it. Here Martha gave an uncomfortable look at her breasts, and acknowledged they were heavier than they had been. There was a bruised, reddish look about them – here came a flood of panic, and then she subsided into perfect trust in Dr Stern. She felt particularly supported by the knowledge that ever since her second visit she and Douglas had followed the prescribed rituals with determined precision. She was free. She continued to revel in her freedom all that afternoon, while underneath she thought persistently of Alice, and wondered why she was now so contented to have a baby, when, as short a time ago as a month, she had spoken of having one with vigorous rejection.

When Douglas returned from the office, she described the day's doings, passing over the nursing lecture as an utter waste of time, and laughing at Stella's frustrated homilies and Alice's vague determination. But Douglas, who had moments, which were becoming increasingly frequent, of remembering that he was a government official, remarked rather officiously that Stella would get herself into trouble one of these days. It was illegal to procure abortions: that was the cold phrase he used. But at this Martha flew into an angry tirade against governments who presumed to tell women what they should do with their own bodies; it was the final insult to personal liberty. Douglas listened, frowning, and said unanswerably that the law was the law. Martha therefore retreated into herself, which meant that she became very gay, hard, and indifferent. She listened to his rather heavy insistence about what she intended to do in place of the nursing course, and understood that he was above all concerned that she should not be in the war – should not go in pursuit of the adventure he himself was quivering to find; he was even more reluctant because of his own daydreams as to certain aspects of that adventure.

He went so far, carried away by the official in him, as to make various sound remarks about the unsuitability of danger for women. She thought he must be joking; nothing is more astonishing to young women than the ease with which men, even intelligent and liberal-minded men, lapse back into that anonymous voice of authority whenever their own personal authority is threatened, saying things of a banality and a pomposity infinitely removed from their own level of thinking.

Martha was first incredulous, then frightened, then she began to despise him. She became even more gay and brilliant; he became fascinated; she despised him the more for being fascinated; he began to resent the offhandedness of her manner and retreated again into the official. She mocked at him recklessly, they quarrelled. As a result of this hatred, they spent a hectic evening, ending up at four in the morning at the fair, where Martha, sick and giddy, revolved on the great wheel as if her whole future depended on her power to stick it out. High over the darkened town – where a few widely scattered windows showed the points where revellers were at last going to bed – plunging sickeningly to earth and up again. Martha clung on, until the wheel was stopped, the music stopped churning, and there was literally nowhere to go but bed. From the bedroom window they could see the lights greying along the street. The native servants were coming in from the location in time to be at work.

She woke with a start; the bed next to her was empty. There were noises next door. Then she saw it was nearly eleven. While she stood in her nightdress, fumbling at her dressing gown, the door began very gently to open inwards. Its cautious movement was arrested; then the person the other side dropped something; the door crashed back against the wall, and Mrs Quest stumbled into the room, reaching out for parcels which scattered everywhere.

'Oh, so you're up,' Mrs Quest said sharply. 'I didn't mean to wake you. I was coming in quietly.' Then, retrieving a last package to make a neat pile on the bed, she added archly, 'What a dashing life you lead, lying in bed till eleven.'

This roguishness aroused in Martha the usual strong distaste. She had covered herself entirely with her dressing gown, buttoning it up tight from throat to hem.

'I thought you must be ill, I peeped in and saw you. Shall I go for the doctor, don't get up, stay in bed and I'll nurse you – for today, at least.'

'I'm perfectly well,' said Martha ungraciously. 'Let's go and have some tea.' Firmly, she led the way from the bedroom, but Mrs Quest did not follow her at once.

Martha sat on the divan listening. Her mother was following the ritual that she had already gone through here, in this room. The flowers had been removed from their vases and rearranged, the chairs set differently, books put into place. Mrs Quest had reassured herself by touching and arranging everything in the living room, and was now doing the same in the bedroom. Martha had time to make the tea and bring in the tray before her mother reappeared.

'I've just made your bed, your nightdress is torn, did you know? I've brought it to mend while I'm here, your bathroom isn't done, it's wet,' Mrs Quest remarked flurriedly. She had Martha's nightdress clutched in one hand. She glanced at it, blushed, and remarked coquettishly, 'How you can wear these transparent bits of fluff I don't know.'

Martha poured the tea in silence. She was exaggeratedly

irritated. The violence of this emotion was what kept her silent; for she was quite able to assure herself that nothing could be more natural, and even harmless and pathetic, than this unfortunate woman's need to lead every other life but her own. This is what her intelligence told her; her conscience remarked that she was making a fuss about nothing; but in fact she seethed with irritation. The face she presented to her mother was one of numbed hostility. This, as usual, affected Mrs Quest like an accusation.

The next phase of this sad cycle followed: Mrs Quest said that it was unfair to Douglas not to sleep enough: she could get ill and then he would have to pay the bills. Martha's face remaining implacable, she went on, in tones of hurried disapproval: 'If you'll give me a needle and thread, I'll mend your nightdress.'

Martha got up, found needle and thread, and handed them to Mrs Quest without a word. The sight of that nightdress, still warm from her own body, clutched with nervous possession in her mother's hands was quite unendurable. She was determined to endure it. After all, she thought, if it gives her pleasure ... And then: It's not her fault she was brought up in *that* society. This thought gave her comparative detachment. She sat down and looked at the worn, gnarled hands at work on her nightdress. They filled her with pity for her mother. Besides, she could remember how she had loved her mother's hands as a child; she could see the white and beautiful hands of a woman who no longer existed.

Mrs Quest was talking of matters on the farm, about the house in town they were shortly to buy, about her husband's health.

Martha scarcely listened. She was engaged in examining and repairing those intellectual bastions of defence behind which she sheltered, that building whose shape had first been sketched so far back in her childhood she could no longer remember how it then looked. With every year it had become more complicated, more ramified; it was as if she, Martha, were a variety of soft, shell-less creature whose survival lay in the strength of those walls. Reaching out in all directions from behind it, she clutched at the bricks of arguments, the stones of words, discarding any that might not fit into the building.

She was looking at Mrs Quest in a deep abstract speculation, as if neither she nor her mother had any validity as persons, but were mere pawns in the hands of an old fatality. She could see a sequence of events, unalterable, behind her, and stretching unalterably into the future. She saw her mother, a prim-faced Edwardian schoolgirl, confronting, in this case, the Victorian father, the patriarchal father, with rebellion. She saw herself sitting where her mother now sat, a woman horribly metamorphosed, entirely dependent on her children for any interest in life, resented by them, and resenting them; opposite her, a young woman of whom she could distinguish nothing clearly but a set, obstinate face; and beside these women, a series of shadowy dependent men, broken-willed and sick with compelled diseases. This the nightmare, this the nightmare of a class and generation: repetition. And although Martha had read nothing of the great interpreters of the nightmare, she had been soaked in the minor literature of the last thirty years, which had dealt with very little else: a series of doomed individuals, carrying their doom *inside* them, like the seeds of fatal disease. Nothing could alter the pattern.

But inside the stern web of fatality did flicker small hopeful flames. One thought was that after all it had not always been that these great life-and-death struggles were fought out inside the family; presumably things might change again. Another was that she had decided not to have a baby; and it was in her power to cut the cycle.

Which brought her back into the conversation with a question on her tongue.

Mrs Quest was talkng about the coming war. She had no doubt at all as to the shape it would assume. It was Britain's task to fight Hitler and Stalin combined. Martha suggested that this might be rather a heavy task. Mrs Quest said sharply that Martha had no patriotism, and never had had. Even without those lazy and useless Americans who never came into the war until they could make good pickings out of it,

Britain would ultimately muddle through to victory, as she always did.

Martha was able to refrain from being *logical* only by her more personal preoccupations. She plunged straight in with an inquiry as to whether her mother had ever had an abortion. She hastened to add that she wanted to know because of a friend of hers.

Mrs Quest, checked, took some moments to adjust to this level. She said vaguely, 'It's illegal . . .' Having made this offering to the law, she considered the question on its merits and said in a lowered voice, a look of distaste on her face, 'Why – are you like that?'

Martha suppressed the hostility she felt at the evasion, and said, 'No.'

'Well, you look like it,' said Mrs Quest bluntly, with triumph.

'Well, I'm not.' Martha added the appeal, 'I do wish you'd tell me . . .' She had no idea what she really wanted to know!

Mrs Quest looked at her, her vigorous face wearing the dubious rather puzzled expression which meant she was trying to remember her own past.

Martha was telling herself that this appeal was doomed to produce all kinds of misunderstanding and discomfort. They always did. And what *did* she want her mother to say? She looked at her in silence, and wished that some miracle would occur and her mother would produce a few simple, straightforward remarks, a few *words* – not emotional, nothing deviating from the cool humorous understatement that would save them both from embarrassment. Martha needed the right words.

She reflected that Mrs Quest had not wanted her. How, then, had she come to accept her? Was that what she wanted to know? But looking at her now, she could only think that Mrs Quest had spent a free, energetic youth, had 'lived her own life' – she had used the phrase herself long before it was proper for middle-class daughters to do so – and had, accordingly, quarrelled with her father. She had not married until very late.

For many years now, she had been this immensely efficient down-to-earth matron; but somewhere concealed in her was the mother who had borne Martha. From her white and feminine body she, Martha, had emerged – that was certainly a fact! She could remember seeing her mother naked; beautiful she had been, a beautiful, strong white body, with full hips, small high breasts – the Greek idea of beauty. And to that tender white body had belonged the strong soft white hands Martha remembered. Those hands had tended her, the baby. Well, then, why could her mother not resurrect that woman in her and speak the few simple, appropriate words?

But now she was turning Martha's flimsy nightgown between her thickened, clumsy hands, as if determined not to say she disapproved of it; and frowned. She looked uncomfortable. Martha quite desperately held on to that other image to set against this one. She could see that earlier woman distinctly. More, she could feel wafts of tenderness coming from her.

Then, suddenly, into this pure and simple emotion came something new: she felt pity like a clutching hand. She was remembering something else. She was lying in the dark in that house on the farm, listening to a piano being played several rooms away. She got up, and crept through the dark rooms to a doorway. She saw Mrs Quest seated at the keyboard, a heavy knot of hair weighting her head and glistening gold where the light touched it from two candle flames which floated steadily above the long white transparent candles. Tears were running down her face while she set her lips and smiled. The romantic phrases of a Chopin nocturne rippled out into the African night, steadily accompanied by the crickets and the blood-thudding of the tom-toms from the compound. Martha smiled wryly: she could remember the gulf of pity that sight had thrown her into.

Mrs Quest looked up over the nightdress and inquired jealously, 'What are you laughing at?'

'Mother,' she said desperately, 'you didn't want to have me. Well, then . . .'

Mrs Quest laughed, and said Martha had come as a surprise to her.

Martha waited, then prodded. 'What did you *feel*?'

A slight look of caution came on to her mother's honest square face. 'Oh, well . . .' But almost at once she launched into the gay and humorous account, which Martha had so often heard, of the difficulties of getting the proper clothes and so on; which almost at once merged with the difficulties of the birth itself – a painful business, this, as she had so often been told.

'But what did you *feel* about it all? I mean, it couldn't have been as easy as all that,' said Martha.

'Oh, it wasn't easy – I was just telling you.' Mrs Quest began to repeat how awkward a baby Martha had been. 'But it wasn't really your fault. First I didn't have enough milk, though I didn't know it; and then I gave you a mixture, and didn't know until the doctor told me that it was only half the right strength. So in one way and another I half starved you for the first nine months of your life.' Mrs Quest laughed ruefully, and said, 'No wonder you never stopped crying day or night.'

A familiar resentment filled Martha, and she at once pressed on. 'But, Mother, when you first knew you were going to have a baby – '

Mrs Quest interrupted. 'And then I had your brother, he was such a good baby, not like you.'

And now Martha abdicated, as she had so often done before; for it had always, for some reason, seemed right and inevitable that Mrs Quest should prefer the delicate boy child to herself. Martha listened to the familiar story to the end, while she suppressed a violent and exasperated desire to take her mother by the shoulders and shake her until she produced, in a few sensible and consoling sentences, that truth which it was so essential Martha should have. But Mrs Quest had forgotten how she felt. She was no longer interested. And why should she be, this elderly woman with all the business of being a woman behind her?

In a short while she returned to the war, dismissed Chamberlain with a few just sentences, and recommended

Mr Churchill for his job. The Quests belonged to that section of the middle class who would be happy and contented to be conservatives if only the conservatives could be more efficient. As it was, they never ceased complaining about the inefficiency and corruption of the party they would unfailingly vote for if they lived in England.

Towards lunchtime she left, with the advice that Martha should go and see the doctor and get a good tonic. She looked dreadful – it wasn't fair to Douglas.

The result of that visit from her mother was that Martha decided again she must not sink into being a mere housewife. She should at once learn a profession, or at least take some kind of job. But this decision was not as firm as it might seem from the energy she used in speaking about it to Douglas.

She was gripped by a lethargy so profound that in fact she spent most of her time limp on that divan, thinking about nothing. She felt heavy and uncomfortable and sick. And she was clinging to Douglas with the dependence of a child. She was miserable when he left in the morning; she was waiting anxiously for his return hours before he might be expected. Pride, however, forbade her to show it, or to ask him to come home for lunch. At night, the loud sad music from the fair was becoming an obsession. She found herself waking from sleep and crying, but what she was weeping for she had no idea at all. She drew the curtains so that she might not see the great wheel; and then lay watching the circling of light through their thin stuff. She accused herself of every kind of weak-mindedness and stupidity; nevertheless, the persistent monotony of that flickering cycle seemed a revelation of an appalling and intimate truth; it was like being hypnotized.

During the daytime she sat with a book, trying to read, and realized that she was not seeing one word of it. It was, she realized, as if she were listening for something; some kind of anxiety ran through every limb.

One morning she was very sick, and all at once the suspicion she had been ignoring for so long became a certainty – and from one moment to the next. When Douglas came home that night she said sullenly, as if it was his fault, that she must be pregnant; and insisted when he said that Dr Stern could not be wrong. At last he suggested she should go and talk to Stella, whose virtuosity in these matters was obvious. She said she would; but when it came to the point, she shrank from the idea and instead went to Alice.

It was a hot, dusty morning. A warm wind swept flocks of yellowing leaves along the streets. The jacarandas were holding up jaded yellow arms. This drying, yellowing, fading month, this time when the year tensed and tightened towards the coming rains, always gave her a feeling of perverted autumn, and now filled her with an exquisite cold apprehension. The sky, above the haze of dust, was a glitter of hot blue light.

Alice was in her pink taffeta dressing gown in her large chair. She greeted Martha with cheerful indifference, and bade her sit down. On the table beside her was a pile of books, called variously *Mothercraft*, *Baby Handling* and *Your Months of Preparation*.

Martha glanced towards them, and Alice said, 'The nonsense they talk, dear, you wouldn't believe it.' She pushed them gently away. Then she got up, and stood before Martha, with her two hands held tenderly over her stomach. 'I'm as flat as a board still,' she remarked with pride. She looked downwards with a preoccupied blue stare; she seemed to be listening. 'According to the books, it doesn't quicken until – but now I've worked out my dates, and actually it quickens much earlier. At first I thought it must be wind,' remarked Alice, faintly screwing up her face with the effort of listening.

'I think I'm pregnant, too,' remarked Martha nervously.

'Are you, dear?' Alice sat down, keeping her hands in a protective curve, and said, 'Oh, well, when you get used to it, it's quite interesting really.'

'Oh, I'm not going to *have* it,' said Martha with energy.

Alice did not reply. Martha saw that she had gone completely into her private world of sensation, and that anything which happened outside was quite irrelevant. She recognized the feeling: what else had she been fighting against during the last few weeks?

After a pause Alice continued the conversation she was having with herself by remarking, 'Oh, well, to hell with everything. Who cares, anyway?' She gave her dry nervous laugh, and reached for a cigarette.

'Well, you look pleased with yourself,' said Martha, half laughing.

Alice frowned as these words reached her, and said, 'Help yourself to cigarettes, dear.'

The morning drifted past. Alice, dim and safe in her private world, smoked constantly, stubbing out the cigarettes as she lit them, and from time to time dropping remarks such as 'It ought to be February, I think.' When Martha roused herself to go, Alice appeared to be reminding herself that she had not been as sympathetic as she could have been. She held the door open, Martha already being outside it, and proceeded to offer various bits of advice in an apologetic voice, the most insistent being that she should at once go and see Stella.

Martha went home, reached for the telephone, but was unable to dial Stella's number. She shrank away from Stella with a most extraordinary dislike of her. She was thinking of Alice; and in spite of her own deep persistent misery, her knowledge that the web was tight around her, she knew, too, that she was most irrationally elated. Anyone would think that you were pleased, she said angrily to herself. With an efficiency which Stella must have applauded, she put on her dressing gown, locked the door, and took the telephone off the hook. She then drank, with calm deliberation, glass after glass of neat gin, until a full bottle was gone. Then she lay down and slept. When she woke it was four in the afternoon, and she felt nothing but a weakness in her knees. She filled the bath with water so hot that she could not put her hand into it, and, setting her teeth, got in. The pain was so intense that she nearly fainted. She was going through with this, however; and she sat in the bath until the water was tepid. When she reeled out, she was boiled scarlet, and could not touch her skin. Having rubbed cream all over herself, she lay on the bed, shrinking from the touch of the sheet, and cried a little from sheer pain. She slept again.

Douglas was rattling at the locked door when she woke, and she staggered to let him in.

Faced with a tousled, bedraggled, red-faced female, reeking of gin, Douglas was naturally upset; but he was informed in a cold and efficient voice that this was necessary. He sat wincing while Martha climbed repeatedly on to the table and jumped off, crashing down on her heels with the full force of her weight. At the end of half an hour he could no longer stand it, and forcibly put her to bed. In a small triumphant voice Martha informed him that if *that* didn't shift it nothing would.

In the morning she woke, feeling as if her limbs had been pulverized from within and as if her skin were a separate, agonized coating to her body, but otherwise whole. Douglas was astounded to hear her say, in a voice of unmistakable satisfaction, that she must be as strong and healthy as a horse. He was unable to bear it: this female with set will, tight mouth, and cold and rejecting eyes was entirely horrifying to him.

'Well,' demanded Martha practically, 'do we or do we not want to have this baby?'

Douglas evaded this by saying that she should go forthwith to see Dr Stern, and escaped to his office, trying to ignore the inescapable fact that Martha was contemptuous of him because of his male weakness.

Late that afternoon Martha entered Dr Stern's consulting room, in a mood of such desperate panic that he recognized it at once and promptly offered her a drink, which he took from a cupboard. Martha watched him anxiously, and saw him look her up and down with that minute, expert inspection which she had seen before. On whose face? Mrs Talbot's, of course!

Dr Stern, kindness itself, then examined Martha. She told him, laughing, of the measures she had taken, to which he replied gravely, looking at her scarlet skin, that she shouldn't overdo these things. But never, not for one second, did he make the mistake of speaking in the anonymous voice of male authority which she would have so passionately resented.

Finally he informed her that she was over four months pregnant; which shocked her into silence. Such was his bland assurance, such was the power of this man, the doctor in the white coat behind the big desk, that the words stammering on her tongue could not get themselves said. But he saw her reproachful look and said that doctors were not infallible; he added almost at once that a fine, healthy girl like herself should be delighted to have a baby. Martha was silent with misery. She said feebly after a pause that there was no point in having a baby when the war was coming. At which he smiled slightly and said that the birthrate, for reasons best known to itself, always rose in wartime. She felt caught up in an immense impersonal tide which paid no attention to her, Martha. She looked at this young man who was after all not so much older then herself; she looked at the grave responsible face, and hated him bitterly from the bottom of her heart.

She asked him bluntly if he would do an abortion.

He replied immediately that he could not.

There was a long and difficult silence. Dr Stern regarded her steadily from expert eyes, and reached out for a small statuette which stood on his desk. It was in bronze, of a mermaidlike figure diving off a rock. He fingered it lightly and said, 'Do you realize that your baby is as big as this already?' It was about five inches high.

The shock numbed her tongue. She had imagined this creature as 'it', perhaps a formless blob of jellylike substance, or alternatively, as already born, a boneless infant in a shawl, but certainly not as a living being five inches long coiled in her flesh.

'Eyes, ears, arms, legs – all there.' He fingered the statuette a little longer; then he dropped his hand and was silent.

Martha was so bitter that she could not yet move or speak a word. All she was for him, and probably for Douglas too, she thought, was a 'healthy young woman'.

Then he said with a tired humorous smile that if she knew the proportion of his women patients who came, as she did, when they found they were pregnant, not wanting a baby, only to be delighted when they got used to the idea, she would be surprised.

Martha did not reply. She rose to leave. He got up, too, and said with a real human kindness that she was able to appreciate only later, that she should think twice before rushing off to see one of the wise women: her baby was too big to play tricks with now. If she absolutely insisted on an abortion, she should go to Johannesburg, where, as everyone knew, there was a hospital which was a positive factory for this sort of thing. The word 'factory' made her wince; and she saw at once, with a satirical appreciation of his skill in handling her, that it was deliberately chosen.

He shook hands with her, invited her to drop in and talk it all over if she felt like it at any time, and went back to his desk.

Martha returned to her flat in a trance of despair. Not the least of her bitterness was due to her knowledge that in some part of herself she was already weakening towards this baby. She could not forget that diving creature, bent in moulded bronze, about five inches long. In her bedroom, she found herself standing as she had seen Alice stand, hands curiously touching her stomach. It occurred to her that this child had quickened already; she understood that this long process had been one of determined self-deception – almost as if she had wanted this damned baby all the time, she thought quickly, and immediately pushed the idea from her mind. But how could she have mistaken those irregular but definite movements for anything else?

When Douglas came home she informed him that nothing would induce her to have this child, with which he at once agreed. She found herself slightly annoyed by this. It was agreed that she should go at once to Johannesburg. Douglas knew of an astounding number of women who had made the trip and returned home none the worse for it.

Martha, left alone next day to make preparations for the trip, did nothing at all. Then her mother flew in. Against all her intentions, Martha blurted out that she was going to have a baby; and was immediately folded in Mrs Quest's arms. Mrs Quest was delighted; her face beamed pleasure;

she said it was lovely, it was the best thing that could possibly happen, it would settle Martha down and give her no time at all for all her funny ideas. (Here she gave a small, defiant, triumphant laugh.) Unfortunately, as she had to get back to the farm, she could not stay with her daughter, much as she wanted to. She embraced Martha again, and said in a warm, thrilled voice that it was the greatest experience in a woman's life. With this she left, wet-eyed and with a tremulous smile.

Martha was confounded; she sat thinking that her mother must be out of her mind; above all she was thinking angrily of the triumph she had shown. She roused herself again to pack and make telephone calls; but they again faded out in indecision. The child, five inches long, with eyes, nose, mouth, hands and feet, seemed very active. Martha sat feeling the imprisoned thing moving in her flesh, and was made more miserable by the knowledge that it had been moving for at least a week without her noticing it than by anything else. For what was the use of thinking, of planning, if emotions one did not recognize at all worked their own way against you? She was filled with a strong and seething rage against her mother, her husband, Dr Stern, who had all joined the conspiracy against her. She addressed angry speeches of protest to them, fiery and eloquent speeches; but, alas, there was no one there but herself.

Sometime later Stella came in, stepping blithely around the door, hips swaying lightly, eyes bright with interest. She had heard the news; the boys were already drinking Douglas's health in the Club.

'Everyone's quite convinced that you *had* to get married,' said Stella with a delighted chuckle.

An astonishing thought occurred to Martha for the first time. 'Do you know,' she cried out, half laughing, 'if I'm as pregnant as Dr Stern says I am, then I must have been when I got married!' At this she flung herself back and roared with laughter. Stella joined her briefly; then she regarded Martha impatiently, waiting for the rather helpless wail of laughter to end.

'Well,' demanded Stella, 'and what are we going to do about it?'

It was at this point that Martha, in the stubborn, calm voice of complete conviction, found herself explaining to Stella how foolish an abortion would be at this stage. Stella grew increasingly persuasive, and Martha obstinate. The arguments she now found for having this baby were as strong and unanswerable as those she had been using, only ten minutes ago, against it. She found herself intensely excited at the idea of having a baby.

'Well, I don't know,' remarked Stella disgustedly at last. 'You and Alice are mad. Both mad, quite mad.'

She rose, and stood poised before Martha to deliver the final blow; but Martha intercepted it by suggesting teasingly that Stella herself ought to start a baby, as otherwise she'd be left out of it.

At this Stella allowed a brief gleam of a smile; but at once she substituted a disapproving frown. 'I'm not going to have kids now, it wouldn't be fair to Andrew. But if *you* want to shut yourself into a nursery at your age, then it's your own affair.' She gave the triumphant and amused Martha a long, withering look, dropped a goodbye, pulled on her gloves gracefully, and went out.

She sustained the sweep of her exit until she reached the street. She had meant to go shopping, but instead she went to Douglas's office. She told the typist to announce her, but was unable to wait, and followed the girl in, saying urgently, 'Douggie – I must see you.'

'Come in, Stell.' He nodded to the typist, who went out again.

Stella sat down. 'I've just seen Matty.'

'Yes, it's a bit of a mess,' he said at once. But he looked self-conscious, even proud.

Seeing it, Stella said impatiently, 'She's much too young. She doesn't realize.'

'Oh, I don't know – she's been putting the fear of God into me. She'll be ill. I wish you'd speak to her, Stell.'

'But I have been speaking to her. She won't listen.'

'After all, there's no danger in a proper operation in

Johannesburg, but messing about with gin and all that nonsense . . .'

Stella shrugged this away, and said, 'She's as stubborn as a mule. She's just a baby herself. She's pleased now, of course, but that's natural.'

Douglas looked up sharply, and went red. His lips trembled. He stood up, then sat down again. Now he was white.

'What's the matter with you?' she asked, smiling but irritated.

'I'll talk to her again,' he muttered. He understood. Now all he wanted was for her to go. For the first time he had imagined the baby being born. He was imagining himself a father. Pride was invading him. It had already swallowed up his small pang of hurt that Martha had made up her mind without him, his aggrieved annoyance at her inconsistency. He felt nothing but swelling exaltation.

Stella had risen. 'You're both crazy,' she said.

'There, Stella . . .' he said, hesitated; then kissed her.

'Well!' she exclaimed, laughing.

'Look, Stell, I'm awfully busy.'

She nodded and said, 'Come and have a drink, both of you, this evening. We'll celebrate. Though I think you're both mad.' With another unconsciously envious look at his flushed, proud face, she went out.

The moment she had gone he rang Martha. Her voice came gay over the air as she announced her conviction that having a baby was the most sensible thing they could both do.

'Why, Matty!' he shouted. Then he let out a yell of pure elation. He heard her laugh.

'Come home to lunch?' she asked. Then she added scrupulously, 'Not if you're busy.'

'Well, actually, I've got an awful lot of work.'

'Oh, very well, we'll celebrate this evening.'

'Actually, Stella asked us over.'

'Oh, but Stella . . .' She stopped.

'We can decide that later.' They each held the receiver for a while, waiting for the other to say something. Then he said, very stern and efficient, 'Matty, you're quite sure?'

She giggled at his tone, and said derisively, 'I've been perfectly sure for a whole hour.'

'See you later, then.' He put down the receiver – and nearly lifted it to ring her again. Something more, surely, must be said or done. He was seething with the need to release his elation, his pride. It was impossible to sit quietly working in the office. He walked across to the door of his chief's office, and stood outside it. No – he would tell him later. He left a message that he would be back in half an hour, and went into the street. He was walking towards the flat, he realized. His steps slowed, then he stopped. On a street corner he stood staring at nothing, breathing heavily, smiling. There was a florist's shop opposite. He was drawn to the window. He was looking at some deep-red carnations. He would send Matty some flowers – yes, that was it. But as he was about to go into the shop, he saw again her face as he had last seen it that morning – set, angry, stiff-lipped. He did not enter the shop. A big clock at the end of the street said it was after twelve. He hesitated, turned, and set off towards the flat after all. He would surprise her for lunch. Then again he stopped, standing irresolute on the pavement. Nearly, he went back to the office. Almost, he directed himself to Martha. He gave another long look at the mass of deep crimson carnations behind the glass. Then he thought, I could do with a drink. He walked off to the Club, where he usually had a drink before lunch.

The first person he saw was Perry at the bar, eating potato chips with a glass of beer. They nodded, and Perry pushed the plate of chips towards him.

Douglas shook his head. 'My ulcer's been playing me up again.'

'The more I ill-treat mine, the more it likes it.' Perry directed very bright hard blue eyes at him, and asked, 'What are you looking so pleased about?'

'We're having a kid,' said Douglas proudly. He knew tears stood in his eyes: it was the climax of his exultation.

'You're joking,' said Perry, polite but satiric.

Douglas laughed, then whooped, so that people turned around to stare and smile sympathetically. 'It's a fact.' He called to the barman, 'Drinks on me. Drinks all round.' In a moment the two were surrounded and Douglas was being thumped over the shoulders and back. 'Stop it, silly sods,' he said, grinning, 'stop it.'

Then Perry, with a wooden face, deliberately reached into his pocket and fetched out papers. 'You'll want to fix this up right away,' he said, pushing the papers towards Douglas.

'Don't work so damned hard,' said Douglas, laughing, pushing the papers back. Insurance policies – Perry worked as manager of a big insurance company.

'The finest policy south of the Sahara,' said Perry. He pulled out a fountain pen and handed it to Douglas. 'Sign on the dotted line.'

Douglas pushed them back at him again.

But as they drank and talked, Douglas glanced over the papers, and as the two men left the bar he said, 'I wouldn't mind having another look at that policy sometime.'

'I'll send it over to you,' said Perry.

'You think it's the ticket, hey?'

'It's the one I'd have if I was starting a kid.'

Perry nodded and was walking away. Douglas thought, It'll be a surprise for Matty. He wanted to take something back to her. He called after Perry, and the two went together to the insurance offices. Douglas signed the documents then and there. He rang up his office to say that he would not be back this afternoon, and went home to Martha. He ran the last few yards of the way, and pounded up the stairs holding the packet of papers in his hand, grinning like a boy with pleasure at the thought of her face when she saw the policy.

Part Two

You must remember that having a baby is a perfectly natural process.

FROM A HANDBOOK ON HOW TO HAVE A BABY

Chapter One

Mrs Quest joyfully ran into the house and announced they were to have a grandchild.

Mr Quest lowered his newspaper and exclaimed, 'What! Oh Lord!'

'Oh, my dear,' she said impatiently, 'it's the best thing that could happen, it's so nice for her. It'll settle her down, I'm so happy.'

He listened for some time to his wife's cheerful planning of the child's future; it was not until the young man was due for university that he remarked uncomfortably, 'It's all very well . . .'

But she swept on, illuminated by decision. The boy – he was to be named Jeffrey, after Mrs Quest's father – was to be saved by a proper education from Martha's unconformities; he would be, in fact, the child Mrs Quest had always longed for, the person her own two children had obstinately refused to become. Her eyes were wistful, her face soft. Mr Quest regarded it with increasing discomfort, for it could not but bear witness to what he hadn't been able to do for her.

'I think on the whole Sandhurst would be better,' she concluded at last. 'We'll see that his name is put down in good time. I'll write tomorrow. My father always wanted to go to Sandhurst, instead of Uncle Tony – it was the great disappointment of his life.'

Mr Quest removed his gaze from the Dumfries Hills, whose blue coils were wreathed in smoke – a veld fire had been raging there unchecked for some weeks – and turned his eyes incredulously on his wife. Then he flung down his newspaper, and let out a short laugh. 'Damn it all!' he protested.

Mrs Quest was gazing at the great blue buttresses of the mountain range. She heard his voice; her smile became a little tremulous. She swiftly glanced at him, and dropped her eyes.

'One may presume the child's parents will have something to say in the matter?' he inquired. Then, dismayed by the pitiful incomprehension on her face, he suddenly put back his head and let out a roar of angry laughter.

'But I mean to say,' she protested, 'you know quite well what she *is*, she's bound to have all sorts of ideas . . .'

'Oh, well,' he commented at last, 'you fight it out between you.' He lifted his paper. 'It will be time for my medicine in five minutes,' he added abstractedly.

Mrs Quest continued to dream her dreams, while she watched the light change over the mountains. It was an hour of pure happiness for her. But her husband's withdrawal began to affect her. Soon the wings of her joy had folded. She sat in silence through supper; and looked like a little girl checked in what she most wanted. After the meal, she went to old chests and cupboards, and took out baby clothes she had kept all these years and unfolded them, stroking them with remembering hands. Tears filled her eyes. Life is unfair, unfair! she was crying out in her heart, that lonely unassuaged heart that was aching now with its emptiness. For what her husband had said meant that, once again, she was to be cheated. She felt it. After a long time she carefully folded the clothes again, and put them away in their lavender and mothballs. It was time for bed. She went out in search of her husband to tell him so. He was not in the house. She looked out of the windows. Light streamed from them down the dark paths of the garden. The moon was rising over the Dumfries Hills. Mr Quest stood, a dark, still shape beyond the reach of the streaming yellow house lights, watching the moon. She left the house and walked through the rockeries, where geraniums were a low scent of dryness rising from around her feet. She put her arm in his; and they looked out together towards the Dumfries Hills, which were now lifted towards the pale transparent disc of the moon by chains of red fire, and swirling in masses of red-tinted vapour.

'Beautiful,' said Mr Quest, with satisfaction. Then, after a pause: 'I'm going to miss this.' It was a half-appeal. Mr Quest, who for years had been playing his part in framing the family's daydreams for escape to England or to the city, was longing for some reprieve now that the move to the city was certain.

Mrs Quest said quickly, 'Yes, but things will be much better in town.'

Their thoughts moved together for a few minutes; and then he remarked unwillingly, 'You know, old girl – well, she is awfully young, damn it.'

Mrs Quest was silent. Now, instead of the charming young man Jeffrey, she could see nothing but the implacable face of Martha.

The drums were beating in the compound. A hundred grass huts, subdued among the trees, were illuminated by a high flaring bonfire. The drums came strongly across the valley on the wind. The taste of wood smoke was bitter on their tongues.

'I'm going to miss it, aren't you?' he demanded savagely.

The sad knowledge of unfairness filled Mrs Quest again, and she cried out, 'But we can't die on this place, we can't die here.'

Against this cry the drums thudded and the crickets chirped.

'It's time to go to bed,' said Mrs Quest restlessly.

'In a minute.'

They remained, arm in arm, looking out.

'My eyes aren't so bad, even now,' he said. 'I can see all the Seven Sisters.'

'Well, you can still see them in town, can't you?' She added, It's getting cold,' as the night wind came sharp to their faces from a rustling glade of drying grass.

'Oh, very *well*.' They turned their backs to the moon and the blazing mountain, and went indoors. At the door he remarked, 'All the same, I wouldn't be surprised if it wasn't more sensible for her not to have this baby.'

'Oh, nonsense,' she cried gaily. But she lay a long time in the dark, and now it was Martha's face she saw, set stubborn and satirical against her own outpourings of joy.

In the morning she rang up the neighbours to see if it was possible to get a lift into town. Nothing was said between husband and wife as she left but 'Do what you can, old girl, won't you?' And she: 'Oh, very well, I suppose you're right.'

Two days after Mrs Quest had heard the news from the bitter Martha, she marched into the flat to see her kneeling on the floor, surrounded by yards of white satin which she was fitting to a crib. Martha swept away her mother's protests that it was absurd and impracticable to surround a baby with white satin, and in any case, why so soon? Martha had already bought flannel and patterns and had cut out nightdresses for the baby.

Mrs Quest ignored the small protesting image of her husband, and disapproved strongly of the pattern for the nightdresses. She finished by inquiring, 'Why not *blue* for the crib?'

'Oh, so it's going to be a boy?' inquired Martha.

Mrs Quest blushed. After a few minutes she conceded, 'Why, are you going to have a girl, then?'

Martha said nothing, and Mrs Quest understood that she had again confirmed her daughter's worst ideas of her. She said with an aggressive laugh, 'Anyway, it's no good making up your mind you want a girl. I was sure you were a boy. I'd even chosen the name – and then look what I got!'

'I know, you mentioned it,' said Martha coldly. She swiftly put satin, flannel, scissors and pins into a drawer, as if concealing them, and faced her mother like – the image came pat to Mrs Quest – an animal defending her cubs.

The older woman said, laughing, 'Well, there's no need to look like *that*. After all, I have had experience and you have had none.'

Again the vision of Mr Quest hovered between them. Mrs Quest, doing her duty, said like a lesson, 'Your father says he thinks you are too young to have a baby, and you should consider what you're doing.'

At this Martha flung herself into a chair, and laughed

helplessly; and after a moment Mrs Quest joined her in an inquiring peal.

'I'll make tea,' said Martha, springing up.

They drank it while Mrs Quest explained exactly how this child should be brought up. Martha said nothing. At the end of an hour she exclaimed abruptly, her voice seething with anger, 'You know, this is *my* baby.' At once Mrs Quest's eyes filled with tears; she was the small girl who had been slapped for something she has not done. Martha felt guilty, and told herself that her mother could not help it. She said quickly, 'You must stay and have lunch.'

Mrs Quest had planned to stay the day. But she rose and said unhappily that she had shopping to do. She left, filled again with the conviction of bitter injustice, her heart aching with love refused.

She went back to the farm and told Mr Quest that as usual he had got hold of the wrong end of the stick, that Martha was quite wild with happiness. Then she went off into a long complaint of how Martha's ideas about children were absurd and she was bound to ruin them.

After listening in silence for some time, Mr Quest rose and took out his writing things. 'God knows why you two have to go on like this,' he said bitterly. 'Why? why? why?' His words drifted out of the window and died among the noises of owl and cricket. He sat stiffly holding the pen between his fingers, staring out of the window to where the Seven Sisters burned low over the glare from the fireswept mountains, a pale smudge against that nearer conflagration which still sent wings of flame up into the great black starry vault of the sky. 'One would think,' he observed to this scene of splendour where his mind dwelt at ease, 'that people would have some sense of proportion, considering the state the world's in.'

A pause. He turned his pen angrily between his fingers. Mrs Quest knitted behind him in silence; she had that evening begun on a jacket for the baby Jeffrey.

'But I suppose it makes no difference one way or the other,' he went on. Mrs Quest, clicked her tongue protestingly.

Mr Quest, with a final, confirming glance at the stars, the fiery mountain, the empty veld, murmured, 'After all – those stars are millions of years away, so they say . . .'

'My *dear*,' said Mrs Quest again, uneasily.

Mr Quest's pen was motionless in mid-air. His eyes were wide at the sky. 'So if one damned foolish girl wants to make a mess of her life . . .' He lowered his pen carefully to the paper and began to write.

When her mother had left, Martha cupped her hands protectingly over her stomach, and murmured to the creature within that nothing would be allowed to harm it, no pressure would deform it, freedom would be its gift. She, Martha, the free spirit, would protect the creature from her, Martha, the maternal force; the maternal Martha, that enemy, would not be allowed to enter the picture. It was as one independent being to another that Martha spoke; and her hands on her flesh were light, as if even this pressure might be an unforgivable imposition.

To Douglas she forcibly outlined the things they must avoid in this child's future. First, even to suggest that the child might be one sex rather than another might have deplorable results – to be born as it chose was its first inalienable right. Secondly they, the parents, must never try to form its mind in any way whatsoever. Thirdly, it must be sent to a progressive school, where it might survive the process of education unmutilated – for Martha felt, like so many others, that progressive schools were in some way outside society, vacuums of progress, as it were. If this last necessity involved their sending the child at an early age to a country where there *was* a progressive school, then so much the better; for a child without any parents at all clearly had a greater chance of survival as a whole personality.

To all this Douglas easily agreed. The ease with which he did agree disconcerted Martha slightly; for her convictions had after all come from the bitterest schooling, which he had escaped. He did remark at one point that the war might make it difficult to do as they liked about schools, but she waved this aside.

Douglas was very satisfied with Martha. There had been

moments in the last few weeks when she had seemed unreasonable, but that had all vanished. She was now gay and amenable, and the whole business of having a baby was being made to appear as a minor incident, to be dealt with as practically as possible. Practicality was the essence of the business, they both agreed; and the completed cot, a mass of icy white satin and lace, was a frivolous note of contrast to the sternness of their approach. For Martha, who was prepared to spend infinite emotional energy on protecting the child from her emotions, it was a matter of principle that the physical requirements should be as simple as possible. She took one look at the lists of things supposed to be needed for a small baby, and dismissed them with derision, as Alice had already done. By the end of a fortnight after she knew she was pregnant, she already had everything necessary to sustain that child for the first six months of its life. They filled a small basket. The child might be born now, if it chose. Martha even had the feeling that the business was nearly over. For she was once more in the grip of a passionate need to hurry. Impatience to be beyond this milestone was a fever in her. The five months between now and the birth of the child were nothing – five months of ordinary living flashed by so fast they were unnoticeable, therefore it was possible to look forward to the birth as if it were nearly here. Almost, it seemed to Martha that strength of mind alone would be enough to rush her through those months; even her stomach might remain flat, if she were determined enough.

In the meantime, she continued to live exactly as she had done before. She would have scorned to abdicate in any way, and in this Alice agreed with her: the two women, meeting at some dance or drinking party in the evening, congratulated each other on not showing anything; retiring into comfortable distortion would have seemed a complete surrender to weakness.

Almost at once, however, and it seemed from one day to the next, the wall of Martha's stomach pushed out in a hard curve, behind which moved the anonymous but powerful child, and Martha's fingers, tentatively exploring the lump, received messages that strength of mind alone was not enough. Besides, while Alice and she, the centre of a group of approving and envious people, insisted gaily that no fuss whatsoever was to be made about these children, that they were not to be allowed to change their parents' lives – and in their own interests at that – it was obvious that both were very jealous of their privacy. Husbands and friends found these women admirably unchanged; during the daytime they retired, and were irritable at being disturbed.

The moment Douglas had gone to the office, Martha drifted to the divan, where she sat, with listening hands, so extraordinarily compelling was the presence of the stranger in her flesh. Excitement raced through her; urgency to hurry was on her. Yet, after a few minutes, these emotions sank. She had understood that time, once again, was going to play tricks with her. At the end of the day, when Douglas returned from the office, she roused herself with difficulty, dazed. To her it was as if vast stretches of time had passed. Inside her stomach the human race had fought and raised its way through another million years of its history; that other time was claiming her; she understood the increasing vagueness of Alice's eyes; it was becoming an effort to recognize the existence of anything outside this great central drama.

Into it, like noises off, came messages from the ordinary world.

For instance, from her father. A few lines in his careful hand, dated three weeks back – clearly he had forgotten to post it.

My dear Matty,
    I understand you are going to have a baby. I suppose this is a good thing? Naturally, it is for you to say. Your mother is very pleased. What I wanted to say was, if there is anything I can do, I shall be glad. Children have a tendency not to be what you expect. But why should they be? Some damned kaffir has let a fire start on the Dumfries Hills. Extraordinarily pretty it is. We have been watching it at nights.

And then the careful close, the basic forms of the letters shaped and formed, with the capital letters all flourishes:

'Your affectionate Father.' After this, hasty and expostulating, one rapid sentence which said all that he had failed to get into his letter: 'Damn it all, Matty, it's so damned inconsistent!'

Martha felt helpless with tenderness for him. She could see him writing it: the pen hovering before each word and dipped so reluctantly into the wells of feeling because duty demanded it of him; his mouth set in duty; and all the time his eyes straying towards the landscape outside. She wrote him a flippant letter saying she was apparently doomed to be inconsistent; she was terribly happy to be having a baby; she couldn't imagine why she had not wanted one!

And there was politics, in the shape of a twenty-page letter from Solly. Solly had been betrayed. The communal settlement, only three months old, had been blown into fragments by the Stalin–Hitler pact. Having read it twice, Martha pushed it aside, with every intention of writing to assuage the unhappiness it revealed. But after a day or so she was left not with the impression of unhappiness: she saw, rather, a dramatic figure on a stage. She did not understand it. If, however, she had remembered that with no personal memory of the Twenties she had succeeded in imaginatively experiencing the atmosphere of the decade from people who had, she might have looked forward to the time when the Thirties would be similarly reconstructed for her. As it was, she could only shrug. Solly – vociferous, exclamatory, bitter, had gone into the Cohen store as 'the lowest-paid clerk', which, he seemed to feel, served history right. Also, he had taken a packing case to the market square where the Africans bought their vegetables, stood on it and harangued them for an hour on how they had been betrayed, they now stood alone, on their own efforts would their future depend.

Apparently this throng of illiterate servants and casual labourers had listened with respect for his efforts, but without understanding, as they should instantly have done, the nature of the revelations being made to them. Solly had been taken off in a police van and – final insult – fined ten shillings for being drunk and disorderly. 'As you know, I consider alcohol degrading.' It all went to show the incredible stupidity of the authorities in not understanding their real enemies, personified by Solly.

Solly stood before the magistrate – as it happened, Mr Maynard – and delivered a fine speech on the historical development of liberty. Mr Maynard, interested but at sea, had suggested practically that it was a pity he didn't finish at the university; such talents should not be wasted. This was the final blow to Solly's pride.

Martha got a letter from Mr Maynard, giving his version of the affair.

. . . A friend of yours, apparently? I took him out to lunch after the case, because of my insatiable interest in the vagaries of the young. His vagaries, however, do seem to me to be out of 'historical context' – a phrase I learned from him. Surely behaviour more appropriate for England or Europe? One feels it is wasted on us. It would appear that he feels there is no hope for the world at all; I find it enviable that people should still care that this should be so. At my age, I take it for granted. He says he is now a Trotskyist. I said that I was sure this would be a great blow to Stalin, but that I would infinitely prefer my own son to be a Trotskyist rather than the town buffoon, it at least shows an interest in public affairs. This annoyed your friend exceedingly. He feels I should have sent him to prison for six months. If I had only known, I would have obliged him. Why not? But, as I pointed out to him, since the sons of our Chief Citizens think nothing of spending their nights in the custody of the police – Binkie was given a 'shakedown', as he calls it, the other night in the company of some of the 'lads' – the hands of the police are hardly the place for conscientious intellectuals. They wouldn't appreciate him, either.

Making feeble elderly jokes of this kind had the opposite effect to that I intended. He remarked darkly that the Revolution (which?) took too little heed of the differences in the degree of consciousness of the ruling classes. He said there was nothing he despised more than a reactionary who imagined himself a liberal. Could this mean me? He went on to say I was making a mistake to underrate him. I took *this* to mean that there must be a vast conspiracy under our noses among the blacks.

My information, however, is that this is not the case. An interesting similarity, this; between the good ladies of the city, who are moaning with horror over their bridge tables about your friend Solomon's exploit, and your friend Solomon himself, whose imagination is no less romantic. However, I was writing to say that

I am delighted you are having a baby. Since you are probably still bathed in the sweats of the honeymoon, you will not agree with me when I say that children are the only justification of marriage. I should like to be godfather to your (I hope) daughter. Naturally, I hasten to say, without the benefit of religion. If I'm not mistaken, this would be against your principles? I should like, however, to be 'in' on it. I wanted a daughter more than anything.

This last sentence touched Martha deeply, coming as it did after the painful self-punishments of the rest of the letter. It was to the writer of that sentence she sent an affectionate reply, ignoring the rest.

Almost at once various other letters arrived, and, her nose being as acute as it was to sense any form of spiritual invasion, she was becoming aware that the people who are sucked irresistibly into the orbit of marriage are by no means the same as those who respond to the birth of a child. Mr Maynard, for instance, could be witty about marriage, but not about daughters. Mrs Talbot was never anything but tender about daughters, sighed continually over the children she had not had, sent a charming note of congratulation to Martha, but for some weeks saw very little of the young couple, for she had become absorbed in the wedding of a friend of Elaine's, who needed all her attention. Various elderly ladies, scarcely known to Martha, rushed into her flat, folded her in their arms, offered her their friendship, and lingered, talking about their own children with the wistful, discouraged look which always made Martha feel so lacking.

Above all, the elder Mrs Knowell, who had done no more than send sprightly telegrams of congratulation from the other end of the colony about the wedding, suddenly arrived in person. That creature in Martha which was the animal alert for danger against her cub waited tensely for the arrival of a possible enemy; and the other raw nerve was sounding a warning: this woman was likely to be a forecast of her own fate. For – she had worked it out with mathematical precision – since men were bound to marry their mothers, then she, in the end, would become Douglas's mother. But she was committed to be like her own mother. And if the two women were not in the least alike? That did not matter; in its own malevolent way, fate would adjust this incompatibility too, and naturally to Martha's disadvantage.

As Mrs Knowell entered the room, Martha's defences went down. They had been erected in the wrong quarter. She had been expecting something gay, jolly, with the self-conscious eccentricity of the letters and telegrams. Mrs Knowell stood hesitating, kissed Martha carefully, and took her seat like a visitor. At once she took out a cigarette. Martha unconsciously curled out of sight her own stained fingers, and looked at the big, rather nervous hands, soaked in nicotine. This was something altogether different from what she had been waiting for! Mrs Knowell was a tall woman, big in the bone, yet with thick flesh loose about her. She had heavy brown eyes, the whites stained yellow; she wore a mass of faded yellow hair in a big untidy bun. Her skin was sallow, and as a concession to what was expected of her she had put a hasty rub of yellowish lipstick across a full sad mouth. She wore a yellowish-brown dress. Nervous exhaustion came from her like a breath of stale air. She watched Martha as she made the tea, and made conversation, in a way which said clearly that she had come prepared not to interfere or infringe. It positively made Martha nervous. Her talk quite contradicted the heavy watchful eyes: it was gay and amusing; this was the personality which enabled her friends from what she herself referred to as her 'palmy' days to entertain her with a warm amused affection as a persistent *enfant terrible*. That gay old child, flitting erractically from one house to another, dropping in on a bridge game from a town seventy miles away, or suddenly taking flight in the middle of a two-week visit on an irresistible impulse to see a friend at the other end of the colony, was a creation of such tact that Martha found herself undermined by pity and admiration.

Mrs Knowell was not of the first generation of pioneering women. She had ridden in covered waggons in the months-long journey from the south, but without need to take cover against hostile tribes. She had lived in the remote parts of the country, but the rifle which leaned against the wall was against wild animals and not a native rising. Her husband had been farmer, miner, policemen, businessman, as opportunity offered; he had made several fortunes and lost them in the casual way which was then customary. She had borne eight children, and kept two alive. The daughter in England was married to a small-town solicitor; they kept up a bright and entertaining correspondence.

Mrs Knowell had succeeded in imposing on everyone who knew her this gallant and independent old lady, the jolly old girl; yet, if that heavy yellow stare, that tight defensive set of her limbs, that tired dry undercurrent to her voice meant anything, it was that her battles had been fought not against lions and flooded rivers or the accidents of a failing gold reef. She was in every way of the second generation; and Martha, impulsively ignoring the 'amusing' remarks, as if she were insulted that such a fraud should be offered to her, spoke direct to what she felt was the real woman, out of her deepest conviction that anything less than the truth was the worst of betrayals, and more – that this truth should be an acknowledgment of some kind of persistent dry cruelty feeding the roots of life. Nothing else would do.

Mrs Knowell responded slowly, with a nervous gratitude. She tentatively mentioned the baby; Martha talked of it without defences. Mrs Knowell, released by this new baby into her memories of her own, spoke of them as she had obviously intended not to do. She began talking of the way they had died – blackwater, malaria, a neglected appendix. She began telling a long story, in a heavy, slow, tired voice, of an occasion when she had found herself alone on a farm, fifty miles from anywhere, her husband having gone to buy some cattle. She had been pregnant with her second child, her first having died. She had slept each night with locked and barricaded doors, a revolver under her pillow. In the day she had been frightened to move away from the house. Martha could imagine it, the lonely farmhouse, blistering in the heat, the empty veld stretching for miles all around. 'Of course,' said Mrs Knowell, smiling drily, 'I never told Philip I was lonely.' Into this loneliness had come riding a young policeman on his rounds. 'He was so kind to me, Matty – he was so kind.' Martha, who had been expecting the story to continue, found it had reached its conclusion. Mrs Knowell stirred herself, and remarked, 'I don't know why I'm telling you this, I never talk about it.' Martha, who was triumphant at that admission, which it was her need, for some reason, to gain, replayed, as it were, in her head, like a recording, that story of the weeks of loneliness, in the light of that final 'He was so kind to me' – and found it enough.

She was being very kind to Mrs Knowell. She liked her enormously, and knew Mrs Knowell liked her. It was understood that Mrs Knowell would stay to lunch, would spend the afternoon with Martha, and in the evening the three of them would go out somewhere. Into this scene burst Douglas, cheerfully rubbing his hands, and embraced his mother with the words, 'Well, Mater, what have you been up to?'

There was a short pause, while the currents changed, and Mrs Knowell visibly rallied the bright old lady. She offered some hilarious stories about the people she had just been staying with. Her weeks in that house had been one long picnic of jam-making, bottling, pickling. She had cut her finger – she wagged it before them, laughing. Now she was departing south, and had taken the opportunity to drop in and see the dear children.

Douglas invited his mother to admire Martha's health and attractiveness. She did so. Both Douglas and Martha became offhandedly practical about the whole affair; Douglas began to tease his mother about her preoccupation with such old-lady-like things as embroidered pillowcases and lace-edged dresses. Mrs Knowell preserved her amused sprightliness for a while, but became noticeably silent, while Martha chattered brightly, in a hard voice, about unhygienic sentimentality – this was not at all as she had been alone with her.

After a while Mrs Knowell suggested wistfully that it was such fun to make things for a new baby; and saw them exchanging glances in tolerant silence.

'But it is!' she cried out. 'I'd love to have the chance of making little things again.'

'Now come off it, Mater,' said Douglas cheerfully. 'We're not going to have any of *that*.'

After a while she got up and remarked that as she was going to play bridge with Mrs Talbot that afternoon she must hurry away.

Douglas, relieved, teased her about being a frivolous old woman. She bravely announced that she had taken one shilling and sixpence off Mrs Talbot the last time she had played with her.

In a flurry of jokes, kisses, promises to meet soon, she departed. Martha was left with the memory of those yellowing tired eyes resting on her in hurt disappointment. She felt a traitor. And yet, by themselves, they had understood each other so well!

Douglas was speaking with grateful enthusiasm about his mother's capacity for enjoying herself so much at her age – Martha reminded herself that, after all, Mrs Knowell was only fifty. Douglas went on to remark practically that at least they needn't expect any interference from her, she always had far too much on her own plate to bother about other people. Martha was on the point of repudiating this comfortable evasion of the truth, but let the moment go.

Mrs Knowell departed from the city that evening, after sending a small parcel by Mrs Talbot's houseboy, containing a dozen long muslin dresses, exquisitely embroidered and tucked, with a note saying; 'These were Douglas's when he was a baby. I offered them to my daughter, but she said they were not practicable. But if you can't use them, then they'll do as dusters. I really haven't time to see you dear children again, I must get off to the Valley, they're having a picnic on Sunday, and I wouldn't miss that for worlds.'

Later, Mrs Talbot remarked that Mrs Knowell had been as erratic as ever: she had promised to stay a week, and left after half a day. She was really so wonderful for her age.

Martha was sitting down the next morning to write a nice letter to the old lady, to make some amends for the unpleasant way she knew she had behaved, when a native messenger arrived from Douglas's office. There was a note saying:

'Well, we're off! War's just been declared.' After the signature, the words, 'Matters appear extremely serious.'

Martha tried to *feel* that matters were extremely serious. Outside, however, a serene sunlight, and the pleasant bustle of an ordinary morning. She switched the wireless on – silence. Then the telephone rang. Alice, in tears, repeating angrily, 'And now Willie's bound to go and I'll be alone.' Then Stella, who also wept: the situation demanded no less.

But, having put the receiver down, she stood listening to the silence as if there was something more, some other *word* that needed to be said; she heard now that same dissatisfaction in the voices of the two women who had ceased speaking, and were doubtless engaged in busily telephoning others to find whatever it was they all needed. 'They say that war has been declared, Matty?' It was this incredulous query which floated in her inner ear. She was extremely restless. She looked at the blue squares of park and sky which opened the walls of the flat, and it seemed menacing that nothing had changed. She went out into the streets. There, surely, the war would be visible? But everything was the same. A knot of people in sober argument stood on the pavement's edge. She approached them and found them talking about the prices of farm implements. She walked through the streets, listening for a voice, any voice, speaking of the war, so that it might seem real. After a while she found herself outside the offices of the newspaper. There clustered a small crowd, faces lifted towards windows where could be seen the large indistinct shapes of machinery. They were hushed and apprehensive; here danger could be felt. But Martha saw after a minute that they were all older people; she did not belong with them.

She went home to the wireless set, which was playing dance music. It was now lunchtime, and she wished Douglas might come home. At the end of half an hour she was disgusted to find herself making angry speeches of reproach to him in her mind – a conventional jailer wife might do no less! Nothing, she told herself, was more natural than that he should find the bars and meeting places of the city more exciting than coming home to her. She would do the same in his place. And so she waited until afternoon in a mood of impatient expectancy; and when the door at last opened, and he came in, she flew at him and demanded, 'What's the news? What's happened?' For surely something must have!

But it appeared that nothing had happened. In both their minds was a picture of London laid in ruins, smoking and littered with corpses. But it seemed that while they thought of London, of England, the imaginations of most were moving far nearer home. Douglas announced ruefully that women were already sitting shuddering in their homes, convinced that Hitler's armies might sweep down over Africa in 'a couple of days', and more – the natives were on the point of rising. In any colony, a world crisis is always seen first in terms of native uprising. In fact it seemed that the dark-skinned people had only the vaguest idea that the war had started, and the authorities' first concern was to explain to them through wireless and loudspeaker why it was their patriotic task to join their white masters in taking up arms against the monster across the seas in a Europe they could scarcely form a picture of, whose crimes consisted of invading other people's countries and forming a society based on the conception of a master race.

Douglas was stern, subdued, authoritative. Martha was only too ready to find this impressive. Almost, she found her dissatisfactions fed. But it was soon clear that Douglas too was waiting for that *word*, that final clinching of emotion. He moved about the flat as if it was confining him, and suggested they should drop across to the Burrells. They met the Burrells and the Mathews coming in. They went in a body up to the Sports Club, where several hundred young people were waiting for the wireless to shape what they felt into something noble and dramatic.

By evening, the hotels were full. To dance would be heartless and unpatriotic; but to stay at home was out of the question. The bands were playing 'Tipperary' and 'Keep the Home Fires Burning' to packed, silent masses of people who seemed to find it not enough. They stood waiting. They were waiting for the King's speech, and with a nervous hunger that began to infect Martha. The pillars of the long, low white dance room were wreathed in flags; when the band struck up 'God Save the King' the wind of the music seemed to stir the Union Jacks hanging bunched over their heads. When the slow, diffident voice floated out over the crowd, it was noticeable that a stern, self-dedicated look was deepening on all the faces around her. Douglas, she saw, was standing to attention, his face set and proud. So were Willie and Andrew. Alice, however, appeared miserable; and Stella, whose facial muscles were set into a mould of devoted service, was steadily tapping her small gold-covered foot, not impatiently, but as if preserving some rhythm of her own. As for Martha, she found these three young men, stiff as ramrods, with their fists clenched down by their sides, rather ridiculous. After all, she was pointing out to herself, even while her throat muscles tightened irritably against an unaccountable desire to weep — she resented very much that her emotions were being roused by flags, music and solemnity against her will — after all, if any of these young men were to be asked what they thought about the monarchy, their attitude would rather be one of indulgent allowance towards other people's weaknesses. She glanced sideways towards Alice, and Stella; involuntarily they glanced back, and, not for the first time or last time, acknowledged what they felt by a small, humorous tightening of the lips.

The speech was over. The enormous crowd breathed out a sigh. But they remained there, standing, in silence. The courtyards were packed, the bars crammed, the big room itself jammed tight. For some people it was clear that the word had been said — they were released. A few groups disengaged themselves from the edges of the crowd and went home: mostly elderly people. Everyone else was waiting. The band again struck up 'Tipperary'. Then it slid into a dance tune. No one moved. Stern glances assailed the manager, who stood in acute indecision by the pillar. He made a gesture to the band. Silence. But they could not stand there indefinitely; nor could they go home. Soon people were standing everywhere, glasses in their hands, in the dance room itself, the verandas, the bars, the courts. The band remained on its platform, benevolently regarding the crowd, their instruments at rest. At last they began playing music which was neutral and inoffensive; selections from *The Merry Widow* and *The Pirates of Penzance*. And still no one went home. The manager stood watching his patrons with puzzled despair. Clearly he should be giving them something else. At last he approached a certain visiting general from England, who was standing at the bar. This gentleman climbed up beside the band, and began to speak. He spoke of 1914. The date, and the words Verdun, Passchendaele, the Somme, were like a bell tolling, and led to the conclusion of the speech, which was: '. . . this day, September the third, 1939.' Heightened and solemn it was; and the hours they had been living through, so formless and unsatisfactory, achieved their proper shape, and became a day they would remember always; it could be allowed to slide back into the past, and become another note of the solemn bell pealing the black dates of history.

There was nothing more to be said. The general, with a long, half-appealing look at his audience, as if to say 'I've done my best,' climbed from the platform, hastily adjusting his tunic. The band rose and gathered their instruments. Now they could all go home.

As the Knowells, the Burrells, and the Mathews reached the pavement, Stella remarked in a humorous, apologetic voice that she thought she was going to have a baby. It fell flat.

Alice said pleasantly, 'That's nice, dear.' She clutched her husband's arm, and said, 'Do let's go home.' Her voice had risen in a wail of tears.

The days went by slowly, as slowly as if people had been wrenched out of a habit; as to live in exactly the same way as before was in itself something unexpected and impossible. A ship was sunk thousands of miles away. An army crossed to France, arousing in the older people memories that apparently fed them with certainty about what was going to happen next. In Britain, the Government bickered, and the newspapers put it into the language of dignified disagreement. Anticlimax deepened. It was as if the date for the beginning of a tragic winter had been announced, and a late summer persisted in shedding a tentative sunlight.

Martha went back to her divan. Where the bright pinnacles of the trees in the park, persistent green against the persistent blue, showed in the open squares in the white wall, Martha sat watching patterns of sunlight shift and lengthen across the floor, watching the blue convolutions of smoke from her cigarette dissolve into a yellowish haze. Sometimes she stretched out her arm and received the warmth of the sun direct through her skin on behalf of the new creature within; it seemed to her that the sudden glow was answered by an increased vigour of its movements. Or, smoothing down the cotton stuff of her tunic over the swelling mound she watched the wall of flesh pulse, or how the weight of flesh distrubuted differently − as if a sleeper turned in his sleep. It was as if on the floor of a dark sea a half-recognized being crouched, moving sometimes against the change of the tides. Or she looked at the blue vein on her wrist and thought it swollen, and was glad because its larger weight of impurities guaranteed the fresh strength of the new red current that fed the infant. She had succumbed entirely to that other time. She had even tried to remember the flood of excitement that had swept through her, and so short a time ago, at the words: Only five months, four and a half months, four months ... For now these seemed immensely long epochs; she could hardly see the end of a day from its beginning.

She was alone from early in the morning till dark. Douglas was spending all his time with the boys, rocking delightedly on every fresh current of rumour. It was understood that he was going on active service very soon. He felt guilty in his own delight in it. He even felt uneasy because Martha concurred so easily. For he did not understand that five months, in this new scale of time, seemed so immensely long. It was as if he was planning to leave her in a distant future. Naturally he would go! To put any pressure on him not to would be unpardonable − she would always refuse to play any such role. But the fact was, the outside noises of war seemed like increasingly distant thunder.

One morning there came a little note from Mrs Talbot saying it would give her great pleasure if dear Douglas and Matty would come with her to the station to see a friend off to England. Douglas reported that Elaine had become engaged to a young man from the Cape.

The long grey station was hot with evening sunlight. The train, that perfect symbol of the country, stood waiting. Behind the engine stretched the coaches; one or two white faces showed from the windows of each. At the extreme end, there was a long truck, like a truck for cattle, confining as many black people as there were whites in the rest of the train. In between, a couple of ambiguous coaches held Indians and Coloured people, who were allowed to remain provided no white person demanded their seats.

Halfway down the train was a concentration of white faces. These were young men, the sons of fathers who had been able to afford their learning to fly, but not to risk their jobs before war actually started. Outside the windows stood groups of well-dressed elderly people. At a window away from the others leaned a youth of perhaps twenty, not more. He was slight and pale, with a shock of light straw-coloured hair. His face was sensitive and intelligent, his eyes direct and blue, very serious. Elaine stood beneath, looking up at him. So isolated were they, that when Mrs Talbot appeared at the station entrance, in an impulsive movement of love which would carry her across to join her daughter, she was checked. Her eyes overflowed. She turned to Douglas and held out her arms, in a helpless gesture of emptiness, before slowly letting them fall.

Douglas at once went to her, laid a hand on her shoulder, and said stoutly, 'Bear up, Mrs Talbot.'

Her whole body shook; she let her head droop beside his for a moment; then she raised a sad face. 'It's awful – they've only been together a few days.'

She looked across to where Elaine and her lover still gazed at each other. She took a step forward, and stopped as if afraid to disturb them. Douglas supported her and led her towards the window. Mr Talbot emerged from the entrance.

He nodded at Martha formally; again she felt herself instinctively shrink away from him. He was now looking at his wife. Douglas, with a small bow, released Mrs Talbot to her husband's protection; but as Mr Talbot showed no signs of supporting her as she needed to be, Douglas replaced his comforting arm. Martha watched Mr Talbot's hard close look at his wife. Again she felt shrinking discomfort, which was almost fear. Experience gave her no clue to that jailer's look; but she could not remove her puzzled gaze from that saturnine pillar of a man who stood erect, dark, concentrated with watchfulness, just behind his wife. She felt protective towards Mrs Talbot. He remained perfectly still, watching, while his wife allowed her head to fall in a momentary gesture of despair on Douglas's shoulder, and while Douglas squeezed and patted her shoulders consolingly and exchanged with her a smile of intimate sympathy. Finally Mrs Talbot took two helpless steps forward by herself, and was within the orbit of the lovers. Elaine smiled quietly out from that charmed circle at her mother; but immediately turned her eyes back towards the young man.

A few paces away a score of youths were saying goodbye to their families, who were preserving a brave cheerfulness which was becoming increasingly unbearable.

The engine suddenly let out a long shriek. Elaine gathered herself up in a movement as if she would fling herself after her lover, but she let herself sink back. Mrs Talbot was now clinging to the girl. The train moved; the sunlight flashed along its windows. A chorus of goodbyes broke out. They all watched the boyish, grave, charming face; then he lifted his hand in salute, and withdrew: the window was empty. Elaine remained standing on the extreme edge of the platform, stiff in the arms of her mother, gazing after the train, while the groups of people dissolved about them. Mrs Talbot was weeping openly. Elaine seemed to awaken, she smiled at her mother, put her arm about her, and walked beside her to the arched entrance: they went out of sight. Mr Talbot, whose gaze had never left his wife, nodded formally to Martha, gave a stiff bow to Douglas, and strode after the two women.

Douglas remained gazing after the train, whose smoke was settled in sunlit clouds over the platform. Martha, who knew he was feeling nothing but envy of the young men who soon would be in the Air Force in England, looked away from him. Close by, she saw Maisie, shaking the hands of an elderly couple who were urging her to come home with them. Their smiles were stiff and determined: Maisie had married their son that morning. They had been prevented by the taboos from saying that she was of the wrong class; now it was appropriate that their son's wife should come home 'at least for the evening', as they repeated disapprovingly. 'He would have wanted it,' the lady murmured, sighing, to her husband.

Maisie was standing lazily before them, her weight slumped on to one plump hip, her loose fair curls shining in a haze of sunlight. There was an ink mark on her yellow skirt. She was repeating with a forbearance as marked as theirs, 'Thank you, thank you so much, but I have an appointment this evening.' Her face continued polite; theirs were increasingly resentful. At last, putting an end to it, she said directly, 'I am sure you mean it kindly.' And hurried away.

Her face changed into a strained blank gaze. Through it came a glimmer of recognition. She came walking towards Martha, the good-natured blue eyes heavy with shock. Martha instinctively put out a hand to steady her as she came to rest, still looking after the train.

'So they've gone, eh?' Maisie said. She was incredulous.

Douglas said kindly, 'Bad luck, I'm sorry.'

She looked through him, turned the round blue eyes on Martha and said, 'We got married this morning. I said to Dickie, "What's the point? It makes no difference to us, and it only gets *them* down."' She jerked her shoulder towards her parents-in-law, who were standing hypnotized, listening a few paces off. 'I said to him, "After all, with their ideas from England, they can't help it, so why get them all upset for nothing?" But he'd got a bee in his bonnet, so I married him. Men are romantic, aren't they?' she ended on an inquiry, wanting confirmation from Martha. The parents-in-law were exchanging looks in which, as Martha could see, their intention to show a democratic forbearance was rapidly vanishing under fury that this young woman should have no idea of her good fortune. Maisie, who had forgotten them, went on: 'As long as it made him happy, I don't mind. I wouldn't mind having a baby, really,' she added, frankly inspecting Martha. 'You don't show much, either, considering.'

Her eyes moved past Martha to where the railway lines curved gleaming out of sight. Her mouth fell open, like a child's. 'They've gone,' she muttered again.

The parents-in-law exchanged another look, and moved away heavily with a look of patient endurance.

Martha and Douglas took an arm on either side of Maisie and moved her towards the entrance. She was heavy and inert.

Outside the station she seemed to recover. She shook herself free calmly, and remarked, 'I've got a date tonight with Binkie. I don't really feel like it, but Dickie wouldn't like me to sit at home and mope.' She nodded and smiled. The blue eyes were solemn and puzzled. 'I suppose everyone else knows what the war's for,' she remarked resentfully, as she turned away with a final wondering stare at the station, 'but it's more than I do.'

With this she walked off past the car where her new parents-in-law were sitting. She offered them a polite unhappy smile, and slightly increased her lazy amble along the street which led to McGrath's. She was late for her date with Binkie.

Chapter Two

Stella was now explaining to both Alice and Martha that it was the duty of young married couples to have children while they were young: their duty to the children, who would naturally prefer to have parents who were brothers and sisters to them. No one contradicted her. She went on to insist that to have a baby now, while the men were on active service, was the essence of good planning: the nursery stage would be over by the time they got back. To which Alice replied irritably, 'They haven't gone yet, for crying out loud!' And Martha, 'But Stella, that isn't what you *said*.'

Stella drew herself up; indignation flashed from every line of her charming body. She retreated to her own flat, sulking. As usual, neither Alice nor Martha seemed to understand the gesture. She emerged, at the end of the week, in full dresses, with a look of warm loosening fulfilment. After many hours before the mirror she had decided to pile her hair loosely on top of her head, like a busy mother too occupied to bother with personal attractions. Presenting herself thus, she earned from Alice the good-natured remark, 'You look lovely, Stell.' And from Martha, 'But, Stella, why do you rush into smocks when you aren't even showing yet?'

Stella wept. Martha and Alice looked at each other in complete amazement. They offered handkerchiefs and the advice to take things easy.

Martha was feeling that of the three of them it was Stella who was really enjoying herself; for zest, always Stella's quality, was the one thing which neither she nor Alice possessed.

She was essentially divided. One part of herself was sunk

in the development of the creature, appallingly slow, frighteningly inevitable, a process which she could not alter or hasten, and which dragged her back into the impersonal blind urges of creation; with the other parts she watched it; her mind was like a lighthouse, anxious and watchful that she, the free spirit, should not be implicated; and engaged in daydreams of the exciting activities that could begin when she was liberated.

Into this precarious balance burst Mrs Quest again and again, bright-eyed, insistent, stating continually that the deepest satisfaction in life was maternity and that Martha must sacrifice herself to her children as she had done, concluding always with the triumphant remark, 'You won't have time for all your ideas when the baby is born, believe *me!*'

To which Martha reacted with a cold, loathing determination that she must keep brightly burning that lamp above the dark blind sea which was motherhood. She would *not* allow herself to be submerged.

To Douglas she cried continually, 'Why can't she leave me alone?'

But one day he entered on a scene where Mrs Quest, irritable, impatient, and insistent, was demanding that Martha should order a certain pattern of jacket rather than the one she preferred, while Martha was logically arguing that in Iceland, or perhaps it was Chile, babies wore no jackets at all, and therefore – He collapsed into a chair and laughed until his face was wet. Mrs Quest regarded him with smiling forbearance. Martha, however, felt she had been betrayed. She looked forward to when her father would come into town; he, she was convinced, would support her against the forces of tyranny.

It was not long before the household had been moved, and she received the message she expected. Mrs Quest said that her father had something important to say to her; she must come over at once.

Martha therefore walked across the park, and found Mr Quest seated under a folded mass of purple bougainvillaea, which in its turn was shaded by branches of jacaranda in full bloom. The masses of light-mauve blossoms swayed over him; occasionally a flower detached itself and floated down. Mr Quest, from a distance, looked as if he were seated in a clear blue lake.

'I wanted to say something to you, what was it?' he demanded, conscientiously turning his eyes on his daughter. He examined his future grandchild with the frank appraisal of a countryman, and remarked, 'You're shaping nicely, all things considered. I can't remember what your mother said I should say, but you wouldn't take any notice anyway, so it doesn't matter, does it?'

Martha sat down. The house was of red brick, with verandas flung out all around. A golden shower climbed the pillars in front, and laid heavy green arms over the corrugated-iron roof. Through the windows could be seen the furniture from the farm. Martha felt a sadness which she understood was shared by her father when he said, 'It's all very well, we had a bad time on the farm, but I feel so damned *shut* in, with all these streets.' The park opened its acres of green and flowers immediately across the street, the garden was shadowed by shrubs and trees from the bisecting street, but Martha felt an exile, as he did. She did not know how much it had meant that her parents, at least, had been on the land. Some balance had been upset in her. That fatal dichotomy, soil, city, had been at least held even by thinking of her father working his land. Now she felt altogether cut off from her roots, even more so because she disliked the idea of actually living on a farm so much.

'It's not that I enjoy all the inconvenience,' went on Mr Quest, looking over at her for confirmation. 'It's not that at all. I don't see any point in lamps instead of electric light, or being miles from doctors, or no shops near by. Some people seem to enjoy that sort of thing. But, damn it all, I liked knowing what was going on – you can't even see how the rain comes and goes here. I liked watching the rain coming across the hills.'

Martha assented. What she was feeling was something like disloyalty: she could not share with her father her love for that particular patch of soil the farm, which in fact he was now aching after. She probed, 'But it wasn't the same for you as England, was it? You know, when you used to go rabbiting in the fields, and then the horses – you told me, you remember?'

She waited. It worked, as it always did. Mr Quest, eyes narrowed at the hard blue area of sky overhead, sighed. Then it was as if he expanded in water. He let himself fall back in the chair and stretched his legs in front of him luxuriously. 'Ah, well, now, that was a different thing altogether!' He looked at her suspiciously, and asked, 'But I told you, didn't I?'

'I don't think so,' said Martha quickly.

'I thought I had.' He removed his eyes from her face, suppressed any thought that she might be tolerating an old man, and remarked, 'The rain is different there – things smell after rain. There's nothing like the smell of the earth after rain in England.' To Martha, for whom the smell of this African earth after the first rains of the season was the keenest pleasure of the year, it was as if a door had been shut: she had invited it. 'And then those long evenings, not like this damned country, where the night shuts down on you like – like – I can't bear being shut *in*,' he said.

He continued to talk about England. He did not once mention the African farm on which he had lived for all those years. Martha listened, circling her stomach with her forearms, while with one half of her mind she saw a boy running wild across an English farm, fifty years before, and ran with him, tasting faint and exquisite dews, feeling long lush English grass around her ankles. With the other, she was indulging in the forbidden pleasure of nostalgia. The pang of lost happiness was so acute it shortened her breath. Then she asked herself if there was any moment of her childhood she would choose to live again, and she could only reply that no, there was not. If she burrowed back under the mist of illusion, she had felt a determination to continue, a curiosity perhaps, an intention to endure, but no delight. Yet that uncomfortable antagonistic childhood had over it a shimmering haze of beauty, it tugged at her to return.

She broke across her father's rambling monologue to inquire, 'Were you happy as a child?'

He was checked. The bright vague eyes clouded over – irritation at being brought back to this garden, this sky. 'What I liked best,' he remarked, 'were the horses. They don't have horses here, not like *those* horses!' He looked at her again. 'Oh, yes,' he said practically, 'I've remembered what I wanted to say. Your mother thinks that you ought to come and have your baby here. Then she can look after you both.'

He looked steadily at her. She looked at him.

'You must do as you think best,' he said hastily. Then, after a long reflective pause, he inquired, 'Did I ever tell you about the time I went to Doncaster with Bert's black mare?'

Soon after this, a letter, rather wistful, arrived from Mrs Knowell, saying that if she wouldn't be in the way, she would like nothing better than to come and nurse mother and baby.

Martha immediately booked a room in the nursing home which she had sworn never to enter because it was almost inevitable that she must.

As for Alice, after discarding Dr Stern as a possible assistant in the process of birth, which she felt she understood well enough to dispense with one, she gloomily accepted him with the remark that she supposed one doctor was as bad as another. She too hastily booked a room, after representations from her grandmother that she should instantly move to the city where that old lady was living, several hundreds of miles away.

'Really,' she remarked with her familiar good-natured giggle, 'you'd think that they'd be pleased to be finished with the awful business, instead of rushing to start all over again with us.'

The mere act of booking a room seemed to bring the day of birth nearer; Martha felt it was positively unnatural that the actual number of days on the calendar remained the same.

The rainy season began. The child would be born towards its end. Again she felt the discrepancy between the shortness of the rainy season, a handful of brief months in any ordinary scale of time, and the crawling days which she had to live through. She was consumed several times a day by a violent upsurge of restlessness. She could not keep still. She could not read. Above all, she felt there must be something wrong with her, to feel like this. For at the back of her mind was the vision of a woman calm, rich, maternal, radiant; that was how she should be.

She was very much alone.

Douglas, together with Willie and Andrew, was going through a crisis of his own. For authority had spoken, and as a result several hundreds of young men had achieved uniform. But not their age group. And it was the first time they had understood they were not the boys of the town, the golden youth. That was over. It had been a shock to find themselves thrust aside by these younger men. They were wearing the humorous resigned look of middle-aged men called 'sir' for the first time by their juniors. They would, however, be called up very soon, they already felt themselves to be cut off, in spirit, from the civilian population, and they filled the bars and clubs every moment they were free of work.

To Martha, Douglas suggested she should spend her time with Alice. To Alice, Willie said that Martha was a nice kid, and just the ticket as a companion. But for a long time the two women did not meet in the daytime. They liked each other, they understood each other very well; but something prevented them from mingling their daytime lives. It was that both felt they must be in some way unnatural; they did not want to expose what they felt to the other.

Then, one very hot morning, when Martha was seated under the square of blue sky, such a passion of rebellious restlessness took hold of her that she leaped up, ran downstairs, and got into the car. She was going to do something she had often been tempted to do before. She was going to look at the nursing home. It was five miles. She parked the car on a small ridge half a mile from it, and looked longingly across the valley to where the building stood, neat in its white paint and green shutters, on the opposite ridge. She felt that looking at it thus might bring the day nearer. She felt that looking at it made her one with the mysteries it sheltered.

Nevertheless, the sight of it awoke some unwelcome and far too familiar thoughts. Scrupulously visualizing first a male child and then a female one, she shaped that unborn being, now heaving and bubbling continuously in its cage of ribs, into – Binkie Maynard, perhaps? Or one of the hockey-playing maternal amazons of the Sports Club? That was even more intolerable. Yet even as she shuddered away these possibilities, she was reminding herself that never, at any time, had she had the intention of becoming what Solly so easily dismissed as a petty-bourgeois colonial, yet here she was; so it followed that the child was doomed, also.

It was very hot. The whitish dust of the road glittered. Heat poured down from masses of black cloud. In a haze of glare, a yellow dazzle focused into her eyes. It was a car, gathering shape in seething clouds of white dust. She knew the car – Alice's, now slowing to a standstill. The two women looked at each other. Both blushed; then they smiled confessingly. Alice awkwardly jumped out of the car, a tall, lean creature from whose light frame of bones protruded grotesquely her child. Martha joined her. They examined each other frankly, and exchanged heavy sighs which said that while they knew they were committed to this absurd process, they at least intended to remain ironical spectators of it.

'I thought I'd come and have a look at the place,' Alice said, and giggled suddenly.

Martha joined in with a laugh. 'I can't bear the way time crawls,' she complained, with a watchful eye on Alice's reaction. 'I can't bear any of it! I could scream!'

But Alice looked understanding and relieved. 'Neither can I. I wish I'd never started. If I'd known it was going to take so long . . .'

They looked across the intervening wastes of yellow grass to the grove of blue gums, the white shining building where lay fortunate women, already delivered of their burdens. They stood there a long time, gazing at the promised land, until Alice said irritably, 'Oh, well, I suppose this is just stupid.'

Martha assented, and they returned in their separate cars to Martha's flat. The barriers had gone down.

Now they spent their days together. They did not talk much. They smoked, sewed a little, or amused themselves by balancing some objects on their stomachs, such as a box of matches, until a thrusting limb or a butting head knocked it off on to the floor. Long periods of inactivity caused Alice to remark helplessly, 'I suppose the little so-and-so's asleep. Well, good luck to it, it doesn't know when it's lucky.' This was a reference to her misery because Willie, like Douglas, was so seldom at home.

Some person high in the Government, exasperated beyond endurance by the importunities of the young men, had cried out, 'For God's sake, find something for them to do. Keep them quiet until we know what to do with them.' As a result, the men of Willie's and Douglas's generation spent every afternoon after work deploying on a red dust square with various obsolete weapons, under an old sergeant from the last war who resented this occupation bitterly: he wanted only to be sent to the front somewhere. After an hour or so's drill the men went to drink. They were soldiers. They returned to their women late in the evening, cheerful strangers. Or at least that was how Martha felt.

Alice greeted Willie with sardonic hostility; later she might weep and cling to him.

Martha was scrupulously undemanding, but inquired who had said what, until Douglas said impatiently, 'Oh, it was all just as usual.'

It was a heavy rainy season that year. Many afternoons the square was a squelching mass of water and red mud. Once Martha and Alice drove up to watch, which they did in derisive silence. The drill was impossible, so the soldiers were scrambling and fighting across the mud, throwing great handfuls of it into each other's faces, yelling and whooping, knocking each other over.

It was painful to the women, seeing their men turned into willing savages. They never told their husbands they had been up to watch. They never mentioned it again to each other; they did not even like to think of it. There was some sort of disloyalty to their husbands, and to their marriages, in remembering how the men had fought among the mud puddles with each other, their eyes gleaming with savage joy out of mud-streaked faces, because they were not allowed to go off and fight some enemy.

The women were very close together. It rained endlessly. They felt enclosed behind a high misty grey curtain which shut out everything.

Martha had no satisfaction from this rain, which drenched down and was stopped by surfaces of concrete, surfaces of brick. Half an hour after the storm, the town was clean but dry; the water had been repelled and was flooding off into swollen gutters away from the streets. In the park opposite, the soil received it, small acres of greenness in a waste of impervious streets. She leaned at a window, looking out into the swirling mists that arose faintly about the hard glittering rods which caught a gleam of light from a window, or a car nosing far below. She was helpless with melancholy, inert with waiting; for on such afternoons both women stiffened and listened at every sound outside, the men might perhaps be coming home, since it was surely impossible to drill. But the hours went by, it was dark before they came.

One afternoon Douglas rang to ask if the girls would stretch a point: he and Willie wanted to go on to some celebration. He was speaking in the overcontrite, almost mockingly pleading way men use when they band together against the impositions of their women. He had never spoken so before; Martha had always winced with angry distaste at hearing Willie speak so to Alice, or Andrew to Stella. Now, because Douglas was with Willie, in that atmosphere of men escaping their wives, he put on that tone with her. She was furious that he could do it. She assured him, gaily, that of course he must go out with the boys, of course she didn't mind — as she always spoke on these occasions. But when she put the telephone down she was angry. It was all intolerable. She was shut in here, in this flimsy little flat, by the rain, because of the baby in her stomach, forced to accept that falsely humble voice from a young man who by himself would never think of using it: she was the wife of one of the lads. That was all.

Alice had sunk back into a chair, her face bleak and discouraged. 'Oh, well,' she said after a moment, with a bright unhappy laugh, 'I suppose I don't blame the buggers. I suppose if I were a man I'd find us dull, too.' The two women looked at each other, acknowledging frankly in this moment that they wished they had never married, wished they were not pregnant, even hated their husbands. They looked out again into the grey thick rain.

'Let's go out in it,' said Martha on an impulse. Alice's face lit; she waited, though, for Martha to encourage her. 'We'll go and drive in it,' Martha said again excitedly.

Alice sprang up. They were now restored to their own self-respect. For to go out in the rain would be a gesture of defiance to their husbands, who were now so full of prohibitions and firm masculine attitudes about getting cold or tired; they had adopted this attitude because they were so little with their wives. The women had accepted the counterfeit, which was better than nothing.

They ran downstairs, hesitated a moment in the doorway, which glittered with stalactites of rain; then ran straight out into it, leaped across the gutter and dived into Alice's car. The cars stood side by side in the gutter, water to the wheel-hubs. Alice swore, because the size of her stomach made it hard to fit comfortably behind the driving wheel; then she stiffened her body and jammed it back repeatedly against the seat until it slid back. Her face was set, her eyes hard and lost-looking. She was putting far more force into the action than it needed. Martha saw that Alice, like herself, was thinking wildly that perhaps even now she might have a miscarriage, might be released from a position they found all at once humiliating and intolerable. Alice swung the car around and began driving recklessly through the downpour. The streets were a drumming haze of water; the headlights drowned in a wet yellowness half a dozen yards ahead. The water sliced up from the wheels in a beautiful solid, gleaming curve fringed with scattering white.

Alice took the road to the nursing home. On the small rise opposite it, they parked the car. They were shut into a small dry space inside the swirl and squelch of the storm. Through the greyness came a movement. It took shape, and they watched a single African workman come past, the water splashing up from his bare feet. His khaki pants clung to him. The water poured over his chest. He held his arms clenched across in front, for a little warmth, and walked head bent, his body tensed in a shiver. His eyes moved sideways towards the car, then returned to the road ahead. He was concerned with nothing but getting to shelter.

When the darker blot of his shape had been sponged into the downpour, Alice looked at Martha and said, 'Well?'

She began taking off her clothes, with rapid clumsy movements. Martha did the same. They held the door half open, for a last look for any possible invaders, and then plunged across the road into the long grass on the other side. Immediately they were to their knees in water held by the rough wells of saturated grass. Martha saw Alice, a long distorted female shape, pallid in the grey rain, before she vanished. She heard a shout of exultation. Then she too ran straight onwards, stumbling through the wet, dragging waist-high grass that cut and stung, through the deep drench of the rain which came hard on her shoulders and breasts in a myriad hard, stinging needles. She heard that same shout of triumph come from her own lips, and she ran on blindly, her hair a sodden mat over her eyes, her arms held out in front to keep the whipping grass off her face. She almost ran into a gulf that opened under her feet. It was a pothole, gaping like a mouth, its red crumbling sides swimming with red water. Above it the long heavy grass almost met. Martha hesitated, then jumped straight in. A moment of repugnance, then she loosened deliciously in the warm rocking of the water. She stood to her knees in heavy mud, the red thick water closed below her shoulders. She looked up through the loose fronds of grass at the grey pit of the sky and heard a mutter of thunder. She was quite alone. A long swathe of grass had been beaten across the surface of the water, and around its stems trailed a jelly of frog spawn. A bright green frog sat six inches from her face, watching her with direct round eyes and a palpitating throat. The rain drummed on the surface of the water in a fury of white prancing drops. Martha put out her hand towards the frog. It took a clumsy leap into the froth of water, and came up to cling with its small human hands to the ends of the grass, watching her anxiously. Martha allowed herself to be held upright by the mud, and lowered her hands through the resisting water to the hard dome of her stomach. There she felt the crouching infant, still moving tentatively around in its prison, protected from the warm red water by half an inch of flesh. Her stomach stretched and contracted; and the frog swam slowly across the water, with slow, strong spasms of its legs, still watching Martha from one bright eye. In the jelly spawn were tiny dark dots of life. She could see a large snail tilting through the grass stems, its pale-brownish shell glistening and beautiful, the horned stalk of its head lifted high. Then, across the white-frothed surface of the pool, she saw an uncoiling in the wet mat of grass, and a lithe green snake moved its head this way and that, its small tongue flickering. It slid down over the red pulpy mud, and, clinging with its tail to a clutch of grass, it allowed itself to lie on the surface, swaying its vivid head just above the water.

Thunder shook the clouds again; and Martha looked up and felt a lightening of the dark enclosing grey. She could hear nothing but the drumming of the rain, see nothing but rods of shining rain; but certainly it was clearing. All of a sudden she was panic-stricken. She must get back to the car before the rain stopped and she was exposed and visible. She struggled out of the pool, while the snake pulled back on its spring of a tail away from the rocking water and flickered its tongue a little. The frog hopped into the middle of the pool with a splash. She was red to her armpits; and she stood still, while the rain came down and drove the red off her into the grass and she was clean and shining. Carrying her belly proudly, she walked blindly back to where she thought the car might be. At last she came on to the road, and saw with a fresh panic that there the rain was sending down its last big drops. The car was a hundred yards away. Suddenly she felt that there might be hidden eyes anywhere in the trees or the grass. She ducked low into the stinging grass, and ran crouching along its verges until the car was opposite. She dived across the road and into the front seat.

Almost at once Alice appeared, looking apprehensively up and down the road. She too flung herself over the exposed road and into the car. They looked at each other, holding their mats of sodden hair away from their faces. They went off into fits of laughter at the sight of their large, aggressive swollen stomachs, streaked purple and red, resting with such self-satisfaction on their slender white legs. But they were covered all over with minute red scratches from the grass, and fragments of wet grass clung to them. Outside the car, the rain had stopped, and a wash of strong orange sunlight was coming fast over the low, beaten grass, which was already slowly lifting itself frond by frond, as the heavy sparkling drops sprang off. The women took their petticoats and scrubbed themselves. In a moment they were dry enough to put on their clothes – in the nick of time – for a crowd of labourers came along the road, gave a curious glance at the two bedraggled young women, and then averted their eyes.

They drove back through heavy sultry sunlight which dragged shining clouds of steam from the earth. Eveything was saturated; everything shook off water; the road was still running a foot of water.

'Those potholes are probably filthy,' said Alice all at once, with a nervous laugh.

Martha was thinking the same. Back in the neat enclosed car, with her clean clothes about her, that plunge into the wet soiled veld seemed to her exaggerated and unpleasant. But there was no doubt they were both free and comfortable in their minds, their bodies felt relaxed and tired; they did not care now that their men preferred other company to theirs.

As soon as Martha was home she rushed to wash off the experience in a deep clean bath. She now hated to think of the mud of the vlei in her pores. 'Not,' she remarked to the crouching baby, 'that it makes any difference to you whether it's clean or dirty water outside, does it?' The child lurched, and the whole balance of Martha's stomach changed as it went into a new position. The skin on the lower slopes was breaking into purple weals; on the upper part of the thighs were red straining patches. Her breasts were heavy, bruised-looking. But the woman who only a few months before had enjoyed such ecstasies of self-worship had apparently died. She felt no more than a pang for the lost perfection. She traced the purple stretch marks with one finger, and felt something like satisfaction mingled with half-humorous appreciation of the ironies of her position. She reminded herself that she would never be perfect again. She told herself that never again would she look herself over, finding not one mark or faulty line on her body. It was gone, that brief flowering. It crossed her mind that perhaps, when it came to being old – at thirty or even sooner, for she was still proudly revolting away from the thought of being old – when it came to that moment of renunciation, perhaps she would feel no more than this amused ironical appreciation? But it was an intolerable thought, to be pushed indignantly away.

Later Willie and Douglas came in. It was nearly midnight and they were rather drunk. They played the role of humble apologetic husbands for a little; then Willie went off to Alice, and Douglas reverted at once to his usual self. 'Sorry, Matty,' he said nicely, 'but I didn't want to miss it – I knew you wouldn't mind.'

By now she did not; the fact that she didn't was making him uneasy, she saw. An old instinct came up, and she found herself grumbling humorously: who would be a woman, stuck at home, while the boys go off and have fun. He brightened as he listened. Then he came over to her and put his arms about her.

Chapter Three

Weeks before the babies were born, the two women sat waiting, while each twinge, each shift of pressure, a pang down the thigh, caused them to alert: was that the beginning of the pains? For both women had scorned Dr Stern's calculations, and had arrived at dates a week earlier than his.

'It might as well be born now,' said Alice. 'I've only got to give the finishing touches, so to speak.' From which Martha understood that her feelings were shared, an incredulous relief that she had so far successfully sheltered the creature and it was now a human being. The fact that it might be born safely now was merely a step to believing that it would be.

But every morning they awoke to deserts of time. Both would turn over, to sleep away another hour or so. At least when they were unconscious time resumed its proper shape.

Then Martha's self-allotted period was up. A day passed, then another. She rushed in a frenzy of disappointment to the other extreme, and exclaimed that there was no reason at all why she should not have to wait another month. Alice reached her day and passed it. Both women slumped into an irritated depression which made them snap at each other; they found each other repulsive to look at, exasperatingly self-absorbed. After spending every day together for months, they withdrew into solitude, alone with their swollen discomfort like animals in a cave.

One morning Willie rang to say that Alice had started pains at twelve the night before, and now had a son. At this announcement, making the extraordinary adventure so banal, Martha fell into a state of sullen resignation. She drove out to see Alice, entering the nursing home with the feeling of a rightful inmate unjustly treated as a visitor, and found her seated bolt upright in bed, looking flushed, bright-eyed and very pretty, her black hair curled for the first time in months. She greeted Martha with casual triumph, and announced that nothing would ever induce her to have another baby, and if women knew what they were in for, they'd think twice. Martha heard this as if it were meant for someone else. If she had ever thought of childbirth as an ordeal, it was – she was convinced – because people were weak-minded enough to allow it to be one. She watched the gay and elated Alice with a hurt conviction that she was betraying her, Martha, by so completely repudiating the condition she had been in only yesterday. She might never have been so clumsy, heavy, waddling, misshapen.

Martha went home in despair. She informed Douglas that she was convinced the child would not be born for at least another month. Douglas pointed out that Dr Stern had predicted tomorrow. But Martha scorned Dr Stern. The contrast between Alice, now two beings, and herself, still one, was too great. Having finally given up, or so it seemed, the intention ever to have a baby at all, she spent the evening sorting books that would provide the basis for a study course on economics. She was sitting on the floor surrounded by them, when there was a small stabbing pain in her vitals. She frowned with alert concentration; then told herself that she was sick of imagining that every twinge was the herald of the end. She was about to get undressed when she felt another. There was no doubt it was of a completely different quality from all the other stabs and twinges. She prowled cautiously about the room, admonishing the child to keep still, so that she might listen better to the activities of her muscles. The child was seething and striving like a wrestler. It was momentarily still on the third stab of pain. Martha was lifted on a wave of excitement; she cried out, 'Hurray, this is it!' and, like some sort of savage creature, proceeded to dance in heavy lopsided triumph around the room. Never had she felt such a soaring elation as this.

Douglas, who was on the point of sleeping, awoke at once,

inquired practically if she was sure, and began to dress. He was delighted. It was a moment of pure delight for both of them, being alone thus, the lights of the city dimming all around them, while they were setting off on such an adventure. Martha announced her intention of walking to the nursing home. Douglas's satisfaction in a wife who had such a carefree attitude was submerged in concern. She was put into the car, together with the case which had been packed for the last two months, and driven rapidly to the home. She had established, by the time she had reached there, that the pains were coming every five minutes; it troubled her that this was not what the book said was correct.

The nursing home was flooded with light. From some room down the corridor came a subdued chorus: several scores of babies were yelling there. A door opened; the orchestra swelled up into a cacophony of protest. It shut; the sound subsided again. A very young nurse came hurrying past. She saw Martha, exclaimed, 'Oh, damn, here's another!' then suggested impatiently that Martha should sit down and wait. Martha sat obediently, while the distant orchestra swelled up and down as the door opened and shut; and nurses in uniform went hurrying past, carrying half a dozen bundled babies each, with the satisfied proficiency of waiters balancing several piles of plates at once. Finally a large, fat nurse went briskly past, wheeling a tea trolley with six bundles of babies on the top layer and six on the bottom. Martha saw a dozen twisted searching heads, a dozen open mouths nuzzling for absent breasts. Doors opened and shut. The sound of hungry crying diminished. All at once there was silence over the building; the unshaded lights glared down into an intensity of stillness, long white corridors, gleaming emptily away in all directions.

At last there emerged an immensely tall, thin, springlike woman, a long white glazed pillar of efficiency, from which peered two calm, brisk dark eyes. She laid her hand on Martha's shoulder, consideringly, rocked her slightly back and forth a little, then said, 'Let me see, what's next? Oh, yes, of course, the forms.' Martha and Douglas were invited into an office, and found themselves engaged in that indispensable preliminary to every vital activity – filling in forms in triplicate. Douglas complied efficiently; Martha felt disappointed that this adventure should be interrupted by such banalities. When it was over, Miss Galbind told Douglas that he must go away and ring up in the morning. 'Be a good boy, don't ring up every five minutes – we're coping with the Easter rush.' While Martha subdued her indignation that she was included in anything so ordinary as an Easter rush, Miss Galbind received Douglas's conscious grin with a relieved and even coquettish smile. Encouraged, she proceeded, 'Why you young people restrict your fun and games to certain times of the years, I can't think.'

Douglas laughed. The two stood together, laughing; while Martha waited on one side. She had decided that she wanted Douglas to go; she noted that while Miss Galbind was made ageless by the uniform – she could not be more than thirty-five – it also enabled her to call Douglas a good boy and to flirt with him.

Douglas squeezed her shoulder encouragingly, and said he would go off and find Willie so that they might give it a bang. With this he departed, rubbing his hands. A nurse came rushing down the long brightly lit corridor, calling out for Miss Galbind, who again invited Martha to sit down and wait a while – 'Unless there is any hurry, dear?' She went off on her soundless springlike feet. Martha was again left alone in the entrance hall. She walked up and down for some half an hour, from the big door that stood open, like a door of a sanctuary, showing the star-crowded sky and the distant glow of the city across the ridge, to another door – large, white, closed, on which was painted 'No Admittance'. She was listening to the rhythm of her muscles. Five minutes to the second. She was extraordinarily impatient; it seemed to her intolerable that nature should be thus bound by the clock; all the needs of her being demanded that this baby should be born forthwith, without any further nonsense. In her mind, it was already born. A nurse who came past, holding her face down tenderly to a white silent bundle, aroused in Martha a flood of impatient tenderness. It was reassuring to see that busy young woman in a moment of love snatched from the white-glaring, painfully shining, bare, heartless efficiency. Martha wondered if Alice was asleep. She wished she might go and talk to her. She looked longingly towards the door of her room, but did not dare to go towards it.

At last another nurse came hurrying along, and said in a harassed way that she was terribly sorry to leave Martha so long, but there were five babies being born, there wasn't a bed to put Martha in just now – would she mind filling in time by having a bath?

Martha was shown into a bathroom, and told to ring the bell if she needed anything. She was undressing when a second nurse put her head around the door and said hopefully that she could see from Martha's face that she was the sensible sort, not like some, who carried on in a way you wouldn't believe. As she spoke, a door opened somewhere near, and Martha heard a woman screaming on a high note, 'Mother . . . Mother . . . Mother . . .'

'Listen to that!' said the nurse, a girl of perhaps twenty, with a round, pink, disapproving face surrounded by light wisps of shining fair hair. 'And she's only just started.'

Martha understood, from the fresh face, and the voice, that the girl was newly from England; she at once felt the appropriate reaction: What right has *she* to criticize *us*? Besides, she was such a baby, thought Martha, from the immense superiority of her proud belly, her primed breasts.

The girl gave Martha another encouraging smile, and said that if everybody was as sensible as Martha, life would be much easier. With this she left her alone.

Martha flung her cotton smock off, with the triumphant thought that she would never have to wear it again. She heaved herself into the deep hot water and looked at her stomach. It was now almost square, mottled and streaked purple, glistening with strain. The baby was as tense as a knot; and Martha's every muscle was braced with the intention of hurrying the process. She lay stiff in the water, her eyes on the watch. Five minutes. Five minutes. Five minutes. The pains came steadily, like the strokes of a bell, and, each time, Martha's whole body tensed against them.

She lay there for nearly an hour; the water was getting cold. The woman across the corridor was moaning steadily. The noise was beginning to get on Martha's nerves; or rather, her intention that it should not succeed in fermenting in her an angry irritation. Five minutes — Martha found herself exhausted, and lapsed into tired indifference. It was into this lull of absence that there shot a new intense pain, strong enough to make her catch her breath. She got quickly out of the bath, and put on the ugly calico garment provided for her. She caught a glimpse in the steam-dewed mirror of a fat, bedraggled shining-faced slut with a look of frowning concentration. She combed her hair, and made up her face. Thus armed, she walked out into a deserted corridor, still gleaming timelessly with regular white lights. Lines of shut doors stretched to either side. She walked to the right, and was met with a door marked 'Labour Ward'. She stood there, listening to the woman moaning inside. It opened abruptly, and a nurse came out, who, seeing Martha, pushed her gently to one side, and then ran fast down the corridor and out of sight. Martha walked back in the other direction and found herself in front of an open door. Inside were half a hundred white cradles, silent under a low shaded light, and at a long central table sat the fat nurse whom Martha had seen wheeling the loaded trolley. She exclaimed, 'What are you doing here?' then glanced keenly at Martha's face, and said in a different voice, regulated to kindness, 'You fed up with waiting?' She regarded Martha cautiously over a poised needle. Then she inched the needle into the white stuff she held, and pushed it away over the shining table. Everything in that room shone, even in the subdued light. The walls were very white, the floor black, with pools of shining light moving over it. The cribs were white, the nurse's glazed uniform was white. Piles of white napkins, white baby clothes, were stacked everywhere. Martha suddenly found herself gripping the table's edge.

The fat nurse walked unhurriedly towards her, laid a hand on her shoulder, and waited till she straightened up. 'That's right,' she approved.

Again there was a keen, impersonal glance. Martha felt

there was something in her face which should not be there, for the nurse said, 'Cheer up, you'll have got it out by this time tomorrow. Nearly over!'

Martha felt her lips tremble. She would have liked to fling herself on that fat shining bosom. The impulse annoyed her.

'Can I see Mrs Burrell's baby?' she asked timidly.

The nurse hesitated, then stepped along the lines of cradles. At the foot of each was a name on a card. She nodded to Martha, who followed her, and bent over a tightly stretched white blanket, where showed the top of a small red head that was crinkled and covered with loose dark fuzz. A powerful stirring of tenderness came into Martha; she resisted it; she felt it to be dangerous to her intention of concentrating on getting her own baby born.

The fat nurse sat down again, pulled the white stuff towards her, and said, 'You'd better get back to your room, you know.'

'I haven't got one yet,' said Martha forlornly.

'Dear me,' said the nurse. 'Well, we're so full – it's the war. There's a crop of babies suddenly that took us all by surprise.' She was sewing steadily, her needle going with flashes of light through the white stuff.

Martha drifted out again, and was standing in the corridor when the pink English girl came hurrying along. 'Oh, there you are, you shouldn't have got out of that bath without me, you know,' she reproved. 'The doctor wants to see you.'

Martha followed the pink nurse, who led her into another room marked 'Labour Ward', and said, 'You'll just have to make the best of this. There's nowhere else to put you till morning.'

It was another gleaming white room, this time with the lights bulging down from the ceiling like eyeballs. There was nothing in it but trolleys full of sharp instruments, and two very high, very narrow white beds.

'Lie down,' said the nurse, sharp with impatience.

Martha climbed with difficulty on to one of the high narrow beds, and almost at once Dr Stern came in.

'Well, Mrs Knowell? You girls all insist on having your babies in the small hours.' She knew him well enough by now to understand that he had said this many times before. Once again she submitted to those skilled impersonal hands, while he remarked that it was a good time of the year for having babies, she had done well to arrange things thus. He then removed his hands, said, 'Fine, fine,' and turned to depart. Martha, who had half believed that this was nearly over, demanded how long it would be; at which he remarked absorbedly, on his way out, that she must be a good girl, and be patient. The door swung silently shut behind him, and she was alone.

For some time she lay stiff on the very narrow slope of the bed, and waited. In this position, it seemed that the pains were worse. Or rather that she could not command herself as well. She climbed down, and walked up and down the deserted room. Now it was every four minutes, and she was doubled up with them, shutting her teeth against the desire to groan, cautiously unfolding herself again. She noticed she was wet with sweat. It was very hot in the room. She went to the window and looked out. Across the faintly moonlit veld, the glow from the city burned steadily, swallowing a glitter of stars. The stars vanished in another hot wave of pain. This time she found herself crouching on the floor, astonished and indignant at the violence of it. The pain had swallowed *her* up; and dismay at having lost guard caused her to return to the bed, where she might keep her attention on the process, keep that sentinel alert against the dark engulfing sea. Tight, stiff, cautious, she felt the baby knot and propel itself down; it recoiled and slackened, and she with it. The pain had changed. She could mark the point at which, just as it had abruptly changed its quality a couple of hours before in the bath, so now it ground into a new gear, as it were. It gripped first her back, then her stomach, then it was as if she and the baby were being wrung out together by a pair of enormous steel hands. But still she kept that small place in her brain alive and watchful. She would *not* give in. She lay like a tight spring, with half her attention given to not rolling off the bed, or table – which was so narrow she could not have turned on it – and concentrated.

The baby-faced nurse hurried in, and inquired, 'How are

you doing?' And hurried out again. Martha, engulfed in a pain, most passionately resented that uncommitted virgin with her determination not to be disturbed by suffering. But it was to the practical cool little voice that she was submitted; and when, at some indeterminate time later, the nurse came back, to say that Martha was being a good girl, and in the morning she would have a comfortable bed, she was able to achieve a humorous gasp that she wouldn't mind a comfortable bed now.

'Well, what can we do?' demanded the pink girl. 'We can't help it if all the babies decided to get born at once, can we?' She vanished again, remarking, 'We've got three of them out, that's something. Let's pray no more of you come in tonight.'

Martha no longer had the energy to achieve a mild amusement. The small lit place in her brain was dimming most alarmingly with the pains. Every time, the light nearly went out; always, it flickered precariously and shone up again. Martha noted that something new was happening to time. The watch that lay six inches from her nose on her crooked arm said the pains were punctual at two minutes. But from the moment that the warning hot wave of pain swept up her back, she entered a place where there was no time at all. An agony so unbelievable gripped her that her astounded and protesting mind cried out it was impossible such pain should be. It was a pain so violent that it was no longer pain, but a condition of being. Every particle of flesh shrieked out, while the wave spurted like an electric current from somewhere in her backbone and went through her in shock after shock. The wave receded, however, just as she had decided she would disintegrate under it; and then she felt the fist that gripped her slowly loosen. Through the sweat in her eyes she saw that ten seconds had passed; she went limp, into a state of perfect painlessness, an exquisite exhaustion in which the mere idea of pain seemed impossible – it was impossible that it could recur again. And as soon as the slow flush of sensation began, the condition of painlessness seemed as impossible as the pain had seemed only a few moments before. They were two states of being, utterly disconnected, without a bridge, and Martha found herself in a condition of anxious but exasperated anger that she could *not* remember the agony fifteen seconds after it had ended. She was now lying almost naked, her great tight knotted belly sticking up in a purple lump, watching with fascination how it contracted and strained, while she kept alert the determination not to lose control of the process; while she was lit with curiosity as to the strange vagaries of time and, above all, and increasingly, almost to the point of weeping fury, that all her concentration, all her self-consciousness, could not succeed in creating the state of either pain or painlessness while its opposite was in her. It was a complete failure of her, the free spirit: how was it possible not to remember something that had passed ten seconds before, and would recur so soon? The anger at her failure was strong enough nearly, but not quite, to quench that part of her mind which must stay alert. She sobered herself. When the wave of pain had receded, and she lay spent, she was grimly flogging her mind to *imagine* the quality of the pain that had just gone. Impossible. And when she was writhing in the grip of the giant fist, she was gasping with determination to *imagine* no pain. She could not. With all her determination, she could not. There were two Marthas, and there was nothing to bridge them. Failure. Complete failure. She was helpless with rage. She heard the pain-gripped Martha cry out, 'Oh, God, oh God!' and she was curious at the ancient being in her that cried out to God. Damned liar, coward, idiot! said Martha to herself from across the gulf. It only needs that you should call out 'Mother!' And behold, Martha, that free spirit, understood from the exquisite shore of complete, empty non-sensation that she had been groaning out 'Mother, Mother, Mother!' Without a flicker of feeling in any part of her body, she felt the tears of failure roll down her face; and looked up through them to see the pink nurse looking down at her with unmistakable disappointment.

'Well, dear,' said the girl disapprovingly, 'it's no good carrying on like that *yet*.' Her plump little hands, tightly sealed in pink rubber, went plunging into Martha's body. 'Not nearly yet, you know,' she remarked, regarding Martha while she grunted and rolled in another pain. 'And anyway,' heard Martha, the young bright voice coming distorted through hot agony, 'we've got to get this other baby born before we can attend to you. Do you think you could hold it a bit?'

Martha saw the door open, and a stretcher wheeled in. Suddenly the room was filled with people. She saw a woman, similarly grotesque, inhuman, grunting, being rolled over on to the other narrow high table, while Dr Stern and a couple of nurses stood about with a look of intent concentration. Then the white screens went up and hid them. Martha looked away, and submitted to another trial. The woman on the other table seemed to be having pains about every half-minute; what Martha's determination could not achieve, her nerves could: she suffered in her flesh that other woman's pains, like a counterpoint, a faint but faithful echo of her own, in jarring opposition to her own rhythm. Suddenly the sounds of striving flesh ceased, a faint smell of chloroform was in the air; Martha found herself avidly breathing it in. Instruments clinked; she heard Dr Stern's voice giving orders; she heard the stiff rustle of starch. There was a gasp, and a baby started crying.

'For God's sake,' nagged Martha to her child, 'get yourself out of there quickly.' The child, however, was crouched waiting for the next spring forward; and Martha watched the flesh shrink and harden in the new contraction. This time she heard herself give a shriek. She no longer cared at all. All she fought for was to drag herself as soon as possible out of each gulf, not to give in more than she had to.

A long time passed; she rolled her eyes to the window and saw that it showed grey light; a single white star hung quivering; it faded; a pink flush crept up the sky. She heard the sound of a wet brush on a floor. It was a native woman, on her knees with a scrubbing brush. The screens had gone from the other white bed. Martha tensed and groaned, and the native woman raised her head, looked over, and smiled encouragement. There was no one else in the room. Martha could hear the cacophony of screaming babies from the other end of the building.

The native woman gave a quick look into the passage, and then came over to Martha. She was young, her dark face polished and smiling. She wore a neat white cloth on her head. She laid her wet dirty hand on Martha's striving stomach. 'Bad,' she said, in her rich voice. 'Bad. Bad.' As a fresh pain came, she said, 'Let the baby come, let the baby come, let the baby come.' It was a croon, an old nurse's song. Martha trembled with exhaustion, and tensed herself, but the woman smiled down and sang, 'Yes, missus, yes, let it come, let it come.'

Martha let the cold knot of determination loosen, she let herself go, she let her mind go dark into the pain.

'That's right, missus, that's right, that's right.'

Suddenly the hand was withdrawn, leaving a cold wetness on her stomach. Martha looked, and saw that the native woman was on her knees with the scrubbing brush, and the young pink nurse stood beside her, looking suspiciously at the scrubbing woman. The brush was going slosh, slosh, wetly and regularly over the floor. Martha listened to the sound as if it were the pulse of her own nature, and did not listen as the pink nurse lifted her legs, levered them energetically up and down, and said, 'That's the stuff, push!' Later, Martha heard the bright voice calling from the door, 'Yes, doctor, she's ripe!' The room was full of people again. She was sucking in chloroform like an addict, and no longer even remembered that she had been determined to see the child born.

When her eyes cleared, she caught a glimpse of Dr Stern holding up a naked pallid infant, its dark hair plastered wet in streaks to its head, mouthing frustratedly at the air. Martha momentarily lost consciousness again, and emerged, feeling it must be years later, to see Dr Stern, in the same position, still holding the white baby, which looked rather like a forked parsnip and was making strangled, grumbling gasps. Two nurses were watching him. They looked triumphant and pleased. This humanity comforted Martha. She heard one say, 'A lovely little girl, isn't she?' Then the pink nurse bent over her and began lifting handfuls of Martha's now slack stomach, and squeezing it like oranges. Martha shrieked, with the intention of being heard. 'Oh, drat it,' said the nurse; and the dome of white chloroform came down again over Martha's face.

This time her eyes opened on a scene of white beds, and faces leaning against white pillows. After a time, she realized that she was pillowed at last in comfort. Five woman were in the other beds. Excitement flooded her, and she attempted to sit up. The lower part of her body announced that it was bruised and sore, and did not want to move. Martha raised herself on her hands and the woman next to her asked how she felt. Martha was struck by the lazy self-absorption of that voice. She said she felt fine, and the woman nodded. But her eyes were on the door. It opened, and the pink nurse entered with five babies balanced all over her arms. They were yelling, with hungry open mouths. The babies were plopped neatly one after another on to the beds, and gathered in by the waiting mothers. The pink nurse, empty-armed, arrived at Martha's bed, and inquired, 'Well, how are you?'

'Where's my baby?' asked Martha anxiously.

'She's having a nice rest,' said the nurse, already on her way out.

'But I haven't seen her yet,' said Martha, weak tears behind her lids.

'You don't want to disturb her, do you?' said the nurse disapprovingly.

The door shut. The woman, whose long full breast sloped already into the baby's mouth, looked up and said, 'You'd better do as they want, dear. It saves trouble. They've got their own ideas.'

Martha, cheated and empty, lay and watched the other women suckle their babies. It was intolerable that after nine months of close companionship with the creature, now announced as a girl, she might not even make its acquaintance. There was something impossible in the idea that yesterday the child had been folded in her flesh and it now lay rooms away, washed and clothed, in a cradle with its name on it. It made her uneasy; she wanted to see it – she even felt irrationally that the child might have died at birth and they were lying to her.

Then she remembered the moment when she had seen it lifted, mouthing and struggling for air, and winced suddenly with remembered pain. She had entered on a new state. The shadow of the pain she had felt, though not the terrible intensity of it, threatened her. She must not think of it, as otherwise the bruised flesh of her stomach began to contract in remembered waves of pain. Also, the absolute peace of those moments between the pains had gone. She was sore and aching, and her body was gripped tight in a stiff roll of stuff, under which she could feel the slack flesh folded together.

The babies lapsed into content all round her, and she watched them being taken away. The elation she felt, the achievement, slackened into disappointment.

When Douglas came in that afternoon, beaming, rubbing his hands with pride, smelling strongly of beer, her intention to appeal to him vanished in dislike. He announced with pride that he and Willie had been giving it a bang with the boys all night, he had not been to bed, he had rung up the home at half-hour intervals until Miss Galbind had told him he was a nuisance. He said, too, that the baby was fine.

'I haven't seen her,' said Martha faintly.

'Oh, well, they know best,' he said.

At this moment Mrs Quest entered, tremulous with emotion, and said that the baby was beautiful, but that she was quite sure the nurses had no idea how to treat a new baby; she had a good mind to go to the matron. At this Martha reacted with the announcement that the nursing-home people certainly knew what they were doing.

When Douglas and Mrs Quest left, Martha lay and quivered with anger and frustration. It was late afternoon. For the third time she saw the white bundles brought in and handed to the mothers, while she lay watching.

Late that evening, after the babies had been fed for the last time, Miss Galbind briskly entered and asked if everyone was happy, and Martha inquired when she could see her baby.

'You want to see her, do you?' inquired Miss Galbind

reasonably. 'Oh, well, I suppose you may as well.' She departed, having shed friendly good nights around the room; and Martha raised herself, waiting for the moment.

But it seemed Miss Galbind was in no hurry; half an hour crawled by, while Martha watched the door. At last the pink nurse entered, with a tight white bundle, and deposited it carelessly on the bed. 'There's your daughter,' she announced. 'Five minutes, now.'

Under the jealous inspection of the pink nurse, Martha turned back the flap of blanket, and saw a tiny flushed sleeping face. Again curiosity flooded over into a passionate protective tenderness, and she held the baby close; but the nurse, restless hovering at the side of the bed, decided it was enough.

'Now then,' she announced, 'you'll have enough of her in the next few months, I bet!' And with this she deftly removed the bundle, and went out with it, switching off the lights.

The other five women had already laid themselves down for the night. Martha, who to her fury once again discovered that she wanted only to cry, looked around for support. She caught the eye of the woman in the next bed, who said kindly, 'It's no good getting upset. They'll let you have her in the morning, I expect.' She turned herself carefully on to her side, and shut her eyes, in an obvious determination to submit to the routine and get it over. She remarked, with closed eyes, 'This is my third. I always say I'll never come here again, but it's easier on the whole. You can do what you like when you get home, that's a comfort.' She began breathing deeply.

Martha lay tensely awake. She heard a car drive up: another baby was due to be born; but already the condition of waiting for a baby to be born seemed far behind. She felt a calm superiority over the women who still had to go through with it. But when, later, doors opened and shut, feet hurried, and a woman began moaning down the passage, she had to bury her head in the pillow, because each moan seemed to drag a wave of pain out of her own stomach. She could not sleep. Excitement was beating through her. She was longing for the morning – perhaps then she might be allowed to feed the baby. The women slept heavily all around her, reminding her, with their heavy breathing, of cows on a dark hillside. But her mind was at the other end of the building, in the room full of babies. She watched the stars move across the windows, and wished they might hurry, hurry, hurry to the dawn. Then a baby began crying, a faint persistent wail, and soon they were all crying. The women began stirring and listening in their beds.

The woman in the next bed said in a resigned voice, 'Well, they're as tough as anything, that's a comfort.' She was lying tense; Martha saw she was crying. This upset her – the mother of three, calmly resigned, had given her strength to bear her own childish impatiences.

'What's the matter?' asked Martha anxiously. Then: 'Are the babies hungry?'

The woman gave a weak laugh through her tears, and said, 'They can't be hungry till six. It's against the rules.' Then she turned herself over with another cautious heave, and remarked, 'I always cry like a leaking tap for weeks after I have a baby. Don't take any notice.'

For a while Martha saw how the women turned and tossed, listening; then the chorus of crying dimmed and they slept again. Martha heard the cocks crow, and then again. She could see the Seven Sisters, a faint clustering glow over a spiring black gum tree. The babies began to scream again. It was nearly dawn. The sky was lightening. The women sat up, blinking, as the lights came on and a bright gay voice shouted, 'Get ready, girls.' It was morning, though the stars were shining outside. It was half past four.

'What's funny is this,' said the woman next to Martha, with tolerant good nature, 'it's supposed to be six, but even the nurses can't stick it out, so they stretch it a bit.'

Half an hour passed. 'My breasts are dripping,' said one woman. 'Every morning my bed's flooded,' said another. Martha was helpless with envy. Her breasts were still limp.

This time six small yelling bundles came in on a trolley. Martha received her daughter with trembling eagerness. The baby was crying; it looked, to Martha, distressed, hot and miserable. She took the little thing, and held the yelling round mouth to her nipple. It moved in sudden desperate silence this way and that, eyes showing anxious gleams of blue, and then – miracle! – the lips fastened and began to suck. Strong waves of suction passed through Martha and into her womb with contractions of pain. She did not expect this, and moved uncomfortably, gripping herself against it. The baby sucked steadily, small slits of hazy blue showing in the tiny red face. Martha daringly undid the tight roll, and the infant fell loosely into the shape of a baby, so that Martha was able to hold it to herself comfortably, instead of in the shape of a papoose. She moved it over to the other breast, admonishing both to be quick and supply milk.

Miss Galbind came springing silently in, and stood watchfully over Martha. 'All right,' she announced, after a minute, 'she's a good sucker.' With this she removed the child, rolled it again into the papoose of white blanket, and said, 'That's enough for a start.' She went out, the baby tucked under her arm like a long parcel sticking out behind.

'Don't worry,' said the woman in the next bed, giving Martha an amused look. 'You can do anything to a baby, even bounce it.' Martha therefore lay back and refused to worry. She had accepted this woman as a guide; she was able to because she disliked the discipline as Martha did, and yet could dismiss it all as another of those unaccountable bureaucratic stupidities thought up to plague honest females – that was her attitude. Martha found the tolerant matron – she was perhaps thirty – frightening because she had three children and was so satisfied to be a maternal housewife, but at the same time inexpressibly comforting. Through her, Martha was accepted into this community of women, all so much older than herself, all absorbed into the rhythm of eating, sleeping and nursing.

When Mrs Quest and Douglas entered that afternoon, it was as if foreigners had come from a strange country. A gay message from Alice in the next room meant more than Douglas's talk of parties and the Club; and Mrs Quest's announcement that it was absurd to feed babies to the clock found Martha calmly determined that everything was as it should be.

Next morning, when she woke, her breasts were heavy, and she received the baby with pride that she had milk for her. She was now in a state of settled calm elation, she could not conceive that she had ever imagined anything but a girl child, or a child in the slightest way different from this one. A faint warning voice from the well of fatality did remark that a girl child was in the direct line of matriarchy she so feared, but it left her indifferent. This tiny, delightful creature, with its exquisite hands, its small round red face, cuddled with such perfect trust to Martha that she could not believe she could be anything but good for it, and to it.

She was now very uncomfortable with the pressure of the milk. Her breasts were swollen like two full skins attached to her body. Her determination, fed by the book, that it was her duty to femininity to preserve the shape of them fell before the surging plenty nature offered. In the night she woke, hearing the yelling roomful of babies down the corridor, and her breasts swelled and stung in answer; and she found her sides wet with useless milk. In the morning, the women would sit up in bed, helplessly laughing, as they supported their enormous breasts with her hands and let the milk spurt away in streams into the cloth that had bound them. And the babies, who had been restless and hungry for several hours, would come fighting to the engorged breasts and choke there. The faint sweet smell of milk filled the women's nostrils all day.

Soon Martha found herself light and easy in bed; slipping her hands down under the tight hard cloth over her stomach, she pulled in the muscles and felt them respond, a hard wall under the rolls of fat. Then the woman in the next bed announced to her doctor that five days in this factory was enough. She climbed unsteadily to her feet, and went. Martha noticed with a pang of apprehension that this woman, who in her bed had seemed so light and easy, on her feet was heavy and shapeless – a veritable wet nurse of a female. She missed her when she had gone. They put into her bed a girl having her first baby with precisely Martha's looks of determined cheerfulness, under which showed anxiety. It upset Martha, that hard gaiety. Then Alice came to see her from the next room; and she saw her as not at all radiant and pretty, as she had been on the first morning after the birth, but pale, tired, bedraggled, with a loose stomach and full clumsy hips; Alice was unhappy. Her helpless giggle rang out repeatedly as she complained that she couldn't stick these damned women in uniform – the Lord help her, she said with a shocked smile; if she thought she had been as inhumanly efficient as that when she was a nurse, she'd hang herself. It was clear that she felt she had.

She complained they were never left in peace for half an hour together. If it wasn't cups of tea or bedpans, it was visitors, babies, or having to wash, she said; she couldn't sleep at night for listening for the babies crying. She burst into tears herself, and Miss Galbind, entering hastily, said, 'Now, really, Mrs Burrell! Surely you should know better than that.' Alice was led away, sobbing.

Martha was quite shocked at this collapse. The next day, however, she found herself heavy, languid, tired; the wings of elation had folded under her. She thought that when she got home she would be ugly and shapeless; she would be bound for months and months of servitude, without any escape from it; she found herself regarding the infant Caroline with a detached scrutiny that resulted in the faint, bored thought that this was a baby like any other, of no interest to anybody, not even herself. She would certainly grow up to be like these women about her, a dull housewife with no purpose in life but to continue the cycle of procreation. Martha found herself disliking the child, hating her swollen breasts, and filled with disgust at the way milk flowed over her a dozen times a day like a tide. She found herself no longer seated up in bed, bright and animated, chatting to Douglas about the parties, questioning him about what So-and-so had said, but lying flat on her back with no desire ever to sit up again.

Miss Galbind came in to ask how she did, and she was astounded to find herself in tears. But it seemed Miss Galbind found nothing surprising in this.

'It's the reaction, dear,' she explained; and Martha, who could never feel anything but resentment at the idea that her emotions might be the result of predictable chemical processes in her body, said, 'I don't care a damn what it is, but I wish I'd never had a baby at all.'

Miss Galbind listened and clicked her tongue, clearly because she felt it might do Martha good to be disapproved of. Martha found that her things were being collected together, and she was invited to get out of bed and walk next door. Miss Galbind said it would be nice for Martha and her friend Mrs Burrell to be together and cheer each other up.

Martha found that she and Alice had been put in a kind of enclosed veranda with glass around three sides. The sun came streaming into the white, shining place. Alice lay in bed on her back, looking up at the ceiling. She rolled her eyes towards Martha, and remarked indifferently, 'Oh, so it's you.'

'It looks like it,' said Martha, grimly.

Miss Galbind looked from one to the other, and remarked, 'You'll both feel better in a couple of days.'

Martha got into the new bed and lay flat. From depths of utter indifference to life, the two women lay and looked at a ceiling whose flat emptiness seemed to mirror their condition.

After some time Alice remarked, with a shocked giggle, 'I hate that damned brat, and that's the truth.'

'So do I,' said Martha at once.

A pause. Then Alice let out a small, resigned chuckle, as a suggestion that she might, at some future time, be prepared to find her present mood ridiculous.

Martha said, 'We might just as well be a couple of cows.'

Into this shared misery suddenly entered Stella, with a cheerful matronly smile, bearing flowers, her plump body graceful even now in its folds of dark silk. Martha looked at her, and noticed that her reaction to the sight of Stella's protuberant stomach was one of repugnance; Stella was as distasteful to her as poor Caroline now was.

Stella looked at the two women and stopped abruptly.

'What on earth is wrong with you? It's the first day they'd let me in, I've been every day to ask.'

'It's no good coming to see us,' remarked Alice flatly. 'We both wish we were dead.'

Stella gave them a shocked look, then sat midway between them, as if she were distributing her friendship equally.

'What's the matter? The boys said you were doing fine, and I've seen your babies. They're lovely. I do wish I'd started when you did, I'd have got it over by now.' She was looking anxiously from one to the other; and recognition of duty to a fellow woman stirred in Alice and Martha simultaneously: they aroused themselves and thanked her for the beautiful flowers she had brought.

'Did you have an awful time in labour?' she asked, with bright eyes.

Alice said indifferently, 'Oh – mine just fell out.'

Martha said honestly, for now, at this wide distance of five days, she could barely remember the experience, 'There's nothing to it.'

After a pause Stella said jealously that Dr Stern said she had narrow hips. Since there was only the disapproving silence that she was used to from these two unaccountable women, and which confused her, she went on to demand practically. 'If it's easy as all that, why are you going on like this? And look at your hair!' she added disapprovingly. 'You look awful, both of you.'

Almost, Martha and Alice were stirred into their duty to be attractive at all costs. But they subsided again into lethargy. Quite soon, Stella flushed with shocked disappointment, got up and said that if she had got it over and done with, they wouldn't find her behaving like this! 'It's not nice for your husbands,' she concluded on the familiar note, which succeeded only in eliciting a faint giggle from Alice and an exasperated sigh from Martha.

She was on the point of leaving, when both women felt guilty, and Alice spoke for them both when she raised herself in bed and said appealingly, 'Now, look here, Stella, don't take any notice. We're in a bad mood.'

Stella brightened, glanced gratefully towards them both, and left radiant with happy maternity.

They slumped back into the comfort of their beds.

'Poor Stella,' remarked Alice. 'Little does she know.' Then she giggled, and suddenly burst into tears. She cried out that she wished she had never got married, she knew now that she had never loved Willie at all; she couldn't understand how she had been so crazy as to tie herself down to being nothing but a piece of livestock to be stuffed three times a week, and then swollen like dropsy, and then a cow streaming with milk, and her breasts were so sore she couldn't bear it. 'Look at these silly bitches,' she said, meaning the nurses, 'all they have to think about is boyfriends, and going out, and earning money and having nice clothes – they've got some sense, at least.' Half crying, half laughing, she continued until the babies were brought in. Then she stopped herself, and fed her child with an air of tired endurance.

But later that afternoon Martha saw that she was being bad-tempered with Willie, and felt envious, because this was evidence of more emotional energy than she could command. Next morning, when the stars were extinguished as the electric light came plunging on, she noted that Alice immediately shot up in bed, then sat regarding her chest, which was padded tight in wads of wool, with a grim smile. She stripped off the wool, exposed the two knotted swollen breasts, and then remarked cheerfully, 'Oh, well, who cares?' She combed her black hair, applied lipstick, and announced to Martha as she lit a cigarette that life wasn't as bad as she had thought.

From which Martha deduced that by the next day she, too, might be over 'the reaction'. And so it proved.

But, in her gay competence of the next morning, she knew that she was left with a certain uneasiness. Nature, that great mother, might have done better, she felt. To remove the veil of illusion, to allow the sustaining conviction of necessity to fail, even for a moment, must leave her female children always helpless against a fear that it might happen again, and with as little warning.

Chapter Four

On the same afternoon, Alice and Martha stood on the steps of the nursing home, expelled from the community of women back into ordinary life, each carrying a white bundle of baby, each clinging tightly to her husband's arm.

Willie remarked that there were dozens of aunts and so on waiting to welcome Alice home. She murmured, 'Oh, God!' and emitted her high, helpless giggle, looking inquiringly towards Martha for support; for Douglas had just told Martha that she must expect a similar ordeal. That it would be an ordeal was an axiom with them all.

Martha was just about to get into the car, when another drew up. She saw an immensely large young woman, surrounded by older women, go towards the building. She recognized Marnie Van Rensberg. She ran after her and stopped her. At first Marnie did not seem to recognize Martha. Then she and her mother exclaimed and kissed her. Mrs Van Rensberg was in black – black lace hat, black crêpe, an enormous black bag stuffed with knitting. Marnie was as broad as a bed, and smocked in pink roses. Her honest, happy face beamed under crimped fair hair.

'You've got a lovely baby, Matty,' she said enthusiastically and for a moment Caroline passed from one to another of the attendant sisters and aunts. Then Marnie seemed to stiffen; she clutched her mother's arm for a few seconds, then she cried out, 'Oh, Mom!'

'Quick,' said Mrs Van Rensberg. She hurried Marnie into the home, both women sending warm smiles back towards Martha as they went. Marnie's, however, rather strained. The flock of women entered the building; and were received by Miss Galbind. A young man, stiff in his Sunday suit, stood on the steps. Presumably the husband. He passed his hand nervously over his plastered-down hair, and went in. The steps were empty.

Martha went back to the car. Douglas said that they had all agreed it would do the girls good to drop in for a drink at the Club before going home. The Burrells' car was already departing down the avenue of frangipanis. Alice was turning to wave and smile back at Martha. Thus had they so often set off on one of those long nights of dancing. But it was not the same.

'Perhaps we could go to the Club after Caroline's asleep?' suggested Martha.

But Douglas said, 'No, the boys want to give the kids the once over. Just for a minute – It'll do you good after being cooped up for so long.'

They arrived therefore on the veranda of the Club among the bare brown legs and the beer glasses, and were vociferously welcomed. Both babies had been celebrated continuously for some days now; their actual appearance was felt, at least by the mothers, to be an anticlimax. After a few minutes Martha's look at Alice received support for she rose, slightly unsteady, and said that it was time the little so-and-so was fed. Martha made a similarly cheerful remark; for a few minutes the two women stood clutching their babies amid a knot of admiring girls, and then the young couples separated to go home.

Next morning both were visited by the nurse appointed by the authorities for this purpose. Sister Doll, armed with pamphlets, charts, scales and an insistence that to 'pick up' a crying child, or to feed it five minutes before the clock said it should be fed, would be – her tone, shocked and grave, conveyed it – no less than a crime against nature. Alice and Martha exchanged ribald scorn at Sister Doll over the telephone, but the fact was that their lives were now regulated by her weekly visits, periods which were broken not into days and nights, but into shorter intervals by the clock striking six, ten, two, six, ten.

They would sit, both tense in every nerve, in their separate flats, with their eyes on the clock, their breasts tingling with milk, while the infants screamed in their cradles for an hour, two hours, three hours – until the second hand touched the hour, and they might spring up and lift the child to be fed. The strain of it was something to be acknowledged only in half-humorous grumbling remarks over the telephone.

Alice, much weaker clay than Martha, broke first. She rang up one morning to announce, in the hushed shocked tones of one who is prepared to take the burden of a sin on herself, that she had fed the child in the night. Martha was silent and censorious.

Martha would lie awake for hours, listening to Caroline crying, smoking cigarette after cigarette, and responding gaily to Douglas's admonitions that she should bear up – for he sometimes woke. The most she would do was to feed the child a few spoonfuls of water, as the nursing home and Sister Doll recommended, in the hopes that it might be deceived into thinking itself fed. Those nights were a torture. She could not understand why the crying should so work on her nerves. Caroline had only to stir and let out a single cry, for Martha to spring tinglingly awake. She tried to pretend it was a child belonging to some other woman; after all, the baby through the wall in the next flat cried often, and Martha did not hear it. But it was good for Caroline to cry, Sister Doll said so; and her character would be ruined for life if Martha was to give in.

After a few days Alice – now almost hostile in her determination to break the taboos – rang up to say briefly to hell with everyone, she was putting her son on the bottle, she couldn't stand it any longer. Martha received this too with polite disapproval.

But now she began to worry that her own milk was getting less. She worried all through the day, listening, as it were, to the activities of her breasts as she had listened to the movements of Caroline in her body. By four every afternoon, with Caroline already screaming for food, she would anxiously hold her breasts, still limp and half empty; she would even, desperate with worry, lift the baby from her crib half an hour before the clock allowed, with an instinctive feeling that the warmth of the little thing against her might encourage the flow of milk.

Then Sister Doll weighed the child and found that she had achieved half an ounce of flesh less than was proper. Martha was quite frantic, and began drinking milk herself, pints of it, and horrid preparations of baked flour which were supposed to assist the process. And still Caroline cried, and Martha's nerves vibrated in extraordinary response, as if the child were connected to her flesh by innumerable invisible fibres. That energetic, angry wail seemed to scrape direct on her backbone like a sharp fiddle on a bone. She would hang over the crib, hands locked behind her back to prevent them from reaching out to the child, watching the scarlet little face moving open-mouthed from side to side to find the breast, while her heart beat with anxious pity.

She would not, however, weaken like that traitor Alice, who had routed Sister Doll, and fed her child not only from the bottle, but regularly in the middle of the night, a practice which was bound to ruin its stomach. 'Oh, well, dear,' said Alice forbearingly, to Martha's disapproval, 'I suppose you are right, but I just couldn't stick it, that's all.'

And Martha looked secretly at the small Richard, and agreed that he seemed to be surviving under the treatment remarkably well.

From one day to the next, Martha changed front. Caroline let the breasts go without protest. She was taking the bottle inside twenty-four hours, and Martha had tied up her suffering breasts with linen – their work was over.

Peace at last.

Mrs Quest looked at Caroline with an odd little smile, and then remarked with the bright guilty laugh in which was the note of triumph that always stung Martha, 'I suppose you've been starving her as I starved you.'

And now Martha was free again, she proceeded to starve herself. By dint of literally not eating anything, she had lost twenty pounds at the end of six weeks. Better, she had regained that slimness which had been hers before she had married. Looking incredulously into the mirror – for she never looked into one without preparing to be surprised at what she might see there – she confronted a slight, firm young woman with high breasts, a determined mouth, and tawny-coloured hair in rough curls all over her head.

She was herself, though a new self; and Caroline, as the rules said she ought to be, was content to take milk from bottles at stated hours. The nights were calm. Martha was lifting her head to look about her, with the burden of maternity properly regulated and herself free to see what life might have to offer, when authority spoke again: all of Douglas's generation were whisked into uniform and into a camp just outside the city. It was said they might train there for some months; that was the rumour. Martha was adjusting herself to a life which would receive a husband released for afternoons or an occasional weekend, when a fresh surge of rumours settled into a decision.

All the men were to be sent at once up north. At one stroke, two evenings from now, several hundred of them, the junior civil servants, administrators and executives, the clerks and the businessmen and the lawyers – that firm masculine cement that held the community safe and steady – would be sent away. After the long months of waiting for precisely this moment, of eagerness held in check but fed steadily by the phrases, the ritual dancing and drinking, it was as if a bell had struck, but on the wrong note. For, while it was understood that the boys would be given a bang of a send-off, and the clubs and the dance halls dedicated themselves for the occasion, it was observable that there was a curious look of uncertainty, even anticlimax, on faces hitherto lit by wild excitement.

Late that last evening, in the crowded gilded halls of McGrath's Hotel, while the band played from its bower of ferns, Binkie Maynard, his fat body encased in tight khaki, sat at the head of a long packed table, fingering a glass, his heavy reddened face solemn with thought.

'I don't get it,' he observed, frowning. '*They* must know something we don't.' Heads nodded around the table; to relinquish authority to *them* would come easily to none of these men. 'I mean to say, what's the good of just getting us together and sending us off? Where are we going to be trained? It's not good enough, they don't tell us anything.'

'It's wartime, kid,' observed Maisie, who sat, plump and fair, beside him, smiling maternally.

'Well, but all the same. They're pushing us around. I'm not going to fight a parcel of . . .' But complete lack of information made it impossible to finish. 'I mean to say, I'm all for fighting the Huns – ' He paused; the words had given off the wrong echo. 'The Jerries, I mean,' he amended carefully. 'They've got to be put in their place. They want to take our colonies away, that's all they're after. But there's the Wops – they're not even worth fighting as far as I can see.'

There was a pause. The fifty people listening waited hopefully for that one word from the pastor of their days of youth which would allow them with good grace to board that train the next day. The violins, which had been sobbing through the changes of 'Black Eyes', stopped, were joined by a drum, and swung into 'Run, Rabbit, Run'. That song, whose impertinent, cocky mood expressed a Britain whose vigour was still in mortgage, sounded an alien note here. Half the table took it up; it petered out weakly.

'It's all very well,' concluded Binkie indignantly, his black locks untidy over flushed civilian brows, his buttons undone, his shoulder tab crooked – Maisie reached over to straighten it – 'it's all very well, but somebody's messed something up, that's what I think.' Instantaneous agreement. It was the anguished wail of the administrator who must become a pawn, the administrator who has no reason to have much faith in the process of government.

'What I mean to say,' pursued Binkie with difficulty, 'it's not fair!'

The band had exhausted 'Run, Rabbit, Run', and offered 'The Siegfried Line'. It was no good – the mood was wrong. The violins retired a little, the drums and saxophones came forward and stood looking at Binkie.

Binkie tipped back his head, drained his beer, and produced automatically, 'Well, to hell with everything!' Then, in a chant: '*I'm* all right, are *you* all right?'

The crowd chanted back, 'We're all right, we're all right!'

Binkie, having abandoned the difficulties of politics to his betters for the duration, climbed on a chair. He raised his arms; his tunic strained; a button flew off and Maisie stooped to pick it up.

'Isn't he a crazy kid?' she crooned admiringly.

The room stilled, grinning at the familiar sight, waiting for the moment when those commanding arms would descend.

'"Roll Out the Barrel"!' shouted Binkie; and the obedient orchestra crashed into the familiar tune, as Binkie's arms descended, releasing the din of thumping feet and yelling voices.

Nobody went to bed that night. All over the city next day wives and mothers waited for the hour of sunset in the condition of hypnotized calm that the hilarious mood of the men made necessary.

The train was to leave at six. By five-thirty the long grey platform was packed. The train was waiting, its empty windows like so many frames waiting to be filled, and the sky over it tumultuous with a gold-and-crimson sunset. A band was playing, hardly audible in the din of talk and singing. A warm breeze smelling of sun and petrol stirred a hundred yellow streamers that idled above the heads of the crowd, which parted, shouting greetings, as the men in uniform came roaring through. They were all drunk and singing. With them came the girls, running alongside, singing and flushed with the same intoxication.

Someone had blundered again, for there were only five minutes before the train was supposed to leave. A wave of khaki washed up over the train; the frames were filled with grinning soldiers. The relatives and friends shook themselves out into groups below the windows. The band was playing 'Tipperary'.

There was a sardonic cheer. Binkie and Perry appeared on the roof of one of the carriages, and stood swaying there, grinning, arms outstretched.

'Go it, Binkie!' shouted a shrill voice. 'Give the Jerries stick!' roared the female chorus. Meanwhile the sober families smiled steadily.

Binkie and Perry were doing a war dance, and singing

'Hold Him Down, the Zulu Warrior'; while the band joined in half a bar behind. A group of officers, smiling but cautionary, appeared at the edge of the crowd; and Binkie and Perry clung to each other in a parody of fright, and staggered up and down like clowns on a tightrope. The officers were shouting some orders; Binkie craned forward, blinking foolishly, one hand behind his ear. His foot slipped, someone shrieked; he rolled down over the roof into the crowd. Perry staggered back and forth like a man trying to get his balance, his great handsome blond face wooden with deliberate stupidity; then he took a neat nosedive off into a group, which caught him. For a moment Perry and Binkie were tossed up and down, yelling and laughing, while the officers gesticulated futilely on the edge of the crowd.

The train shrieked. Douglas, who was holding Martha's hand out of the window, was laughing appreciatively at Perry and Binkie. She held up her face, he bent to kiss it; but the train jerked forward a foot, and they both laughed, while their eyes met in regret that it was impossible to be serious at this last moment. Two paces away, Binkie and Perry were locked in embrace, singing in thick wobbling voices, 'Kiss me goodbye ...' But the crowd took it up seriously for a few bars; then someone shouted, 'Get on the train, you silly buggers, it's going.' Mr Maynard stood forward and held out his hand to his son. Binkie dropped his fooling, and came to meet him, looking responsible. Mrs Maynard, blinking away tears, impulsively flung her arms around him in a convulsive embrace. Binkie remained still, then made a joke in her ear, so that she stepped back, grimacing with laughter as the tears fell.

Binkie and Perry began running down the creeping train in slow motion, with exaggeratedly lifted legs and pumping arms. The train stopped again. A sardonic cheer from the soldiers in it, who were leaning out waving beer bottles. Perry and Binkie swung themselves on to the back bumpers. The train jerked, nearly flinging them off, then let out another shriek, and began to move in earnest. It rumbled along the platform with its burden of soldiers, who were hanging from their waists in every window or clustered on the foot plates. As the train gathered speed, Binkie and Perry appeared on the roof of the last carriage, through a cloud of filthy grey smoke. They were dancing and waving beer bottles. An epoch was going out to the strains of 'Roll Out the Barrel'; and the crowd on the platform left facing the empty rails were silent.

The band stopped, then played 'Show Me the Way to Go Home'. The crowd eddied and thinned. In a few moments there remained a group of young wives with babies, looking with determined stoicism after their husbands. A group of girls who had run some way along the train now returned, wild-eyed, untidy, tipsy. Maisie was among them, and she greeted Martha cheerfully as she passed, with 'So now we're all girls without men. What a life, hey?'

Stella, Martha and Alice looked at each other, and smiled; smiled steadily. The train, a black snake blotched with khaki, was now far away over the veld. A wave of blue gritty smoke came drifting back. The sun, a heavy orange ball, dropped behind the mountain, and the white station lights came on. Yellow flags still idled under the roof; the band had gone.

Alice's face was white; but all she said was, 'So that's that.'

Stella suddenly collapsed into tears, and was led away by her mother. Martha and Alice left the station. Mr Maynard stood on the pavement, beside a car where his iron-browed wife was weeping over the driving wheel.

'There, there!' he was saying. 'There, there!' As Martha went past, he looked at her, suddenly produced a heavy sarcastic smile which was like a grimace of pain, and observed, 'So much for the happy warriors!'

'Oh, the foolish, foolish boys,' Mrs Maynard cried out. 'They'll all kill themselves before they even get to the fighting.'

'I think not,' said Mr Maynard patiently. He had turned back to her, and Martha went on with Alice. The two women lifted their infants into their respective cars, and drove away home.

Part Three

When a person dies for his country, then you can say he loves it.

TURGENEV, On the Eve

Chapter One

The skies of Africa being for the most part blue and clear, and eminently suitable for aeroplanes, there were few cities in the subcontinent that did not hastily throw up on their outskirts camps of Nissen huts, hangars, runways and temporary houses, surrounded by fences and barbed wire and as self-contained and isolated as those other towns outside the city, the native locations.

For weeks before anything changed, the local inhabitants would drive out of a Sunday afternoon to watch the building; for weeks nothing was spoken of but that the Air Force was coming. That phrase, together with those others now constantly used by the newspapers, like 'Knights of the Air' and 'our boys', evoked in the minds of the population, which was now after all mostly female, an image of a tall graceful youth fitted neatly into sky-blue cloth. Certain poets were partly responsible for this charming figure – the newspapers are not to blame for everything. Besides, this was the period of the Battle of Britain; a need for heroism, starved so long, was being fed at last; it was as if the gallant youth from 1914 had donned a uniform the colour of the sky and taken wing. Their own young men who had left the colony in search of adventure were mostly dead, and killed in the air. The air was their medium, they felt. Useless to ask a country separated from the sea by hundreds of miles to think of itself as a breeder of sailors; and of that mass of young men who had departed north for land fighting, few had as yet actually fought. When they did, when those deaths and wounds were announced, the shock of it would breed a new image; in the meantime, it was an air war, and it was fitting that this colony should be asked to train airmen.

More than this lay behind their impatience for the moment when 'the boys' should actually arrive. Few of them had not been brought up with the words 'Home' and 'England' continually in their mouths, even if they had not been born there; it was their own people they were expecting – and more: themselves, at one remove, and dignified by responsibility and danger. They knew what to expect: the colony was being fed month by month in peacetime by immigrants who were certainly of the stock which produced rather graceful young men, even if they changed in so few weeks into people like themselves – not charming, not – but the word 'effeminate' was one the Battle of Britain made obsolete; it was conceded that the war and the number of deaths in the skies over London made those more sheltered cousins the equals of any veld adventurer or horizon conqueror.

But before an aeroplane can be sent into the air with its proper complement of highly trained young men, there must be so many others on the ground to provide for the welfare of both. It was this that the local people had not taken into account.

Suddenly, overnight, the streets changed. They were filled with a race of beings in thick, clumsy greyish uniforms; and from these ill-fitting cases of cloth emerged pallid faces and hands which had – to people who above all always had enough to eat and plenty of sunshine – a look of incompleteness. It was as if nature had sketched an ideal – that tall, well-fed charming youth, so easily transformed into a tough hero – and, being starved of material to complete it with, had struggled into what perfection it could. That, obscurely, was how they felt; they could not own these ancestors; their cousins from Home were a race of dwarfs, several inches shorter than themselves. They were not burnt and brown, but unhealthily pale. They were not glorious and rebellious individuals – for, above all, emigrants to the colonies have been that – but they had the look, as they strayed cautiously and curiously about the shallow little colonial streets, of a community whose oneness was only emphasized by the uniform.

In short, they were different.

It never entered their heads to apologize for being different.

They made no effort to become like their hosts.

Worse than anything, the faces of these new guests – a colonial people instinctively feel themselves as hosts – expressed nothing but a patient and sardonic criticism. They were unwilling guests.

These groundlings, dumped arbitrarily into the middle of Africa, strayed about the town, noted the two cinemas, half a dozen hotels, a score of bars; noted that the amenities usual for ten thousand white inhabitants were to be stretched to provide for them in their hundreds of thousands; noted that women would be in short supply for the duration; and, with that calm common sense which distinguishes the British working man, decided to make themselves as comfortable as possible in circumstances fully as bad as they had expected. For a time the grey tide ebbed back from the city into the camps that were surrounded by the high, forbidding fences.

Not before a number of disturbing incidents had occurred. For instance, several innocent men had brought Coloured women into the bars of an evening, and had violently resented being asked to leave. Others were observed offering black men cigarettes on street corners, while talking to them, or even walking with them. It was rumoured that quite a number had actually gone into the homes of the servants of the city, in the native location. But this was not the worst; it was felt that such behaviour was merely the result of ignorance; a short acquaintance with local custom would put things right. No, it was something more indefinable, something inarticulate, an atmosphere like an ironic stare, which, since it was not put into words, could not be answered.

A group of airmen might be walking down the street, hoping that some diversion might offer itself, when their attention was drawn by the sound of a wild and urgent motorhorn. An expensive car stood by them, into which a couple, smiling with fervent goodwill, urged they should enter. They climbed, therefore, into the car, and were whisked off to McGrath's Hotel, where drinks were called for all round. The orchestra still played, war or no war, from its bower of ferns. The native waiters came round with trays of beer. All was gilt and imitation marble. And this couple, so eager to be kind, were kindness itself. But why this positively effusive hospitality? Why? They might almost have been guilty about something. They talked about England: Do you remember, do you know, have you ever been to ... But, but! the colonial's England is not the England that these men longed for, not the pubs and streets they were exiled from. They were kind enough not to point this out.

That *but* was felt like a piece of grit in the mouthful of honey which was this chance to be welcoming hosts. How seldom do colonials, starved in their deepest need to be hosts, get the chance to take to their bosoms not one or two but twenty thousand grateful guests at once? All over the city, in bars and hotel lounges and even in private drawing rooms, could be seen – in that first week or so – a couple, man and wife, entertaining anything up to twenty polite but determinedly inarticulate groundlings, who drank and ate all they could, since the pushed-around are entitled to take what crumbs fate offers them, but certainly did not return that loving approval which is what hosts most essentially ask in return. Yes, this was a fine country; yes, it was a grand town; yes, it was a wonderful achievement for half a century. But. But. But.

The tide receded. It would return. Thousands upon thousands more men were arriving every week from Home. From those first tentative contacts it was clear that there was a situation which should be faced by those whose task it was to administer and guide.

In every city there is a group of middle-aged and elderly women who in fact run it. The extent to which they are formally organized is no gauge of their real power. The way in which they respond to danger is that gauge; and from the frankness with which they express their intentions can be measured the extent of the danger. To students of 'local politics' let there be recommended the activities of the mothers of the city:

About a week after the first grey tide, there occurred a conversation between Mr Maynard and his wife, not on the pillow – they had not shared one for many years – but at the breakfast table.

Mrs Maynard was the leader of the council of matriarchs. She was fitted for it not merely by character. The wives of prime ministers, Cabinet ministers, governors, mayors, because of the necessity that they should be above struggle and party strife, are precluded from certain positions. Far from envying such women, Mrs Maynard rather pitied them. She could have been one had she chosen. As it was, she was the daughter of an English family who for centuries had occupied itself with 'public work'; she was a cousin to the existing Governor, her husband was a third cousin to the Prime Minister of Britain; but he was only a magistrate; she was, so it was hoped it would be considered, not only reliable, but above all independent. Nothing she said would be taken as from the Government or a political party.

She remarked over the sheets of the *Zambesia News*, 'It is quite disgraceful that the authorities are not doing anything about it.'

Mr Maynard laid down his paper and asked, 'About what?'

'Millions of poor boys brought into the country and nothing whatsoever done for them.'

'You exaggerate slightly, I think?'

'Well – fifty thousand, a hundred thousand. One thousand would be bad enough.'

'There are cinemas and canteens in the camps, I believe.'

'You know quite well what I mean.'

Mr Maynard stirred his coffee, and remarked, 'Even in peacetime men outnumber women.' He added, 'I assume you are not suggesting a brothel – the churches wouldn't stand for it.'

She coloured and tightened her lips; this mask of annoyed rectitude vanished as she smiled with dry appreciation. 'Personally I'd rather brothels than – but that isn't what I meant.' She frowned and said, 'We should provide entertainment – something to keep them occupied.'

'My dear Myra, save your trouble. Every woman in the town is already lost. Wait until the pilots arrive.'

'I am thinking of the blacks,' she said, irritated. A short pause. Then, as it were, thinking aloud, 'I heard from Edgar that they have no idea at all how to treat natives. Not their fault, of course, poor things. I suggested to him a course of lectures on native policy, that sort of thing, *before* they arrive in the country.'

'So you are not concerned with the morals of our wives and mothers?' He smiled at her, the heavy urbane eyebrows raised.

She returned an equally bland smile. 'I am concerned with both. The first thing should be a dance hall, with canteens, ping-pong – something like that.'

'I have just understood that you intend me to sponsor it – is that it?'

'You would do very well,' she suggested, for the first time with a touch of appeal.

'No,' he said decidedly.

'You've got to do something. Everybody's doing something.'

He continued to stir his coffee, and to look at her. It was a challenge.

It was met. 'We are at war, you know!' she cried out at last, from her real emotions. She was now flushed, indignant, and with a hint of quivering softness about brows and mouth – a reminiscence of a certain striking dark beauty.

He smiled unpleasantly; apparently he felt this to be a victory.

But she did not attempt to quell her emotion. 'Your attitude is extraordinary, extraordinary!' she said, lips quivering. 'Don't you care that we are at war?'

'I care very much. But not enough to run a refined club for the boys,' he added. Then: 'I shall confine myself to keeping the native population in its place. Nothing could be more useful than that, surely?'

They exchanged a long married look, which held dislike, and respect. The two faces, both heavy, black-browed, commanding, confronted each other from opposite ends of the long table. It was, as always, a deadlock.

'Then I shall ask that old stick Anderson to run it.'

'An admirable choice.'

She rose, and went towards the door. His raised voice followed her: 'As regards the problem of the dear boys and the native women, it is my personal view that – regarded from a long-term point of view, of course – a few thousand more half-caste children would be a good thing. It might force the authorities to provide better amenities for them. As things are the Coloured community provides more petty criminals than any other section of the population.'

This was designed to annoy. But one of the minor pleasures of power is to exchange in private views which would ruin you if your followers ever had a suspicion you held them. Mrs Maynard let out a short dry chuckle and said, 'There are surely simpler ways of getting better housing for the Coloureds than infecting all our boys with VD.'

Two days later a paragraph in the paper announced that three entertainment centres for the Air Force personnel were to be opened shortly under the experienced patronage of Mr Anderson, late of the Department of Statistics, a well-known public figure.

A second grey tide flowed abruptly over the town. Not quite so grey: the idea of the blue air fed a tinge of blue into those stiff uniforms, and now the hungry expectations of the people were assuaged, for these were the cousins, the welcomed relatives from Home – these, the aviators in person, recognizably the same species as themselves. They were perfectly at ease in drawing rooms, clubs, bars and dance rooms, where they at once appeared in their hundreds; and the city, long accustomed to indulging its young men in whatever follies they might choose to use, found nothing remarkable in their behaviour. They brought with them an atmosphere of dedication to danger, of reckless exuberance which – as every woman in the city soon had reason to know – was covered by a most charming modesty; and this in its turn was a mask for a cynical nihilism which was more dangerously attractive than even recklessness. If the note of the First World War was idealistic dedication, succeeded by its mirror image, sarcastic anger, then the symbol for this period of the Second World War was a cynical young airman sprouting aggressive but flippant moustaches capable of the most appalling heroism, but prone to surprising lapses into self-pitying but stoic despair, during which moments he would say he hoped he would be killed, because there was no point in living, anyway. The truth of the morale of any army is most likely to be discovered between the sheets.

The danger of this mood, felt like a heightened pulse in the town, was expressed to Mr Maynard at the breakfast table thus:

'It's all very well, but we have to think of our boys up north.'

'I expect they are taking care of themselves in their own way.'

'Have you heard about ...' Here followed the names of about a dozen young women. 'They are all losing their heads.'

'Provided they don't lose them too far, I daresay all will be well at the armistice.'

Mrs Maynard looked sharply at him, tightened her lips, held his eyes steadily with her own. When this couple had come together in 1919 after years of separation, there had been incidents to overlook on both sides. Not forgiven – no. Mrs Maynard could not forgive him that he had overlooked so easily. Yet what had happened? Nothing – she had never been unfaithful to him. There was simply a photograph of an officer, a cousin, among a bundle of old letters. As for him, he could not forgive that there was nothing to forgive. She had always fulfilled the letter of every agreement. But there burned in this handsome matron's heart a steady flame of romance: he knew it. She had given her heart to the dead and was thus free to deal with life as she felt was right. She had never done anything to be ashamed of.

After a few moments, he smiled and inquired, 'What do you propose to do about it, my dear?'

Mrs Maynard paid a number of visits, received others, was a good deal on the telephone. As a result, many young women got letters from various organizations suggesting that they might spend their time on such and such a form of war work. Strings invisibly tightened. Mrs Talbot, wan and beautiful with her daughter's grief (the *fiancé* had been killed in the air over London during the Battle of Britain), dropped in to see Martha and suggested she should join the organization of women connected with the civil service.

Martha hardly listened. Such was her naïveté that she thought it odd, even interfering, of Mrs Talbot, who had nothing to do with the Service. She gave Mrs Talbot tea, told her what news there was of Douglas – very little, save that he had just finished leave with the boys in some town in Abyssinia. And that meant – Martha calmly stated it, apparently not noticing Mrs Talbot's indrawn breath – that he was probably having dozens of love affairs. Happening to glance at Mrs Talbot, she frowned slightly, and added that he was perfectly entitled to do so; they did not believe in jealousy. Mrs Talbot was searching for the right words to express her disturbance of mind, when Martha, unaware that any were needed, began talking of something else. Martha's advantage in any such encounter was always her assumption that Mrs Talbot (for instance) was bound to agree with her; any suggestion that her view might not be the right one was met with a critical, almost incredulous stare.

Some days later, Mr Maynard himself came to see Martha. Mrs Maynard had said that she intended to visit personally a number of girls who were not pulling their weight. Mr Maynard had said hastily that he would see to young Matty Knowell himself. It was an instinct of protectiveness which he did not analyse.

As he climbed the stairs to the flat, he heard a child screaming; he had to knock several times before he was heard. Martha admitted him and asked him to sit down, announcing brightly that they would have to shout through the noise, if he didn't mind.

Mr Maynard did mind. He said he was prepared to wait. He disposed his large body on one of the small chairs, and watched. He was adjusting his ideas to the fact that Martha was no longer a girl with a baby, that his godchild-without-the-benefit-of-religion was now a personality. He saw a small lively girl striving energetically against the straps that bound her to a high chair, her cheeks scarlet and tear-stained, her black eyes rebellious. Caroline was small-limbed, dainty, with a fine pointed face – a delightful creature. On the platform before her was a heavy china plate, and on that a squelch of greyish pulp. Martha, planted on her two sturdy legs, faced the child like an antagonist, her own lips set as firmly as Caroline's, who was refusing the food she was trying to push in between them. As the spoon came near, Caroline set up an angry yell, and bright sparks of tears gleamed through squeezed lashes; then the small white teeth closed tight on the metal. Martha was pale with anger, trembling with the contest, even caught the child's nose until the mouth opened, and thrust in the spoon, leaving a mass of that unpleasant-looking pulp. Caroline choked, then began to cry differently – a miserable, helpless wail. Martha winced, then fumblingly loosened the straps, and caught Caroline up. 'Oh, Lord,' she cried helplessly, 'I don't know what to do!' Caroline was twisting in the embrace; Martha set her on the floor, where she stood holding a chair and yelled defiance at her mother. Martha lifted her with an impatient movement, and took her out to the veranda, came back and shut the door. Silence. She passed her hand across her eyes, reached for a cigarette, lit it, and sat down. She was now pale, tense and exhausted.

'Is all this really necessary?' inquired Mr Maynard.

Martha laughed unhappily, and said that the book ordered that if a child would not eat it should not be forced, but Caroline had not eaten a mouthful for days.

She took great gulps of smoke, but seemed to be sitting on edge, as if waiting for the slightest sound from Caroline.

'She looks very well on being starved,' observed Mr Maynard.

Martha frowned, and was silent. He was reminding himself of that time – so long ago – when Mrs Maynard was engaged in rearing Binkie. He could recall only his violent distaste at what had seemed an indefinite period of smells and mess; he remembered his puzzled respect for that tidy and fastidious lady his wife, who had apparently found nothing distasteful in soiled napkins and dribbling mouths. Now he looked at the high chair planted in the middle of the room, bathed in sunlight from the window. Scraps of brownish vegetable mush clung to it. There were bits of the stuff on the floor around it. Flies were settling over the plate. 'Can't you remove that unpleasant object?'

Martha looked at him inquiringly, and then at the chair. She shrugged at male queasiness, and remarked, 'If I take the chair out and Caroline sees it, she'll start screaming again.' But she lifted it outside, without incurring any protest, hastily wiped the bits of mess off the floor, and sat down again, still smoking. Mr Maynard observed that she was looking very attractive. She wore a slip of a yellow dress showing brown bare legs, brown well-shaped arms. Her fingernails and toenails were painted. She was scarcely recognizable as the pale plump schoolgirl he had married to her husband. She looked very young, self-contained, hard, unhappy. The dark speculative eyes watched him as if he might turn out to be an enemy.

The shell of bright confidence dissolved as she remarked humorously, 'I believe firmly that children should be removed from their parents at birth in their own interests.'

Mr Maynard's thoughts, which had left the infant Caroline, were thus returned to her. He said that children survived anything, in his experience. And returned to considering the fact which appeared to him to be confirmed by Martha's careful attractiveness, that rumour must be right.

'What are you doing with yourself.'

'Nothing much.'

'Having a good time?' he probed.

She said humorously, in a way which grated out resentment, that since children had to be fed three times a day and put to bed at half past six, there was scarcely much time left to enjoy oneself.

Mr Maynard could not remember being discommoded by Binkie's infancy, so he again dismissed Caroline. 'Do you go out much?'

'No,' she said, biting it off. And then: 'I am reading a lot.'

But he did not take it up. He lay propped on the angles of

the slight chair, like a broad solid grey plank, and observed her from his heavily accented eyes. He was convinced that no young woman living alone with a small child would go to the trouble of curling her hair and painting her twenty nails, unless it was for the purpose of attracting a man. He dismissed the reading as he dismissed Caroline, and came direct to his point. 'It is being said that you are having an affair with an officer in the Air Force.'

'I have no doubt of it.' She was flushed with anger. 'If I were, I think I should be perfectly entitled to.'

'I am not arguing the matter from its principles,' he began, regarding this as an admission. 'I am merely suggesting that there are ways of doing things.'

'Hypocrite!' Martha snapped out; then stiffly smiled. Her eyebrows were knitting and reknitting as if, above her gulfs of anger, tendrills of thought attempted to engage.

Mr Maynard coloured slowly; such was the power of Martha on him: she paid no tribute at all to the authority he felt he enshrined. 'My dear young woman, what is the point of infuriating people if an ounce of tact would save you from it?'

It appeared a fresh outburst was imminent; then she laughed and said, 'As a matter of fact, I haven't had any love affairs with anybody.'

'Having acknowledged your rights in the matter – ' he began, with humorous conciliation, but was interrupted.

'Do you know what happened?' inquired Martha, poised on the verge of what she meant him to think an amusing story.

'I can't wait to hear.'

'Well, I don't go out at nights much, because of Caroline.'

'Why don't you ask your mother to take her?'

'*No*,' said Martha quickly. 'Well, I asked the woman across the corridor to watch her. She never wakes at night. There was a dance at McGrath's – an officers' dance, of course,' she added disgustedly.

'Well, why not?'

She hurried past this point. 'So they laid on the girls, as

usual. You know how they ring you up and ask you if you'll be one of the girls.'

'I don't see why not. As long as the boys are content to be boys, why shouldn't the girls oblige?'

She giggled. Then: 'Well, you know how they go on – but I suppose if there is one thing we've all had plenty of experience in it is coping with the boys on the tear.'

Mr Maynard coloured again, and shifted his limbs uncomfortably. 'Quite.'

'There were half a dozen at my table – you know, all very *English*.' She paused for words, while Mr Maynard wondered what the word 'English' meant to a girl, certainly English by parentage, who had never been in England.

'I am at a loss.'

'Soft,' said Martha, dismissing it. 'You know, those deprecating types with moustaches.'

'I hardly think it is the right word to use *now*,' he observed.

She looked confused and guilty, but persisted, 'Well then, heroes one and all, I know. But what is heroism, then?'

'Can't we leave that fascinating social question aside for the moment?'

'It's easy enough to let yourself be killed.'

'There are hundreds of thousands of men who are doing everything to see they will *not* be killed – I do hope you don't admire them more.'

'I didn't say so,' she said sullenly.

Mr Maynard waited.

'About twelve o'clock I was landed with one of them and he was terribly drunk. I mean, really drunk. He was swaying all over the table. I got a waiter to hold him upright. But all his brothers in arms were dancing or in the bar. I couldn't think of anything to do. So I pushed him into my car and brought him here. Well, I could hardly take him into the men's washrooms, could I?'

'I suppose not.'

'So I brought him here and he was duly sick. Then I put him to bed on that divan there, and went to bed myself. About three in the morning, a vast horde of them burst in to claim him. Very solicitous they were about his condition. It appeared he was due to fly at five. He nearly pranged the morning before, he told me ...' She tailed off. A note of defiant pity that had appeared in her voice must be disowned, apparently, for she continued, 'They all thought it a hell of a joke.'

This was the end of the story. Martha was scarlet with remembered humiliation. After a pause, Mr Maynard said, 'I don't see what you expect — you want to have it both ways.'

'Why?' she inquired reasonably. She lit a cigarette. 'If you want to construct a story that I am having an affair with the Air Force out of that interesting little incident, then you're welcome.'

'I don't see why I should apologize when you think you're entitled to an affair any time you like.'

'But I didn't!'

'When your practice catches up with your theory, all I want to suggest is a little more discretion.'

'Did you come here to tell me that?' she asked, amazed.

He moved his limbs again, and said, 'Well, no.'

First she appeared angry; then, unexpectedly, moved. She leaned towards him and asked, stammering slightly, 'Why — why do you care what I do?'

And again Mr Maynard, having got through the defences of this armoured young woman, could not face the emotion he had found. He took a quick glance at her direct, inquiring eyes, averted his own, and remarked, 'My dear girl, you can all go to the devil for all I care.'

He was surprised and contrite that her eyes filled with tears. She got up abruptly, went outside, and returned in a few moments with the sleeping child. She sat, holding her in her arms, smoking over the soft nestling head. Mr Maynard saw that ancient symbol, mother and child, through a pale blue fog shot with sunlight. He was extraordinarily moved. Martha seemed to him altogether more amenable, conciliating — safe, in fact — thus disposed.

He remarked, 'A charming picture.'

Martha was first puzzled, then embarrassed. She at once

sprang up, and deposited the baby in a receptacle outside the door.

'Why did you do that?' inquired the elderly gentleman. 'I meant it.'

She looked at him sardonically. 'I am so glad you find it so satisfactory.' Then: 'It's against the rules to cuddle a baby out of hours – the book says so.'

At this point the door opened, and Mrs Quest came in. 'Matty, why don't you put your name on the door, I keep telling you – ' She saw the magistrate, and greeted him warmly.

'I'm just going,' said Mr Maynard, 'having spent a delightful half-hour with your daughter.'

'She's an awful scatterbrain,' said Mrs Quest instinctively, avoiding compliments to her own like a peasant afraid of the evil eye. 'Have you ever seen such a mess as this place is in?' She began to set it to rights forthwith. Martha sat on the arm of a chair puffing out smoke and looking stubbornly ironical.

'Would you like to come with me to a meeting of that Left group tomorrow night?' inquired Mr Maynard.

Martha brightened. Mrs Quest's face glazed – the pillars were rocking. She looked timidly at Mr Maynard and said, 'You don't mean that batch of Communists – someone said yesterday they have the CID at all their meetings.' She gave a short scandalized laugh.

'Oh, I don't think it's as bad as that,' Mr Maynard soothed. He looked inquiringly at Martha.

Mrs Quest said, 'I'll take Caroline, and you can go with Mr Maynard; it's very kind of him.'

Martha said nothing; she was looking angrily at her mother.

Mr Maynard recognized the existence of one of the female situations which it was his principle to avoid, and said to Martha, 'I'll pick you up tomorrow about eight – see you then, goodbye, ladies.' And departed.

'I really don't see why you don't get a boy,' said Mrs Quest irritably.

'Why should I have a servant when I've nothing else to do?'

'Everyone has one.'

'That's apparently final.'

'Besides, you don't do the housework — I've never seen such a mess.'

'Well, I live in it.' But now appeared that old enemy to decision of character, who pointed out to Martha that this argument was ridiculous, not because she was not entirely in the right, but because it sounded so *banal*. She retreated to the divan which not so long ago had supported the inebriated limbs of the Air Force officer, and watched her mother sweep and tidy the flat.

Mrs Quest, relieved by 'doing something', began to chat good-humouredly about Mr Quest — who was much better these days, he had dropped one of his medicines yesterday — and went on from there to Mr Maynard, who must be misinformed about the Left crowd, because a man in his position couldn't afford to get mixed up with such people.

'Oh, Mother!'

'But everybody knows . . .' This was lost as she bent under a corner table to retrieve fallen papers. Martha sprang forward to take them from her. Mrs Quest gave them up suspiciously. Martha put them into a drawer in such a way that she might have been accusing her mother of looking at them. Mrs Quest, hurt, said she had no intention of prying into Martha's private concerns. This reminding her of nearer preoccupations, she inquired offhand, 'And what's all this I hear of your going out gallivanting in the evenings?'

'I can only imagine.'

'I thought you said you weren't going out — what did you do with Caroline?'

'She was not neglected, if that's what you mean.'

'It's all very well,' cried out Mrs Quest, from the depths of her heart, 'but when I dropped in yesterday, she was quite alone and crying. As I told Mrs Talbot at bridge yesterday, you are really quite irresponsible.'

Martha was now alert with anger. 'I was only out for

twenty minutes buying vegetables. And what's it to do with Mrs Talbot?'

'You should get a boy, and then you wouldn't have to go out shopping. It's ridiculous, they'll deliver, anyway.'

'I thought you said it was dangerous to have a boy in a place where there was a small girl, because he was bound to rape her?'

They were now on the verge of a real battle, when Caroline let out the sudden, startled wail of an infant woken too soon. Martha got up, but, seeing that her mother was there before her, sat down, telling herself it was all unimportant and she should learn not to mind.

Mrs Quest brought in the small girl, and sat crooning over her, with an access of tenderness that touched and disarmed Martha; but Caroline was striving like an unwilling captive in the arms that held her. Mrs Quest laughed ruefully and set her down, and she unsteadily staggered back to the veranda, while the two women watched her with the same small, proud smile, in which was a touch of regret.

'She's very small for her age,' said Mrs Quest dubiously. 'I hope you are giving her enough to eat.'

Martha jumped as if stung. Mrs Quest rose hurriedly, and said she might just as well take Caroline now for a few days, it would give Martha a rest. Martha nearly protested, then allowed herself to slide into apathy – for why not? Then Mrs Quest added that Caroline needed to be fed up a little, and Martha turned away helplessly, silenced by the knowledge that she was certainly a failure, she could no more manage Caroline than Mrs Quest had managed *her*. Grandmothers, she reflected, falling back with relief on the abstraction, are better with their grandchildren than with their own children. And she even dwelt wistfully on a charming picture, Mrs Quest tenderly relaxed with Caroline, a picture that had the same soothing, ideal quality as that Mr Maynard saw when he looked at *her* with the child.

In a few minutes Mrs Quest had left with Caroline, and the flat was empty. Martha was, as always, uncomfortably surprised that as soon as Caroline was away from her it was as if she had never had a child at all; whereas as long as they were together that invisible navel string twanged like a harshly plucked string at every movement or sound the child made. She sat down and consciously tried to pull herself together; she felt herself to be a hopeless failure; she was good for nothing, not even the simple natural function that every female should achieve like breathing: being a mother. As she sat there, her eye came to rest on a half-closed drawer from which papers protruded. She jumped up, and, without reading what she had written, tore them up. It was a letter to Douglas. She had fallen into the habit of writing him long letters about – as he put it – what she really felt. The letters that reached him, however, were amusing accounts of Caroline's development, Alice's struggles with her son, Stella's enjoyable sufferings in childbirth. Pride forbade her to post her 'real' letters, which were in effect passionate complaints that he had ever married her if he intended to leave her at the first opportunity; despairing admissions of incompetence with Caroline; and her hatred of the life she led.

The letters she got from him filled her with dismay she would not acknowledge. The incidents of his army life he found as humorous as she did hers. Besides, he continually urged her broad-mindedly, as was the spirit of their compact, to get out and have a good time; which she interpreted, from a deeper instinct than she would admit to processing, as the voice of guilt itself.

She was about to sit down and describe the visit of Mr Maynard in terms which would make him sound like an avuncular priest, when the telephone rang.

She approached it with caution. Since that moment three nights before when six or seven young men had burst in to claim their comrade, it had been ringing with suggestions that she might go to this dance or that. She had reacted with stiff coldness. She was hurt that the victim himself had made no sign. She had not told the whole truth to Mr Maynard. Thomas Bryant had collapsed on to the divan in more than alcoholic breakdown. He had wept on her breast like a child – he had lost his nerve, he would never be able to go up again, he wished he had been killed when the aircraft had tipped over on its wing that morning. Martha had cradled him, and felt such a depth of emotion that afterwards she could not bear to think of it. It was terrible to her that weakness should have so strong an appeal. And yet it had been a perfect intimacy – for the few minutes before he went limp into sleep. That he should *not* have rung up seemed to her like a slap in the face. Now she took down the receiver, and a hearty embarrassed voice thanked her for holding his head; it was a jolly good show, he said. Then, after a short pause, he said it was a lovely day; Martha laughed in amazement; encouraged by this sound, he invited her for dinner that night. Martha agreed at once.

She ran off to prepare her dress and herself for the occasion: it was shortly after midday. While she bathed and curled her hair and anointed her body, her whole being was dedicating itself anew. She might have never been the wife of Douglas and the mother of Caroline. Her fantasies of the night ahead centred on the intimate talk, a continuation of that existing intimacy, a complete truthfulness which would sanctify what would follow. This, however, never approached even the threshold of consciousness. At the most she imagined a kiss. But until the kiss, fantasy must sleep. She was crying out for a romantic love affair; she had been waiting for months for just this moment; not for one second had the idea entered her head. There is no such thing as a female hypocrite.

When Thomas Bryant entered the flat at eight that night, she had been dressed and ready for over an hour. This was one of the evenings, she knew, when she was beautiful – though why the spirit of attraction should visit her as it did, she did not know; no man had ever explained it to her.

She welcomed him casually, like an old friend; she saw at once he did not recognize her. He looked uncertainly about the flat, and then at the divan on which he had slept.

'Mrs Knowell?' he inquired formally.

Martha laughed involuntarily; saw his startled shamed look; then hastily covered for him: he remembered nothing of what had happened, and she must not tell him. 'It was a terrible evening, wasn't it – we were all drunk as owls,' she remarked flippantly, and saw the relief on his face.

'I'm very sorry,' he said. 'You must let me make amends.'

She offered him a drink, and he arranged his length carefully on the divan, as if he distrusted it. He was very tall and rather slight, though broad-shouldered. He was fair, with a clear, ruddy English skin, and blue eyes inflamed by flying and late nights. They observed Martha with approval. The boys had told him she was a nice little piece; it was an understatement. He could not remember ever having seen her before; he remembered a crowd of vaguely amiable girls. He had decided to take her out to dinner somewhere where he would not meet his friends, behave pleasantly, take her home early, and take care not to see her again. Something like that was owed to a woman whom he remembered dimly as a maternal and practical presence. Now he changed his plans instantly: he would take his prize among his brother officers.

Martha, examining him, saw that he wore his uniform carelessly; that his whole person expressed a sort of humorous resignation to the absurdity of uniforms and war – a studied, self-conscious repudiation of anything serious, particularly his own death, which, since his training would be complete in a couple of weeks, was not likely to be delayed longer than a few months at most. She felt a pity for him which was betrayed even in the way she handed him a glass of whisky; he might already be a figure on a war memorial.

He tossed it down, and said, 'Let's go.' He stood up. 'Shall we dance instead?'

She said immediately she would love to. Somewhere in her was spreading a shadow of desolation. She felt insulted. She became very gay.

All the way to the camp he asked her minute questions about the make of the car, its performance, how much it cost to run. She thought of cars as objects invented to take one efficiently from one place to another; she had never really believed anyone could be seriously interested in such matters. He was offering her the merest small change of conversation; and she answered politely.

At the gates in the great black fence, the sentry stood aside as the young officer held out a piece of paper. There was a newly built hall, surrounded by ranks of parked cars. They entered the hall. It was already full. A band of uniformed men played from a platform.

Martha looked around and knew all the women present. A year ago, they had been dancing in the arms of the local men; now they were moving with equal compliance in the arms of the Air Force, and using with perfect ease the new language. She saw Alice dancing past. She waved. Alice waved back, then stopped, spoke to her partner, and came over.

The young officer stood aside politely while Alice took Martha's elbow and said, 'Hey, Matty, so we're back in circulation – it's awful, isn't it?' She let out her high giggle, and added, 'I'm browned off with everything. I don't see why we shouldn't – God knows what Willie's up to up north.'

Martha, who had felt a stab of jealous shock on behalf of the absent Willie, now agreed instantly that Douglas always said she must go and enjoy herself. At this Alice suddenly smiled, the women smiled ironically, exchanged a look, and separated.

Thomas Bryant returned to Martha, and edged with her around in the space between the dancers and the tables. She suddenly stopped. She had thought of this as going out with Thomas Bryant; she had imagined being with *him*. She saw a long table, around which sat a dozen young officers, half of whom had rung her during the last week. She looked at Thomas, unconsciously reproachful. He glanced curiously at her face: she was scarlet. He avoided looking at his friends, who had already made a space for them, and led Martha to another small table. They sat. Her back was now to the other table. Glancing at him, she saw him looking over her shoulder at his friends. She turned swiftly, and saw them grinning at him; his face expressed a half-sheepish triumph. She hated him. When he summoned the black waiter and suggested champagne, she said she would drink lemonade. They got up to dance, like two wooden things.

He was drinking heavily again. After a few dances, he had sunk into the collective wash of emotion; the whole roomful of people was dancing in the anonymous throb of music. That was what he most wanted, she could see: not to have to think, to let himself go into it, to let his mind flow out and away from the terrible necessity of his days. And he wanted to be with a girl whose face he would not have to remember next day. Well, then, he would. She loosened and danced in the beat of the drums.

Quite soon, a grinning young man tapped Thomas on the shoulder. 'Why don't you come and join us?'

He looked awkwardly at Martha; she said at once, 'Why, we'd love to.'

At the end of that dance she went easily with him to the other table. She disliked him now so much it did not matter what she did. She was now that woman who says, 'So that's what you want me to be – very well, then, I'll show you how well I can do it.' She danced cheerfully with the young men to whom she had been so cold on the telephone. Choosing a moment when Thomas was at the bar, she asked one of his friends to tell him she had a headache – she chose the most casually insulting formula she knew – and left, quickly, to find her car. She was now trembling – with cold, she told herself. It was a cold night, the great stars glittering in their patterns as they had on so many dancing nights.

As she got into the car, she saw two people sitting in the back seat. A young woman, lazily disposed in one corner, supported the head and shoulders of a young officer who lay stretched along the seat. Martha peered through the half-dark and saw that the girl was Maisie. Both were asleep.

She sat for a while, watching the bright soft dresses of the women flowing against the neat close shapes of the men as couples passed up and down the steps in the yellow light that fell from the apertures of the hall. Then she grew impatient, and leaned over and shook Maisie's bare white shoulder.

Maisie woke at once, opening her eyes straight into Martha's and smiling in her easy friendly way. 'Hey, Martha, have we been asleep?' She looked down at the man, whose face was half buried in her bosom, and yawned. 'I picked your car because I knew you wouldn't mind. Lord, this boy's heavy.'

'Who is he?'

'He's the Air Force.'

'Well, of course.'

'You know, Matty, I like these English boys, don't you? It'll be awfully hard to go back to our own after knowing them. They treat us quite differently, don't they?' A pause, and another yawn. 'I never get any sleep. They read more books. They talk about things. They've got culture, that's what it is.'

Maisie's husband had been killed flying in Persia. That had been six months before.

'He's very nice, this one,' she went on reflectively. 'He wants to marry me. Men are funny, aren't they, Matty? I mean, the way they are always wanting to get married. I suppose it's because they are going to get killed.'

'Are you going to marry him?'

'Well, I suppose so, if it's going to make him happy. I don't see the sense in it, myself. I look at it this way: Supposing he doesn't get killed after all – a lot don't, they just finish their turn, and then go to the ground. Well, then, he'll be English, and he'll want to live in England. But I like it here and then we'll be married and have to get divorced.' She shifted herself, with infinite gentleness, into a different position, carefully catching her lower lip between white teeth as his head rolled into the crook of her arm. He opened his eyes, stirred, sat up.

'This is Matty. I told you – she's all right.'

'How do yo do?' inquired an educated English voice.

'How do you do?' said Martha.

'Do you mind giving us a lift back to town, Matty? That's why we came into your car. Don hasn't got to fly tomorrow. He's got a weekend pass.'

Martha backed out, and drove through the big gates past the sentry. 'When are you getting married?' she asked.

'Tomorrow,' said the young man promptly, in a tender

proprietary tone, to which Maisie responded good-humouredly, 'Oh, you're a crazy kid.'

Martha observed in the mirror that they were once more embraced, and was careful not to speak again. She was feeling cold and lonely and left out. Now she regretted behaving so stiffly with Thomas.

She was able to drive to Maisie's room without having to ask for instructions. She stopped outside another white gate, banked with shrubs whose glossy leaves glinted in the starlight. She waited for them to realize that the car was no longer in motion.

Maisie came unhurriedly out of the embrace, saying, 'Thanks a lot, Matty, do the same for you sometime.' As she got out, linked to her young man, she inquired politely, 'And how's your Douggie?'

'He's doing fine.'

'Did you hear that a crowd of our boys tore Mogadishu to pieces a while back? You know how they are when they get into one of their moods.'

Don politely thanked Martha. 'It's very kind of you.'

'Not at all.'

He bent his head over Maisie's fair gleaming curls as they walked into the house where she had her room. Martha watched them going inside, cheeks laid together, dancing a half-mocking half-dreamy sliding step. She wished that her principles would allow her to cry. But this would not do; she efficiently let out the clutch, and drove herself back to the flat, feeling herself to be the only cold, sober, isolated person in a moon-drugged city given over to dancing, love and death. She felt as if she had shut the door against her own release. Then she remembered that tomorrow night she would be taken to a meeting packed full – she hoped against hope – of dangerous revolutionaries. She was enabled to retire to bed alone with philosophy.

At half past seven the following evening, Mr Maynard folded his napkin and rose from the dinner table, although the meal had reached only the roast-beef stage and there were guests.

'Spending an evening with your chums?' inquired his wife

briskly. The word 'chums' was the one she used to deprecate that group of elderly gentlemen who were Mr Maynard's favourite company, and whom she felt as an irritating but not dangerous comment on her own activities.

'No, I'm dropping down to the Left people.'

The ladies let our arch little cries of dismay. They were Mrs Talbot, pale in clouds of grey chiffon and pearls; Mrs Lowe-Island, her stubby, sunburnt sixty-year-old body upright in pink taffeta; and Mrs Maynard herself – sage-green lace and an amber necklace that fell to her waist.

Mr Maynard was prepared to forgo his pudding, but not his brandy; he sipped it standing. Mrs Lowe-Island, born to be that indispensable lieutenant who must say and do what her superiors find beneath them, cried, 'Now that everything is so serious, and the Huns are attacking us in North Africa, I can't see how anyone can waste time with a bunch of agitators – it's encouraging them.'

Mr Maynard smiled, and set down his brandy glass. Mrs Maynard was absorbed in her pudding, but it was to her that he remarked, 'Even with the Huns at our gate, I feel we might keep a sense of proportion.'

Mrs Maynard took another spoonful, but Mrs Lowe-Island said indignantly, 'They might sweep down over the whole continent in a couple of weeks.'

'I'm sorry you have so little confidence in our armies.'

'Oh – but we know Hitler is quite unscrupulous.'

Mr Maynard laughed. He was on his way to the door.

His wife inquired, 'You are taking that Quest girl?'

'You don't mean that young Mrs Knowell?' exclaimed Mrs Lowe-Island.

'She's a sweet girl,' said Mrs Talbot reproachfully. 'She's a darling thing – and so artistic!'

Mrs Lowe-Island quivered. Mrs Maynard spooned in the last of her pudding in a way which said that the cook would be spoken to about it in the morning, and firmly rang the bell.

From the door, Mr Maynard saw that in the centre of the living room stood a card table, with fresh packs of cards laid out; while on subsidiary tables here and there were piled dockets of papers, files, lists, pencils: his wife intended to indulge both her passions that evening.

'Who's your fourth?' he asked.

'Mrs Anderson.' The name was merely dropped.

'Ah,' Mr Maynard said, and looked curiously at his wife.

'Mrs Anderson is such a sweet, dear woman,' said Mrs Talbot, fingering her thick pearls. 'Now that her son is in uniform, she's taking such an interest in things. And when she's always so busy, too.'

'Busy,' cackled Mrs Lowe-Island, flushing angrily. 'We could all be busy if we took as much interest in men as she does.'

'Oh!' breathed Mrs Talbot.

Mrs Maynard turned her head slightly, and surveyed the areas of wrinkled burnt skin about the ruched pink taffeta. 'I should say that men took an interest in her,' she observed suddenly, her lips compressed over a laugh. Mrs Talbot and she exchanged a rapid malicious glance.

A short pause, while Mrs Lowe-Island looked from one to the other, smiling sourly. She blundered on: 'I hate to think what she spends on clothes.'

Mrs Maynard now surveyed the small puffed pink sleeves on Mrs Lowe-Island's upper arms, and remarked, 'It is so pleasant to sit through a dull committee with a woman like Mrs Anderson, who is always a thing of beauty. It's a rare talent to dress suitably for one's age – it seems.'

Again Mrs Lowe-Island appeared puzzled. Mr Maynard inquired, 'So she's already on committees, is she?'

'She is coming to talk things over tonight,' said his wife discouragingly.

'What! In the inner councils already!'

'Her husband is being so efficient with the recreation centres,' said Mrs Talbot.

'I can imagine. And what's she providing – the entertainment?'

Mrs Maynard frowned. 'Mrs Anderson is really very efficient.'

'I was always convinced of it. There's nothing I admire more than that kind of efficiency. The art of living in a small town is one of the most difficult to acquire. Or perhaps it is inborn?' Here he looked full at Mrs Talbot; her eyes veiled themselves, she faintly coloured.

Alert to danger, Mrs Maynard glanced from one to the other, and said energetically, 'Perhaps you and Mrs Talbot might discuss it later – privately. As you usually do,' she added, with a pleasant smile. 'Because you are going to be late for your meeting.'

She saw Mrs Lowe-Island's small black eyes fastened on Mrs Talbot. Mrs Maynard rose, and laid her hand lightly on Mrs Talbot's shoulder. 'Bless you, dear,' she said. Mrs Talbot's face did not change at all; her shoulder shrank away slightly, then stood firm under the slight pressure.

Mr Maynard was looking warningly at his wife. She met his eyes, and raised her heavy black brows mockingly. Then she allowed her hand to slide away from the grey chiffon shoulder, and went towards the living room. They all followed her.

It was a long, low-ceilinged room, painted white, with pale rose-and-green hangings. It was a room appropriate for tea, cards and gossip; and in the middle of it stood Mrs Maynard, upright, hands on her hips, looking at her card indexes and files.

'Mrs Brodeshaw is probably dropping in later,' she informed Mr Maynard.

'So the Players are extending their scope?'

'Not Mrs Player, Mrs Brodeshaw,' Mrs Lowe-Island said, and stopped. Her stiff bulky little body quivered under the pink taffeta; the tolerant silence was another affront. She looked from one to another discreet face, and dropped into an ingratiating smile.

'I wish success to your councils,' Mr Maynard said, and strode off across the veranda.

'I do think it's odd that Mr Maynard should go to the meetings of those people.'

'So boring, I should have thought,' said Mrs Maynard casually. She seated herself at the card table, split the seal off a pack, and remarked, 'It wouldn't be a bad thing if we could get a representative of the Left League, Book Council, whatever it is.'

'Oh, yes, they are such terribly sweet people, really,' urged Mrs Talbot.

'You keep in touch so cleverly with everything.'

Mrs Lowe-Island flushed again and insisted, 'They tell me they have niggers at their meetings.'

Mrs Maynard half closed her eyes, and remarked, 'Aggie, dear, there are parts of Africa where *Africans* sit in Parliament.'

'But we don't want that to happen *here*.'

'It surely depends *how* it happens?' Her smile at Mrs Lowe-Island was an invitation to allow the mills of thought to begin to turn; but Mrs Lowe-Island snapped, 'I wouldn't sit down in the same room with a kaffir.'

'No one has asked you to yet.'

Mrs Lowe-Island swelled; then the round reddened little face twisted itself into a smile; the small black eyes wavered, uncertain.

'Will you cut?' inquired Mrs Maynard.

'What I think is,' breathed Mrs Talbot, 'everybody should get together and learn to like each other. I mean, when you meet anybody, you like them *really* ... I don't see why people should dislike each other, and all this bickering...'

'Bless you, dear. Would you like a higher chair? Your pearls are getting mixed up with the cards.'

Mr Maynard, having looked at his watch and discovered he was late, amended his pace very slightly, and made his way under the moon-filled branches of the trees which lined the avenues that led towards young Mrs Knowell.

His mind was working comfortably along two different channels. He was thinking that in the 'Left Club' or 'Socialistic League' – his contempt for the organization was demonstrated by the fact that he could never remember, or rather, refused to use, its proper name – were some very able men, who, if the Government had any sense, would be made use of in this national emergency. For the purposes of his dissatisfaction he chose to think of the Government as some clearly defined machinery with which he had nothing to do. Besides, he was an amateur, a looker-on, a dropper-in; he was not implicated. Therefore he turned over in his mind the names of the men in question like a woman fingering silks she had no intention of buying. But there rose the vague thought, One might have a word with old Thompson-Jones.

At the same time, he was conscious of a steady chagrin which he defined as due to Martha. He was a handsome man; many women had found him so; Martha was an attractive young woman; there was nothing in the laws of nature to prevent her from thinking of him as a man; it was clear that never, not for a moment, had she done so. To that woman who makes a man feel for the first time that he is getting old is due a regard which is not so easily defined. He remembered the moment yesterday when she had leaned forward and asked emotionally why he cared about her; and thought of it as an opportunity lost. He knocked on the door of the flat, and waited, suitable remarks preparing themselves on his tongue.

Martha appeared at once, so that he was reminded he was late; and he apologized. He thought she looked very young, and rather appealing. He turned out the light for her, shut the door behind her, and, as they descended the broad stone stairs, tucked her arm under his. She suffered it to remain there a moment, then it dropped out from its own weight.

'You'll be cold,' he remarked. She wore one of her slips of coloured linen, arms and legs bare.

'But it's so hot,' she said.

He conceded to himself that for him a coat was something one put on when one went out in the evening. For Martha there was a different approach, apparently. He reflected that his wife had sets of clothes suitable for occasions; he could deduce from what she wore what she intended to do. That sage-green lace, for instance, was essentially for bridge with ulterior purposes; whereas, had she worn bunchy silver brocade, he would have diagnosed a late intimate call from the wife of the Prime Minister, or even the Governor's wife.

Whereas Martha might have been going shopping, for a picnic, or to the pictures.

She continued to walk beside him in silence. The moon was large, clear silver, directly above them. The little town was glaring white, black-shadowed, everything sharp and defined. The road glittered saltily. The street lamps were round bright-yellow globes.

'Do you often go to these meetings?' inquired Martha.

'Occasionally.'

'What are they talking about tonight?'

Mr Maynard considered. 'I don't know.' Then, seeing her surprise: 'The deficiencies of education, I believe.'

'Well, that should keep them busy.'

'Surely education's better than it used to be?'

She was puzzled. 'Oh, you mean in *England*.'

'You consider they should discuss education here?'

'We live here.'

Mr Maynard considered this in silence.

Aggressively she said, 'They just talk and talk.'

'I apologize,' he began, bringing unnecessary batteries of sarcasm to bear, 'for taking you to a function of which you disapprove so strongly.'

And now she slipped her arm into his. 'It's very sweet of you. It really is.'

At once he tightened the grip of his elbow intimately. She impatiently pulled hers away, then shot him an apologetic and embarrassed look. 'It's so hot,' she said again.

As they turned the corner of a street into that small area of the town which was the business area, she stopped and looked down a few hundred yards of shop fronts and office blocks. 'It's growing with the war, isn't it?'

He had never really considered it as a town at all; he tried to see it through Martha's eyes, and failed. 'You've never been out of the colony?' His voice was compassionate.

She burst out, 'I hate it. I loathe it. I wish I could take the first train out of it. It's like a – Victorian novel. They talk about their servants at tea parties, and say the lower orders are ungrateful. They even go so far as to pay them twelve pounds a year, like our grandmothers, and say they are spoilt. It's all so boring, things happen the same way over and over again. And in fifty years' time, people will be saying about now, "How backward they were then!" But in the meantime, they fight and make speeches and write articles over every sixpence, and all the time with moral language, religion, and all the rest of it. What's it all about, that's what I want to know? It's all so stupid and unnecessary.'

'We'll be late,' he said, walking forward hastily – not away from the idea, which seemed to him sensible, but from the emotion she put into it. 'For a girl of your age, I can think of better things to care about.' There was no reaction to this. After a while he conceded, 'I admit that this place is only to be borne by those, like myself, who have had their fill of big cities and know that there is really very little difference – We turn in here, I believe.'

They were now in the street which lower down became very disreputable and petered out in the slums where the Coloured people lived. They entered a large old, ugly building, and began to mount a spiral iron staircase that was lit by one dull-yellow electric bulb.

'I worked here once,' said Martha.

'When?'

'Oh, about two years ago.' Clearly, it might have been a decade. 'You know what's so awful about you?' she inquired angrily.

'I shall be pleased to be told.'

'You don't really care about anything.' She was sullen and aggressive. Then, looking at him, she was overcome with discomfort, and let out a short embarrassed laugh which was half flirtatious. 'Well, you don't, do you?'

They stood now on the second landing, which was in the darkness. Above them, over several twists of the iron stairway, came a glimmer of yellow. Doors stood shut and discreet all around them. There was a faint stale smell of urine.

Mr Maynard suddenly put his arms about Martha, kissed her, and said, 'So, I don't?'

She gave him a cold shocked look, pulled away, and went up the stairs in front of him. He followed resignedly.

On this third landing, the doors which studded the dim and dirty corridors stretching away all around them showed brown and peeling under that dingy yellow light. One door stood open, light spilled out, there were people inside. On the door was 'Contemporary Politics Discussion Circle' in small white letters on the cracked brown paint. They entered. The meeting had already begun. They slipped into empty spaces separated from each other. Martha looked around, and saw faces she had seen before.

It was a large room, with discoloured whitewashed walls, a bare board floor, yellow electric light bulbs hanging from loosely knotted flex. There were rough wooden benches all around the walls. A plain wooden table stood at one end, and from behind it spoke a long, bony, bespectacled figure – Mr Pyecroft himself. He was speaking with great deliberation, mouthing over the long, many-syllabled words. There were about twenty people present, among them three young men in the grey-blue uniform.

On the walls hung two portraits, one of Mr Nehru and one of Lenin. She had never seen a picture of Lenin before, and the name had had a flavour of something unpleasant, furtive, shady. She saw a strong man, gazing calmly into the future over his little pointed beard. The contrast between the two images confused her. She began to listen to what was being said. Mr Pyecroft was talking about the provisions for education for village children in Wales in 1910; and although occasionally a match scraped or feet shifted, everyone was listening absorbedly. Martha thought that in 1910 Lenin was alive; she saw him against the background of Tolstoy and Chekhov; in 1910 children in Wales were suffering conditions not much better than Russian children – why, then, had there been no Lenin in Wales? And the way African children lived now . . . she looked around the room. If there existed a Lenin here, presumably he would be in this room? She looked from face to face, and her spirits sank; and she had again ceased to listen.

Opposite her she saw a small dark girl smiling, and

recognized Jasmine. She smiled back. Jasmine's eyes turned with a look of inquiry towards Mr Maynard, and Martha felt herself grow hot. She saw Mr Maynard through Jasmine's eyes. She was embarrassed. He was seated on his part of the wooden bench stiffly, taking more room than anyone else, arms folded, legs stretched out in front, eyes lowered to the floor. The dark, decided face showed no sign of emotion of any kind. Yet from time to time he lifted the bold hazel eyes and looked with a peculiar intentness at various people: Mr Pyecroft himself, Mr Perr, Mr Forester. This intent gaze made Martha uncomfortable, as if she were responsible for it; then, seeing a derisive, critical smile on Jasmine's face, and one that was meant to be noticed, she reacted in the other direction: in comparison with these careless, nondescript people. Mr Maynard was impressively dignified and sure of himself. If *he* were cut across, he would show solid clean grain right through; he was all of a piece.

But Mr Pyecroft was still talking. He was now in Scotland and quoting a passage from Scott. People stirred and livened and laughed as Mr Pyecroft read; a fresh current of life ran through them, and they shifted themselves more comfortably for another effort at listening.

Then Martha saw everybody's eyes turn towards the door. A tall, stooping man stood there smiling; he was an African, dressed carefully in shabby clothes that had been darned and patched everywhere. He carried a briefcase under his arm. Mr Pyecroft stopped for him; he had continued talking as Mr Maynard and Martha came in.

Everyone nodded and smiled, made way for him beside them. Half a dozen packets of cigarettes were at once stretched out towards him. He seated himself between Jasmine, who smiled at him like an old friend, and a small fair woman whom Martha remembered seeing before somewhere. He accepted a cigarette, and looked towards the speaker; at once everyone, reminded of their obligations, did the same. But Martha continued to look at him. This was the first time in her whole life, and she was now twenty-one — the first time in a life spent in a colony where nine-tenths of the population were dark-skinned — that she had sat in a room with a dark-skinned person as an equal. Again her spirits lifted, and she felt these were people to live and die for. She looked with envy at Jasmine, and at the fair woman on the other side, who had been whispering something to him. She was a tiny, thin creature, with fair braids wound around her head. She had a small, round, bright-coloured face, small brown quick eyes, a big generous nose, a wide emotional mouth. On her other side sat a large, fattish young man, pale, with black-rimmed spectacles: Jewish obviously, and very much an intellectual. From her whispering to the African, she turned to him, the young man, and they exchanged a warm, intimate, deep smile. Martha saw they were in love; passion shone out all at once from the dingy room, and even from the measured sentences of Mr Pyecroft. Martha warmed to them, warmed to them all. Then, directed by another cautious sardonic look, this time from the tiny fair girl's young man, she looked towards Mr Maynard, who was steadily regarding the African under his heavy brows.

Martha caught a whisper from near her: some women were talking. One said, in a low humorous voice, 'That's Magistrate Maynard – he fined Mr Matushi two pounds or twenty days last week.' 'Dirty bastard,' came the reply. A great many eyes turned towards Mr Maynard, who was impervious to such atmospheres, obviously, for he remained calm and absent in his space of bench, a monument of detachment.

Mr Pyecroft had raised his voice. 'And now for my conclusions,' he said. He took off his spectacles, paused, laid down his papers. Eyes which had been directed at Mr Maynard, at Mr Matushi, centred on him again. Martha found herself gripped by what he was saying. The dead statistics, cautious assessments, hedged facts, were flowing together outwards on words that had the nobility that emanated from the picture of Lenin, from the couple in love, from Mr Matushi. She listened as if to her own deepest voice speaking. People, said Mr Pyecroft, were warped and twisted by the system; vast capacities for good lay in everyone; only the tiniest proportion of humankind had ever been given what was needed to raise them from brutes; he painted a picture of the world crowded with miserable, stunted, light-starved creatures, like animalcula writhing under a stone which needed only to be removed. But by Mr Pyecroft? If one shut one's eyes and listened to the words, then anything was possible, any belief, any vision of good; if one looked at him, that cautious lean gentleman, with his humorous, almost jaunty self-deprecation, the vision collapsed. He was finshing an extraordinarily moving description of new and ennobled humanity with the dry phrases, 'And so much for the set piece of the evening; now I'll leave the subject open for discussion.'

People stirred, and moved their limbs about: those benches were very hard. No one was eager to begin. After a long minute's silence, Mr Pyecroft remarked humorously that it appeared he had exhausted the subject. At once Mr Perr, in considered words, presented what he described as 'a small contribution'. It appeared that Mr Pyecroft had misquoted some figures from Scotland. Then the young pale Jew next to the fair girl began to speak. His English was slow, correct, and he would pause without embarrassment for as long as he needed to find the exact word. He asked them to consider the following proposition: In countries where there had been education for the working classes for any length of time, no revolution had been achieved. Revolutions occurred in countries where the masses had 'never been made – ' he hesitated over the word – 'moulded – formed,' he brought out triumphantly, 'by the ruling classes.' Could there, then, be a case, he asked them to consider, for progressives such as themselves to fight against popular education instead of for it?

There was a small laugh around the room: it was an embarrassed one. Mr Pyecroft smiled indulgently, and asked their good friend Boris from Poland to remember that this was a general discussion on education; it was not in their province to discuss the techniques of revolution.

The young man Boris said sarcastically that he should have thought it was a key question. A short silence ensued; Martha saw that the fair girl looked with passionate support into his eyes, and even touched his hand with her own. He remained passive but bitter for a few moments, until he flashed out a warm, grateful smile at her. Various people looked at them tolerantly, but with a touch of malice, as Martha noted angrily.

Since there seemed to be no further contributions, Mr Pyecroft asked their good friends and visitors from the Air Force to contribute. Two looked at the floor to avoid the invitation. One, a bulky shockheaded mechanic, got up and said that he would like to take up Boris's argument, with which he disagreed, but he was forbidden while in uniform to discuss politics. Here he gave a rather sarcastic laugh, which provoked sarcastic laughter from everybody. He proceeded to describe his own education, which had finished at the age of fourteen, in London. When he modestly sat down, he was regarded with interest and compassion by them all: here was the subject of their discussion in person, the working man from England.

All this time, Mr Matushi had been listening intently. Now he stood up and asked leave to speak. They all leaned forward to listen. He began by saying that he had heard with gratitude the address given by Mr Pyecroft, he was sure everyone would be grateful to him for the trouble he had taken. But what had interested him very much was what the last speaker had said. Because it was always surprising and interesting to hear that white men were not always well educated and doing only nice work. (Here people looked at each other self-consciously, but with a certain satisfaction.) A great many of his people would not believe that in England white men lived in bad houses, and with not enough to eat, and had to dig coal and make roads. He wished very much that a great many of his people could hear what the last speaker had said. Then perhaps – he said this with a gentle humour – they might not be so hurt by the newspapers when they said all black men were centuries in evolution behind the white men. But what he really wanted to say was this: There was a problem that interested him even more than the wonderful and intelligent lecture of Mr Pyecroft. It was the question of the education that African children were given – if you could call it an education, he added apologetically. It would give him great pleasure, he would be very grateful, if that problem could be discussed.

He sat down and looked at them in his characteristic way: patient, dignified, but stubborn.

Mr Pyecroft at once rose, thanked Mr Matushi for his contribution, and said they would certainly have a discussion on African education very soon. Here he looked at Jasmine. 'In a month's time, Miss Cohen?'

Jasmine said it must be two months' time, since there was another meeting already arranged.

Mr Pyecroft looked around, his hand resting on the table before him. 'If no one wants to say anything?' he began; but Mr Maynard remarked, 'I should rather like to say something.'

Close attention was focused on him. 'I will be brief. The assumption behind the speaker's very interesting address was this and I want to challenge it: that education is a good thing. There is no evidence at all that sow's ears can be made into silk purses. Popular education in Britain has existed, such as it is, for some decades; are the people better or happier as a result? I doubt it.'

There was a chorus of 'Oh! Oh! Oh!'

Mr Maynard waited until it had subsided, and said, 'Is there any evidence whatsoever that a person educated in one way rather than another will have different qualities, different abilities? And is there any evidence that the mass of human beings are better than brutes?'

He paused. Everyone exchanged ironical glances. There was also a feeling of discomfort, due to his repeated use of the word 'evidence': there was that gap between him and them that is always filled by silence; it was as if a peasant had asked them to prove that the world was round.

'I would be the first to admit that I am an avowed reactionary,' said Mr Maynard urbanely. There was a relieved laugh.

Mr Perr the statistician rose eagerly. 'This is my province,' he said, and they laughed again. He was a thin, dark man, with close gleaming black hair and pale gleaming cheeks with a ruddy patch on each. He held himself in such a way that he looked as if he might suddenly fold up like a hinged ruler. He quoted statistics plentifully from various countries, which – if it were necessary – proved to everyone that Mr Maynard was talking nonsense; Mr Maynard was obviously unimpressed, however. He smiled ironically until people began chanting all around him in lugubrious tones, 'The more things change the more they remain the same,' and 'Everything is the same under the sun.'

'That is my contention,' remarked Mr Maynard.

The deadlock might have been prolonged indefinitely, to peter out, as they do, in frustrated anger and hostility. But Mr Matushi, who had been regarding Mr Maynard with a sorrowful face, stood up and began passionately, in marked contrast with his controlled speech of a few minutes before, 'Our friend Mr Maynard says that people don't need to be educated. Well, I know that our people suffer from not being educated. Perhaps Mr Maynard has had too much education – then he doesn't want other people to be educated. All I know is that our children want to go to school, they want to learn, and they cannot because there are schools for a tiny number of them only.'

'You misunderstand me,' interrupted Mr Maynard.

'Oh, no, no, no, I don't misunderstand you, I understand you very well,' cried Mr Matushi.

'Mr Matushi . . .' said Mr Pyecroft urgently, half rising from his seat.

Mr Matushi hesitated, looking around him at faces which for the most part regarded him with interested compassion. He slowly seated himself. 'If I am out of order, I am sorry.'

'I think we should close the meeting,' said Mr Pyecroft. 'Are there any announcements?'

Jasmine rose, in her demure, self-contained way, and laid a slip of paper before him, and returned to her seat.

Mr Pyecroft read the slip, and then smiled in a way which prepared them all for a joke. 'The next meeting, which will take place here four weeks from tonight, will be addressed by Mr Dunhill.' There was a titter. 'Mr Dunhill, who, as we all know, is from the CID, has asked to address us on the comparative incidence of crime in industrial and agricultural areas in Britain.'

They all laughed loudly, and looked at a smooth clerkly man who sat, self-conscious, in a corner. 'It's a hobby of mine,' he muttered.

Could this be all that was meant by the gossip that the CID attended all their meetings? Martha felt indignant and let down.

'It is now ten o'clock,' said Mr Pyecroft. 'Before I close the meeting, there is the little matter of funds.'

Discreet tolerant smiles were held while Jasmine, who had apparently been secreting it about her person, produced a cocoa tin with a jagged rent in its lid. It went from hand to hand about the room, to the accompaniment of the small tinkling of falling coins. This incident, like every other, seemed to provide everyone here with the comforting sense of repetition, the safe, the familiar. These people, who all knew each other so well, who exchanged understanding glances at a word, who knew at once at which points to laugh in discussion – these people had been meeting once a month for years, to reassure themselves that their ideas were shared by enough others to make them valid; for years they had discussed education in Chile, or medicine in India; and for years respectable tea tables had been humming with talk of their dangerous activities. Martha found herself succumbing to something rather like fear: the old fear as if nets were closing around her, that particular terror of the very young. This was such a small town – the size of a small market town in England, so they said; and yet it was possible for so many different groups to form themselves, to lead their own self-contained lives, without affecting, or so it seemed, the existence of any other. She was instinctively shaking herself free of this mesh of bonds before she had entered them; she thought that at the end of ten years these people would still be here, self-satisfied in their unconformity, talking, talking endlessly.

All about her she heard small jokes, half-finished phrases that needed only an understanding laugh to complete them.

People were rising, going to find particular friends, making plans to meet for sundowners, tea, or children's tea parties.

Jasmine had crossed the room and stood before her, smiling in her quiet friendly fashion. 'It's nice to see you here,' she began, and involuntarily shot a questioning look towards Mr Maynard, who was talking to Mr Perr the statistician. Mr Perr laughed; it had a note of flattered eagerness which Martha found unpleasant. She saw that Jasmine was observing the couple satirically.

'Did you enjoy it?' she inquired, turning her critical but patient attention back to Martha.

'Why England, why not Africa?' burst our Martha hotly.

Jasmine smiled her agreement, saying, 'Well, there are some of us who feel the same way . . .' She glanced round, looking at Boris. 'This crowd are a waste of time,' she added. Someone grasped her arm. She smiled hastily at Martha, saying, 'I'll get in touch with you,' and turned away, having thus dismissed the organization for which she had been acting as secretary for some years.

Her place was taken by the fair girl, Betty, who eagerly clasped Martha's arm, searching her face with warm brown eyes; behind her stood Boris, smiling.

'Well?' demanded Betty urgently. 'Jasmine's told us about you – we're pleased to see you here. How about coming to tea with us, and – '

'You are overwhelming the poor woman,' said Boris humorously, in his clear, correct voice. Betty fell back, laughing, looking at him with eyes full of love. For a moment they smiled at each other, in a way which isolated them from everyone else in the room. A pang of pure envy shot through Martha: she immediately saw their relationship as something lofty, beautiful, on a plane infinitely higher than anything she herself had ever known.

Boris withdrew his eyes from Betty with difficulty, and said with the slow humour which made him sound pompous, 'If you would care to come to tea with us and discuss certain matters? There might be a place, for instance, for a discussion group which is not quite so – cautious?'

'They're really too scared to live,' flamed Betty. 'They're

so scared of the word "Left" that they won't even use it in their name, and – '

They both fell back as Mrs Perr came forward, shouldering them aside absently. Martha saw them exchange humorous glances.

Mrs Perr, a tall, thin dark woman, with hair cut straight around her face like a Dutch doll, loose straight discordantly coloured clothes, and a large dry orange mouth, looked closely at Martha and said, 'Oh – we've met before.'

'Yes, about two years – '

'Well, we're pleased to see you again. I'll ask Jasmine to send you notices of the meetings.'

'Thank you very much.'

Mrs Perr narrowed her eyes at her for a moment, in a way which suggested that she was mentally ticking off items on a list, and said, 'And, of course, there's the Book Club, if you want to join that.' She glanced over her shoulder, frowned, then smiled with pleasurable malice. Betty and Boris were leaning against the wall on the other side of the room, talking in low voices, face to face. It was not only Mrs Perr who smiled in that discreet, faintly malicious way. 'Betty does the books, but since she's been in love they're neglected. Betty!' she called.

Betty slowly turned and blinked across at them, her small, warm, delicately pink face illuminated.

Martha saw that Mr Maynard was looking at her impatiently across the room, and said, 'I'll have to go, anyway.' She smiled apologetically at Mrs Perr, whom she disliked quite finally for being malicious about love, and joined Mr Maynard.

They went out into the long, dim, dusty corridor. The laughter and talk from the room they had left became a unit of cheerful sound, and Martha stopped, afflicted by the desire to return and belong to the warm community.

'And how did that strike you?' inquired Mr Maynard affably.

Martha was not going to confess to the criticism that was at the root of her confused disappointment: while they were a community, each of them seemed anxious to repudiate the others to an outsider at the first opportunity.

'That man Perr has real ability,' observed Mr Maynard. 'And so has Forester.'

'And not Mr Pyecroft?' Martha could see no difference between Forester, Perr and Pyecroft, all of them as far as she was concerned equally verbose, self-satisfied and elderly.

'Pyecroft has a head on his shoulders, but he's got bogged down in this talking shop. It's all very well as an amusement, but not as a lifework, after all.' He added, 'There is a certain type of man who leaves the common rooms and lecture halls of Britain simply because he will strike enlightened communities like this one as the last word in education and intellectual daring.'

Martha was digesting this when he said, 'I've never been able to understand why left-wing women choose to be so unattractive. A remarkable phenomenon.'

'They might have better things to do.'

'Conceivably.'

Martha was thinking of the imposing Mrs Maynard, who clearly regarded clothes as so many badges of office. She was wondering how Mr Maynard saw his wife, when feet hesitated behind them. It was Mr Matushi.

'Ah, Matushi,' exclaimed Mr Maynard, 'I'm glad of the opportunity to talk to you.'

They were on the dark platform of iron which was the landing on the second floor. This was where he had tried to kiss her. She would have liked to go quickly past it. But she waited calmly while Mr Matushi descended. She noted that Mr Maynard did not use the 'Mister', which the others had been so careful to do; she most bitterly resented, on Mr Matushi's behalf, the casual, authoritative manner of Mr Maynard.

Mr Matushi was now standing quietly on the landing, drooping his length from his shoulders: he was a head taller than even Mr Maynard.

'I understand you regard yourself as a kind of leader of your – compatriots?' Mr Maynard inquired.

'Yes, I think that is so.' The voice was soft, firm, a little hesitant.

'Well, then – there's this question of the war. Would you like to represent your – followers, on a committee for raising funds, eh?'

Mr Matushi appeared to reflect. Then he said, 'Our people all support the war against fascism.'

Mr Maynard let out a surprised grunt. 'Eh?' It was the word 'fascism'; as far as he was concerned, England was fighting Germany again. 'So, you do, do you?'

'Our people are well aware of the danger Hitler represents to the civilized world.'

'I don't suppose that more than half of one per cent know who Hitler is.'

'In that case, it is not ... democratic' – Mr Matushi hesitated delicately over the word – 'to make them soldiers in this war, is that not so, Mr Maynard?' He stooped before Mr Maynard, stubborn, gentle, expressing with every line of his body an infinite willingness to wait.

Mr Maynard looked at him heavily, and said, 'Be that as it may, it would be appreciated if a well-known and acknowledged leader – a man like yourself – would represent your people on the committee.'

Mr Matushi smiled gently. 'Perhaps there might be a better man for the position? A person like myself, fined in the courts, might not be – acceptable?'

Mr Maynard's black eyebrows shot up, and he said severely, 'Matushi, if you don't keep the law, it's my job to fine you. That's all there is to it.'

Mr Matushi was smiling, biting his lips, smiling again; he shook gently with laughter. 'But, Mr Maynard, you are a very good magistrate, we all know that; we all know you as a very just man.'

There was no resentment in his manner, not even the impertinence which Mr Maynard was certainly looking for – nothing, apparently, but that genuine bubbling amusement. Suddenly he stopped his long body from the slight pervasive shaking, and said, 'Mr Maynard, our people will do everything they can in this terrible war. They will fight well. It is only fifty years since we were honourably defeated by your soldiers. Our soldiers have already gone to fight with your soldiers against fascism for democracy.' He waited, stooping and smiling.

'Good night, Matushi,' said Mr Maynard.

'Good night, sir.' He stood to one side while Mr Maynard and Martha went down the stairs before him, and then followed at a polite distance. They reached the street.

'What did you fine him for?'

'For not having a pass after nine o'clock.'

Martha was silent with hostility.

'I don't make the laws, I am their servant.'

Martha laughed angrily.

He looked at her in surprise. 'Personally I should be in favour of issuing educated men – comparatively educated, that is – with a special pass to exempt them from carrying other passes. I believe it is under consideration now.'

'Why not abolish passes altogether?'

'Why not? I suggest you put pressure on your Parliamentary representative to that effect.'

Martha laughed again.

'I am firmly of the opinion that the sooner a middle class with privileges is created among the Africans, the better it will be for everyone. Unfortunately, the majority of the whites are so bogged down in intelligent considerations such as that they wouldn't have their sisters marrying black men, that they are too stupefied to see the advantages of such a course.'

Martha was several years from understanding this remark, and felt herself to be as stupid as that majority he had dismissed so contemptuously.

They proceeded in silence down the empty moonlit street, Mr Maynard strolling along, putting one firm leg before the other under a heavy, massive body, hands behind his back, narrowed thoughtful eyes directed ahead. 'They are all the same, these African agitators. You can buy any one of them for ten shillings.'

'Has Mr Matushi been bought?'

'They all overreach themselves, if you give them time.'

'One of these days they'll fight you with their bare hands.'

'I don't doubt it. In the meantime I shall continue to do my duty in that station of life into which it has pleased God to call me.'

Martha considered this for a time; and then inquired, really wanting to know: 'I don't see why you go to these meetings?'

For the first time, Mr Maynard showed signs of discomfort. He said hastily, heavily humorous, 'I'm an interested observer of life.'

'You behave as if you were God,' said Martha at last.

They had reached the pavement outside the block of flats.

'If you are genuinely interested in uplifting humanity, which is right and proper at your age, then there are many things you could do.'

'Oh no, you don't,' said Martha abruptly. Mr Maynard raised his brows. Martha was embarrassed because of the hostility that had sounded in her voice; she did not really understand what she had said. 'It was very sweet of you to take me out,' she said like a schoolgirl.

'So you have already said. Are you going to ask me up for a drink?' he inquired, facing her massively, so that she had to look up into his face. She felt him to be powerful and dangerous; she remembered him on the second landing. She said, 'Caroline wakes so early in the mornings.'

Up went those brows. 'But I thought Caroline was with your mother?' Then he said, 'Well, I won't obtrude myself. Good night.' He turned and went striding off along the street.

Martha went indoors in a ferment of embarrassment. He had made her feel gauche and unaccomplished. Yet there had been nothing of the ironical gentleman about him on the second landing among closed doors and the unpleasant, disreputable smell. She felt that the incident had been an insult to both of them. If she chose to remember it, she would never be able to feel liking for him again. She proceeded to forget it, with the vague thought, I suppose it's because he's so old; that generation – kissing hastily on staircases is the sort of thing they did.

She proceeded to think of Mr Matushi; she could not

understand his extraordinarily gentle amusement. If I were Mr Matushi, she thought angrily, I would . . . But she could think of nothing but that she would have slapped Mr Maynard's face. Which would have earned him a sentence for assaulting a white man.

She went to bed in a mood of severe self-criticism.

As for Mr Maynard, he strolled through the moonlight, hands behind his back, and the memory of Martha's nervous hostility rankled. He felt he had been encouraged and then rebuffed. He proceeded to comfort himself by thinking of various romantic episodes. At the same time, he reflected on the meeting; he dwelt particularly on that moment when Mr Perr had laughed when he remarked that he could not understand why left-wing intellectuals always insisted on being so uncomfortable when they met. The grateful, almost obsequious note in that laugh caused another, but quite disconnected, image to float into his mind: the face of old Thompson-Jones, Minister of Finance, with whom he would be playing golf tomorrow.

Chapter Two

The two rooms at the top of the block of flats were filled with light from the sky as soon as the sun, splendid, enlarged and red, swelled up over the horizon of suburb-clotted hills, pulling behind it filaments of rose-and-gold cloud. By half past five fingers of warm yellow were reaching over the big bed, over Caroline's cot. Martha lay warm in the blankets, listening to Caroline wake. She always woke the moment the child first stirred, as if an alarm had gone off; she woke instantly if Caroline murmured in her sleep at night. Caroline gurgled, and strove with her limbs until the covers were off. She sat up. Martha, through eyes kept half closed, saw the tiny energetic creature in its white gown rolling over and stretching, two small rosy feet playing in the air, while the voice tried itself: a soft chuckle, then a deep, self-absorbed murmur; silence, and a sudden shriek of triumphant vitality as the cot shook and rattled with her movements. The low meditative murmur began again; Caroline, crouching on all fours, looked steadily at the white blanket while she listened to her own voice; there was a look of thoughtful surprise on the small face. She dropped sideways, rolled to her back, her legs stuck straight up, she grunted and puffed while her face reddened. She lay there, rocking her legs from side to side, silent for the moment, apparently waiting with docile patience to hear what new sound her throat would bring forth. A high single note, like a bird's; another, a fifth lower; a long silence, and again a triumphant yell. Caroline clambered resolutely to her feet, clutched the edge of the cot, put her chin on it, and looked out of the window at the sun. The big yellow ball swam now in a clear sky. Caroline blinked at it; beads of sweat clung under her short black curls. She squeezed her eyes shut, and rocked, humming, from one foot to another, the sun sharply etching her rosy face with shadow and warm light. She opened her eyes cautiously; the sun still filled her eyes with its dazzle. She turned her head slightly, and, frowning with determination, put up a clenched fist over one eye, and opened the other at the sun: it was still there, hanging in the blue square of the window. She stretched out one fist and spread it into a shaft of yellow light that swam with golden dust; the small fingers moved wildly, then clutch! They shut on nothing. Caroline looked down, puzzled, at her empty palm. She tried again; her hand went clutch! clutch! at the mote-filled sunlight. Then she stretched out both hands to the sun, a look of desperate desire on her face. She let out a high, angry, baffled yell and shook the bars of her cot furiously. She lost her footing, rolled over, and lay on her back, legs waving comfortably in the warm sunlight, contentedly trying out her voice.

Martha shut her eyes and tried to sleep again. She could not. There was this band of tension, felt deeply as a web of tight anxiety, between her and the child. Every moment, every sound Caroline made reverberated through Martha. Relax! said Martha to herself, but she felt tension in every limb. She was waiting for that moment when Caroline's high shriek peremptorily sounded the summons for the day to begin.

And yet, during those three days while Caroline had been with her grandmother, Martha had slept, waked, gone about living as if Caroline did not exist, had never existed. Not for a moment had Martha felt anxiety; she had scarcely thought of the child. She came home; and again Martha was caught up into the rhythm of this other small life. Her long day was regulated by the clock to Caroline's needs; and she went to bed at night exhausted by Caroline's experience.

She lay now, eyes closed to a narrow slit, the sun making rainbows on her eyelashes, so that she might see it as Caroline had just seen it, and knew that her reluctance to get out of bed was simply boredom at the thought of the day ahead. She wished it were already the end of the day, and

Caroline safely in bed and asleep. Then her, Martha's, life might begin. And yet the hours of evening were as restless and dissatisfied; she always went to bed early to put an end to them. Her whole life was a hurrying onwards, to get it past; she was back in the tension of hurry, hurry, hurry; and yet there was nothing at the end of it to hurry towards, not even the end of the war, which would change nothing for her.

At this point in her reflections, she again told herself to relax: her inability to enjoy Caroline simply filled her with guilt. Yet she could not relax into Caroline; that would be a disloyalty and even a danger to herself. Cycles of guilt and defiance ruled her living, and she knew it; she had not the beginnings of an understanding what it all meant.

Caroline was now chanting steadily, with a note of urgency in her voice that Martha knew. Her limbs involuntarily stiffened; she made them lie loose.

Caroline bundled herself over, dragged herself hand over hand up the bars of the cot, rested her chin on the rail and looked at her mother. Martha saw the small, white-gowned girl, her alert bright black eyes shrewdly watching her. Caroline let out a shriek of warning and waited. Martha suddenly laughed, won over into tender amusement. Caroline surveyed her mother for a moment, and shook the bars like a monkey. In an instant, Martha had swung her legs over, lifted Caroline out and set her on the big bed.

The book prescribed rusk and orange juice. Martha fetched them. Caroline staggered around the room on her unsteady little legs, sucking the rusk into a sticky fawn-coloured paste.

The small white-painted room was filled with sunlight, like a glass bowl full of quivering bright water. Martha took a bath: the bathroom was shot with needles of sunlight; the water rocked in the white bath in spangles and opals of light. Then she dressed swiftly in one of the brief coloured dresses that gave her so much pleasure to wear. How lovely to wear so little, to feel her brown smooth limbs coming out of the slip of coloured linen; she was all free and her own again; she was light and supple, and the stains and distortions of pregnancy belonged to another epoch. How lovely then to wash the little girl, and see her in her fresh pretty cotton dress, the delicate pink feet balancing so surely and strongly over the floor.

By seven every morning Martha and her daughter were dressed and ready for the day, and they ate breakfast together; or rather, Martha drank tea and painfully did not care that Caroline would not eat.

Ever since the day Mr Maynard had entered on the unpleasant scene of Caroline being fed, when Martha had seen it sharply through his eyes, she had forced herself, and with an effort that exhausted her, *not* to care about Caroline's eating. She must break this bond! That was how she felt it: as something compulsive and deadly that would most certainly affect the child's whole future. So Martha no longer cared, on principle. But at the beginning it had not been so easy. She prepared the messes suitable for Caroline's age, set them on the wooden platform before the child, put a piece of linoleum under the high chair, and retired with a cup of tea and a book, forcing herself not to look at her.

And now what contests of will followed! Caroline had been used to a forceful pillar of a mother standing over her with a glinting hard spoon full of stuff that she *must* eat, no matter how she tightened her lips and turned away her face; now she saw this woman – and from one day to the next – sitting away from her on the other side of the room, not listening to her cries of rage and shrieks of defiance. Caroline picked up the bowl of porridge and flung it on the floor so that the greyish mess splashed everywhere; Martha turned a page and did not look. Caroline sparked her black eyes at Martha, let our short sharp cries of anger to *make* her look; then she picked up a mug of milk and poured it all over herself. Martha remained indifferent in her chair; but there was a tight-lipped tension about her that Caroline knew. She paddled her hands in a lake of soiled milk and rubbed them in her hair, singing our her defiance. And suddenly Martha became a whirlwind of exasperation. She jumped up and said despairingly, 'Oh, Caroline! You are a naughty, naughty girl!'

The little girl, with blobs of porridge on her face, her hair plastered and dripping with milk, gurgled out triumphant, defiance. Then she found herself lifted roughly from the chair; she yelled angrily while Martha held her kicking under her arm, and bent to fill the bath. She was dropped into the water, soaped hastily; she felt herself whirled into new clean clothes, and then she was dropped into her wooden pen, where she soon forgot all about it, and began playing with her toys.

In the meantime Martha was scrubbing porridge and milk off the floor, the furniture, herself. She was sick with disgust at the mess. She was asking herself why she had endured months of that other mess with only occasional lapses into distaste; a period when napkins and then clothes and blankets had been wet and dirty, without difficulty: the book had said so. The book and she had been admirably justified: Caroline was now, as the phrase went, perfectly clean. But that had been no problem; the battle centred on food. What is it all about? asked Martha in despair. She was furious with herself for losing her temper. She could have wept with annoyance. She was saying to herself, as she wiped off milk and grey pulp, Oh, Lord, how I do hate this business, I do loathe it so. She was saying she hated her daughter; and she knew it. Soon, the hot anger died; guilt unfailingly succeeded. Outside, on the little veranda which was like a wired cage projecting out into the sunlight – the sun was now pouring down from over the trees in the park – Caroline was cheerfully gurgling and singing to herself. Inside the room, Martha was seated, tired and miserable. Her heart was now a hot enlarged area of tenderness for the child whom she was so lamentably mishandling.

She went out on to the veranda. Caroline, in her short bright dress, looked up with her quick black eyes, and made an inquiring noise. She was snatched up and held against Martha's bosom. At once she began striving free; Martha laughed ruefully and put her down; she staggered around the room, singing to herself.

But she had eaten absolutely nothing. Martha produced rusks, and left them surreptitiously about the room. Caroline seized on them and began chewing vigorously.

'Oh, Caroline,' sighed Martha, 'what am I going to do with you?'

She was forming the habit of talking to the child as if to herself. The small brain was receiving the sound of a half-humorous, resentful, grumbling, helpless voice rumbling away over her head.

'My poor unfortunate brat, what have you done to deserve a mother like me? Well, there's no help for it, you'll just have to put up with it. You bore me to extinction, and that's the truth of it, and no doubt I bore you. But as far as I can make out, one of the most important functions of parents is that they should be suitable objects of hate: if psychology doesn't mean that, it means nothing. Well, then, so it's right and proper you should hate my guts off and on, you and I are just victims, my poor child, you can't help it, I can't help it, my mother couldn't help it, and her mother . . .'

After a silence the voice went on, rather like Caroline's own meditative experimental rumblings and chirpings: 'So there we are, and we'd better make the best of it. As soon as possible I'll send you to a nursery school where you are well out of my poisonous influence. I'll do that for you at least.'

By nine in the morning, it seemed always as if long stretches of the day had been lived through. And yet it was three hours till lunchtime. Martha sewed – she and Caroline had dozens of cheap pretty dresses. She watched the clock. She cooked little messes for Caroline. She leafed hopefully through the book – or rather, whichever one of them seemed most likely to provide what she wanted – to see if she had overlooked some pattern of words that might help her to feel better. And at the least she felt she was being honest, that virtue which she was still convinced was the supreme one. Somewhere at the bottom of her heart was a pleasant self-righteousness that while she was as little fitted for maternity as her mother had been, she at least had the honesty to admit it.

She would watch lunchtime approaching with helpless

despair. But she was determined to break this cycle of determination, which always ended in her own violent anger and Caroline's rebellious screams.

She learned to put Caroline's food in front of her and then go out of the room altogether. When she came back, she forbade herself to notice the unpleasant fly-covered mess on the high chair. She quickly lifted the child out, and washed her, and set her back in her pen without saying a word. Day after day, Martha lay face down on the bed at every mealtime, her fingers stuck in her ears, reading, while Caroline yelled for attention next door. Slowly the yells lessened. There came a point where the child received her food and ate it. Martha returned from her exile in the bedroom, the victory won. She had succeeded in defeating the demon of antagonism.

And now she was able to cook the food and serve Caroline with it and not care if she ate it or not. And, of course, now it was eaten. And Martha existed on hastily cut slabs of bread and butter and tea. She could not be interested in food unless she was cooking it for someone with whom she would share it afterwards. Women living by themselves can starve themselves into a sickness without knowing what is wrong with them.

Then she became perversely sad because she had won the victory. It seemed that something must have snapped between her and her daughter. It increased her persistent uneasiness, which expressed itself in those interminable puzzled humorous monologues: 'It's all very well, Caroline, but there must be something wrong when you have to learn *not* to care. Because the trouble with me is not that I care too much, but that I care too little. You'd be relieved, my poor brat, if you knew that when you were with my mother I never thought of you at all – that's a guarantee of your future emotional safety, isn't it?' Silence, while Caroline pursued her own interests about the room; if the silence persisted, however, she cocked a bright inquiring eye towards her mother. 'But what I can't understand is this: Two years ago, I was as free as air. I could have done anything, been anything. Because the essence of the daydreams of every girl who isn't married is just that: it's the only time they are more free than men. Men *have* to be something, but you'll find when you grow up, my poor child, that you'll see yourself as a ballet dancer, or a business executive, or the wife of a Prime Minister, or the mistress of somebody important, or even in extreme moments a nun or a missionary. You'll imagine yourself doing all sorts of things in all sorts of countries; the point is, your will will be your limit. Anything'll be possible. But you will not see yourself sitting in a small room bound for twenty-four hours of the day – with years of it in front of you – to a small child. For God's sake, Caroline, don't marry young, I'll stop you marrying young if I have to lock you up. But I can't do that,' concluded Martha humorously, 'because that would be putting pressure on you and that's the unforgivable sin. All I can promise is that I won't put any pressure on you of any kind. I simply *won't care* . . . But supposing that not caring is only the most subtle and deadly way of putting pressure on people – what then? . . . But what is most difficult is this: If you read novels and diaries, women didn't seem to have these problems. Is it really conceivable that we should have turned into something quite different in the space of about fifty years? Or do you suppose they didn't tell the truth, the novelists? In the books, the young and idealistic girl gets married, has a baby – she at once turns into something quite different; and she is perfectly happy to spend her whole life bringing up children with a tedious husband. Natasha, for instance: she was content to be an old hen, fussing and dull; but supposing all the time she saw a picture of herself as she had been, and saw herself as what she had become and was miserable – what then? Because either that's the truth or there is a completely new kind of woman in the world, and surely that isn't possible, what do you think, Caroline?'

All the morning, sunlight moved and deployed around the flat. After lunch the sun had moved away; the rooms were warm, airless, stagnant. And then Martha put Caroline into her push-chair, and filled in the time by wheeling her around the streets for an hour, two hours, three hours. Or she sat in the park under a tree with dozens of other young mothers and nannies, watching the children play. This period of the day seemed to concentrate into it the essence of boredom. It was boredom like an illness. But at six in the evening, Caroline was washed, fed, and put into her cot. Silence descended. Martha was free. She could go out, see people, go to the pictures. But she did not. She sat alone, reading and thinking interminably, turning over and over in her mind this guilty weight of thoughts, which were always the same. Those people who have been brought up in the nonconformist pattern may shed God, turn upside down the principles they were brought up to; but they may always be relied upon to torment themselves satisfactorily with problems of right behaviour. From these dreary self-searchings there emerged a definite idea: that there must be, if not in literature, which evaded these problems, then in life, that woman who combined a warm accepting femininity and motherhood with being what Martha described vaguely but to her own satisfaction as 'a person'. She must look for her.

Then one day she saw Stella in the street. They exchanged the gay guilty promises to come and see each other which people do who are dropping out of each other's lives. Afterwards Martha thought that Stella looked very contented. She had changed. Two years ago she had been a lithe, alive, beautiful young woman. Having a baby had turned her into a stout and handsome matron, very smart, competent and – this was the point – happy. Or so it seemed in retrospect. Thinking wistfully for several days about Stella's unfailing self-assurance, in whatever role life asked her to play, turned her, for Martha, into a symbol of satisfactory womanhood. On an impulse then she dropped Caroline in the house across the park with her mother, and drove out to the house in the suburbs where Stella now lived with her mother.

It was a very bright sparkling day, with a tang of chill in the air. The sky was glacially blue. The white houses in their masses of heavy green foliage shone in a thin clear light, with a remote, indrawn look, as if prepared to be abandoned by warmth for a short season. The wave of painful emotion that is a clearer sign of changing seasons than the loosening of a leaf or a clap of thunder after seven months' silence entered Martha suddenly with familiar and pleasurable melancholy – winter was coming. In such a mood, to inquire from Stella how one should live appeared absurd; nostalgia imposed different values – nothing mattered very much. Suppressing it, she drove on through the avenues, turned outwards over a narrow road through a shallow grass-filled vlei, and entered a new suburb; the town was spreading fast under the pressures of war. This suburb was a mile of new bungalows scattered hastily over a rock-strewn rise. Stella's mother's new house was at its limit; beyond stretched the unscarred veld; and the garden was bounded by heaps of granite boulders tangled over by purple bougainvillaea. The bungalow was small, but no longer a colonial bungalow. The veranda was a small porch, and there were green shutters to the windows, and there was a look of glossy smartness about it. Martha parked the car, went up prim steps, and rang the bell, feeling like someone paying a visit.

Stella appeared and cried out a gay welcome. She was wearing a handsome scarlet housecoat, and her dark braids fell down her back. In the living room her mother was playing with the baby. The room looked like an illustration from a magazine; it was all cream leather and red carpet. Through the cream-shaded windows a stretch of sere drying veld looked in and disowned the alien. Martha felt a sharp dislocation in her sense of what was fitting, as she always did with Mrs Barbazon, who, with her careful dark eyes, seemed a stray from the capitals of Europe.

Stella flung back her dark braids carelessly, and, with her new look of matronly contentment, sat down, watching her child – a little girl, dark-eyed, slender, pale. Both women were competing for Esther's attention. Mrs Barbazon was holding up her crystal beads and swinging them before the infant's moving eyes. Stella leaned forward and offered the end of one of her long thick plaits. Esther reached out for it, and with a satisfied smile, Stella lifted her on to her own lap.

'How's Andrew?' asked Martha.

Without lifting her eyes from Esther's face, Stella said,

'Oh – I haven't had a letter recently. I don't know.' This was hard and careless.

'I heard from my brother that he'd met him somewhere up north.'

Stella looked up quickly, searched Martha's face, asked, 'What did he say he was doing?'

'Oh, nothing much, just that they'd met. My brother's with the South Africans.'

'This terrible, terrible war,' said Mrs Barbazon.

'Oh, they seem to be having a good enough time,' said Stella, with a careless laugh. Her face looked set for a moment; then she smiled at Esther, and began tickling her cheeks with the soft brush at the end of the braid.

'And how's Esther?'

Mrs Barbazon, smiling reminiscently, opened her mouth to give information. Stella cut in first with a story of how the child had crawled this morning across her bed. Mrs Barbazon said, 'You should let her sleep with me – you'd get some rest.'

'Oh, I've nothing else to do, and you're a good girl, aren't you, Esther?'

There was a silence. Martha felt the room oppressive. She could see that both women were devoting their lives to Esther; it was a close, jealous, watchful household.

'And are you having a good time?' asked Mrs Barbazon, in a way which told Martha they had been discussing her unfavourably.

'I've got my hands full with Caroline.'

'Oh, there's no time for anything else with a baby in the house.'

'I had a letter from Andrew last month,' said Stella casually. 'He says the boys up north are all demoralized because their wives and girlfriends are unfaithful to them with the Air Force.'

'It's a terrible thing,' said Mrs Barbazon, 'when our men are sacrificing everything to fight, and the women have no loyalty.'

Here there was an inexplicable long look between Mrs Barbazon and Stella; the older woman rose, and said, 'I'll make some tea, the servants are out.' She left the room with a small wistful smile in the direction of Esther.

As soon as her mother had left the room, Stella set the child on the floor and gave her attention to Martha. She asked if Caroline was walking yet; when Martha said yes, she said quickly that a year was early to be walking, from which Martha deduced that Esther had fallen behind schedule in her achievements.

Martha looked at Esther with detached criticism, in which was concealed the distaste that women feel for other women's babies while they are still closely physically linked with their own. Esther, she decided, was listless and heavy compared to the ceaselessly mobile Caroline.

Stella began talking of how she had had to wean the child after three months; her health had not permitted her to stand the strain of breast-feeding; as she spoke, she unconsciously felt her now plump breasts with both hands. 'Having babies ruins the figure, ruins it.' She looked over at Martha and said, 'You've lost the weight you put on.'

'I didn't lose it,' said Martha grimly, 'I starved it off.'

'Oh, I could never diet, I'm not strong enough. Anyway, Andrew always said he wished I was fatter.' Stella sighed, and her face fell into dissatisfied lines. The beautiful dark eyes looked strained and shadowed. The remote exotic gleam had gone; the seductive quality that Martha had so envied, that had showed itself in her every glance and movement, had completely vanished; she was a good-looking housewife, no more.

The doorbell rang. Stella's eyes gathered life; she half rose, then said, 'But I'm not dressed!'

'Leave it – I'll go,' said Mrs Barbazon from the kitchen.

Stella stood with her hands to her hair.

'You'd better get yourself dressed,' said Mrs Barbazon, as she came through to go to the door. There was a disapproving note in her voice which caused Martha to glance curiously at Stella.

A look of anger crossed Stella's face, then went. 'Oh, yes, I can't be seen like this,' she said, and went out quickly just before Mrs Barbazon came back with a young officer.

He was a big, bulky, fair-headed man, blue-eyed, Northern-looking. He sat down, while Mrs Barbazon moved and fussed about him. She sat down and began questioning him with the touching, self-immolating devotion which was what she offered to her daughter, about how the flying had gone yesterday, had he been sleeping better?

'Stella's just getting dressed. You know what things are with a baby in the house.'

The newcomer, reminded of the household's obligations, clucked at the baby. Mrs Barbazon, seeing him occupied, went out and quickly returned with a tea-waggon. She began pouring.

A gay voice was heard outside. 'Mother, where's my hair-brush?'

'I don't know,' Mrs Barbazon spoke sharply. She stood looking at the doorway, with the teapot held suspended in her hand. Stella, in a dress of apple-green linen which showed her apricot-coloured arms, was standing in the doorway, her loosened masses of hair about her face, apparently oblivious of the officer.

'Ah, there it is. Naughty Esther, you had it.' Stella reached for the hairbrush, holding back her heavy hair with one hand. 'Why, Rupert, is that you?'

Mrs Barbazon steadily poured tea, her lips compressed.

'You know how things get all over the place, with babies in the house,' said Stella with her jolly laugh. She stood in front of the big man, who had risen and was awkwardly facing her, and began brushing back the loads of glistening hair that slipped with a hiss over her shoulders. He could not keep his eyes off it. Her small smooth face emerged from the frame of falling hair, and Martha saw that the spirit of attraction had lit it again; Stella looked as she had done before the baby. She smiled and asked how he did, while he said, 'Fine, fine, thank you,' and his eyes followed the movement of the hair. She held the scene for a few moments longer; then, with a final swift toss of her head backwards, which flung the hair into an oiled, iridescent, dead-black curve, she said, 'Excuse me, I'll just finish dressing.'

The three sat and made conversation while the officer's

eyes rested on the door through which Stella had gone. She returned in a few moments, the black hair done up demurely in its heavy knot, and sat down near him. Little Esther began tugging at the green linen. Stella put her hands down once or twice, and then said hastily, 'Let's call the nurse – she can go out for a bit.'

Mrs Barbazon rose, picked up Esther, and went out. She did not return.

Martha soon got up and said she must go and feed Caroline.

At once Stella said, 'Do come and see us again, Matty. You're a naughty girl, forgetting your friends like this.' But she was looking at the officer even as she spoke; Martha felt something like pity for the big likeable man with the candid blue eyes.

Stella came with her to the door. 'He's a nice boy,' she remarked. 'We try and make him feel at home. It must be hard for them, so far from their families.'

Martha laughed. Stella looked at her, puzzled.

'He's a really nice boy. Mother says she feels towards him like a son,' she went on, smiling a small, dreamy and quite unconscious smile.

Martha urged Stella with false animation to visit her soon. Stella again berated Martha for being so unsociable. They exchanged urgent invitations for a few moments, and parted, disliking each other.

Martha was feeling extraordinarily foolish as she drove home. The reaction against Stella sent her back to Alice. The two women had in common a basic self-absorption that made it possible to forget each other for weeks and meet again easily without any embarrassment. They understood each other very well. They would seek each other out for the sole reason that they needed a safety valve; they would discuss in humorous, helpless voices, for an hour or so, their boredom, the tediums of living alone, the unsatisfactory nature of marriage, the burden of bringing up children, and part in the best of humours with the unscrupulous and buccaneering chuckle that came of being so ruthlessly disloyal to everything they were.

Then each retired again into isolation. Alice was half crazy with being alone. She was very thin, her hair hung limp about her face, she neglected her clothes. From time to time she exclaimed defiantly, 'Oh, to hell with everything,' and rang up Martha to say she was going out with the Air Force. Martha always assured her that this was the least of her rights. Alice pulled out an old dance dress, combed her hair back, scrawled some lipstick across her face. She then set herself to be the life and soul of whichever party she happened to be at. Returned to her flat by some ardent young man, she allowed herself to be kissed and caresssed for a while, as if she owed this to her self-respect, and then said, 'Oh, well, that's that – thanks for a lovely time.' With which she departed indoors, with a hasty apologetic wave. She never saw any young man for a second time. On these occasions Martha was likely to be rung up at three in the morning by Alice, who concluded her desperate, gay, rambling comments on the party by 'The point is, once you've been married there's no point in it. I don't enjoy anything any more.' And then, firmly: 'But if Willie thinks I'm going to sit at home weeping for him, he'd better think again, after what I heard he was up to!' With this, she let out her high fatalistic giggle, and wished Martha a good night.

Chapter Three

The airstrip was an irregular stretch of glistening white sand
in the dull-green bush. As the aircraft turned in to land, the
shadow of its wings dipped over an acre or so of tin-and-
brick bungalows. The soldiers in the aircraft peered down
past the tilting wings and suggested Lower Egypt, Abyssinia,
Kenya, Uganda. It seemed that they had all seen this shanty-
town in the bush many times before.

The aircraft bounced a little as it landed, then slewed to a
stop. A thick cloud of white dust drifted up. The door was
kept shut till it cleared. Then they descended – half a dozen
men on their feet. An ambulance was already motoring
across the half-mile between here and the red-brick shack
that was an office, to pick up the stretcher cases. The half-
dozen stood on one side hopefully while the stretchers were
slid inside the white car, but it drove off immediately. They
walked across the white glisten of the strip, sand giving with
a silken crunch beneath their boots, then through low dun-
coloured bushes towards the office. Small paper-white butterflies hovered over the bushes, or clung with fanning
wings. There was a hot, spicy smell of leaves. Over the
squashed remains of a chameleon, spreadeagled on the sand
like a small dragon's skin pegged out, was a thick black clot
of ants. A stray kaffir dog, his skeleton showing clear through
tight skin, lay in the pit of blue shade outside the veranda.
They stepped over the dog and went in.

It was a single room. A South African sergeant sat behind
a small deal table. A black man in a sort of orderly's uniform
stood at ease beside him. The sergeant was pouring a glass
of water from a bedroom decanter. He tipped back his head,

poured the water into his mouth, wiped his hand across his mouth, looked at them and said, 'So there you are.'

Douglas said half facetiously, 'Where are we, we'd like to know.'

The sergeant thought, concluded that the information could not subvert the course of the war, and offered cautiously, 'Nyasaland.'

The men exchanged startled, bitter glances. 'Pretty far from the front,' said Douglas, his face hard.

A quick glance from the sergeant. He said officially, 'Are you OK till you get into town? There's a car coming for you.'

He nodded at a bench set against the wall. They did not immediately sit down. They stood tense, looking at each other, at the sergeant.

'Sit down,' said the sergeant again, authoritative but uneasy.

They slowly walked over, dropped their packs by the wall, sat. Six men, all tough soldiers, very burnt, apparently fit for anything. Yet here they sat. They sat and waited with the patience which a year in the Army had taught them. Indeed, for that year they had done little else but wait. They had marched, drilled – and waited; slept under canvas or in the open – and waited; they had been told nothing, knew nothing. For the first time in their lives they had been *pushed around*; they were expected to wait. And now things were really happening up north, and they were back only a few hundred miles from home. They waited. The small brick room, unceilinged, was roofed with corrugated iron; the heat poured down. The brick at their backs burned through the thick khaki; they sat away and forward from the wall, looking out of the doorway into the sunlight. The aircraft looked like a small silver insect glittering off sunlight. It was apparently abandoned. A pair of hawks circled above on steady wings.

Douglas, at the end of the bench, blinked regularly out into the dazzle. Beside him sat Perry, legs sprawling in front of him, the big blond sun-reddened body tense. Douglas heard the breath coming fast and irregular, and glanced swiftly sideways; Perry was staring angrily at a map of

Africa nailed to the brick wall opposite. Arrows of black ink showed the offensives and counter-offensives in North Africa. Their unit was – so they believed – combining with the Australians against Rommel at that moment. Perry's mouth, when closed, was a hard, lipless line; when slightly open, as now, it had a spoilt and peevish droop.

Douglas muttered with warning cheerfulness, 'Hey, take it easy, man.'

Perry moved his legs, showing mats of wet hair on the reddened skin where they had adhered together. Sweat was dripping steadily off all of them. 'There's been a balls-up, a mucking balls-up.' The tone was one they all knew; legs shifted, bodies eased, all along the bench. The sergeant, seated behind his table, was writing a letter home, and did not look up.

Douglas got up, went to the table, reached out his hand, laid it on the decanter, and looked at the sergeant, who nodded briefly. Douglas took glass and decanter, and went along the line of men with it. Before he reached the end, the water was finished. He handed the decanter to the black orderly, who submerged it in a petrol tin covered with a wet sack that stood in a corner, and handed it back, dripping. The water hissed into the brick floor. Douglas returned the things to the table, and sat down again.

Perry's mouth and chin were wet with water. He raised his fist and rubbed it over the lower part of his face, then let it drop. The fist hung clenched. He banged it several times against the edge of the bench, and left it hanging. He looked at the map and said, 'They told us we'd be examined. They've balled us up. What are we doing in this God-damned dump?'

Douglas hastily agreed, 'Bloody mess,' and looked at him with entreaty.

Perry writhed his big body frustratedly and jumped up. He went rapidly to the table, snatched at the decanter as the sergeant instinctively jerked up his head, dived at the petrol tin, filled the decanter, and poured it all over his head and shoulders. The sergeant turned his head to watch, then went on writing. Perry dumped the decanter down under the man's nose.

'Oh, sit down, damn it,' the sergeant muttered uneasily.

Perry grinned slightly, and sat. They waited. The bricks hissed as the water sank in. Water dripped off Perry's neck and hair.

A lorry came bumping across the airstrip. But it swerved over to the aircraft. A couple of Africans got out, uncoiled a black hose, and began feeding petrol into it. The two hawks were now black specks high in the grey-blue air. The air between here and the aircraft swam in lazy hot waves. Then the aircraft began to shake. It turned, and trundled away up the strip for the take-off. They watched it turn and come roaring down the strip past them, and up. In a moment it was away over the trees, and its silver glitter was absorbed in the vast glitter of the sky. The two hawks continued to wheel on level wings.

'Mucking bastards, leaving us behind,' said Perry suddenly, and his voice cracked.

The sergeant's cheek muscles showed tense, but he went on writing fast.

Perry got to his feet with slow deliberation, and slouched over to the table. 'Sarge?'

The sergeant laid down his pen and looked at him. 'Steady on, man,' he said warningly, 'I'm not responsible for it.'

Perry, his face scarlet, his tunic soaked, drops of sweat and water scattering, leaned forward, suspending a big red, hairy fist over the table. 'I'm not going to be messed up,' he said, in a quiet voice.

'I'm not messing you up,' said the sergeant steadily. He looked past Perry to the bench, where the men sat watching. There were half-grins on their faces. The man at the far end, nearest the door, a lanky youth with a bony freckled face, was smiling hilariously. He looked as if he were about to cheer.

Douglas remained seated for a moment, but then got up and came forward, laying his hand on Perry's shoulder. 'Now, come on, man, don't take it out on him.' He sounded embarrassed.

Perry kept his shoulder still, then flung off the hand with a sudden heave. Douglas stood back a pace. Perry leaned both his fists on the table, and stared straight into the sergeant's face. 'I'm going to break everything up if I don't get some sense out of you.'

The table leaned over, the sergeant put his hands down to steady it, it slid roughly over the lumpy brick tight against the sergeant's stomach. He was now pinned back against the wall. The orderly stood, arms folded, watching with interest.

Perry deliberately pressed the table forward against the sergeant, who was pale and gasping, and trying to push it back again. 'You mucking pen-pushing bastard . . .' Using all his strength, he forced the edge of the table into the sergeant. Ink, pens, paper, glass, decanter, went rolling and crashing.

Douglas made a movement of his head towards the others. After a hesitation, three of them rose, leaving the cheerful boy alone, and came over. 'Now stop it, damn it, man,' said Douglas.

Perry gritted his teeth, and heaved. The sergeant had lost his footing, and was pinned in mid-air against the wall, straining for breath. His boots scraped wildly at the floor. Douglas nodded at the three; all four gripped Perry by the shoulders, with a sort of weary good humour, and pulled him back. A moment's scrape, struggle, heave – then Perry came staggering back, the sergeant found his feet, the table shot away. The sergeant stood blinking, trying to get back his breath without showing he had lost it. He smoothed down his tunic, pulled up the fallen chair, and sat down. He nodded at the African, who began picking up things off the floor.

'Look at him,' gasped out Perry, 'sitting there on his fat arse, pushing a pen.' He shook off his captors, who had their hands laid warningly on various parts of his upper body. He looked at them, grinning. They grinned sheepishly back. Then they all turned suddenly at the sound of a wild cry of laughter from the youth who had remained sitting. His face was flushed and incoherent, his eyes lit with a blue glare. He stamped his boots a few times on the floor, let out an

'Hurray!' and all at once sat looking at them doubtfully, as if he did not know them.

'For God's sake,' said Douglas in a rapid warning under-tone, 'he'll be off again.' Immediately, all five returned to their places on the bench, leaving a small space between the youth and the man next to him. Perry leaned back against the burning wall, and began a low hissing whistle between his teeth, to the tune of 'Begin the Beguine'. From time to time he banged his big fists on his knees, in a considering way. His mouth drooped slightly open; but he looked cautiously over the youth, who was now staring straight in front of him, his clear blue eyes clouded with wonder, at the map on the wall. The African was sweeping the mess of glass, ink, and water from the brick with a fibre broom. The sergeant sat moodily, arms folded on the table.

'I could have you court-martialled,' he observed bitterly at last.

No one said anything. Perry continued to hiss out 'Begin the Beguine'.

'I'd be within my rights to have you court-martialled,' insisted the sergeant.

'Discipline,' said Perry. 'Discipline is what this war needs.' He turned his big head slowly towards the sergeant. He surveyed him steadily.

'Oh, for God's sake,' said Douglas impatiently. 'Don't start again.'

The sergeant glanced involuntarily through the square in the wall that called itself a window, and exclaimed, 'Your car's coming.' His voice was eager with relief.

Perry lapsed back against the wall, his lips stretched in a small ugly grin.

A large army lorry stopped outside. The soldiers stood up, stretching themselves. When the distracted youth did not move, the man nearest to him unceremoniously heaved him up: he stood for a while, vaguely looking, then began with hasty officious movements to straighten his clothes and arrange his pack.

A young woman leaped down from the driver's seat, landing with a skid in the white sand, and came forward.

She was clumsy in khaki, her cap on the back of her head, wisps of pale damp hair hanging beside her face.

At once Douglas let out a whoop, and began thumping her on her shoulders, while she stiffened herself, laughing, saying, 'Hey, hey, steady now, boys.' They crowded around her; she was one of the girls from the Sports Club. They had played hockey with her, danced with her, made love to her all through their glorious youth. 'It's fine to see you here, Bobby,' said Douglas. She received their kisses on her offered cheek.

She was a rather tall, lumpish girl, with pale fatty cheeks which were stained wild pink in patches from the heat. Her grey eyes were slightly protuberant. She had acquired a mannish stride and a new hearty voice. 'Well, pile in, boys.' She made a half-serious salute to the sergeant – who returned a grin and a nod – and turned towards the lorry. 'Here, aren't you coming?' she shouted cheerfully at the youth, who had sat himself down again on the bench, and was watching the proceedings from a distance. Douglas significantly tapped his head, and she gave a stare of startled distaste at the youth. One of them went back, helped him to his feet, and came with him to the back of the lorry. He was heaved in. Bobby, Perry and Douglas stood beside the front seat.

'What the hell are you doing in this dump?' asked Douglas. 'We heard you'd got up north.'

'Join the Army and see the world. If I'd known I'd land in this mucking hole . . . But they're sending me up north next month, this bleeding place is being closed down.' This slightly hoarse, good-fellow's voice, the way she carefully seasoned in her obscenities, caused Douglas and Perry to involuntarily exchange a look.

Perry suddenly remarked, 'For Christsake, we haven't seen a woman in months.' He sounded injured.

Bobby's pale cheeks crimsoned irregularly. She looked at them in appeal. Douglas, embarrassed for her, said quickly, 'It's pretty good to see an old pal here, Bobby.' She looked now in gratitude, then turned away, and climbed up into the cab. Douglas was about to climb up beside her, when Perry laid his arm across, like a barrier, and grinned at him fiercely. For a moment Douglas glared. Then he smiled, let out a short laugh, and said, 'Go ahead.'

Perry hoisted himself up beside the girl, shouting down, 'You'll be seeing your wife tomorrow.'

Douglas looked annoyed. He said through his teeth, 'You'd better let up, Perry, I've just about had enough of you.'

Ever since Perry had been officially informed that he had an ulcer, he had been breaking out. Douglas had been watching over him like a father. It was his turn to feel injured. He walked moodily back to the end of the lorry, and jumped in. There was no window between the back of the lorry and the driver's seat. But they could all hear Bobby's loud boisterous laugh, increasingly uneasy, as the lorry turned, bumped across the bush-covered sand, found the strip, raced along it at sixty and, with a swerve that sent them sprawling, turned on to a rough track that wound through the bush. They were silent, crouching with their backs against the sides of the lorry, holding tight as it bounced and rocketed. The youth with the wild eyes had stiffened himself and was glaring at them all in turn. They were all afraid of him and ashamed to be afraid. The trees were growing thinner, and shacks of brick and tin flashed past. Then it was a proper street, tarmac, where the heat coiled and quivered, and stretches of whitish sand on either side; then Indian stores and native eating houses. Now they were in a broad empty space of dust, whose surface eddied and stirred. There was a biggish new white building, with a couple of jacaranda trees shading it. The lorry stopped with a jolt. They swore angrily under their breaths as they banged themselves on the sides. Bobby's loud and boisterous voice invited them to descend. They did so in silence.

Under one of the trees a native woman sat in the dust, draped in red cloth. She was suckling her baby. She looked at them indifferently. Some dogs lay stretched under the other tree, looking as if they were dead. The men stood in a group around Bobby; she seemed hot and flustered, and would not look at Perry, who was grinning savagely.

'Now, who's got what wrong with them?' she inquired. 'We've got stomach and respiratory separate.'

They all laughed disgustedly.

'For crying out loud,' said Perry. 'What, two beds each?'

'Well, Perry,' said Douglas, 'we're together.' They stood off to one side.

Bobby looked at the other four. 'What's wrong with you?' Their faces tightened. 'Oh, very well,' she said hastily. 'I'll show you where to go. Perry and Douglas – over there, that house there. The doctor'll come over.' She quickly turned her back on Perry, and went off with her four into the big building, the youth lagging behind and looking around him suspiciously.

Perry and Douglas crossed the dust towards a small wire-enclosed house. 'Bloody skirts,' said Perry.

'Oh, go on,' said Douglas awkwardly. 'She's a nice kid.'

Perry spat and began whistling between his teeth.

The shack had a veranda closed in by greenish gauze. It was raised; three red cement steps led to the gauze door. On the steps sat a native orderly. He sprang up and stood to one side, quivering at attention. Perry heaved his shoulder dispassionately into the man's chest without looking at him, swung open the door and went in. The man saved himself from falling by clutching at the door-frame, nimbly straightened himself, and sat down on the steps, brushing whitish patches of dust from his khaki. He reached out for his hand piano where it had fallen beside the steps, and began playing it.

Inside on the veranda were four iron beds covered with neatly folded red blankets. There was no one in sight. Behind the veranda was a single room with a table and a chair in it. On the table stood a glass jar with some thermometers slanting up.

Douglas slung his pack on to one of the beds, took off his boots, and lay down on another, closing his eyes.

Perry heaved his pack beside the other, and let himself down flat on his back, his dusty boots side by side on the blanket. He waited, hands behind his head, a dangerous immobility about him.

It was about two in the afternoon. They had landed four hours ago. No one came. The expanse of dust outside the green gauze remained empty. Half a dozen native women came past with their children, chattering in their shrill voices. From a big msasa tree that shaded the veranda a pigeon was cooing regularly. The iron roof cracked in the heat. The hand piano tinkled.

'For crying out loud,' began Perry suddenly.

Douglas hastily opened his eyes, swung his legs down, said, 'I'll see if they can get us a bite.' He called the native orderly. 'Hey, Jim, where's the doctor?'

The orderly pointed at the other building cheerfully.

'Can you get us something to eat?'

'Yes, baas. Right away, baas.'

He went through into the inner room, through that into the back. Silence again. The pigeon cooed on and on.

He came back with a tin tray. Fried eggs, bacon, fried bread. Perry raised himself, looked at it, looked at him.

'We have ulcers,' he said. 'Ulcers – diet – no fat.' He flipped his hand up against the tray. It jerked, the plates slid, the orderly caught at it, steadied the plates into their pattern, turned his back and was staring out through the green gauze at the sky.

'Can you boil us some eggs?' asked Douglas quickly.

'Boiled eggs? Yes, baas, right away, baas.' The orderly went out with the tray at a half-run.

Perry did not move. He was looking at an officer walking across the dust towards them, who came up the steps, pushed the door open impatiently, then carefully closed it behind him. Perry turned himself over in one movement, and lay looking at him. Douglas, who had been going to salute, stood up, then sat down again.

'You're the ulcers, are you?'

'That's me,' said Perry. 'Just one big ulcer.'

'Sorry I didn't get over before – was fixing those other chaps.' He sat down on the edge of Douglas's bed, and looked at them. He was rather slight, with rough fair hair, grey straight eyes. He was reddened and sweating.

'You're English,' remarked Perry.

'Yes, I am actually.'

Perry turned on his back and lay looking at the iron roof.

The doctor smiled rather tiredly and said, 'Well, how are things where you've come from?'

'Read the newspapers?' asked Perry.

'Pretty bad,' said Douglas.

The doctor glanced at Perry quickly, then more slowly at Douglas.

'When am I going to be examined?' asked Perry dangerously.

'There's been a bit of a balls-up,' said Douglas apologetically. 'We shouldn't be here.'

'What happened?'

'Well, it's like this – '

But Perry swung over again, and poked his head forward at the doctor: 'He's got it in for me. I'll get him when the war's over, I'm warning you. Officer – well, he won't be an officer when the war's over, he'll be my junior clerk.' He dropped his head back again, and let his two fists dangle on each side of the narrow bed. They swayed back and forth over the floor.

'How about sleeping for a bit?' said the doctor. 'Then we'll talk about it.'

'I'm not going to sleep. I'm going to be examined – now.'

Douglas again smiled his small apology. Perry's sideways flickering eyes caught the smile. 'And I'll get you too, Douggie old pal. Arse-licker, that's all you are. Always were.'

Douglas yellowed, but kept his steady, rather nervous smile.

The doctor sat in thought. He sighed unconsciously. Of the four men in the other building, three had threatened him and the commanding officers, then broken down and wept. Secret cabals of influence worked against them; life itself had it in for them. But he, Doc, was a good type who understood them. He had given them sedatives, and tomorrow they would go home with battle fatigue. The crazy youth had been quite amenable, then suddenly began climbing out of the window, shouting that he would kill himself. He was now under guard. He was all in line with what the doctor knew and could handle. But he could not understand these colonials, so tough, masculine, violent – and then the sudden collapse into self-pity. It seemed a well of self-pity lay in all of them, ready to overflow at any moment. Caught by accident in South Africa at the beginning of the war, he had been with South Africans all the time. They every one of them got drunk or broke down at some stage or another and confessed to a vast grievance against life. Extraordinary, he thought, remarkable. He looked at Douglas, and considered. Douglas filled him with confidence. He looked a round, humorous, cheerful soldier of a man; the round good-natured face was frankly boyish. The doctor felt he could rely on him. He turned to him and asked, 'Tell me what happened?'

Perry stiffened, rolled his eyes sideways, but did not move.

'Well, I've had trouble with my stomach off and on for years,' said Douglas, with a wary look at the braced Perry. 'It flares up from time to time. I had a sudden bad go last week. Usually I just shut up about it and diet myself as well as you can on army food. But it was a really bad go – they got me into hospital. I'd only been there half an hour when orders came to evacuate. I was never examined. They flew a bunch of us down to the next town. We were evacuated from there again almost at once. The next thing was, we were all shoved on to a plane, and here we are. I'm sure I could carry on in the Army. I'm quite fit apart from the ulcer, and it's not bad.' He ended on a frank appeal.

'You can't feed an ulcer in the Army,' said the doctor pleasantly. 'And you're better out.'

Douglas's mouth was bitter. 'No one examined me, I was just pushed off.' Suddenly the lips quivered. He turned away, blinking. God help us! thought the doctor, astounded – here it is again.

Perry had slowly risen, was sitting on the edge of his bed. 'Hey, what about me? What about me, Doc?' He rose, fists clenched.

Deliberately ignoring him, the doctor said to Douglas, 'Get

inside a minute, I'll call you.' He was embarrassed at what he was going to do.

Douglas hesitated, then rose, then stood still. He was staring like a child at the doctor. At last he turned and stumbled indoors.

Perry, crouching low, was on the point of springing at the doctor.

'Damn it,' said the doctor easily, 'take it easy, now.' His voice was deliberately kind, paternal.

Perry quivered all over, then sat. His lower lip, thrust out aggressively, worked. Tears sprang from his eyes. The doctor moved over and put a hand on his shoulder. Perry seemed to swell, then subsided. The doctor sat beside him, arm lightly across his shoulder, and began to talk, in a low, persuasive voice.

Douglas, standing behind the gauze door, looking suspiciously out, was amazed and upset at the scene. Then he turned away, and sat on the table inside. He could still hear the doctor's almost maudlin voice soothing Perry like a child. He could hear Perry heaving up great sobs and complaining that the officer had it in for him, the sergeant had it in for him, he'd never had a chance.

The back door cautiously opened; the orderly's head came around it. He came in with a tray of boiled eggs, and laid it before Douglas. Seeing a dangerous gleam in Douglas's fixed blue stare, he hastily slipped out again.

The sentimental murmuring had ceased. Douglas looked out. Perry was lying face down on the red blankets. His fists, hanging down each side of the bed, were being banged slowly and with method on the floor – there was a streak of blood on the knuckles. The doctor was standing upright, filling a syringe against the light. Then he swiftly bent, jabbed the needle into Perry's forearm, and moved quickly back: he expected Perry to attack him. But Perry was whimpering, face down, 'You're a good chap, Doc, thank you, Doc.'

Douglas saw the doctor shut his eyes, sigh, and open them again, as he stood motionless, syringe in hand. If he sticks that thing into me I'll kill him, thought Douglas. But the doctor dismantled the syringe and put it away. Then he stood up and braced himself: there was still Douglas. He came into the inner room. Douglas stood waiting for him belligerently.

'He'll sleep for a couple of hours and then he'll be all right,' said the doctor cheerfully.

'You're sending us home?' began Douglas, standing square in front of him.

The doctor suddenly snapped, 'Yes, I am. I'm sick to death of the lot of you. You've no right to be in the Army in the first place. How did you get in? Told a lot of lies, I suppose. Bloody clever.' He paused, and added, 'Hundreds of pounds spent on you, you crack at the first strain, and you have to be sent back home. What do you think this is, a picnic?'

Douglas looked at him incredulously. Seeing the familiar swelling and reddening, the working lower lip, the doctor snapped, 'Oh, shut up, shut up, shut up — go to hell and shut up.'

'Who's in charge here?' said Douglas after a pause, the official in him coming to the rescue.

The doctor stared, laughed angrily, and said, 'You can go and see Major Banks if you like — he's over there.' He pointed at the building opposite, picked up his case, and went out past Perry without looking at him. He strode across the dust and vanished into the building. Douglas looked at the eggs; he was unconsciously grinding his teeth. Then he followed the doctor out.

A deep shady veranda surrounded the main building; off it rooms opened. Inside one of them sat Major Banks under a spinning electric fan, dealing with piles of papers. He looked up, irritated, as Douglas strode in, slamming the door. His eyes narrowed. Douglas stopped in the middle of the room, saluted hastily, came forward.

'Well, Doug, how are you?' said the Major, rising and holding his hand out over the table. Douglas shook it. They had known each other for years. 'Sit down.' Douglas sat. He was looking at the papers, the files, the ink banks, the paper clips: the fetters from which he had escaped.

'The doctor's been talking to me about you,' said Major Banks.

Douglas allowed himself a bitter smile. But he accepted a cigarette with a 'Thank you, sir.'

Major Banks was a lean, fibrous, olive-skinned man, with very keen, bright, light-blue eyes: they looked odd in that burnt face. 'Active service's out, Doug,' he said finally. 'But if you want me to fix you up on the administrative side, I'll do it.'

'Thanks,' said Douglas with hostility.

'You're wise. I'll be spending the rest of the war in happy spots like this one – nice prospect.'

'If I've got to sit behind a desk I'd rather do it at home.'

'They should never have let you go, anyway. I know your chief was sick when you left.'

'They didn't let me go. I worked a point,' said Douglas, grinning proudly.

'So I gathered,' said the Major drily. He added, 'How's your wife – she'll be glad to see you.'

'Oh, she's fine, fine,' said Douglas proudly. 'We've a kid, did you know?'

'Lucky chap. Well – perhaps you'll join me for a drink later.'

'Alcohol's out – I've got an ulcer.'

'Bad luck.' The Major picked up some papers.

Douglas rose. He saluted; the Major casually, half jocular, returned it. As Douglas reached the swing doors, someone started shouting from a room near by. He stopped. The sound was disturbing for a reason he could not define.

'That's your pal, Simmons,' said the Major. 'He's gone clean off his rocker. Still, it's just as well to get the crocks out of the way before the fighting starts.'

Douglas went red. He looked with helpless affront at the oblivious Major, now bent over his papers. The shouting stopped. Silence. He slammed the door again, walked out across the square and entered the little gauze-covered house. Perry was lying face downwards, exactly as he had been, the unclenched hands knuckled loose on the floor. He was deeply asleep. The native orderly was back on the steps with his hand piano. The soft, brooding, tinkling melodies went on and on together with the pigeon's cooing. Douglas sat on the edge of his bed and sank into thought. His mouth was dry with loss. It seemed to him that everything he had ever wanted was being snatched from him. All his adult life he had sat in an office; now after a year's brief reprieve he was being sent back to it. He could see his future life stretching ahead, nothing unexpected, nothing new from one year's end to the next. Holidays every five years or so, retirement, death. He felt like an old man.

The year of discomfort and boredom in the Army was already arranging itself in a series of bright scenes, magical with distance. He thought of the men whom he had known all his life, been to school with, worked with, played with, now up north in 'the real thing' at last. It seemed that his whole life had led without his knowing it to the climax of being with those men, his fellows, his friends, parts of himself, in real fighting, real living, real experience at last. And he was out of it. A few days before it started, he had been kicked out. A crock, he thought bitterly.

His eyes rested on Perry, sprawled out loose a couple of feet away. There was something childish about those big open fists resting on their knuckles on the floor, something appealing and childish about the closed lids fringed with sandy lashes. Tenderness, a warm protectiveness, filled him. He thought, He'll have a stiff neck lying like that. He got up, and, using all his strength, turned the big man over on his back. He was winded when he'd achieved it. He stood up, panting. His eyes were wet; he'd be out of uniform in a couple of days. Never again would he know the comradeship of men. Never. Never. He shut his eyes to steady himself. He opened them at last and looked out. It was very still out there. Thick black shadows lay stretched over the sand now. A couple of scraggy hens scratched below the steps. The orderly had dropped off to sleep, sprawled over the steps, the hand piano hanging from his fingers.

The insignificant, dreary little dorp seemed to him what he was returning to – this would be his life now. There stirred a small thought of Martha; he let it die again, and a pang of fondness for her went with it. What he felt for Martha was nothing, nothing at all compared with his year among soldiers. Rage filled him. He was filled with a need to tear, to destroy – he stood still, fists clenching and unclenching, his mind teeming images of destruction. Next morning he would be put on the plane home; he would step straight off the plane into domesticity and the office from eight to four.

A sharp pain stabbed in his stomach; he remembered he had an obligation towards himself. He went inside, and spooned out two of the cold wet eggs on to bread, and began to eat the insipid mess with disgust. He saw a pepper pot standing on the tray, and shook pepper violently all over the eggs, with a savage delight in disobeying prohibitions. Feeling slightly sick at last, he went back to the veranda, thinking he might sleep. Then he saw across the square a black-lettered sign on a small store: 'Joseph's Bar'.

He walked over and went in.

A fat, pale Greek youth was wiping glasses behind the bar. There was no one else in the place. Douglas asked for ginger beer and sat down. There was a single round table against the wall opposite the bar counter, with half a dozen upright wood chairs around it. In peacetime an occasional merchant or government official passed through; the bar was used by them and the local storekeepers.

Douglas took a mouthful of the prickly tepid ginger beer and let it stand. A loud offhand voice was heard just out of sight. Then Bobby came slowly past the open doorway. Her pale hair was now tidy, and bobbing up at the ends. She did not look in. Douglas called out, 'Hey there, Bobby.' She gave a start, but began to smile before she saw him. Douglas grinned proudly at the thought that she must have watched him enter the bar.

She came in and sat down. She was flushed with the heat. She asked for a whisky, and Douglas's mouth filled unpleasantly as she began sipping it. Then she crossed her legs, blew out smoke, and fixed her pale-grey eyes attentively on him. The top buttons of her tunic were undone. Under it he could see a thin pink strap, rather grubby, loose on her shoulder. He felt a mixture of tenderness and repulsion at the sight.

'So you've had it – bad luck,' she remarked in the jocular loud voice which she had decided was suitable to her role as female soldier. But she looked sympathetic.

Douglas began to talk. After a while she asked after Martha. He produced photographs. Caroline stood on two sturdy legs smiling attractively up at her father from the small card square.

'That's a fine kid,' Bobby said sentimentally, and refixed her eyes on his at once. In her attitude was something touchingly devotional. She appeared to be saying that she was completely at his service.

She ordered a second whisky. His ginger beer was still nearly full. He almost succumbed, and then said, 'I'd better be strong-minded, hey?'

'That's the ticket,' she said. 'Mucking bad luck.'

It grated on him; he thought of Martha as a contrast. But the thought of Martha was not balm at all. The truth was, he had been relieved to get away from the atmosphere of bottles and napkins, and, more than this, from Martha's extraordinary tension during those months, when competent gaiety followed irritated exhaustion, and both seemed in some subtle way a criticism of him. But a more recent doubt was working in him. 'Heard any news from home?' he asked her casually.

'Lazy sods, they don't write. But I got a letter from Bogie – you remember Bogie? She says she's having a wonderful time with the boys from Home.'

Douglas said with a quick laugh, 'Yes, they all seem to be giving it stick, all right.' But his gaze still rested on her face with persistent suspicious inquiry, and she went on:

'I heard that Bella's marrying the Air Force, old Sam's breaking his heart over it.'

'Pretty bad show, that.'

'I heard news of Matty, come to think of it. She was at a dance at the air camp.'

'Oh, yes, she told me about it,' he said with an effort, frowning.

'Matty was always one for the boys. Lucky Matty, she hasn't got a figure like a sack of potatoes,' she said, and laughed painfully.

'Oh, you do fine,' he responded after a pause. He looked unhappily round. 'I think I'll be a devil and have a drink,' he said. He went over to the fat silent Greek, who polished glasses and watched these evidences of world war with an unquenchable curiosity. He fetched back two whiskies.

'Here's to the Army,' he said with quiet misery. He drained his down, and sat grinning at her. 'Well, I'm all right, how are you doing, are you all right?'

She drained her third quickly, and responded to the rallying call. 'Oh, I'm all right, I'm fine, are you all right?'

He took the two glasses to the counter to be refilled. She watched him, smiling maternally. He came back and this time sat in the chair next to her. 'Let's give it a bang. Let's give it stick.'

'Oh, you're a crazy kid.'

She began questioning him again about up north, with an eager determination to hear every detail, prompting him when he hesitated on the edge of something he would normally gloss over for a woman. It was as if she were taking part by proxy. She listened, her pale-pink lips slightly open in a wistful greed. At first he was gruffly disapproving, then he let it go and softened to her. Poor old Bobby, she was having a bad time in this dorp, she was a nice kid.

A shadow fell over them. Perry stood at the door, stooping inwards. Behind him the sun was sending up a last wild flare of red into the soft grey sky. The dust expanse had shrunk and dimmed. A group of Africans walking through had a soft and distant look in this thin light, and their voices were high and excited: they were hurrying to get indoors before the night came down.

Perry looked at them. Douglas noted that he was rather yellow, his eyes were inflamed, but he seemed quiet enough. He looked at the whiskies and said, 'That's an idea.' He went to the bar, nodded at the Greek, drained his glass with slow determined thirst, handed the glass back. He leaned on his elbow watching them. He took his second glass and stood there holding it for a while untasted, while the Greek took an oil lamp off the iron hook suspended from a rafter in the middle of the room, removed the glass funnel, lit the wick, fitted back the funnel, and hung the lamp up again. It swung steadily. A drop of paraffin dropped to the brick floor, then another. The smell of paraffin was strong.

The Greek returned to the other side of the counter. Perry still leaned there considering the seated couple, as if from a long distance. He looked very handsome beside the pale, fat youth with his sad olive-coloured eyes; conventionally handsome — square-jawed, hard-mouthed, strong. He was looking now direct at Bobby, and she shifted uncomfortably under it, fiddling with her bobs of pale hair.

'Come and sit down, man, damn it,' said Douglas.

Perry at once came across and sat down, as if he had needed an invitation. He gazed steadily at Bobby until she met his eyes.

'So you'll be going on up north?'

'Yes, next month.'

'Following the Army?'

'That's my job.'

'Nice work if you can get it.'

She gave a nervous look at Douglas, who laughed and said, 'Come off it, Perry man.'

Perry laughed, a calculated silent heave from his chest, and fingered his glass while he looked at Bobby. She had wriggled her chair an inch nearer to Douglas, but she was looking, fascinated, over at Perry and she was flushed.

The orderly came in, addressing Perry and Douglas equally. 'Baas, shall I bring your dinner here?'

'Get out,' said Perry.

'It's OK, Jim,' said Douglas quickly.

The man backed and vanished into the now thick dusk.

'What've you got to eat?' said Perry loudly to the barman.

'We don't cook.'

'So, you don't?'

'There's the mess. Since the war started there's been only the Army.'

Perry's jaw was thrust out. Seeing it, Douglas appealed,

'Couldn't you do us something? We're fed to the teeth with army grub.'

The Greek hesitated.

'I want roast chicken, roast potatoes, vegetables, and some jam tart,' said Perry. He looked steadily over the bar.

The Greek said, 'I'll go and ask my father.' He hurried out.

'Ruddy dago,' said Perry. 'Bad as kaffirs.' He lifted his glass. 'Here's to Civvy Street.'

They all drank. Douglas looked over at Bobby with a tinge of grave reproach. The thread of sympathy that had held them was snapped. She could not take her eyes off Perry. Douglas moved his chair back to the wall, and comforted his glass between both hands. He was beginning to feel the alcohol.

Bobby took a moment's alarm at being left to Perry. She drank hastily, and spilled some. Perry reached out his large paw and brushed drops off her shoulders. She shrank away.

'Well, and how's the war been treating you?' he asked, on a personal, insulting note.

'Oh, fine, fine. But it's mucking boring here, though.'

'Mucking bad luck, muck everything, hey? You should meet the Ities. They've got a far wider range. You should hear their language when they get going. Shouldn't she, Douggie?'

Douglas looked away, dissociating himself.

'You mucking well should meet the bleeding Ities, then you wouldn't have to restrict yourself to bleeding mucking.'

She looked at him with a helpless fascination still, and let out her short gruff laugh.

'Let up, man,' said Douglas again, disgusted. 'Stop it.'

Perry took no notice. 'Still, you've not done too badly here, there's the Major and the doctor and the sergeant.'

She took his direct gaze and said, 'You don't do too badly, either. There's nothing you can tell me about what the boys do away from their wives.'

'But I'm not married, so that's all right. Thank God. She'd be lining the beds of the Air Force.'

She forced out another laugh. He leaned forward, gripped

her wrist and said, 'Remember Christmas night three years ago at the Club – remember?'

'And so what?' she said, laughing.

He released her, frowned and said softly, 'We had a good time then, didn't we?'

'Those were the days,' said Douglas, half jocular, half wistful; they instinctively lifted their glasses to the good old days. Then Perry reached out his enormous arm over the bar, tilted the whisky bottle standing on it, caught it as it heeled, and brought it triumphant to the table.

The young Greek entered with a tray. Roast beef sandwiches, mustard pickles, Marie biscuits, Cheddar cheese. He set it before them and retired silently behind the bar.

'Have some roast chicken,' said Douglas cheerfully.

They ate. Perry, steadily watching Bobby over his busy knife and fork, began reminiscing about the bang they'd had this night last week. Douglas played along with him. When it came to how Perry and half a dozen Australians had wrecked the brothel, Douglas smiled uneasily, but Bobby was laughing her good-fellow laugh. Perry stopped, and said disgustedly to Douglas, 'What do you think, she'd have liked to be there.' He leaned over, pushed his face against hers and said, 'So you'd have liked to be with us, hey?'

She pulled back her head, and said, 'Oh, cut it out, Perry, you're getting me down.'

'Nice girl,' he remarked companionably to the roof. 'Nice girl, this one.'

Douglas leaned over to her, and whispered, 'If you want to make your escape, then go, Bobby. He's been kicked out of the Army, that's all that's wrong with him.'

She turned a small, rather offended smile. 'I know, poor kid.' She at once drew back towards Perry. Her lips were parted. She passed the tip of a pink tongue across them.

Perry was looking at the doctor, who had just come in. The doctor nodded at them all, and stood by the bar.

'Come and join us, Doc,' said Douglas.

'Thanks, but I'm on duty.' He asked for a brandy, and stood leaning by the bar, watching Perry. He said nothing, however.

'How are the boys, Doctor?' asked Bobby, one professional to another.

'Bedded them all down for the night. The plane's leaving at six tomorrow morning.' He looked steadily at Perry and Douglas.

Perry ostentatiously tilted back his glass, emptied it, filled it again.

'Six o'clock,' said the doctor sharply. 'And anyone who's not ready can spend another three weeks here. If that tempts you.'

'We'll be ready, Doc,' said Douglas.

The three were set in hostile defiance against him; they were looking at him across a barrier of half-drunkenness.

'Parsons everywhere,' said Perry to Bobby intimately. 'Have you noticed it? Everywhere you go in this world – parsons. Hate their guts. Only to smell a parson half a mile away gives me guts-ache.'

She looked apologetically but defiantly at the doctor.

'An English parson – they breed them in England.' Perry jumped up, and grabbed her wrist. 'Come for a walk?'

She hesitated, then rose, brushing down her tunic. He flung down four pound notes on the table, and pulled her by the wrist after him onto the veranda. Outside there was a steady beam of moonlight.

Douglas watched Perry and Bobby walk unsteadily over to the gauze veranda opposite, heard the gauze door slam. He looked pathetically at the doctor. 'Let's have a party, Doc,' he said. 'Come on, Doc, let's give it stick.'

'Sorry. I've got a raving lunatic on my hands tonight. I don't know quite . . . If I send him down on the plane with you tomorrow' – he looked, exasperated, at Douglas – 'surely five of you ought to be able to look after one boy like that. He'll be under drugs.'

'Oh, let him cut his ruddy throat,' said Douglas cheerfully. 'Who cares? Do you care? Do I care? No one cares.' He reached out his arm to stop the doctor as he went past. 'Come on, Doc, let's all cut our throats.'

'If I were you, I'd get myself to bed,' said the doctor from the doorway, with a harassed but pleasant grin. 'For God's sake – you'll be in hospital if you drink like that.'

"Who cares?' began Douglas again. 'Do you care ...' But the doctor had gone. Douglas turned his head carefully and focused at the Greek. 'Do you care?' he asked him.

The Greek grinned unhappily.

'Come and have a drink.'

The young man hesitated, then came over.

'Sit down, man, sit down.'

He sat, and poured himself a drink.

'Are you married?'

'No, I've got a girl at home.'

'Where's home?'

'Greece,' said the Greek apologetically.

'You don't want to get married – what do you want to get married for?' Douglas laid his fist on the shoulder opposite him and thumped it. The Greek continued to grin, watching him uneasily.

'Nothing but bitches, all of them.'

'I'm not married – sir.' In a country where all white men are equal there are perpetual problems of etiquette.

'Call me Douggie.' He kneaded the fat young shoulder a little more, then held both hands around his glass and stared in front of him. 'What's your name?' he inquired at last, with difficulty.

'Demetrius.'

'Fine name, that, very fine name.' He lapsed away into a glass-eyed stare, then recovered himself. 'Let me show you my wife,' he said, fumbling with his breast pocket. 'I've the finest wife in the whole of Africa.' He produced a wallet and dropped a bunch of snaps on the wet table. 'Tck, tck, tck,' he clicked his tongue reproachfully. 'Now, now, Douggie, that's very clumsy.' He fished a photograph of Martha out of a pool of whisky, and laid it before the Greek. Martha, in shorts and a sweatshirt, had the sun in her eyes and was trying to smile.

Demetrius courteously pulled out his wallet, and laid on the table a snap of a dark beauty sitting on a rock and dangling her feet in a pool. She and Martha lay side by side while the two men concentrated on them.

'You've got a fine wife, I've got a fine wife, we've both got fine wives,' pronounced Douglas. He hiccupped and said, 'Excuse me, I'm going to be sick.' He got up, and went out to the veranda, holding on to the wall.

When he came back, the Greek was back behind the counter, and the table in the corner was wiped clean. Douglas sat, looked about, finally located him and said, 'You've gone. They've all gone.'

'It's getting late, sir.'

'I want to have a party,' said Douglas obstinately. His eyes swam, focused together on a bit of white on the floor. He bent, retrieved the snap of Martha from beside his feet, wiped it back and front on his tunic and put it into his top pocket. He remained sitting and swaying. He stared at the wall and blinked.

Demetrius wiped a few more glasses. Then he went out. In a moment he came back with himself twenty years older. The two Greeks conferred for a moment, then the father came over and said, 'You'd better get to bed, sir.'

'I'm staying here!' The table jumped as Douglas crashed his fist down.

'But we're closing the bar. I'll help you across to bed, sir.'

'I'm staying here. I can't go to bed, because my best friend is in bed with my wife.' His lower lip swelled and trembled.

The two men looked at each other, at him, and shrugged. Demetrius reached up and turned down the lamp. They went out. Douglas let his head fall forward on to his arms. His arms slipped forward until the upper half of his body lay over the table. It was now dark in the bar. A dim square of moonlight lay on the floor. It moved slowly back towards the door, slipped through the gauze and became one with the blaze of moonlight outside.

Later, Demetrius came in wearing striped pyjamas, carrying a candle. He shook Douglas twice. Then he left him, closing the gauze door with a simple hook on the inside, and sliding over a heavy door of wood.

A few minutes later Douglas sat up. It was very dark, and

rather chilly. His head was clear again. He shook the wooden door in its groove, then went to the window. It was shut on the inside with a hasp and a hook. He fumbled at it a little; raised his fist and smashed it into the glass. A low tinkle came from outside. He heaved his shoulder into the pane; it flew out. He fell out with it and rolled over on to the earth four feet below. He got up unhurt under a big tree that filtered moonlight all over him. He turned himself till he faced the small gauze house, and concentrated on getting his feet to take him there. There was a small yellow glimmer coming from inside it. Overhead the moon was a great sheet of silver light. He gained the steps, climbed them, pulled open the gauze door, went in. It was light. Moonlight lay like white sand over his bed. On the one next to it he could see Perry's big body. It was in movement. He went through into the inner room.

The orderly was sitting drowsing at the table. His head was nodding and swaying over a book. Douglas focused his aching eyes to see what the book was. It was a child's reading primer, soiled and dog-eared, open at a page with a cheap coloured picture of spring lambs frisking on an English meadow and a little yellow-haired girl offering them some pink flowers. The large clear print opposite said: 'Mai-sie is six. Mai-sie likes to go for a walk in the spring mea-dow. She loves the lit-tle lambs. They love her. When Mai-sie gets home, she will do her lessons. Mai-sie works hard at her les-sons. She can read. She can write. Mai-sie lives in a cottage on the hill near a sheep-fold. Her fa-ther is a police-man.'

'Poor sod,' remarked Douglas aloud, with a mixture of compassion, contempt, and a sort of twisted envy.

A small cheap alarm clock on the table said it was half past eleven. He had slept for about two hours.

He went back to the veranda. He sat on his bed. Perry was murmuring with sentimental exasperation, 'Oh, come on, give us a break, kid, give us a break, kid.' Bobby, invisible except for one khaki-covered arm lying across his shoulder, was quite silent. A hand, fat and very white in the moon-light, looked innocent and pathetic.

It gave Douglas vindictive pleasure that matters were not going entirely to Perry's satisfaction.

After a while he felt his head roll; he let himself fall over on the bed and was asleep at once.

He knew he was dreaming unpleasantly. There was danger in the dream. He was in the aircraft with Perry. Perry was at the controls. They were at an immense height. Looking down, he saw pretty rivers, peaceful green fields. That was England. Then he saw a tall brown purplish mountain. That was Africa. It was important to keep them separate. He saw that Perry was hunched and straining over the controls. The aircraft was slipping sideways through shrieking wind. Perry was grinning and saying, 'Give us a break, give us a break, give us a break.' The ground was slanting up and very near the purplish hairy mountain. Douglas woke as they crashed, immediately rising on his elbow and shaking his head clear of the dream. It was dawn. Through the gauze a clear greyish sky lay like a stretched sheet. A few yellowish streaks fanned out from the reddish hushed glow where the sun would rise. Perry was lying on his back, asleep.

Inside the room the orderly moved about, and a primus stove hissed.

A lorry stood outside the administration building opposite. Bobby leaned beside it, apparently waiting. The white ambulance car came driving around the edge of the building and parked beside the lorry. Some native orderlies and the doctor came out and began sliding stretchers into the ambulance with rolls of blanket on them that were the casualties.

Douglas lay down again, rolling his dry and swollen tongue around his mouth. Today he would go home. He would walk into the flat and greet Martha. Tenderness for Martha and his small daughter filled him. The gay flat with its books and flowers seemed very attractive. And he would be back at his desk in Statistics in a week. They would be pleased to see him. He was a kingpin of his section, and everybody knew it. He dozed off for a moment, thinking of Martha and how that night he would be lying in bed with her. Voluptuous fantasies slid through his mind. He was asleep again; but almost at once someone shook him.

'Come on, get up, kids,' said Bobby's bluff voice.

Douglas sat up. Perry was leaning on his elbow looking at Bobby, who refused to meet his eyes. She said hurriedly, 'We're leaving in twenty minutes,' and went down the steps with her free manly stride, pale hair bobbing on her fat white neck.

'Mucking bitch,' said Perry dispassionately. He got up. Douglas was already stuffing things into his pack.

The orderly came out with boiled eggs on a tray. 'Good morning, baas, good morning, baas,' he said cheerfully. The reading primer was sticking out of his breast pocket.

'Morning, Jim,' said Douglas, rubbing his hands. He felt elated and optimistic.

They were eating their eggs when the doctor came over.

'How are you feeling?'

'Fine, fine.'

'You don't deserve it.'

'Oh, come off it, Doc.'

The young English doctor smiled. 'If I put the schiz on to the plane, will you keep an eye on him? He's well and truly drugged.'

'The ulcers will look after the schiz,' said Perry. 'Leave it all to us.'

'Thanks. I've got to get him out somehow. There isn't even a nurse to send with the stretcher cases. They'll be all right. They're not too bad. It's only a few hours. You'll be there before lunch. This place is packing up soon, anyway.'

'Bloody silly place for a hospital,' said Douglas.

'It isn't a hospital. It's a transfer casualty.'

'Whatever it is.'

'Well, I didn't choose it,' said the doctor, automatically clearing himself of responsibility like everybody else. 'Could you get yourselves into the lorry, gentlemen. Please.'

Douglas and Perry slung their packs on and flipped some silver to the orderly, who caught it with one hand.

'Thanks, baas, thanks, baas.'

They strolled over the dust to the lorry, which was now throbbing gently all over. Bobby was already in the driver's seat.

'You can have her,' said Perry to Douglas. 'I don't want her.'

Douglas hesitated. He did not want to drive the four miles with Bobby. But he went round to the front and climbed up beside her. She was being curt and official this morning, so he did not have to talk.

The lorry at once bounced off and away past the tin shanties into the bush. The sun was just coming up. A large red ball clung to the edges of the trees, stretched like a drop of water, then floated clear. By the time they reached the airstrip it had grown smaller, yellow, and was throwing off heat like a flame thrower. They were sweating already. Bobby drove them straight to the aircraft. The ambulance was driving away from it as they came up.

Bobby shook them all by the hand, Perry last, in an off-hand, soldierly way. She at once got back into the lorry and drove off, shouting, 'Give my love to the home town.'

In the plane they had to wait. At the last moment a large saloon car drove up. The doctor got out, went round to the other door, and helped out the sleepy limp-looking youth. He half pushed him up the steps into Douglas's arms. Douglas and Perry hauled him in, and slumped him into the seat by Perry. He slept at once, looking very young and boyish, with his ruffle of damp fair hair on his forehead.

The doctor came in, took a last look at the stretcher cases, and said to Douglas, 'Keep an eye on them, there's a good chap.' He saluted and skipped thankfully down the steps and off to the car.

At once the plane swung round and began lumbering away to the end of the strip. It turned. Over the brick shack a funnel of white silk rippled out. As the aircraft roared past and up they could see a cloud of fluttering butterflies around it, like flying ants around a street lamp.

In a few minutes the bush was stretching empty beneath them. Perry was sitting beside the sick youth. He slipped sideways. Perry put his arm around him. The young flushed face was lying back on his shoulder.

Perry was watching a drift of wet cloud making rainbows in the bright sun, and humming 'Roll Out the Barrel' between his teeth, the shrewd hard blue eyes narrowed and abstracted, the mouth tight, the jaw solid. He shifted himself once or twice carefully to take the weight of the boy more comfortably, then settled down himself with his eyes shut. Douglas went back to talk to the stretcher cases.

About midday the plane touched down, and the boy was lifted, still fast asleep, on to the ambulance.

Chapter Four

As Douglas walked past the iron-and-brick offices at the airport, he saw a man he knew behind a table. He went in. 'How's tricks?' he asked, grinning with pleasure as he watched the face clear through surprise into welcome. They slapped each other around the shoulders for a few minutes, laughing. Then Douglas said, 'How about giving me a clearance to get home and see my wife?'

The friend remembered he was also authority, hesitated, then said, 'I suppose it's all right – come back this afternoon.'

Douglas walked out towards the gates of the airport. He could see Perry and the others nosing around the open doors of the offices to find old friends who might similarly release them. He thought he should wait for them. Then he quickly went out into the road. He stopped in surprise. Only a year ago, the tarmac had crossed an empty grass-filled vlei to the airport. Now it was bordered on both sides by new suburbs of little villas. He felt like Rip Van Winkle. He began to walk the three miles to the centre of the town. Soon a car drew up beside him, to give a lift to the soldier. A new mode of manners, this; he climbed in, and, although five minutes before he had felt like a civilian, allowed himself to be treated with the affable but rather wistful friendliness civilians offer to uniforms. They were talking all the way in of how the influx of thousands of Air Force personnel was unbalancing the country – they had practically taken it over; you could not get into cinemas, hotels, dance halls. One said that the money they brought with them made up for it – the country was on a boom of prosperity. They might have been talking of occupation troops. Then Douglas saw the pavements full of grey-blue uniforms, and felt a stranger in his own town. It happened that the car passed the big block where his department was housed. On an impulse he asked to be set down.

He walked into the department and was greeted thankfully by his chief, who asked if he could start work next day. Warmed and flattered, Douglas mentioned the red tape that would have to be unwound before he could put on his own clothes again. His chief waved all this aside: five minutes on the telephone to the suitable person would settle all that. He settled it forthwith; the interests of the country demanded that Douglas need do no more than pay a call for form's sake at a certain office the next day. Douglas began to feel himself at home.

There was still a slight undercurrent between him and his chief: after all, he had gone over the man's head to get into the Army. At the end of an hour it had vanished. They had discussed problems of reorganization — there were precisely half the people in the office that there were in peacetime, with twice the amount of work. Then, in the deferential, rather boyish way which he used when asking for things that were his right, Douglas mentioned various personal financial matters; the chief suggested they might lunch over it. They went to the Club. In the bar were Perry and the others. This was the last chance they had of playing the part of old campaigners to older men who had been prevented from going to the wars. They took it. At three, the chief said this was all very well, but he had to get back to work. Douglas went with him. The financial situation was dealt with in half a dozen sentences on the pavement edge.

Then he turned to walk home. He was a little drunk. It occurred to him that he had been in the town five hours, and Martha might be hurt that he had not rung her. I'll give her a surprise, he thought, deciding to forget the five hours. As he neared the block of flats, he saw a young woman wheeling a child coming towards him. He thought like a soldier, Not bad, not bad at all! Then he saw it was Martha. He stopped and watched her approach with a proud and proprietary smile. She was slimmer than she had been, and rather pale. She was wearing a short, tight, flowered dress, and red sandals that showed brown bare feet; and looked, in short, attractive. She was staring vaguely in front of her, and as he moved to block her way she frowned discouragingly at the soldier. Then she froze, looking at him for a long moment while she turned white, and then, suddenly, bright pink. Blinking slowly, she came to life with a stiff, nervous smile.

They embraced. For both there was something false and unpleasant in this embrace. They separated, and took refuge from the difficulties of the moment in Caroline. Douglas bounced the child up in the air a few times: he was deeply moved at the sight of this pretty little girl who was his daughter. When he set the laughing child carefully back in the push-chair, he said to Martha, 'Nice work – you've made a good job of her.' He was gazing proudly at her. He was thinking that this was a wife and child to be proud of. He even glanced around to see if anyone was watching. But people were hurrying by: the streets were much fuller than they had been – strangers, always strangers. He thought it would be nice to take Martha and Caroline up to the Club of an afternoon.

She smiled uncomfortably at his compliment, however, and lifted the front wheels of the push-chair around in a way which jerked Caroline so that she clutched the handrails with both hands.

'Hey, you're giving her rather a bouncing, aren't you?' he asked; but received no reply. They walked back to the flats, a couple of hundred yards away.

'Why didn't you let me know you were coming?' she asked carefully.

'Well – I thought I'd drop in.' He laughed and rubbed his hands. 'And then last night . . .' He launched into an account of how he and Perry and some of the lads had given it a bang last night in G——, a ghastly little dorp in the bush miles from anywhere. Bobby – she remembered Bobby – sent her love. They'd all had a hell of a party, and his mouth this morning was like a parrot's cage. Luckily he'd slept some of it off in the aircraft, but, what with one thing and another, he thought it was quicker to come home himself than to telephone. Martha listened, with a new and discouraging detachment. Douglas felt let down. She had always risen in cheerful complicity to accounts of the boys' activities.

'Will you have to stay in uniform?' was her next question.

'I saw old Keen. He wants me back as soon as he can get me. He's fixed it. I'll be back at the office tomorrow.'

She turned her eyes towards him cautiously. Cautiously she inquired, 'You went to the office first?'

'Well, I was passing – I wanted to have everything fixed to surprise you.'

'When did you get in?'

'About three hours ago' – he softened it a little.

She said nothing. Caroline was twisting herself up on her knees in the chair, and Martha pushed her down with one hand as she wheeled. 'Oh, stop it, Caroline,' she said roughly.

They were in the hall of the flats. Martha undid the straps and lifted the child out. Douglas promptly caught her up on his shoulders. The family party slowly mounted the stairs.

'I've got a fine piece of news,' announced Douglas. 'I asked Keen what he thought of my raising money for a house – he'll fix that. He even knows of a house going for us. How's that?' he ended proudly.

She inquired, after a pause, in the manner of one wishing to give him the benefit of any doubt, 'We'll be moving into a house of our own?'

'That's the ticket – yes. It's a big house, too, Matty. You know it – it's the Rellors' old house on the corner of McKechnie Street.'

'But it's enormous!' exclaimed Martha. She stared at him, appalled.

'But, Matty,' he said in an injured voice, 'we'll have our place, we'll be buying our own place – and there'll be a garden for Caroline. And' – here he rubbed his hands and laughed – 'we'll be having another kid soon, eh?'

Her look was now steady and critical.

'I say, now – Matty!' he exclaimed, clutching at her arm. But they were at their door. She pulled her arm away, and opened it.

On the divan was seated a young man in the blue uniform, reading a newspaper. He stood up, smiling shyly but pleasantly as they entered, looking at them with very clear, very blue eyes. He was rather slight – not tall; his hair was a springy bright brown, though against the pale skin it looked dark. As Martha said hurriedly, 'This is William, Douglas. My husband has suddenly pitched up, William,' he held out his hand with a perfect ease and friendliness.

Martha glanced at the two hands, one white, fine, almost effeminate, the other a large red-brown paw; hairs glinted on it. She was looking at her husband's hands as she said, 'If you'll excuse me, I'll make some tea.' Then she saw Douglas was annoyed at finding a stranger there, and said in a way which made both men look quickly at her, 'If you'd found five minutes to let me know you were coming – ' She bit off, and gave a tight smile. Then she went out, taking Caroline with her.

She dropped the child into the playpen, and, as she began to protest, handed her a rusk. Caroline took it and was quiet. Martha went quickly into the little kitchen. She assembled cups on a tray, and carelessly banged the kettle on to the hotplate. She did not know what she was doing. That sudden vision of the soldier who was her husband had been a shock to her which only now began to make itself felt. She was trembling; she cracked a cup as she dropped it on to the saucer.

Douglas, in khaki with the pack on his shoulder, a red-brown man with fat knees, a good stone heavier than he had been, and reeking of beer, had seemed to her gross and commonplace. His round, rather fat red face, grinning proudly at her, had been a revelation of what he really was. She could not now remember her vision of him of even half an hour before. It was quite impossible that this man should be her husband. She was married to one of the boys; he would always, all his life, be one of the boys. At sixty he would still be a schoolboy. There was no escape from it. The condition of being a woman in wartime, she thought angrily, was that one should love not a man, but a man in relation to other men. Whether it was Douglas with the boys, or the boys of the Air Force, it was all the same – and it was precisely this thing, dangerous, and attractive, which fed the intoxication of war, heightened the pulse, and drugged them all into losing their heads. You loved not a man, but that man's idea of you in relation to his friends. But *that* had been true here, in this country, long before the war. Well, she would not; never again!

At this point, guilt, the unfailing goad, gave a warning twinge, but at far lower pressure than usual. She ignored it, and was very angry. He bounced back grinning into her life after a year without a word or a warning, and naturally went first to the boys – *she* was an afterthought. The lonely, proud, self-contained life she had made for herself was invaded just like that, by his choosing to come: thus Martha, choosing to forget that, after all, he could not help it. And now he would bounce into bed with her; the thought filled her with revulsion. That it should do so succeeded in rousing the saving guilt: she could not stand seeing herself as a bestower of sexual favours, so she hastily began to recreate the coarsened soldier into something masculine and strong and attractive.

She lifted the tea tray and marched with it into the other room. The two men were getting on famously. The sight of Douglas on the edge of the divan with his fat putteed legs sprawling filled her again with derision. He was being the administrator; he was absorbed by a description of how the airmen's sleeping huts were laid out in relation to mess halls and recreation rooms. William was making a sort of map with bits of matches on the carpet. He had a quiet, sensible way of explaining things that clearly appealed to Douglas. Martha poured tea and handed them cups, filled with an anger she could not have explained. The business of drinking tea, however, interrupted the plan of how the air camp would have been laid out if either Douglas or William had been asked to do it; and they again became aware of Martha and were silent.

'Let's have Caroline in?' suggested Douglas.

'No – she must stay in her pen for at least half an hour.'

'But why?' he protested rather wistfully.

'Timetable. She'll be making a fuss soon enough as it is,' she added.

Caroline was already grumbling outside; the noise was irritating Martha, they could see. William was sipping his tea with the obvious desire to leave as soon as he could. In a moment he had set down his cup and got up. 'I must be getting along,' he remarked. Martha and Douglas said nothing to dissuade him. He stood smiling, while his blue eyes were thoughtfully examining Martha and Douglas. 'Do you want to join the group?' he asked Martha direct. 'Shall we send you notices? Or perhaps you'd rather think it over now that things have changed.' This last was a hasty statement in reply to her nervous silence. He gave a long diagnostic look at Douglas, then formally shook hands with him. He went out with a pleasant nod at Martha.

'What group?' asked Douglas uneasily.

'Discussion group,' said Martha shortly. William had dropped in casually twice before. His manner was always friendly, but impersonal: Martha had understood that his coming was because he felt it his duty to support and encourage her towards a different view of life. She had almost decided to join the group that contemplated splitting off the old one in order – as William explained vaguely but firmly – to get down to brass tacks. The phrase appealed to Martha.

'Do you know him well?' asked Douglas jealously. She looked up at him for some time in silence; her eyebrows went up. He coloured up and said firmly, 'What does he mean by the group? A political group?'

She said with a sudden aggressiveness, 'Ever since we've been married you agreed I wasn't only to housekeep and mind babies.'

They were on the edge of a quarrel about the group, since it was taboo to be jealous. 'Well, I didn't say you shouldn't,' he hastened to conciliate. Then, as she preserved silence: 'You know, Matty, I'm in the Service, and I must be careful. You know old John lost his job because of his wife.'

She flushed and said, 'His wife drank, didn't she?'

'Well, but, Matty, I have to go slow.'

'Since I suppose three-quarters of the male population is in the Service one way and another, it seems a useful way of keeping you quiet.'

'But, Matty, we have the vote.'

'The vote!' she said derisively. He was puzzled. They looked at each other across a wider gulf than they knew.

'Anyway,' he said, brightening, 'there'll be so much work to do in the new house, you won't have time.'

'Quite,' said Martha. He shot her a startled, uneasy look. Martha had not, previously, been capable of saying 'Quite'. He smelled the influence of the British invasion. But what was particularly unsettling was her tone, calm and dismissing and fatalistic, as if she accepted a long-foreseen calamity.

'Surely,' he said, in the voice of an injured boy, 'surely you're pleased to have a house of your own.'

Again her eyebrows rose, and she said, 'There's nothing in the world I want more.' Then she burst into laughter, and kissed him on the cheek, moving away immediately as he grabbed at her.

'There's Caroline,' she said hastily. Caroline had in fact begun to yell with impatience. Martha went out. Silence from Caroline. Then Douglas followed her. Martha had gone past Caroline to the bedroom. He made some hasty apologetic noises at his daughter and went into the bedroom.

Martha was arranging Caroline's night things on the bed. She glanced up, startled, as he entered; then seemed to remind herself that he had a right to. He watched her for a while, then went across and put his arms around her from behind.

'I've been missing you, Matty,' he began.

She stiffened and said gaily – and it was the first time he had heard the warm, amused gaiety which was how he had thought of her in the Army – 'Oh, so have I.' She turned round and kissed him. After a moment she pulled away and said, 'Well, I must get Caroline washed.'

'Oh, damn Caroline,' he said huskily. 'Let's forget her for a while.' She appeared not to hear him. He said in an offended voice, 'Where are my civvies?'

'Packed in your trunk. If you'd let me know, I'd have got them cleaned and ready for you.'

'It doesn't matter.'

He found some old flannels, pulled on a sweater. 'It's good to be in my own clothes again – I've put on weight,' he said rather appealingly.

She responded quickly, with, 'Oh, it's not so bad.' But the clothes were straining round him, she thought he looked gross.

'Look, Matty, how about putting Caroline in the car and running up for a drink at the Club?'

She paused and looked at him, Caroline's nightdress in her hand. He could not read her expression. 'You know,' she said, cautiously, 'things are not as they used to be here.'

He exploded in a peevish shout. 'Oh, come on, don't be such a wet blanket.'

The hatred between them then was so strong it frightened them both. Without comment, she reached for a jersey, slipped it on, walked out, picked up Caroline and waited at the door, all in the manner of someone obeying an order. He would have liked to slap her.

They went in silence down the stairs. In the car, he slid with satisfaction into the driver's seat and said, 'It's good to be driving the old bus again.'

She seemed to be very occupied with Caroline, and they drove without speaking to the Club. When they reached the turn, he stopped the car, and looked at the building, smiling twistedly. It stood unchanged in its green playing fields, the large white beautiful house, very dignified, the late afternoon sun shining full on it. He started the car again, and drove rapidly towards it, parked hastily, jumped out, smiling with eagerness. She walked quietly beside him to the veranda.

As they went up the steps she did not look at him, but went hurriedly ahead and found a table. He stood unconsciously staring about him on the steps. His face was sagging with helpless disappointment. The long deep veranda was crowded with people, as it always had been; but they were all new faces, save for some of the girls who smiled and waved at him. The grey-blue of the Air Force filled the place like a – well, it was wartime, after all! He came across to Martha, and sat down clumsily. Martha glanced at his face and then away. He had gone a queer yellowish colour and was breathing hard. This was the real moment of coming home; she was very sorry for him. She did not want to be sorry, it made a guilty maternal love stir in her. She thought determinedly that the lumpish reddened face with its spoilt protruding underlip was that of a schoolboy, but longed to comfort him nevertheless. They ordered beer, and drank it quickly, while Martha kept Caroline near her. In the old days the Club babies went from table to table, lap to lap. Now there was formality and a sense of closed groups who were not willing to be disturbed. A couple of the girls came up and greeted Douglas. Every second word was Air Force slang, and it was clear they had other interests than returning crocks from up north.

Douglas watched a group of girls he had danced and played with for so many years flirting with some young officers, and then remarked, with grumbling good humour, 'I begin to see there's a war on.' He laughed unhappily, and she joined him in relief. The colour had come back to his face, and it wore a look of ironical acceptance.

'We ought to go,' said Martha. 'It's time to put Caroline to bed.' He got up immediately; he was pleased to go.

As they walked down the veranda, various girls called out. 'Well, Douggie, and how's the war?'

'I don't know,' he returned good-humouredly, 'I never reached it.'

When they got home, Caroline would not allow herself to be put to bed. She was delighted to have a father, her father was delighted with her. He played with her. He felt surprised respect at the little person she had become. When he laid her down, he loosened the tiny delicate arms from around his neck reluctantly. She at once climbed to her feet and rattled the bars of the cot, looking at this new man with her black alert eyes.

'We shouldn't have this cot in our bedroom now,' he said, and at once he began pushing it into the other room. Martha said nothing; she felt a pang of loss at her daughter being so unceremoniously removed; then reminded herself that she had not really liked having the child in her room; she was relieved that the cause of the inexplicable tension should be removed a little farther – physically at least.

'Let's go out and have a bite,' suggested Douglas, having left Caroline shouting protests on the veranda.

'We can't go out and leave Caroline,' said Martha promptly. It sounded almost as if she were scoring a point over him.

She was sitting on the edge of the bed, slumped forward, very still, very distant. She had changed a great deal, he decided; and tried to define the change. She felt his eyes on her and turned and looked at him defensively, flashing a guilty smile. At once he was beside her, had clasped her. 'Well, Matty, it would be nice if you were a little pleased to see me.'

'Of course I'm pleased to see you.' But he felt she was stiff under his hands. She seemed to be listening. 'Caroline's not asleep,' she said warningly, meaning that she could not give her mind to love-making while the child's sounds and movements were twanging at her nerves.

He did not understand this, and said stiffly, 'Oh, very well, then let's eat instead.'

She quickly escaped and began to prepare a meal. He lay on his elbow on the bed reading, or rather, looking vaguely at the book while he thought in a wave of bitter longing, Up north now they're in the real thing.

Almost at once Martha produced an omelette and some stewed fruit. She seemed surprised and hurt when he suggested this was not a meal to greet a soldier with. He ate it all in a few hearty mouthfuls, and said, 'Now let's eat properly.'

'But what about your ulcer?'

'Oh, to hell with my ulcer.'

Caroline was asleep, lying loose among her blankets, fists at the level of her head, the small face flushed.

'I'll tell the woman over the corridor,' Martha said, and left him to do so. She was away inside the other flat some time; he listened to the women's voices, and it occurred to him for the first time that Martha had built up a life of her own, with obligations and responsibilities. He heard her say as she came out, 'If you want to go out tomorrow, let me know.'

'Who's she?' he asked her, trying to show an interest.

'Oh – she has a baby,' said Martha evasively.

'She's a friend of yours?'

'A *friend*?' said Martha in surprise.

'Well – do you see much of her?'

'We don't like each other, actually. But she keeps an eye on Caroline when I'm shopping, and I look after her kid.'

'Let's go to McGrath's.'

'Oh, no, not McGrath's,' said Martha nervously, and he flashed out again belligerently, 'I said McGrath's!'

She had been wanting to save him from another disappointment; now she felt meanly pleased that it would serve him right.

At the entrance to the big marble-and-gilt lounge he paused, with a boyish, expectant look on his face. His face changed. It was, of course, filled with the RAF. Not a soul looked up to greet him. He moved stoically through under the gilded pillars. Then he saw a waiter he knew and greeted him like an old friend. The Indian bowed and smiled over his tray of filled glass beer mugs and said it was fine to have Mr Knowell back again.

Douglas and Martha went into the big dining room. Uniforms . . . There was room for them at the end of a large crowded, noisy table. They ate one of those vast meals which must be among the worst offered to suffering humanity anywhere, the southern-African hotelier's contribution to the British tradition in food. Douglas ate steadily, and with great satisfaction, speaking very little.

'Well, I needed that,' he announced at last, laying his spoon down after the Pears au Paris. Then: 'Now, let's have a drink.' They moved to the lounge and drank brandy and ginger beer for an hour, while the band played gypsy music. It was a very good band now. The influx of refugees from Hitler had brought musicians who had played to very different crowds, who played now and remembered Vienna, Munich, Hamburg, Berlin.

When they got home Caroline had hardly moved. The sight of the small white exquisite limbs loosened in sleep always gave Martha acute pleasure. She covered them reluctantly, and went to the bedroom. There Douglas was already naked: a stout young man, very white, with ruddy-brown arms and knees and face. She hung about nervously and then took her nightclothes to undress in the bathroom.

'We haven't any contraceptives,' she announced defiantly as she came back.

'Well, that means you've been behaving yourself at least,' he said, laughing hopefully. She got into bed beside him as if in a room full of strangers, tucking her feet in chastely with the nightgown around her ankles. 'Have you, by the way?' he asked casually.

'As much or as little as you have,' she said quickly, and then, as if she herself found this banner of feminism absurd, added a short unhappy laugh. Mistakenly encouraged by the laugh, he rolled over, prodded her in the ribs and said, 'Ah come off it, Matty. Let's take a chance for tonight.'

'Oh no, you don't,' she exclaimed involuntarily.

'Well, why not? It would be nice for Caroline to have a brother nearly her own age.'

'You see no reason why I shouldn't be made pregnant on the first night you're home?' she inquired in a fine cold voice. But it sounded forlorn.

He lay on his back, arms behind his head, looking at the ceiling. On his face was an ugly, angry look; he grinned after a while with ironic appreciation. 'There's no place like home,' he produced at last.

At this Martha felt a confused sort of anguish, partly because she was unable to compete with the attractions of 'the boys', of whom he was thinking at that moment; partly because she was behaving like the unpleasant female who gave or withheld favours; partly because she thought there must be something very wrong with her not to want him. She turned out the light. There was moonlight splashing all over the bottom of the bed. She saw, for the first time that season, the shape of the big wheel in the window – they must have set it up that morning. She suddenly wanted to cry.

He rolled over, and she understood that he had been by no means discouraged. She set herself to be as compliant as possible; to her astonishment, even a certain pride, he was not able to distinguish the difference between this and the real thing. Afterwards, full of childish affection and a gratitude which grated on her, he said, 'I was careful, Matty.'

'So I should think,' she said, with a sort of bright desperation. She was terrified of becoming pregnant.

The next few days, which were occupied in seeing the house, deciding it was satisfactory, and moving into it, going to parties, giving them, making and receiving visits, were interspersed also with love-making. She was tense with anxiety that she might have become pregnant that first night. The old trapped feeling had her again; she was sleeping badly, although for a year she had slept very well; she was again lying through the nights listening to the sad music of the fun fair, and conscious of every twinge or response of her body as if it might vouchsafe to give up its secrets if only she concentrated on it hard enough. Then she knew she was not pregnant. She was able to give her mind fully to this new task of managing a large house, four servants, Caroline and a husband.

Part Four

He must be a dubious hero, a man with possibilities.

C. G. JUNG, On Marriage

Chapter One

The house was in the older part of the city, at the corner of a block. From its gate one could see a mile in four directions along tree-bordered avenues. The town planners, when faced with a need for more houses, always solved the problem by laying a rule neatly over a map which represented a patch of unused veld, causing a pattern of streets to come into existence which crossed each other regularly at right angles. Everything was straight, orderly, unproblematical; grey strips of tarmac stretched endlessly, the naked earth at either side sprouted grass and wild-flowers. Above, trees: the glossy dark masses of the cedrelatoona, the sun-sculptured boughs of the jacarandas, and, between, those small stiff trees the bauhinias, with their pink-and-white blossoms perched on them like butterflies. It was October, and the jacarandas were purple and the streets were blue, as if they ran water or reflected the sky, which was unrelievedly blue and pulsing with heat.

Inside the gate was a large tree, under which Martha stood looking out. Behind her was a rough lawn, where Caroline was playing with a native girl who now attended to her. Martha turned her back on the tiring glitter of the street, and surveyed the house, which was a series of large rooms casually assembled and surrounded by a wide creeper-curtained veranda, reached by a deep flight of red cement steps. The garden was big and untidy. The garden boy squatted beside a border, gently prodding the earth with a fork while he dreamed of his own affairs. He was a young lad of about fifteen, who from time to time turned admiring eyes towards the girl. She, however, was mission-trained and sat very neat and proper in her clean white dress, legs tucked soberly to one side, her head, outlined in a scarlet crocheted cap, bent over her knitting. She did not look at him, but occasionally called out shrilly to Caroline, who was supposed to stay in the shade. The little girl, in a brief white dress, her wisps of black hair shining iridescent in the sun, was running over the rough grass in bare feet. She stopped when she saw her mother, smiled, took two steps towards her, then turned and trotted off to the garden boy, who laid down his fork and began clapping his hands regularly to attract her.

'Caroline?' the girl called, but did not move.

Martha reflected that the boy was supposed to be digging a bed for vegetables at the back of the house, where, however, he would not see the girl; and she was supposed to be ironing at this hour. If she, Martha, were really efficient, she would at once raise her voice and put things right. But she could see no reason why they should not all stay as they were; so she left the shade of the big tree and went rapidly through the blazing sun to the house. Caroline let out a protesting wail, then lost interest, and began digging with the garden boy's fork, while he watched her, smiling proudly.

Martha gained the veranda, stood behind the creeper, and looked out. The sunlight made her eyes ache. She hastily called to the girl to take Caroline away into the shade, and turned her back on the scene of persuasion and protest that followed. As usual she was feeling uncomfortable; she hated giving orders and was always at a disadvantage with her servants. Since she could not look at Alice, the native nurse, without thinking that she ought to be married and looking after her own children, or at the garden boy without thinking that he should be at school, or at the cook in the kitchen without finding it intolerable that a grown man should be under the orders of a girl a third his age, her voice always had a tinge of guilt when she spoke to them. The houseboy, a young man of twenty bursting with health and energy, was engaged in polishing bits of furniture in the dining room. She stopped to watch him. From where she stood, greasy polish marks showed on the shining table, and she knew that it was her duty to instruct him in polishing tables. She continued through the house to the back veranda. Here the piccaninny – the small black child who was engaged, according to custom, for odd jobs – was playing with Caroline's toys on the steps. Since Martha pretended not to see him, he continued to roll a small green car along the edge of a step, growling like an engine in his throat.

The kitchen was large, equipped with all kinds of modern devices. The cook was putting away the vegetables and groceries which had just been delivered from the stores. She left the kitchen and went towards the large refrigerator which stood on the veranda. She proudly opened it; it was her secret pride that it was always stocked with jars of sauces and mayonnaise, pastry of various kinds folded in stiff white slabs ready for cooking, biscuit dough that needed only to be put in the oven, jugs of iced tea and coffee, ice cream and complicated iced puddings that had taken hours to make. Martha told Douglas with satisfaction that she could serve a meal for ten any time at half an hour's notice, and he was pleased with her. But the cook, who after all existed solely to serve meals for two adults and a child, and was delighted if half a dozen people dropped in, suffered this organization unwillingly. Sometimes Martha told him he might take a few hours off, and cooked what she thought of as her own meals; and then, hurt in his pride, he retired to the back garden, where he watched her disapprovingly. He was a very good cook.

There was nothing to do in the refrigerator, so Martha went to the pantry. This was a room large enough to be a room for sleeping or working in; it was cool, with a gauze window that overlooked the vegetable beds at the back. It had a stone floor, stone shelves, dazzling white walls. There was a delicious cool smell of sugar and spices, the warm fresh tang of new flour. Sacks of sugar, flour, meal, stood along the floor. Martha dipped her fingers through the dry glisten of the sugar, touched soft clinging flour, and gazed along shelves where, in neat tins, were stored the groceries: tea and coffee; the starches in all their amazing variations; corn flour and bean flour, soya flour and the grades of

oatmeals, rapoka meal and pea flour and split peas and
beans; the rices, short and long and wild and cleaned, and
ground and polished – six variations of them; the pastas
from Italy, long and thin, long and fat, and moulded into all
their possible forms, shells and buttons and letters and
animals – these last for Caroline; the sagos and the tapiocas,
and flour of the same; potato flour and lentils, red and brown
and grey, and samp and sugar – all the colours and grades of
it, from the fine thin white to the masses of heavy black
treacle from the West Indies. From the sugar the cans and
bottles shaded through to the exotics: dried cherries and
almonds, coriander and ginger root and preserved and dried
ginger; vanilla and candied peel, and currants and sultanas
and raisins and the fine fresh crystallized fruits from the
Cape. Beyond, jars of preserved peaches and apricots and
plums and guavas; jams, chutneys, spiced mangoes and fruit
syrups.

Martha opened one tin after another, sniffing the stored
exhaling odours with keen delight, while she ran her eyes
along the rows of massed and glistening bottles of fruit. This
was her favourite room in the house. But she shut the door
on its pleasures and went back to the veranda. A large ginger
cat now sat on the steps, patting at the little car as the small
black child rolled it past.

The cook came out of his kitchen and said, 'Madam, what
shall I cook for lunch?'

Martha consulted with him at leisure; he went back to the
kitchen, and she through several rooms to the bedroom. It
was large, with a pleasant high white ceiling, and windows
opening on three sides into the garden. It had a conventional
suite of bedroom furniture, rather ugly, and twin beds
covered in green silk.

She had a choice of three rooms to sit in, but she sat on
her bed, and looked at the white trumpets of the moonflowers hanging outside the window. She thought that she might
very well run across the street into Mrs Randall's for morning tea. She resisted it like a temptation, although she
grumbled humorously to Douglas that these women's tea
parties were driving her crazy. Gossip, gossip about their

servants, she complained; and then their doctors, and how they brought up their children (she did not add, 'And the dullness of their husbands'). The fact was, there was something about these daily orgies of shared complaint, for they were nothing if not that, which was beginning to attract her like a drug.

How extraordinary it was that within a month after Douglas had returned from up north she was in this large house, with all these servants, and supplied with a new circle of friends. For all the wives of Douglas's associates had come to see her, and she had gone to see them.

She was one of a set. She had been now for over a year.

They were all married couples, and the wives were pregnant, or intended to be soon, or had just had a baby. They all earned just so much a month, owned houses which they would finish paying for in about thirty years' time, and in the houses was furniture bought on hire-purchase, including refrigerators, washing machines, fine electric stoves. They all had cars, and kept between two and five servants, who cost them about two pounds a month each. They were all heavily insured.

They took holidays at the Cape once in four or five years, gave sundowner parties to each other once or twice in the month, and went dancing or to the cinema two or three times in the week. They were, in short, extremely comfortable, and faced lives in which there could never be a moment's insecurity. 'Security' was the golden word written up over their doorways, security was so deeply part of them that it was never questioned or discussed: the great climax of their lives would come at fifty or fifty-five, when their houses, gardens and furniture would be their own, and the pensions and policies bore fruit.

But if there is a type of man who instinctively chooses 'the Service', is there, then, a type of woman who inevitably marries him? This was the question that troubled Martha. She was uneasy because she had adapted herself so well to this life; some instinct to conform and comply had dictated that she must quell her loathing, as at entering a trap, which she had felt at the idea of being bound by a house and insurance policies until the gates of freedom opened at fifty. She was instinctively compliant, enthusiastic, and took every step into bondage with affectionate applause for Douglas. But she never felt that she really lived in this house, whose furniture had been chosen by the woman who lived in it before her, whose garden had been designed by someone else. She did not feel like Douglas's wife or Caroline's mother. She was not even bored. It was as if three parts of herself stood on one side, idle, waiting to be called into action.

She was secretly and uneasily curious as to how these other women felt, and therefore did she go to the morning tea parties, therefore did she change her dress, brush her hair, take up her handbag and make her way to the circle of women.

On the veranda of one of their houses was set a circle of grass chairs, a table with cakes and biscuits. The babies crawled around their feet, or played on the lawns outside.

The women looked sharply at each other's dresses and at the food provided, while they discussed economy. Money chimed through their talk like a regulator of a machine. For all the heavy insurances, the mortgages, the hire-purchase, the servants, were made possible because of their ingenuity with money. They could all make attractive and expensive-looking clothes for themselves, their children and even their husbands out of a few shillings' worth of stuff bought at the sales; they continually discussed recipes which might cut the grocers' bills by a fraction; they would haggle at their back doors with the native vendors over a penny like old women in a market place; they all knitted and sewed and patched and contrived like poor men's wives. There were sharp scenes between husbands and wives at every month's end; there was a continual atmosphere of contended silver shillings. They were all perpetually short of ready money, because of their god, a secure and comfortable middle age. They sighed out, 'When we retire . . .' as if they were saying, 'When the prison gates are opened . . .'

Martha could not ask Douglas for five shillings to last until the end of the week without a sharp sense of failure; and, since she had caught herself using a coaxing little voice to wheedle it out of him, she had reacted sharply into a stiff pride which meant she would go without meals secretly if he did not come home for them, to save the few pence they would cost. Yet, while she resented this necessity to spend all her time on running up dresses, petticoats, shirts, and clothes for Caroline on the sewing machine; while she never ceased to be conscious of the time that went on bottling, pickling and preserving, it was all a great pride and satisfaction to her. She found that when she had nothing to do she would unpick an old dress to make it into a new one, for the sheer satisfaction of getting something for nothing; just as she would spend two hours making a pudding that looked like an illustration out of Mrs Beeton, so that she might feel pride in the knowledge that it cost less than the rice pudding the cook would have made in its stead.

It was the time of these women which supported the whole edifice; their willingness to sink their youth in acquiring multifarious small talents, which softened the road to that great goal, comfortable middle age.

Martha had been sucked into the pattern; with part of herself she connived at it. Weeks and months would go by, and then she found herself sitting up in bed at night, sweating with fear, and she would be afraid to go to sleep again: she suffered a mild repetition of that period in her childhood when she would lie awake night after night, rigid in the bed, forcing her eyes open to prevent herself slipping into a terrible dream country. Then it all passed and she became lazy and comfortable, willingly spending all her time making and mending and contriving; and she would say to herself, Yes, I shall have another baby. For that was the crux of it. If she had another baby, she would be committed to staying here; she would live in the pattern till she died. Yet that other Martha who stood idly by all this while, waiting to be used, never believed for one moment that she would stay; it was inconceivable.

Caroline was three years old. Martha knew her female self was sharply demanding that she should start the cycle of birth again. There were moods when a slow, warm, heavy longing came up, when the very sight of Caroline filled Martha with a deep physical satisfaction at her delightful little body and charming little face; and this was at the same time a desire to hold a small baby in her arms again. If she looked at one of her friends' babies in this mood, the craving was painful and insistent, and the adventure of being pregnant filled her entirely. She thought that in nine months from now, if she chose, she could hold in her arms something new and extraordinary – a new creature created from her, Martha. And what was nine months? Nothing! said Martha to herself, forgetting how the nine months of carrying Caroline had been a period out of ordinary time. Yet she did not altogether forget. And she did *not* choose to begin again.

She was looking curiously, and with a certain deep uneasiness, at the peremptory charm of that little individual, Caroline. She knew that before Caroline was born she had seen her as 'a baby' merely, something felt in the deep, driving egotism of maternity as an extension of herself and dependent upon her. Yet here she was, not at all a baby, but a creature who became every day more independent, strong-willed, determined. Caroline was that hard and unalterable fact which turned Martha's life, in spite of a pleasant and helpful nursegirl, into a routine which began at five sharp every morning, when the light first showed, and ended at seven in the evening, when she went to bed. The rhythm of Caroline's needs was in sharp discord with her own; she adjusted herself, she did what was necessary, but it was her sense of duty which regulated her. Being a mother, or rather, the business of looking after a child, as distinct from carrying and giving birth to one, was not a fulfilment but a drag on herself. Yet no sooner had she looked at this fact, admitted it, than the voices of guilt made themselves heard; and they were given sanction by the mood of deep physical tenderness and longing for another baby.

It was a mood which was acknowledged in the circle of women. One of them, picking up a small baby with an eager wistfulness which told everything, would say, half humorous and half resentful, 'I'm as broody as hell again, but I can't start another baby until we've finished paying for the washing machine.'

But it was observable that this same young woman announced a short time later that she had started a baby, and that – with a self-conscious look – it was because she and her husband had agreed it was only fair to have a baby as soon as possible to be a companion to little George or Betty. Which deceived nobody.

This event would be succeeded, not by general discussions, for every physical phenomenon but one was discussed with the utmost frankness in the group – sex was taboo – but by a series of tête-à-têtes about that other cycle of anxiety. There were earnest, anxious discussions in the half-humorous grumbling tone which paid loyalty to the situations they found themselves in. For if young Letty Jones could 'start a baby' when, as they knew very well, she had not meant to, and simply because the sharp physical yearning for a baby had confused her out of her efficiency, then what was to prevent the same thing happening to themselves? If they could not 'plan' this, as they planned everything else in their regulated lives, they felt at the mercy of what they most dreaded. They felt insecure, in short. Besides, having a baby at all, for every one of them, was a nuisance, a painful duty, which must at least be fitted into their lives in the most convenient way. The voice of their female selves was a lure whose ambiguous and double-dealing nature they understood very well – they were not supported by the book for nothing.

Once pregnant, however, there was a compulsive satisfaction in the endless discussions of the morning sickness and the indigestion and the childbeds, in the knitting and making; while what the doctor said provided unlimited material for rivalries and comparisons. Each defended her own doctor with the fervent conviction of disciples; women who shared a doctor tended towards real intimacy on account of it; while more than once sharp words about another's doctor caused periods of 'not speaking' which had to be ended by the united efforts of the whole group.

Yet in spite of the grumblings, the complaints of how

children tie one so, how one can never get out at night without so much fuss about arranging for the cook boy to stay and then he gets grumpy, and nurses are more trouble than they're worth, 'but I must have one or I'll be worn out, my doctor says I'm run down and must take it easy'; in spite of the half-humorous despair that one looks like a sack of potatoes, 'and my stomach's like the back of an American car, and I crave for ice cream and pickles every night, isn't it funny, every night at eleven I go into the pantry and eat ice cream and pickles, and my husband says I'm mad, I'll kill him going on like this, and I get so fat when I'm pregnant, it takes me a year to lose it after and I can't get into my clothes . . .' 'Oh, no, I get so thin, my husband says I'm like a broomstick, and I lose my breasts after the milk, but they say Sister Mellors downtown does massage and you can get your breasts back if you try'; in spite of the satisfaction with which the free women looked at their sister, enormous, clumsy, flushed with heat, distressed with the weight ('She doesn't carry well, does she?' 'Oh, no, well, I don't either, it takes everyone differently . . .' 'All the same, if I looked like a cow, like she does, I'd never have a baby at all') – in spite of all this, there was something irresistibly satisfying about the process of self-destruction, self-narrowing. Which they all believed it to be.

Martha found herself looking at pregnant Mrs du Preez, swollen and hideous, and thinking even while she passed her hands with secret delight over the admirable smooth lines of her own body, How nice, that moment when your stomach pushes out, and you put on a maternity dress. Such is the power of the voice, which was speaking in her more and more often.

But she did not succumb. Douglas was urging her not to put it off any longer. 'It's not fair to Caroline, she'll be too old to enjoy the kid when we do eventually have it.' Recently he had said, half joking, for he was one of those who believe in the absolving power of humour, 'I'll hide that damned thing one of these nights, and that'll make up your mind for you!' She had turned on him sharply, sick with anger and fear, feeling her deepest self threatened. He had coloured and stammered out, 'But, Matty, it was only a joke . . .'

After a while she laughed, and even kissed him. But it had been a moment that had the power to set a strain between them. For some months the subject was avoided. Martha was nervously grateful that he said nothing. She thought vaguely that soon she would have a baby – soon, not now. She did not go so often to the women's tea parties. She would sit on her bed, looking worriedly at an enormous basket filled with socks and shirts she should be mending, and drift off into an abstracted daydream that was like a drug against any sort of action. Or she would take a fork to the back garden, where the vegetable beds lay, and work there for hours on end, letting the heat of the sun drug her into warm, slow well-being. It was as if she were waiting for something.

One morning she was kneeling on an old grain sack on the wet black soil, turning the thick rich tilth over and smoothing it ready for the new lettuces. This being October, the air was so dry she could feel the dampness being sucked up in damp hot waves all around her. She was wondering why she was drawn here so often to do work which the garden boy did so much better, for digging in a tame vegetable bed with a little fork was the barest imposture of 'nature', which was presumably what she was in search of. And why was it that nothing but the veld she had been brought up on, the sere, empty, dry vleis, the scrubby little trees, the enormous burnt windy spaces of the high veld, could satisfy her feeling for what nature should be? Dryness, barrenness, stunted growth, the colours that are fed from starved roots – thin browns and greys, dull greens and sad yellows – and all under a high, dry, empty sky: these were what she craved. The thought of a planned and comfortable country, filled with prosperous villas in green and fruitful acres, was dismaying and distasteful. It was at this point that she heard Mrs Quest's voice raised in command from the front garden. She sat back on her heels, felt a surge of anger rise in her; then she conscientiously set herself to fork vegetables as if nothing were happening.

Two or three times a week, Mrs Quest drove across the few avenues which separated her house from her daughter's, and entered the establishment like a demon of constructive energy – told the cook how to clean vegetables, informed him he was a lazy thief, lectured the nursegirl for laziness, called the houseboy in from under the tree where he was cleaning shoes to confront him with dust under the sideboard, and finally cornered Martha with a list of her deficiencies as a housekeeper. She would then depart, satisfied that she had done what was right, yet conscious that the results were not what she had intended. She told her husband and her friends that Martha ruined her servants, squandered money, and neglected Caroline. She did not really mean any of it, of course. But when she discussed her daughter, these remarks came welling up from some deep crack in her nature; it was almost as if she had never really made them. But they were repeated, finally they reached Martha herself, and she went to Douglas.

He was patiently amused, and urged her to take no notice. Martha, almost in tears, said that her cook was upset, the nurse in tears, the houseboy threatening to give notice.

'Oh, well, Matty, this sort of thing happens in half the houses in town. I am sure the cook understands quite well.'

'I can scarcely go to the cook and tell him my mother isn't responsible for what she does!'

'He won't take any notice. Now, Matty, just pretend to listen, humour the old girl, and keep your hair on!' With this he slid an apologetic kiss on to her cheek and found something else to do. This was particularly galling to Martha because she noticed it was how the husbands of her women friends evaded their complaints about their mothers. For every one of these young married couples had one or two mothers-in-law dependent upon them for emotional satisfaction, pathetic middle-aged women left high and dry by society with nothing to do.

Tolerant humour was infuriating. Pride forbade that she should be humoured, and she had now ceased to appeal to Douglas. More, she had succeeded in preserving a tight-lipped forbearance during her mother's assaults. She kept her complaints for the circle of women, which was the one place where she was really understood.

On this particular morning, Martha was left to fork vegetables for no more than half a minute before Mrs Quest came round the corner of the house in that rapid, forceful way of hers, her face set with determination and disapproval. So dramatic was her arrival, so urgent, that Martha instinctively rose, fork in hand, to face a calamity.

'What on earth is the matter?' she exclaimed.

Mrs Quest stopped at six yards, and said, 'My dear! Do you realize what's going on – you really should be more careful.'

Martha understood that nothing had happened after all, bent to the garden bed, jabbed the fork once or twice in the earth, leaving it upright, and followed her mother as she energetically marched back to the front. As they rounded the corner, Caroline could be heard crying angrily from the veranda. She was standing in the playpen, shaking its bars with both hands. Martha went to lift her out.

'I put her in there, she's safe there,' said Mrs Quest. 'Do you know, she was sitting on the garden boy's lap.' A look of disgust twisted her face. 'And that lazy thing Alice, or whatever her name is, was just sitting doing nothing.'

Martha set Caroline down. The little girl squatted in front of Alice and began wiping the tears off her face, while Alice smiled painfully and wiped the tears off hers. The garden boy, his whole body expressing sullen hate, was forking over some nasturtiums.

Martha was as usual seething with futile anger. But she was determined to show none. She said politely to her mother, 'If you'll excuse me . . .' and walked over to Alice, who saw her coming and bent her face sideways, looking at the earth while she stirred a twig round and round in the red dust. Caroline was sitting on her knees, with an arm around Alice's neck.

'It's all right, Alice,' said Martha awkwardly.

Alice looked up, the whites of her eyes very clear in her round, brown, pleasant face. She smiled, then dropped her eyes bashfully while some more tears splashed out. She was comforted, however.

Martha handed the child a red hibiscus flower, which she took and began to pull to pieces; and then went towards the garden boy. He kept his eyes sullenly lowered, and went on digging. Martha hesitated over various phrases, and finally brought out: 'If you'd like to go to the back, Silas . . .'

He rose, shooting at her a look of such black hate that she winced.

'It's quite all right, Silas, you can play with Caroline if you like.'

'I'm not a nurse for Miss Caroline,' he said angrily. He walked off.

Martha went back to the house. Her mother was not to be seen, but, hearing a loud and agitated voice from the back, Martha ran through the house to the kitchen. There stood the old cook, eyes bent to the floor, holding his face expressionless, while Mrs Quest banged open cupboards and stooped to look under the stove. Martha watched in silence. Suddenly Mrs Quest straightened herself from a prolonged inspection of a bottom shelf, and fished out a piece of old newspaper in which were half a dozen onions and a heel of stale loaf. 'There!' she announced triumphantly. 'They steal from under your nose and you take no notice.'

'I gave Tobias that,' said Martha quickly. But the old man would not look at her.

Mrs Quest sniffed, then pushed the things away from her on the table. 'Oh, well,' she said hurriedly, 'all the same, you don't lock anything up, you just leave them about, you must lose pounds' worth every day.' She looked sharply around the kitchen. Her eyes fell on her daughter's cold and angry face and she flushed up.

Tobias, in a way that was meant to be noticed, tipped the piece of soiled bread into the dustbin, and put the onions on a shelf in the cupboard. Then he carefully shut all the doors which had been left open.

'There's three days' dust under the stove,' said Mrs Quest defiantly. Tobias left the kitchen in silence.

'Would you like some tea?' inquired Martha with difficulty. She was so angry that her chest and throat were constricted with it, and her throat ached. She looked in silence at her mother, who was now standing rather helplessly in the middle of the kitchen with a distressed and guilty face. She could think of nothing to say. There never was the slightest use saying anything.

'Oh, no,' said Mrs Quest quickly. 'I haven't time, and there's your father, and then the Red Cross, I told Mrs Talbot it was getting too much for me, I haven't time.'

As Martha was turning to leave, taking her at her word, she said confusedly, 'Oh, well, then, just a quick cup.'

Martha reached out and plugged the kettle into the wall.

'Why can't Tobias get the tea?' said Mrs Quest accusingly. 'He's paid for it.'

'Because I choose to do it myself,' said Martha suddenly, snapping it out. She looked straight at her mother.

The small guilty blue eyes wavered and fell. 'Oh, my dear,' said Mrs Quest quickly, 'there's no need to speak like that, you are quite hopeless, you know!' This was a gay little laugh. She added, 'It's quite irresponsible to let Caroline be with the garden boy, he might do anything to her and . . .' She hesitated and brought out in a rush of disgust: 'Filthy creatures!' Martha said nothing. She poured a stream of boiling water into the tea leaves, and set the teapot on the tray.

'There's no need to use all that tea for just the two of us,' said Mrs Quest automatically.

Martha, carrying the tray, led the way to the living room. Mrs Quest followed.

It was a very large room in the centre of the house. It was cool and rather dark. The stone floor had rugs scattered over it. An enormous fireplace, which stretched across half one wall, now showed a painted tub of geraniums that were like a gay parody of fire, the soft scarlet flowers splashed over trailing green.

Mrs Quest shot a keen look around the room. She bent to tug a rug into a different position, then collapsed into a chair. She looked uncomfortable. She pulled off her hat abruptly, with a man's gesture, then patted her puffs of grey hair like a woman.

That long fine white hand, corded and knotted with work, affected Martha with pity. She looked at her mother, and thought exhaustedly that after all she could not help it. 'In a different society,' she concluded, falling back on her old prop, 'she would be quite different.' She poured tea and handed Mrs Quest a cup, noting with irritation that she said quickly, 'No sugar,' although she liked sugar in her tea. Mrs Quest's life was a complicated system of self-denials; from the antagonistic way in which this had been said, Martha deduced that giving up sugar was in some way connected with her.

'I've given up smoking for the duration of the war,' said Mrs Quest, 'as a prayer for Jonathan's safety.'

'Good,' said Martha cautiously, after a pause.

Mrs Quest hesitated, then brought out in a rush: 'And I've given up sugar too.'

As Martha did not ask why, Mrs Quest continued, 'And I've given up sugar as a prayer for you.'

Martha abruptly got up and went into the bedroom. She was dry-throated with anger. Mechanically she opened her wardrobe: there hung Mrs Quest's coat and a cardigan. She looked at her dressing table; among her brushes and trinkets lay Mrs Quest's powder bowl. Martha understood perfectly well the force which made her mother, who had been living in her for so many years, bring her coats here and forget them, bring her personal toilet things 'by accident' and forget to take them away for months, suddenly produce a nightdress, long-sleeved, tight-throated, and say, 'You'd better wear this, you'll catch cold.' There was never a time when half a dozen of Mrs Quest's personal belongings did not lie in Martha's drawers and cupboards. But while Martha had long ago understood, and with the tired pity which was the greatest degree of charity she could achieve, why it should be so, she could not prevent herself from feeling angry.

She sat on the edge of her bed, looked at the hanging trumpets of the white moonflowers, and invoked the deity society. 'People like her can't help it. They've been formed in this mould.' And then came, inevitably, the voice of the enemy, pride. How ridiculous, said the small jeering voice. How ridiculous you are, Martha Quest, caught in this silly, banal, *old-fashioned* situation. There's nothing new to be said about it. Martha rose from the edge of her bed, deciding that she would have a sensible talk with her mother. She returned briskly to the other room, where Mrs Quest was sitting stirring her spoon round and round the cup as if there were sugar in it. She tautened as her daughter entered, and looked at her cautiously.

'Now, look here,' began Martha with cheerful common sense, 'I want to say something to you. I think I've said it before – but let's have another shot at it,' she added, with rueful humour.

Mrs Quest brightened and said in an equally jolly voice, 'Well, what is it this time?'

Martha's spirits sank a little, but she said carefully, 'I want you to try and remember what you would have felt if your mother had run your affairs the way you try to run mine. I don't think you'd have liked it, you know.'

Feeling that this reasonable statement should be enough, she looked towards Mrs Quest and waited. Mrs Quest had stopped stirring, but the spoon knocked tinkling against the side of her cup – her hand was shaking. Martha noticed this with despair.

'Well, someone must keep an eye on you,' said Mrs Quest, laughing. 'You're so scatterbrained, and all your servants do as they like with you – and you're ruining Caroline . . .'

Anger spurted up in Martha, she quelled it. 'You brought me and my brother up the way you wanted, don't you think I should be allowed to do the same with my children?' Her voice shook. She saw that at this admission of weakness Mrs Quest eagerly lifted her face and smiled a small triumph, as if she were conscious of an audience. 'Listen to this absurd child,' that smile said.

Martha's jaws were aching. She relaxed them, and said, 'I'm going to ask you, I think for about the fiftieth time, to stop upsetting my servants and interfering with Caroline.' This was with the desperate humour which she despised as she used it. And some demon caused her to add, in what was a cry of despair, 'After all, Mother, I'm twenty-two this month.'

At this Mrs Quest produced a small amused laugh.

Martha looked through her stock of reasonable arguments, and returned to the first. 'You know,' she said with tired irony, 'I can remember hearing you talk to my father – though I expect you've forgotten that – about your mother. You had to put your foot down, I remember your saying. She was domineering, you said.' She added to herself, 'And you were lucky enough to leave her behind in England and took good care she didn't follow you.'

'Oh my dear!' exclaimed Mrs Quest, distressed. 'I and your father were very fond of your grandmother. How can you say such a thing?'

It occurred to Martha that she was being extremely foolish. That it had come home to her so often before, that she apparently had no power to learn by experience, depressed her into silence.

Encouraged, Mrs Quest said in a gay final tone, 'Well, I don't mean to interfere, of course. Anyway, Caroline is my child – grandchild, I mean,' she amended hastily. 'And I'm not going to see her ruined.'

'As a matter of interest,' inquired Martha, her voice shaking, 'how am I ruining Caroline?'

'Well, I mean to say – ' here Mrs Quest became confused – 'well, my dear, I mean to say, she's so small for her age, and you let her go into the sun without a hat, and she's always with those black things – they're so dirty. And all that sort of thing.'

'She looks remarkably well on it,' brought out Martha, determinedly humorous.

'She's very pale and exhausted,' said Mrs Quest.

Suddenly Martha snapped, 'Oh, shut up and get out of here. I've had enough.'

She looked, astounded, at her mother, at this extraordinary phenomenon which she had after all seen so often before. Mrs Quest, that handsome matron with her broad downright face, had collapsed into a small girl. Yes, a pathetic frightened little girl sat there, looking at Martha with small sad blue eyes which slowly filled with tears.

Pity filled Martha. She at once remembered her mother's hard and disappointing life; she said to herself that, while she, Martha, was of a generation dedicated above all to self-knowledge, Mrs Quest knew no such obligations. She was appalled at her own cruelty. She said helplessly, 'Oh, damn it *all*, Mother!' She got up, sat on the arm of Mrs Quest's chair, and put her arm around the collapsed and shrinking shoulders. It was very unpleasant for her to touch her mother, particularly as she felt those shoulders straighten and gain strength under the contact.

Mrs Quest turned and with an abrupt and clumsy movement of affection embraced Martha, saying inarticulately, 'There, dear, I didn't really mean . . .'

Horror filled Martha. She realized that by this one movement of pity she had completely undone what she might have achieved: pity itself was contaminated, then? Not that it would have made any difference, she said to herself between set teeth. And finally, in the voice of the enemy: It's better not to fight at all, better anything than these disgusting scenes.

'Now that we are having a really frank talk,' said Mrs Quest, already herself again, 'I want to tell you – it is my duty – I mean to say, everyone is saying you should have another baby.'

Martha disengaged herself, got up, and moved stiffly away.

'Oh, don't be so *difficult*, Matty. Actually, that's why I've given up sugar in my tea – as a prayer to God you'll see some sense.' She hesitated. 'It's not fair to Douglas, it's not fair to Caroline, you're simply selfish,' she concluded gaily.

'I'm not prepared to discuss it,' said Martha finally, as she sat down.

'Oh, but, my dear, you must – everyone is saying . . .' She hesitated at Martha's look.

'So *everyone* is discussing whether or not I should have another baby?' inquired Martha, with extraordinary calm.

'Oh, well, you know how people talk.'

341

'I do indeed. I'm glad to provide such a satisfactory topic for the bridge tables.'

'Oh, it wasn't bridge. You know we don't play bridge so much now that the war . . . But at the Red Cross yesterday – ' She coloured up and stopped. 'Anyway,' she recovered herself, 'your father was saying to me only yesterday that you're totally and completely irresponsible, and that Douglas should put his foot down.'

'My father said that?' asked Martha quickly, filled with total dismay. Then she reminded herself of previous occasions when she had taxed her father with what he was supposed to have said.

'And I took Douglas aside for a good talk yesterday. I went to his office,' said Mrs Quest, in her moment of final triumph. 'He quite agrees with me.'

Martha felt as if her last support had gone; but she recovered herself, and said coldly, 'You've no right at all to discuss me behind my back with Douglas.'

For a moment the frightened little girl appear in Mrs Quest, looked appealingly through her eyes – then vanished. She set down her cup, looked about her, picked up her handbag. She stood up. 'Oh, dear, I'm so late.'

Martha picked up, from various parts of the room, spectacles, gloves, a library book and a coat, and offered them to Mrs Quest.

'Oh, dear,' she muttered, 'just put that coat in your wardrobe for the time being, I've so much to carry.'

'I'll carry it to the car for you.'

'Oh, no – it'll do another time.'

'You already have one coat and a cardigan in my wardrobe.'

'It's a very big wardrobe,' said Mrs Quest hastily.

'Not as big as all that,' Martha said, and suddenly laughed irresistibly.

Mrs Quest looked at her with suspicion, and said, 'You just keep them, I'll call for them, I'm too much in a hurry, another time.' She sounded flustered. The small girl was strong in her face – a little girl deprived of something she badly wanted.

Martha put the coat on a chair, and saw her mother's face brighten. She shrugged helplessly.

They went out through the various rooms to the front veranda. Alice and the garden boy and Caroline were once more seated under the tree as if nothing had happened. Caroline was lying on her back on the grass, her legs waving in the air, crooning to herself, while the boy twanged at his hand piano. A yellow butterfly hovered over the grass, and settled with fanning wings on Caroline's foot. She felt the tickle, and craned up her head to see. It was comical to see the puzzled little face watching her own motionless foot where the butterfly clung. Alice was knitting industriously.

Martha looked at Mrs Quest to share her pleasure at the scene, but saw there only the familiar look of agonized disgust.

'Oh, Matty,' said Mrs Quest urgently, 'it's so awful, you really must keep that man away from her.'

Martha put her arm in her mother's, and propelled her fast down the garden path towards the car, which was parked outside the gate under a jacaranda tree. The roof of the car was scattered with loose mauve flowers. Mrs Quest energetically whisked the flowers off, got into the driver's seat, and looked past Martha at the group under the tree. Her distress was sincere and painful.

'Matty,' she began again, her voice trembling, 'Mrs Talbot told me you let that black girl sleep in Caroline's room when you go out – they have all kinds of diseases, it's awful.'

'You'll be late,' said Martha briskly.

'Well, you must boil the sheets afterwards.' She offered Martha a small wan smile. The eyes of the two women met in pure antagonism, and immediately separated. Mrs Quest drove off firmly down the wrong side of the street.

Martha returned indoors, past the group under the tree. Almost at once, Douglas arrived for lunch. He went first over to Caroline, offered her a small toy he had picked up for her, spoke a few cheerful words to the garden boy and the nurse-girl, and came in.

As soon as the meal was served, Martha inquired abruptly,

'I want to know if it's true that you and my mother have been having a nice frank talk about me behind my back.'

He shot her an uncomfortable look, took a large mouthful, and swallowed it before replying: 'We did have a talk, yes. She is your mother, after all,' he said sentimentally.

'Quite.' She said no more. She felt it as an intolerable disloyalty.

After some minutes' silence, Douglas said bluffly but uneasily, 'Oh, come off it, Matty, there's no harm.'

'I think there is,' she said, and rang the bell for the next course. The servant came in with a complicated coloured pudding. Douglas cast an approving eye at it, and softened. The servant went out again. 'Now, look here, Matty, something's got into you, and I think you should snap out of it,' he said firmly.

'Just what conclusions did you and my mother come to about Caroline?'

He flushed a raw-beef colour and said hastily, 'Well, she's not looking so well, is she?'

'I neglect her?'

'I didn't say that.'

'What are you saying, then? You know quite well that at this time of the year all children get worn out with the heat.'

'Well, perhaps you might spend more time with her.'

She looked at him in amazement. 'Let's get this straight. Caroline wakes at five. I have her until seven. I supervise her breakfast. I have her while Alice washes and irons. I always supervise her lunch. I have her from four until she goes to bed. I make all her clothes. She never eats a mouthful I haven't prepared myself – ' But at this point she stopped; for she saw quite clearly that this was like an argument with her mother, conducted on two different levels.

'I didn't say – ' he shouted, furious with her and himself. He knew he was in the wrong – he should not have succumbed to Mrs Quest. On the other hand, he felt himself to be insulted and diminished by this cold and logical mood of Martha's.

'I should like you to say, one way or the other, if you agree with my mother that Caroline is neglected.'

'Of course not,' he shouted.

'Well, that's something.'

'You should have another baby,' he said quickly, ducking his head to his spoonful of pudding.

'So I should.'

'I tell you what, Matty,' he urged in a brotherly, man-to-man way. 'Why not pop down to old Stern and talk it over, eh?'

'Because I am sick or Caroline is?' inquired Martha.

'Look here, Matty, let me tell you – I rang up old Stern, as a matter of fact, and made an appointment with him for this afternoon.'

She digested this. 'My mother said you should make me see the doctor, you rang up Dr Stern, and asked him to talk to me for my own good.'

She saw that he was on the verge of a mood which was occurring more and more often: he would suddenly turn from a sensible, masculine, responsible young man, though perhaps an angry one, into a sulky little boy, his lips quivering with self-pity. He was going to do it now. She hastily said, 'I'll go and see Dr Stern, if you like.' She could not bear the sulky little boy, it made her hate him.

'That's the ticket, Matty,' he said, relieved. He rose and said, 'I must be getting back to the office, there's so much work. Actually, I've been thinking I won't come home to lunch. I'll take sandwiches, we're so understaffed.'

She said, 'Very well,' casually.

He looked swiftly at her, dismayed – he seemed to feel let down. 'It'll mean a long day for you,' he prompted.

'I'll miss you terribly,' she said at once, and he kissed her affectionately and went out.

She immediately began chiding herself for her utter dishonesty. The instinct to comply, to please, seemed to her more and more unpleasant and false. Yet she had to reassure Douglas and kiss him before he left if she was not to feel guilty and lacking as a woman.

Pushing aside this problem, she went inside to smarten herself up for Dr Stern. But Douglas was calling her from the veranda. His voice was authoritative. She went out to him.

'Look at that, Matty,' he said with the sentimental note she hated. She followed his self-consciously shocked gaze, and saw Caroline asleep, sprawled on a rug under the tree, while Alice sat over her, moving a frond of leaves through the hot still air.

She looked at him, puzzled. 'What's the matter?'

'She should be sleeping in her cot,' he said, still in that stern, sentimental voice.

'But, Douglas, you yourself suggested that she should sleep under the tree in this weather – it's cooler than on the veranda.'

He gave her a quick, rather ashamed look: the rather fattish reddish face expressed an official indignation, however. 'Why can't you have the cot moved out there?' he asked.

'But the girl stays there, Caroline isn't left,' said Martha helplessly. 'You know,' she added humorously, 'what's happening is this: You're in a mood of disapproving of me, my mother's got under your skin, and you're just looking for a stick to beat me with.' She laughed uncomfortably and looked at him, waiting.

He went dark red, fidgeted; it was touch and go whether he lost his temper. He put his arms around her and said in a muffled, affectionate voice, 'Oh, Matty . . .' She kissed him, feeling like a traitor to herself, and off he went to the car, beaming and happy, giving Caroline as he passed a proud and proprietary look. Alice made a kind of seated curtsy towards the master, smiling bashfully, while she continued to wave the frond of leaves over the sleeping child's face.

Martha went indoors again. She felt that some kind of crisis had been precipitated. But every instinct she had shrank away from it. To wait, that was what she would like to do – to drift on, and then something would happen, she did not know what. A rescue of some kind – someone would say something; she was listening unconsciously for the right pattern of words again. She decided she would go and see her father, there was over an hour before she must be at Dr Stern's.

When she had changed from one brief, tight bright dress

into another, and painted colour into a face she thought was pale and even rather ugly, she went out to the garden with the push-chair. Caroline was now half awake, blinking up at the tree that stretched over her. Her fists were curled up beside her head – she was a baby again. Then she saw her mother, smiled, and became a little girl, scrambling energetically to her feet. Martha put her into the push-chair, and told the girl she was free until five o'clock. Alice gave her that delightful shy smile, which showed white strong teeth, and went off singing to the back garden.

Martha rapidly wheeled the chair through the patches of shade along the side of the street. Petals fell like a slow blue rain from the masses of sun-filled blossom overhead. Caroline watched them, her eyes rather strained with the midday glare. Martha thought anxiously that perhaps the child was not well after all – she was certainly pale. Perhaps she was not eating enough, perhaps she ... Martha stopped herself, and went off along the other track of worry: what was wrong with Caroline was that she, Martha, did not feel the right way about her. Do I love her? she asked herself sternly, looking with steady criticism at the little girl. The emotion of love vanished as she examined it. At this moment she felt nothing but the bond of responsibility. Then she saw Caroline's black eyes turn towards her, and the little face opened in a warm, confiding smile. Martha's heart went soft with tenderness. At this, the other thought came driving in: It would be much better for her if I didn't. I must be careful not to be too much interested in what she does. But even as she was making these resolutions she felt her face soften in a protective smile, and she thought despairingly, Oh, Lord, there's no escaping it, she'll hate me, too. Yet the idea of her and Caroline hating each other seemed absurd.

But the child was certainly pale, Martha thought anxiously. And there was sweat on her forehead. She went faster; only another block to go. The wheels of the push-chair made two bruised tracks through the thick carpet of petals, the light dry scent of them came up all about them, a scent so faint it was like the smell of dryness itself, a ghost merely. The flowers of light, they were: she could see how the sun shaded a single flower from a light dry mauve that was almost white to a deep purple where the shade clung. She handed a blossom to the child and watched her turn it over and over in the sun; she wondered if the little brain was absorbing the same impressions that she did – then she stopped herself. Why should Caroline see what she saw? It was blackest tyranny even to want it or think it. But here she gained the house.

Her father was asleep under a tree in a deck chair, a white handkerchief over his face. Her mother was nowhere to be seen. She hesitated; should she go into the house? But she hated it, with its tasteless furniture and its ugly pictures. But that was not the real truth. She could not see the things that had made the landscape of her childhood – a silver tray, a row of books, the pictures themselves – without sharp pain at seeing them *here*: they belonged to a ramshackle, silent house in the veld, they belonged to memory. She never entered the house unless she had to. She would spend hours with her father in the garden, but could not enter that house without a confused and painful disturbance which she did not understand.

She wheeled the push-chair as silently as she could towards her father; but as she came near, he sat up and pushed the handkerchief from his eyes, and blinked at her, his face stiff and wooden from sleep. Then it lightened into affection. He said cordially, 'Hullo, old chap, nice to see you.'

She put Caroline down to play, and took the deck chair beside her father. 'How are you?' she asked, and waited patiently while he answered the question with preoccupied attention to detail. She gathered that on the whole he was rather better than usual.

'But you don't want to be bored with my troubles,' he said hastily at the end, and asked, equally from habit, 'And how are things with you?'

She hesitated. She realized she had come here to complain to him about her mother. The banality of the thing stopped her. Besides, it troubled him so, any appeal to him. She said, 'Oh, I'm fine.'

But he had noticed the hesitation, and was looking at her keenly. She felt uncomfortable. Nine parts of his time, Mr Quest was safe in his inner world of memory and vague philosophical speculations; but he could come out of it abruptly, and be warm, shrewd, paternal. This, if she wanted, was one of the times. She hesitated again.

He turned his eyes away, and looked at Caroline, who was rolling over and over on the grass. 'That's a nice kid,' he observed, as if seeing her for the first time. Martha laughed, and again those very shrewd and knowledgeable old eyes turned towards her.

'What's the matter, old chap?' he asked.

Martha felt her lips tremble. She was shaking with dry sobs. She saw he was extremely embarrassed – he could not stand tears.

'Oh, Lord,' he was saying, 'don't cry, there's a good bloke.' He handed her his large handkerchief, and she wiped her eyes and smiled.

'You're looking tired,' he remarked, the glinting dark eyes looking right into her.

'I'm fed up,' she said, in a trembling hard voice. 'I'm so bored I could scream. I can't bear – anything!' she concluded defiantly, looking straight at him. She waited for his judgment.

'I've been thinking for some time things weren't right,' he remarked. He fished in his pocket, pulled out the old tin where he kept his cigarettes, and offered her one, lighting it with the careful old-fashioned courtesy he never forgot. 'Of course,' he went on, 'I've not said anything to your mother.' She looked sharply at him, but saw it was the truth. 'She's making various remarks,' he added, embarrassed. 'However . . .'

Another silence. Mr Quest looked down at his hands in a way which was very familiar. They were large, fine, but rather limp hands. He appeared to be surprised they were his hands. He frowned worriedly at them and remarked, 'I really must find my nail scissors, they've got themselves lost somewhere.' Almost, he allowed himself to drift off; then he sighed, and shot her another speculative glance from under the stiff white cliffs of his eyebrows.

'What did you do it for?' he said suddenly, in a low reproachful voice. 'It was so obvious it wouldn't be any good. You weren't even in love with him.'

'Wasn't I?' she asked, surprised. She could not for the life of her remember what she had felt.

'You weren't in love with him, you've never been in love with anyone – anyone can tell it by looking at you,' he said. That last sentence, cool, direct, the judgment of no less than an experienced man, caused her to look at him in respectful surprise. 'I knew then it was a mistake – but no one can ever tell you anything. Can they, now?' he added, softening it with a sort of affectionate irritation.

'Well, so that's that,' he said, directing the irritation against life itself. 'Marriage, I suppose, is a necessary institution,' he went on after a pause, 'but for *you* to get married at nineteen . . .'

'You mean, I've made my bed and I must lie on it?' she inquired reasonably.

She was not at all prepared for what followed; she thought uncomfortably that this man not only knew her much better than she ever allowed herself to think, but seemed always to be a jump ahead of her. 'You must think it all over, Matty. Whatever you do, you must do it sensibly.'

He could only mean one thing. Yet never had Martha said to herself in so many words that she would leave Douglas. She felt that she would, sometime – but to say it was too frightening and definite.

'Think it over. And don't get yourself in the family way again until you're certain,' said Mr Quest firmly. They looked at each other. His eyes held an affection which made hers fill. But it was years since they had shown each other affection. 'I'm very fond of you,' he said in a low, embarrassed voice. 'Oh, damn it all!' he exclaimed, as his cigarette fell on to his trouser leg. He brushed off the sparks, and by the time things had been restored to order the moment had passed.

He collected his thoughts carefully, and observed, 'I never

did like that man. I never could understand how you could marry such a – commercial traveller.'

Feebly Martha said, 'He's all right, you know.'

'Yes, but, Matty! He's – for the Lord's sake, why couldn't you pick a man who *is* a man?' Again Martha felt herself reddening under the experienced male look. 'Anyone could see with half an eye that – However, that's that,' said Mr Quest irritably.

Martha felt ashamed; at the same time she was supported. Everything would be all right, she felt.

He lit another cigarette for her, and smoked his own in silence.

'It's going to rain soon,' he observed, looking at the sky. The banks of dark foliage about them hung limp and heavy. Clouds of mauve blossom seemed to dissolve into the sky in quivering light. The deep blue overhead was packed with thunderous cloud masses.

'The heat's awful,' said Martha, irritated. She could feel herself hot and sticky under her dress. All the same, she liked it: the heat sang through her like the movements of her own blood. 'I've got to take Caroline to the doctor,' she said without moving.

'Anything wrong?' he asked politely.

'Oh, no, she's quite well.'

Mr Quest surveyed his grandchild, who was now industriously pulling lilies off their stems, and said, 'The image of you at her age. Except for the eyes, of course. And the hair. Where did those eyes come from?'

'Douglas's father, I believe,' said Martha. 'Why?', then, noting his look, she inquired, 'What on earth do you mean?'

'Well, I've often wondered,' went on Mr Quest calmly. 'After all, you don't hold with our morals; as far as I can see there's nothing to prevent Caroline being someone else's child.'

Martha was extremely shocked. 'You're not suggesting,' she said indignantly, 'that I married Douglas under false pretenses?'

'I don't see what's to prevent you, if you've thrown over

conventional morality. For the life of me I can't see why you married him – there must be some reason.'

'There wasn't any reason,' she said helplessly.

'Then you must have been in the family way.'

'I was, but I didn't know it.' Here she began to laugh; for some reason she could not think of it without finding it absurdly funny. 'There I was pregnant, and I didn't know it, though everybody else did . . .' She laughed herself out, and sat wiping her eyes.

'I don't see the joke,' he said reprovingly. 'I think it's appalling. However, there's some comfort in the thought that your generation is no more competent than we were – though I don't expect you to see it.'

His look at her held a familiar irritation; the moment of understanding was over; almost at once he blew out a long cloud of smoke, watched it swirl away sluggishly into the blue air, and remarked in that other, introspective voice, 'Did I ever tell you about that time when I came out of hospital and I was sure I was mad?'

He knew that he had; his urgent glance nevertheless appealed that she should let him tell it again. She sat in silence for some minutes listening.

'Anyway,' he concluded at a tangent, 'as far as I can see, everyone is mad. Do you know, Matty, that's the only explanation for the world that I can see – everyone's as mad as hatters.'

She agreed politely, and, after a decent interval, said she must leave for the doctor's. She put Caroline into the push-chair, and then kissed her father's dry, papery cheek. He inclined it towards her absent-mindedly, murmuring, 'Nice to see you, old chap. Drop in again soon.' He looked at her – his eyes held a sly, evasive gleam. 'There was something I wanted to say to you, what was it?'

She did not smile, but said seriously, 'I must go now, Daddy.' For that was his way of saying that if he had come out of his cloud to be her father, give her advice, support her, he did not intend to be reminded of it later. He was not going to be held responsible. There was in his smile, however, a direct mischievous quality, rather comradely, which acknowledged the situation as plainly as words. Now she smiled back, ironically.

As she wheeled the chair away, he said firmly after her, "Mad. All of us. Everyone.' And with this he reached out for a book which lay face down on the grass, propped it on his knees, and began to read.

By the time she reached the doctor's rooms, she was ready to burst out angrily against the advice she expected him to give her. She could positively hear the male complacency with which Douglas had asked him to speak to her. And no doubt Dr Stern had replied in the same tone? 'Women,' they might have said; 'you know what women are.' Somewhere from the back of her mind floated up a memory of those words, and that tone – who was speaking? Why, of course, Mr Quest, with Mr Van Rensberg on the farm. There was that question of masculine laughter – conspiratorial almost, but most certainly deeply offensive. Mr Quest was one thing with men, another with his wife; Mr Quest half an hour before, and for ten minutes, had been something different again. Martha clung tight to that image of a man, and, thus supported, looked over at Dr Stern, waiting for him to put the pressure on. As she phrased it to herself.

But Dr Stern was being as bland as he always was. He examined the child carefully, and pronounced her to be perfectly well. On Martha's insistence, he repeated, 'Perfectly well – I'll issue a certificate to that effect whenever you like!' Their eyes met briefly; there was a comprehension in his which both upset and consoled her.

It appeared that he thought the interview over; but that was not what Douglas had implied. She said suddenly, 'Perhaps I could see you for myself, for a moment.'

He at once nodded to the nurse, yet another young woman in the glazed white overall, who took Caroline by the hand and trotted her off into the next room.

The room was full of greenish light; light slid along the polished surface of the desk; the atmosphere of hushed professional intimacy was being re-established. Dr Stern had a card before him on his blotter. He was looking down at it, his pale flattish face without expression. He was looking very tired.

'Well, Mrs Knowell?'

Douglas must have been telling a lie, thought Martha. Dr Stern shot her a swift assessing glance, then pushed her card away and leaned back in his chair and yawned. 'This weather makes me sleepy,' he remarked conversationally. 'And I was up all night with a baby. I don't know why babies are always born at night – yours was, wasn't it?' Martha waited on edge for him to add some suggestion about her having another; he did not. 'At this time of the year we all feel it. You look a bit done in yourself. I should take it easy, if I were you. And Caroline – all kids get pale and fretful, and we should try to keep them as quiet as possible. I get all my mothers along in October, worrying themselves sick. Just take it easy, take things easy, I tell them.'

Martha noted the recurrence of the word 'all'; Dr Stern was feeding that need in her to be absolved by being like everybody else; it was the need that sent her off to women's tea parties. There was a part of her brain which remained satirical and watchful, even amused, while it tried to analyse the process by which Dr Stern handled her. But the watchful other person did not prevent him from playing her like a fish on a line, she thought.

'You know, Mrs Knowell, half the women who come in to see me have nothing wrong with them, but it doesn't mean to say they don't need a doctor's advice. Now, you, as an intelligent woman, will understand that.'

Martha smiled disagreeably, at the 'intelligent woman'; he saw the smile, but went on, 'I prescribe a bottle of tonic. It does no harm. It might do some good. But I'm not going to prescribe a bottle of tonic for you. Your husband seems worried about you. You would be surprised how often I get worried telephone calls from young husbands.' Here he laughed as if they shared a secret. 'Perhaps it is just as well that husbands are – sometimes a little off the mark?' He waited for her to laugh.

She had frozen, however; it was too clumsy. He noted her

frown, picked up his pen, and began making a series of sharp downward strokes on a scribbling pad.

Martha thought, He can't judge people deeply; what he has got is an insight into how they react. He knows I resent it, but he doesn't know what I resent. But she understood that his technique was working very well. She was feeling with him against the world of clumsy young husbands. She reminded herself that he was not much more than thirty, not much older than herself. And then: He didn't even know I was pregnant when I came to him that time, and yet here I sit putting myself into his hands. For the first time she suspected that perhaps he *had* known she was pregnant, and understood her well enough to let her become too advanced to do anything about it. Perhaps all the women who came here were handled in the same way?

For the women of the suburbs, doctors do not make mistakes. At least, not their own doctors.

She thought of his wife. In the circle of women it was said that Mrs Stern was not good enough for her husband. Martha had caught a glimpse of them together one Sunday afternoon in the park. Mrs Stern was a small dark plump girl with a high-coloured face, who clung to his arm while he strolled across the grass, apparently as weary and patient as always. Martha had envied her. Being married to Dr Stern would be something quite different from being the wife of one of the boys. She had thought that proud anxious clutching of his arm rather ridiculous; now, if she, Martha, had been married to Dr Stern . . .

But he was speaking. 'Before I got married myself I had all kinds of notions. But I've discovered that I'm not quite as clever as I thought I was. It's one thing to give advice from outside, and another to handle things yourself. I am quite sure my wife thinks me the most clumsy of fellows.' He looked up and smiled. It was a pleasant and disarming smile. He shrugged, as if the whole thing was beyond him; and Martha found herself smiling with him.

'Now, look here, Mrs Knowell,' he began in a completely different tone, all his cards on the table, 'you would be surprised, I am sure, at the number of young married women who come here and sit where you are sitting, in just the same mood – you will forgive me for saying that I can see you are in a mood? I don't want to step in where angels fear to tread, believe me. For instance, only yesterday a patient of mine came in and she was crying her eyes out and said she couldn't stand her husband and was going to leave him. There was no other man, nothing like that, she just couldn't stand things any longer. It's the time of the year. And then, it was last week, I think, another patient I've known for years and years – ' he sounded like a tolerant old man, and it occurred to Martha that he could not have known any patient for years and years, he had not been practising long enough – 'well, she was in the same mood. But she was in here this morning, and she's going to have another baby, and she'd got over it. We do get over it and just jog along. When I come to think of it, there isn't one of my women patients who doesn't come in to me a couple of years after her marriage, wishing she was out of it all. It's not much of a compliment to us men, I expect, but there it is, that's life.'

He again offered her his bland, tolerant smile, and she smiled back her appreciation of this life they must all accept, since there was no alternative. She was feeling quite remarkably relieved and consoled. But she could not help thinking, He'll keep it up for a few minutes; just to make sure.

And he did continue, using the words 'we', 'all', and 'everybody' in every sentence. She was both angrily humiliated and perversely appreciative of the situation.

'My wife is going to have a baby quite soon, Mrs Knowell, and, believe me, I shall make a point of seeing she goes right away from me and the child in about a year's time – we should all get away from each other sometimes. I certainly shall not allow her to have a second baby before she has been off by herself away from me for at least a month.'

The words 'I certainly shall not allow' succeeded in conjuring up such a picture of his marriage, such a complacent and uxorious young husband, that the spell snapped. She instantly decided that he had said to Douglas over the telephone, 'Well, old chap, you know what women are.'

'I can't go for a holiday, Dr Stern, it's out of the question.'

This was flat and rather contemptuous. Dr Stern raised those intelligent tired eyes.

'Well, Mrs Knowell, if you can't, you can't. Bad luck, but there it is.'

She stood up. 'Well, thank you, doctor – I mustn't keep you.' She added suddenly, 'I really am feeling tired – perhaps you could give me a tonic.'

He drew the prescription pad towards him and wrote. 'Yes, we none of us feel too good at this time of the year.'

Caroline was brought in by the nurse. Dr Stern escorted Martha to the door and dismissed her with the usual invitation to drop in whenever she liked. She went through the waiting room, which as always was filled with women whose eyes were fixed on his door.

In the street she hesitated outside a chemist's shop, then took out the prescription for the tonic and tore it up; she thrust the pieces into her handbag with a really violent impulse of anger. Everything seemed hateful. It's all so terrible, she was saying to herself. She wheeled Caroline along the pavement, instinctively keeping in the shade. She could not bear to think of the *everyone*, the *we* and the *all*. So everyone had moods in which they ran off to the doctor, that archpriest, who gave them bottles of tonic and assured them they were exactly like everyone else? They went for a holiday, then they began another baby and were perfectly happy? All the same, she said to herself, it is the mood which is the truth, and the other a lie. She could not maintain the conviction long. The irritable exhaustion faded at the idea of having another baby: it was so exciting to have a baby, to produce another human being out of nowhere – out of the hat so to speak! And then it would be all settled for once and for all. No escape then! And in two or three years' time the baby would be just such another little person as Caroline was now, looking at her with judging eyes. A pang of tired fear went through her. She saw it all so very clearly. That phrase, 'having a baby', which was every girl's way of thinking of a first child, was nothing but a mask to conceal the truth. One saw a flattering image of a madonna-like woman with a helpless infant in her arms; nothing could be more attractive. What one did not see, what everyone conspired to prevent one seeing, was the middle-aged woman who had done nothing but produce two or three commonplace and tedious citizens in a world that was already too full of them.

Martha was on the point of sliding off into those familiar reflections about what the women of the past had felt about it, when she was brought up short by the thought of her father. He had put the problem quite clearly; she must face it.

If she was to leave Douglas, for what way of living was she to leave? There's something so damned *vieux jeu*, she thought gloomily, in leaving like Nora, to live differently! Because we're not such fools any longer. We don't imagine that rushing off to earn one's living as a typist is going to make any difference. One is bound to fall in love with the junior partner, and the whole thing will begin all over again. The idea was so unpleasant that she swung round: Not at all; she would submit, as everyone else did.

She began daydreaming. Since there was no woman she had ever met she could model herself on, she created a brooding and female spirit in that large cool house in the avenues, surrounded by a crowd – for, while she was about it, she imagined six or seven children, not just two – a brood, then, of charming children, who fed from this source of warmth and creativeness as at a spring. A picture much more attractive than the cold and critical young woman typing letters in a business office.

One of those warm, large, delightful, maternal, humorous females she would be; undemanding, unpossessive. One never met them, but, if she put her mind to it, no doubt she could become one. She would lapse into it as into a sea and let everything go . . . And, severely suppressing the pangs of pure panic that kept rising in her every moment at the idea of abandoning the person she felt herself to be, she set herself to imagine the house, all its rooms full of children, and she in the middle like a queen ant.

She had reached a corner where she must turn off into the leafy avenues. She was dipping the wheels of the push-chair down off the pavement, when she heard a shrill whistle. There was a note in it which made her glance sharply around. On the opposite pavement stood a group of young men in the grey uniform, and they were whistling after her with mixed derision and admiration. She at once felt herself stiffen and become self-conscious. She turned her head away as the whistles rang out again, with a jeering note in them because of her aloofness, and was furious with herself because of that self-consciousness. She hastily gained the opposite pavement, and turned off into the avenue before her own so as to escape the men and her own embarrassment.

This small episode had destroyed the vision of the brooding mother with the flock of children. She could not regain it. She marched sternly up under the drooping purple jacarandas – the sun had lost its hot white glare, and was beaming out a thick yellow which shaped the jacaranda blossoms into clusters of heavy purple – and was pervaded with a disgust of herself, life, everything, so strong it was like a nausea.

She heard steps hurrying up behind her, heard her name called, and turned to see William approaching. She had not seen him since that afternoon eighteen months ago when Douglas returned.

'Were you with that – mob?' she inquired, sour but smiling.

And he grinned, returning equably, 'Boys will be boys.' For naturally he, the individual, had nothing to do with the group he had been part of a moment before. 'Where are you going?'

'Home,' said Martha, resuming her progress.

William advanced his opinion that Caroline was growing a big girl. Martha agreed. William said it was a long time since they had met. Martha said a very long time. William said he found the weather very trying. Their eyes met and they laughed.

He certainly did not look comfortable. The thick stiff cloth seemed more than ever like a variety of shell. In movement he had a quick lightness, almost grace, but the uniform was too much for him, he looked eclipsed. But from the grey carapace his pale face emerged, now rather flushed, and the very clear blue eyes – not like Douglas's eyes, which were a strong rather muddy blue, but a deep blue, like water or sapphires – were calm and intelligent. His hair was bright rough brown, like metal in the sunshine, under a cap which he wore jauntily, at a rakish angle, as they all did – as if it was a joke that they must wear it at all.

'I'll go with you a little way – nothing better to do this fine afternoon.' And he marched along beside her, hands in his pockets.

'How's the – group?' inquired Martha awkwardly.

'Oh . . . fine.' But he relented and said in a friendly, casual way, 'We did hope you would join us. But of course it is difficult now – we see your difficulties,' he amended, colouring a little.

But what did that 'we' mean now?

'You've broken away from that – the old gang?'

'Well, of course, with this sudden swing, it's easy to get things going.'

'What sudden swing?'

He looked at her swiftly, frowning and incredulous. Then: 'Surely it must be obvious even to the wives of prominent civil servants that there's a change in the atmosphere?'

'I haven't been reading the newspapers,' she said confusedly.

He pursed up his lips a little, was silent; then he saw her apologetic face and inquired obligingly, 'Why not?'

'They're all so disgusting.'

'Oh granted, granted.' But he again relented and said, 'There are other ways of coping with it than not reading them.' His air of disapproval annoyed her. She thought, He's nothing but a boy, anyway. He was about twenty, and she two years older; but she was married and had a child. She felt maternal towards him.

They had reached the house. Through the flowering hedges, beneath its sheltering trees, it looked very large, settled, permanent. The garden boy was chatting with the nursegirl under a tree, the piccaninny was gathering peas in the vegetable beds, the houseboy was sweeping the deep flight of front steps.

'A delightful feudalism,' he remarked pleasantly. 'Truly delightful. And you the chatelaine of it all.' She could not help laughing, though she was angry with him. 'Oh, well, it can't be helped,' he went on, casting calm blue eyes over the place. 'And I'll admit that there *are* worse ways of spending one's life.'

He wanted to be asked in, she could see. But she remembered Douglas: he would be angry. First, she thought confusedly, I must get this business sorted out – for once and for all!

'Give my regards to the old man,' he said.

He meant Douglas. She stiffened.

'Well, so long. If you ever feel like a nice change, you've got Jasmine's telephone number.' And he walked off back to town.

She was feeling mean, because she had not asked him in. Almost, she called him back. But she wheeled Caroline into the garden, and handed her over to Alice, and then went straight to the bedroom. The morning's newspaper was spread on the beside table. She opened it and began studying it.

Since she had last looked at a newspaper, it appeared that the Russians had become heroes and magnificent fighters. They were no longer a rabble of ill-equipped moujiks fleeing before the Nazi hordes. A remarkable change – she had ceased to read the papers because she had been sickened by their gloating tone over the invasion of Russia: everyone was delighted, it was obvious, that their gallant allies were being so thoroughly beaten.

There was an epic battle going on at a place called Stalingrad which was – so some anonymous leader writer said – a turning point of the war.

The local situation had remained static. There were two leaders written with that irritable self-satisfaction which was so familiar, about how the native population did not appreciate what the whites were sacrificing in uplifting them from their savage state, how they did not understand the dignity of labour, how they could not expect to be as civilized as the whites in under a thousand years, for this was the length of time it had required the British people to evolve from mud huts to democracy and plumbing. All this could be taken as read. In the letter columns there was a new and strident note. Two respected citizens wrote at length warning the population that there were agitators abroad who were putting ideas into the heads of the natives; 'certain individuals, inspired from Moscow . . .' The Government should immediately examine these organizations, which, under cover of raising aid for Russia, were, in fact, spreading ideas inimical to white civilization.

This was all very interesting. The advertisement columns confirmed that all sorts of new activities were going on. As well as the usual cinema shows, dances and meetings, there were half a dozen notices of meetings run by as many organizations – Help for Our Allies, Sympathizers of Russia, and so on – on subjects like 'The Constitution of the Soviet Union' and 'Life on a Collective Farm in the Ukraine'.

Altogether there was a feeling of movement, stir and excitement which communicated itself to Martha. But above all was she struck by the difference in tone of the paper from a year ago about the war. She rummaged in a cupboard, and found a pile of dead newspapers. Two years ago, the Russians had been dastardly and vicious criminals plotting with Hitler to dominate the world. A year ago they were unfortunate victims of unscrupulous aggression, but unluckily so demoralized that as allies they were worse than useless. Now, however, they were a race of battling giants.

While not reading the newspapers is a practice to be condemned, there are times when it can yield interesting results. For the thought which naturally presented itself to Martha was, How did the editor of this same newspaper picture his readers? There was no connection between the headlines of two years ago, a year ago, and today.

There was a knock on the door; Alice said she had brought Caroline in to be fed. Martha said that for this once she would leave the child to her. She remained sitting on the edge of the bed, trying to collect her ideas, which were in a state of extraordinary confusion.

It was quite clear that the group, however it was now constituted, were 'doing something' at last. But what? Martha began to indulge in attractive daydreams of herself going among people, like a heroine from an old Russian novel. Common sense told her to desist. If Jasmine, or William, or anyone else had been going among the people, then there would have been a much stronger reaction than a couple of indignant letters to the press. The colour bar made that form of agitation impossible.

Suddenly, and without any warning, that feeling of staleness came over her, a sort of derisive boredom. She could not account for it, but the picture of a small group of people, middle-class every one of them, having meetings, running offices, even going among the people, struck her as absurd, pathetic – above all, old-fashioned. Here it was again, the enemy which made any kind of enthusiasm or idealism ridiculous.

The life she was living seemed dignified and attractive.

But no sooner had she come to this conclusion than disgust rose against it; and she thought with tender longing of these new possibilities; nothing could have seemed more heroic and admirable than Jasmine, William and the rest. Yet almost at once, and in proportion to the strength of her desire to join them at once, derision arose, that stale disgust.

She remained, tossing from one mood to the other, motionless on the edge of the bed, while the darkness came down outside and the street lights shone out.

There were steps in the middle of the house, the door opened, the lights crashed on. Douglas came in. He said in a jolly voice, 'What are you doing, sitting in the dark?' But there was a cautious look on his face.

She roused herself and said, 'Oh, nothing.'

He looked at the mess of newspapers on the bed, and said contemptuously, 'Oh, that rubbish!' – meaning world affairs in general – and she saw that the self-satisfied note in his voice was of the same quality as her own mood of gloomy fatality.

She hastily folded up the papers, with a movement as if she were concealing something from him.

'Is Caroline in bed?'

He opened the door into the next room. Caroline was being watched at her supper by Alice.

He returned, and said sentimentally, 'Matty, surely you can give the child her supper at least.'

She shut down her anger, and remarked, 'The doctor says she is perfectly well.'

'Oh – that's a good thing.' He stood looking at her with a tentative indignation.

'And I'm perfectly well, too,' said Martha abruptly, smiling in a way which she meant to be unpleasant.

'That's good.' This was bluff and hearty; he turned away to hang up his jacket in the wardrobe. 'I've got some news,' he began, still in a bluff voice, which made her stiffen defensively. 'Old Billy in Y — has got leave, and they want me to go down and take his place for a few weeks.'

'Well, are you going?'

He turned sharply, and gve her a consciously reproachful look, biting his fat lips. 'You could come, too,' he said, breathing heavily. 'There's a house.'

'But, Douglas, what are we to do with this one? Just shut it up?'

'Oh, well, if you feel like that . . .'

'How long are you going for?'

'Three weeks.' He looked at her again, sideways. 'What did old Stern have to say?'

'Nothing much – but there really isn't any need to worry about Caroline's well-being.' Again it was a moment when the hatred between them shocked and dismayed them both.

'Well, perhaps, it's just as well we'll – have a break for a few weeks, eh, Matty?' He came over and stood a few inches from her, smiling in appeal.

She at once responded by rising and kissing him – but on the cheek, for her lips, which had intended to meet his, instinctively moved past in revulsion. This revulsion frightened her so much she flung her arms about him and warmly embraced him.

The act of love immediately followed.

There is a type of woman – although whether she is a modern phenomenon or has always existed is not a question for novelists – who cannot bear to be found wanting physically. In Martha's case, it worked like this: her mother had a rooted dislike for all matters sexual; therefore it was a matter of pride for Martha not only to be attractive sexually, but to be *good in bed*. There are hundreds of thousands of young women in our society who when all else fails – they may be inefficient at their work, and bored wives and mothers – find solace in the belief that they are good in bed. Not for one moment have they ever paused in their determination to be better than their parents by flying this particular flag. But they have no hesitation in taking from their parents the romanticism which becomes the moral support not of free love – Martha came too late to believe in that; it was associated with the Twenties and thus had a stale and jaded sound to it – but of a determined hedonism, an accomplished athleticism, since 'the book' lays all doubts and suspicions, above all by the variety and ingenuity of the physical attitudes it recommends. Douglas could hardly be blamed for not understanding the thoroughness of Martha's dislike for him, since that prohibition prevented her from ever expressing it in bed. The moment she did so, it would have meant the complete collapse of the romantic picture she maintained of him. A young woman of this type will expend immense energy on arranging her image of her husband into something admirable and attractive. And this as a question of principle. Such a young woman will confuse all bystanders by being charmingly devoted to her husband, angrily defending him against every word of criticism until the very moment she leaves him. After which she will not have one good word to say for him.

On this particular occasion Martha was irritable and, when she realized it, apologetic. She finally escaped with the abrupt remark, 'I must go and see how Caroline is.'

'Oh, but, Matty, she's got the nurse, and I'm going away for weeks.'

'But she mustn't be neglected,' she said, laughing in a way

which told them both that the moment of reconciliation had been a failure. They ate dinner in silence, avoiding each other's eyes.

Next day, Douglas left for Y—, which was a couple of hundred miles south, a small administrative centre.

They embraced affectionately at parting. Then Douglas said sentimentally, 'Do look after Caroline, Matty.' He added, 'You have so much to give her.' He had taken to using the last phrase, half guiltily, meaning that he knew she intended that what she had to give would not all be swallowed in children and housekeeping, whereas he was determined it should be.

She said involuntarily, 'Don't be so damned dishonest.'

He muttered angrily, 'I hope you'll be in a better temper when I come back.'

After a few moments of guilt, not so much at what she had said, but because she had allowed herself to see him as clumsy and ridiculous, she went indoors, feeling deliciously alone and free.

She read a little, played with Caroline, sewed for a while, as if she had no intention of spending the three weeks of freedom in any other way. Then, without knowing until the moment she lifted down the receiver that she was going to do so, she telephoned Jasmine.

Jasmine was calm, unsurprised, and very efficient about dates and places.

Martha arranged to meet her and William the following evening, to talk things over.

Chapter Two

Martha waited for that first appointment with Jasmine like a girl going to her lover. She was dressed and ready two hours before the time, and was just about to start when Jasmine telephoned to say that unluckily she had an unexpected meeting. But she would meet Martha at eight outside McGrath's so that they might both go to yet another meeting, organized by Help for Our Allies. Jasmine felt, she said in that small demure voice, that Martha would find it interesting.

Martha set herself to wait another two hours, conscious that much of her enthusiasm was ebbing. There is something in the word 'meeting' which arouses an instinctive and profound distrust in the bosoms of British people at this late hour of their history. And then the name 'Help for Our Allies' had a childish sound, with strong overtones of tract and even charity. Martha had lapsed back into her condition of irritated distaste long before the time appointed, and it was with an effort of will that she roused herself to go to the car. She waited outside the hotel for some twenty minutes before Jasmine and William appeared, each carrying armfuls of books and leaflets. There was between these two such a look of shared mission that Martha felt lonely and excluded as she followed them into McGrath's ballroom, which was released for this one evening from mess dinners and war charity dances.

The place was full. Seven or eight hundred people were crowded into the big ugly hall. Martha saw that they were all well-dressed and comfortable citizens, and her confusion was completed when she noticed Mr Maynard and Mrs Maynard seated side by side in the front row – large, imposing, black-browed, and apparently pleased to shed approval on the proceedings by being there.

She was hurried to an empty seat by Jasmine, who at once left her and pushed her way through the crowds to the platform, where she sat at a table with a group of people whom Martha did not know. Looking at her programme, however – it was beautifully printed on expensive paper – she saw that the speakers included two clergymen, two members of the Cabinet, a leader of the Social Democratic Party. These gentlemen beamed protective approval at Jasmine, a small demure figure in bright flowered silk.

Jasmine whispered for a moment to a tall, thin man, the Minister for Native Affairs, who stood up and began to speak. He spoke for about ten minutes about the glorious heroism of our Russian allies, interrupted at every moment by storms of applause. All around Martha people were sitting leaning forward, hands poised ready for the next point where they might clap approval; faces were smiling and flushed. When the tall thin man sat down, they applauded for a long time, and they began again before the next speaker could open his mouth.

Yet were these not the same citizens who had been reading and approving the *Zambesia News* in its phase of, recently, pitying these same heroes for their ragged and enslaved condition, and, not so long before that, execrating them for their barbarity?

To Martha it was quite inexplicable, and she looked for enlightenment towards the wall where William stood leaning together with a group of others. Boris and Betty were there, and some men in uniform. Martha saw that as the applause crashed out and the speakers paused, smiling with the deprecating modesty suitable to such moments, this group tended to exchange glances under eyebrows slightly raised. When they applauded, which they did promptly, it was without that self-abandoning enthusiasm which apparently had everyone else in its grip, but in a measured way. Yet surely if there was any group of people in this room entitled to be delighted, even grateful, that the Soviet Union was being honoured in this fashion, it was this one? Their faces expressed – what was it? It was a sort of patient irony, and to Martha, who was in the first flush of adolescent longing to fling herself wholeheartedly into a cause, their look of irony was like a chill of cold water. She positively hated them for not flinging themselves away in abandoned applause, like the others. Then, turning her eyes back towards the platform, she happened to notice Mr and Mrs Maynard, and on their faces too was precisely that look of reserve; they too exchanged glances, with a tightening of the lips, and they clapped decently and firmly, and as if to a time limit. Martha looked more closely among the throng of eager citizens, and saw that there were several others – a couple of journalists from the *News*, a row of people near the Maynards, Colonel Brodeshaw and his wife – who were similarly doling out their applause to measured limits. From which she had to conclude that there were two groups of people in the room who were in command of themselves and their thoughts, and the look of irony which both had was in fact a rather contemptuous resignation towards the hundreds in the grip of mass emotion.

After about two hours of speeches and applause, Jasmine rose and suggested that they might ask one of the men who were 'actually doing the fighting' to say a few words. William came forward and climbed on the platform. His uniform was greeted with fervour. He waited patiently for silence, his notes held ready in his hand. Then he said that of course men in the Forces were not allowed to take a part in politics, but raising money for our allies was obviously a different matter. He then, with a rapid glance downwards towards his notes, began to speak on that subject which filled Martha's thoughts. He had a quiet, easy, informal way of talking, not at all the professional manner with which they had been wooed for the last two hours, and it was noticeable that there were a few moments' chill. And there seemed to be a few people who considered that an analysis of what he called the campaign of lies about the Soviet Union was not really unpolitical. But in a short while he had the whole crowd roaring with laughter, although there was a note of discomfort in it. He had with him (or rather,

Jasmine produced them obligingly from behind the table) a pile of *Zambesia News* for the past four years, and proceeded to discover and expose the contradictions and improbabilities that newspaper had offered its readers – who were now laughing delightedly, or so it seemed, at themselves. As a final feat, he took a single issue from the year before, and reduced it in a few moments to the most abject nonsense, while the crowd chuckled and the *News* reporters, who were seated at a special table to one side, took notes with expressions of calm and democratic indifference.

William then invited them to learn to read newspapers with more discrimination. He pointed out that until perhaps two months before there might have been twelve people in the whole colony – excluding the men of the Air Force, of course, he added involuntarily, causing a small chill to fall for a moment – who knew that Soviet tanks were not made of cardboard and that the Soviet people were not abject serfs. And these twelve people – he would say twelve for the sake of argument – were better informed not because they were in any way more intelligent than the ladies and gentlemen now seated before him, but because they had learned to treat the newspapers with the suspicion they deserved. As for the heroism of the Soviet people – but here the applause crashed out again, and he waited for it to stop. There were piles of books and pamphlets at the door, he concluded, and he invited them to buy them on their way out. With this he smiled, and retired from the platform by jumping lightly down from it to the floor, a feat which earned fresh handclapping and a few appreciative jeers from some men in uniform at the back. To which he responded with a half-mocking bow, and made his way to the table next to the door, where he seated himself behind barricades of literature.

Jasmine got up and thanked 'our young friend from the Air Force' for his contribution, and appealed for money to buy medical supplies 'for our gallant allies'. In a few moments the sum of over a thousand pounds had been collected; bank notes and cheques appeared everywhere, and the air was thick with the sound of chinking silver.

The meeting was over. Martha, crushed in a jam of people by a pillar, saw Mr and Mrs Maynard go past. Mrs Maynard was saying, 'I think one might drop a word in the right quarter.'

Martha squeezed through to the table, which was now nearly empty of its books and pamphlets, and heard one of the men in uniform, a tall, dark, hollow-faced man with a satirical look, remark, 'Well, what a performance – but it was the wrong audience.'

'Not for collecting money,' returned Jasmine with a small satisfied smile. She turned and saw Martha, who was waiting to be gathered in then and there to the bosom of this group of people where she knew she belonged. But Jasmine merely said, 'Well, what did you think? Not bad, considering.'

'Oh, it was marvellous!' said Martha indignantly. 'Come and have some tea with me,' she added hopefully.

'I can't, I have a meeting,' said Jasmine at once. Then, as Martha looked disappointed, she said, 'I'll ring you tomorrow.'

With this Martha had to be content. She was pushing her way out in the tail of the retreating crowd, when William came after her and said, 'Can't we sell you some lit?'

'What's lit?' she asked.

'We feel you should do some reading.' And with this he handed her some books. 'That will be twelve and sixpence.'

She found the money hastily and with difficulty, reflecting that to him she was rich: he was not likely to understand the god, middle age, for whose sake she was always short of money. Then she thanked him. Her look was such that he forgot for a moment that she was a soul to be saved.

He asked intimately, 'Well, did you like it?'

'Wonderful,' she said again eagerly.

He smiled, and said, unexpectedly blushing, 'I'll come and see you tomorrow afternoon – if you're free.'

She left, feeling like a child left out of a party, because they did not at once invite her to that meeting to which they would all now go. But the way William had blushed made her feel it would not be long before she would be one of them.

At home she glanced cursorily into the nursery, where Caroline was asleep in her cot, and Alice beside her on the divan. Then she retired to her bed with the books. She read through them one after another; the dawn was coming up red behind the moonflowers when she had finished.

She had a very confused idea of what she had read; she was content to leave the mass of facts and figures until later. But behind these dull bricks of truth rose the glorious outline of a view of life she had not suspected. The emotion that gripped her was mostly rage: she was twenty-two; she had been born during that revolution, which, to say the least, had been important in the world's development, and yet this was the first time she had been told anything about it. Her rage was even greater because she had been such a willing accomplice in this process of not thinking. For there had been plenty of moments when she might have fitted a few facts together to make a truth. She had not. Her upbringing, her education, her associates, the newspapers, had all conspired to bring her to the age of twenty-two, an adult, that is, without feeling more about what was going on in the socialist sixth of the world – which happened to be the title of one of the books – than a profound reluctance to think about it at all.

Even now, as she sat there, still dressed, on the edge of her bed, she had two clear and distinct pictures of that other part of the world – one noble, creative and generous, the other ugly, savage and sordid. There was no sort of connection between the two pictures. As she looked at one, she wanted to fling herself into the struggle, to become one of the millions of people who were creating a new world; as she looked at the other, she felt staleness, futility.

What, then, was the cynicism that certainly afflicted all the people around her who thought at all? It no longer seemed even mildly attractive. With one sudden movement of her whole being she discarded it, and committed herself to the other. It was as if her eyes had been opened and her ears made to hear; it was like a rebirth. For the first time in her life she had been offered an ideal to live for.

But the immediate political emotion of anyone shaken suddenly into thinking is anger: she was filled with rage at having been cheated; she felt as if she had been lied to, led by the nose, made a fool of, all her life. She was as angry with herself as she was with the people whom she saw in this beautiful naïve moment of awakening as an organized and cynical group who consciously devoted themselves to deceiving her and her generation out of their birthright. What she wanted, in short, was some sort of revenge: if the first political emotion of people like Martha is anger, the second is blind anarchy; if anyone had asked her in that moment to take a gun in her hand and go out to destroy those people who had been making a fool of her, she would have gone without a second thought. Luckily, however, there was no one to make any such demand.

Instead she went to the front veranda, where the day's *News* had been flung down, and opened the paper to find the report of last night's meeting. It merely said that a large sum of money had been collected for our gallant allies at a well-attended meeting. She threw it aside, and went to Caroline. She bathed her, fed her, despatched her to the garden with Alice, and waited for Jasmine to ring her. Time went past and Jasmine did not ring. Martha therefore rang Jasmine. The small quiet voice said that she could not come to see Martha, because she had a meeting. It was then ten in the morning.

In the last twelve hours, the banal and tired sound of the word 'meeting' had quite vanished for Martha; and she sat and thought wistfully of those adventurous gatherings from which she was shut out. She saw Jasmine on the platform yesterday, so efficient, so self-effacing, devoted. Nothing could have appeared more glamorous than such a role.

The outward form of her day was untroubled by the violence of her impatience. She looked after Caroline and attended to the housework as usual; she felt herself to be a completely different person. Later she remembered that William was coming. She did not want to see William. She wanted Jasmine, who had, like herself, been brought up in this country, fed on the colour bar and race hatred. For William things seemed altogether too easy; he had been born, or so it seemed, with pamphlets in his hand and clear convictions in his head.

When he arrived, she offered him tea like a hostess, quite determined to say nothing to him of what she felt; besides, he was nothing but a boy. He shed packets of books and papers on to chairs, removed his jacket, flung down his cap. He would never be anything but a civilian. He was one of the thousands of British soldiers who went through the war out of intellectual conviction: it was a war against fascism and it was his duty to fight. But he never felt anything but a civilian dressed up. The difference between men like William and the passionate soldiers of the war could be seen the moment those other groups entered the colony to train as pilots – the Greeks, the Yugoslavs, the French, the Poles.

As things were, William had an afternoon off between doing clerk's work for the Air Force and addressing a meeting on Hegel, and he was prepared to take an interest in Martha.

In the camp it was said, with the mixed pride and contempt appropriate for occupation forces, that the women in the town were a pushover. His tone towards Martha was of a tentative gallantry, but Martha at once reacted against it. She felt that this commonplace flirtatiousness was nothing less than an insult to the revolution itself. She was cold and polite. He instantly became – as she put it – sensible, and she was able to like him again.

He began talking of the meeting last night – not a bad show at all he considered; but she interrupted him. 'Look, I want to know . . .' Her tone was warm and eager, startling in contrast to the coldness of only a minute before. 'I've been thinking – well, if there's something going on, I want to be part of it.'

'What makes you think anything is going on?' he inquired.

'Oh, don't be silly,' she said crossly.

He reflected for a moment, perched on the arm of a chair,

and seemed embarrassed. After a while he suggested, 'You could join the committee of Help for Our Allies.'

'Oh, Lord,' protested Martha.

'But it's very important work.' Then he confirmed her instinct that there were further degrees of initiation, by remarking, 'How about Sympathizers of Russia?'

She felt snubbed. 'Look,' she said, direct, humorous, but resentful. 'You don't have to – flannel, like this. If there's a Communist group, I want to join it.' She leaned forward eagerly, as if expecting to be absorbed into it that very instant.

'But there isn't one,' he said.

She did not believe him. Seeing her disappointment, he said, 'There really isn't. I can't go into it all now, but it's not as easy as that.'

She was remembering the group of people against the wall the night before; they had the appearance of a welded whole, with their exchanged glances and shared understanding.

'Besides,' he went on, in a light but uncomfortable voice, 'what would the old man say?'

'Old man?' she said stiffly.

'Wives of civil servants really can't do this sort of thing.'

'You talk as if he were an idiot,' she said angrily. 'He's progressive. He – reads the *New Statesman*,' she concluded triumphantly.

But at this he let out an involuntary and delighted chuckle, and got up, with the unmistakable air of a man escaping from a situation.

'Don't go,' she said quickly.

He sat down again slowly, looking at her very seriously. He had half hoped to have a casual affair with her – though without any intention of being disappointed if he did not. He was a very practical young man, and he understood quite well that this warmth, this eagerness – she was looking at him now with an earnestness that he found quite delightful – would make anything casual impossible. But he had sized up the state of affairs in the colony within a week of arriving in it, and he had no intention of getting involved in this mess of broken marriages and passionate love affairs. His plans for the future were definite, and did not include burdening himself with a spoilt colonial woman.

But she was attractive; and that eager sincerity was warming him out of common sense. He was on the point of being in love with her.

As for Martha, she had understood that he was not at all a mere boy, a child. On the contrary, compared with Douglas it was he who was the man. He was not like the immature young men that emerge from the universities, he was not like the boys of the Club. He had come from something quite different: a small, decent, upper-working-class family with roots in the labour movement. He had gone steadily and sensibly through school, and afterwards taken courses at night schools to study what he needed to know while he learned printing. The war had given him leisure, which he devoted to philosophy and physics. He was not ambitious, but he knew what he wanted. Which was to get through the war, take a few more courses, and qualify for what interested him – he wanted to be an engineer. In due course he would make a sensible marriage.

Martha asked, in that eager way which invited him to share with her the exquisite and unique experience which was his life, 'Tell me, I want to know, how did you join the Communist Party?'

'I was never a member of the Party,' he said at once.

She wilted away from her eagerness as if finally disillusioned. She appeared critical.

He found himself piqued; unpleasant to lose this approval so soon! He set himself to explain. 'I didn't approve of the Party's policy during the phony war. So I didn't join. I had reservations.'

The way he said 'the Party' struck her as comical. Not for the first time. After all, at least half the reporters, writers, civil servants, etc. – the intellectuals, in short – have at some time or another been in, around, or near the Communist Party, and ever afterwards they refer to it as 'the Party' as if there could never be another, even while most passionately engaged in pretending they know nothing of it. But William might say 'the Party' in that familiar, easy way; he was not in it. Her vision of him had collapsed. From being a whole-hearted crusader, he had become a cautious dealer in reservations. She had been regarding the alert, intelligent young face topped by the metal-bright hair as if it had been the face of the revolution itself; now she listened to a quiet analysis of the Stalin–Hitler pact and the phony war and heard a note she knew far too well; it was this: if William had been in charge of policy during that period, it would not have been as inefficient, clumsy and inadequate as it had been with other people in charge.

Martha frowned. She was thinking uncomfortably that she was doomed to be, not attracted to – she would not admit that yet – but *with* people who administered other people; more, people who were the dissatisfied administrators whom Fate or – and here she carefully tested the new phrase – The Logic of History did not recognize for what they were, by nature far more efficient than those whom Fate or Logic actually chose as its servants. There are people, warm-hearted and enthusiastic, but unfortunately liable because of these very qualities to a prolonged juvenescence: Martha could not bear that people tended to fall into types. It was to Douglas rather than to William that she remarked grudgingly, 'Well, that may be so, but perhaps you wouldn't have done any better yourself if you'd been running the show.'

He stopped himself in a long sentence which dissected the reasons why Harry Pollitt was right and not wrong in his first assessment of 'the line' – he used the phrase with a sort of jaunty respect – and his look at Martha changed. That warmth and enthusiasm of hers must be met. He wavered, and fell over on the wrong side of his barrier of caution. It was in a new voice, humorous, light and intimate, that he said, 'No, Matty – I would have been *much* more efficient.'

She laughed at once. They looked at each other – and then away. It was too early for either of them to acknowledge that their hearts were beating fast.

He rose, and said, 'I must be downtown in half an hour.'

'I'll run you down in the car,' she said at once.

He refused quickly – it was imperative that he should be alone to think. But he smiled intimately at her before he left, swinging his pack over his shoulder, and cramming on the little cap which made him a soldier again.

He walked rapidly off, as if really in a hurry, until out of sight of the house, and then strolled comfortably under the trees. He was thinking that he had been irresponsible to encourage Martha about that Communist group she had set her heart on. The truth was that he did not know himself what was happening.

Some months ago, when Hitler attacked the Soviet Union, the left wing of the old discussion circle had suggested setting up Help for Our Allies. This was given immediate approval. Quite soon there was an organization with an office, typewriters, filing cabinets and a letterhead on which appeared the names of about fifty prominent citizens. On the committee, which was very large, were all the members of the discussion circle, from Messrs Perr, Forester and Pyecroft down to Boris Krueger and Jasmine.

But no sooner was this running satisfactorily than the minority – Boris, Betty, Jasmine and their allies – seethed into activity with a new organization, Sympathizers of Russia. These two organizations, even to an unsophisticated eye, offered food for thought. The left wing of the Help for Our Allies formed the committee of the Sympathizers, together with a whole ferment of new people, chiefly from the Air Force, who regarded the first committee with calm contempt as cautious temporizers. For a while Jasmine had been secretary of both organizations. She was so efficient that it was a pity to waste her.

About two weeks ago, a new dissatisfaction had set in.

It had begun at the moment when Mr Perr, in a humorous voice which nevertheless reeked of suspicion, remarked at a meeting of the Help for Our Allies Committee that the said committee had no intention of being run by a Communist faction. At this, eyes had met all around the long table, some hurt, some puzzled. No one knew of a Communist faction. As for the majority of the committee, simple people who were unpolitical on principle, they were upset, and found it all unpleasant. For they did not understand the law that people like Mr Perr who have been called Communists in popular gossip spend nine-tenths of their time proving their bona fides by attacking Communists. That committee meeting left an unpleasant taste in every mouth. As for the left wing itself, Jasmine, Betty, Boris and William, they made inquiries of each other, and concluded that Mr Perr was suffering from the mania only to be expected of him. At this point, a certain Jackie Bolton, sergeant, administration, recently posted to the city from another down south, took them to tea at a certain café downtown, and informed them they were a lot of skulking petty bourgeois who refused to face up to their responsibilities. He, Jackie Bolton, was about to form a Communist group, and invited them to join.

But, while all their hearts leaped to this proposal, they did not at once agree. 'Matters should be discussed,' said Jasmine. That was three days ago.

Since then there had been a tense atmosphere in all the committee, and people tended to go off in pairs talking earnestly, looking at other couples similarly engaged with suspicious inquiry. No one knew what was going on; but they felt instinctively that Jasmine was the key to everything. Jasmine patiently cautioned them all: They must be responsible and sensible, they must not do things in a hurry. As for herself, she felt a Communist group to be premature.

Sergeant Jackie Bolton waited for twenty-four hours, and then spoke to William in the mess. 'That crowd in town are all useless,' was the burden of his message. He invited William to meet him at Black Ally's Café to talk it all over.

It was to this interview that William was going. He was feeling very uncomfortable about it. To a young man like William, who, as has been said, was sensible and matter-of-fact, there was something disagreeable about Jackie Bolton, who was the tall, dark, hollow-cheeked, saturnine man whom Martha had noticed exuding sarcastic disparagement at the Help for Our Allies meeting. William did not like heroics – Jackie was heroic on principle; William did not like intrigue – Jackie breathed out conspiracy with every word he spoke; he did not like drama – Jackie was dramatic. But he was going to meet him nevertheless; he could not refuse, because of that bond which, during the war, was stronger than any other, that between men wearing the same uniform.

Black Ally's was filled with aircraftsmen – it was by consent a place for the Air Force – and William entered the sordid little café with a feeling of being at home. The two men removed their caps, unbuttoned their jackets, and settled down to plates of eggs and chips.

Jackie was confidential and conspiratorial, with his large urgent black eyes, his hollow bony face, his manner of silent laughing – he would heave with laughter, without letting out a sound. He wanted to start a Communist group, led by himself, from certain men in the Air Force and a few sound types, from town, excluding 'all the Jasmines and Bettys and Borises', who were nothing but social democrats of the worst kind, and infected with Trotskyism to boot.

William listened in silence. He wanted to commit himself. The phrase 'those types in town' was a bugle of solidarity. He was strongly bound to Jackie by the feeling of being in exile, and their good-humoured contempt for this city. He almost agreed. Then Jackie remarked that he had never been a member of the Party. He added that he considered himself a freelance of the revolution. William was chilled by that phrase. He hesitated and temporized and tried to change the subject.

He said that Matty Knowell was ripe – meaning politically; but the sergeant gave it another meaning by heaving his hollow shoulders soundlessly; and William smiled stiffly – he was on the borderline still; Matty was not yet his girl, but on the other hand he felt a strong current of sympathy for her. He frowned and said he thought Jackie was altogether too sweeping; there was Jasmine, for instance: 'She's a good type.'

'Better than the others,' admitted Jackie. He added, laughing, 'I had supper with her last night.' William felt no sexual loyalty towards Jasmine, so they were able to pursue this point. They remained there for about two hours, taking the taste of the camp food out of their mouths with repeated orders of eggs and chips, drinking cup after cup of very strong tea. By that time it had been agreed that Jasmine had possibilities; Matty was to be sounded by Jackie that evening. They were both capable of education; so were all the men in uniform who had ever shown the slightest interest in politics. The male civilians, however, were all beyond hope.

They would have, they reckoned, some fifteen or twenty people as a nucleus. But still William would not commit himself. He left the sergeant with the promise that he would think it all over. He walked away uptown from the café, and already Jackie's influence was waning. He found himself distrusting the man. He decided to ring up Jasmine herself, and abide by her decision.

He rang her up from the nearest telephone. She was due at a meeting in an hour, she said, but could give him twenty minutes of her time afterwards. The calm sense of the girl's voice satisfied William that he had done right.

On the same afternoon there was another encounter, between two men who have not yet been mentioned.

The Help for Our Allies Committee was sitting. Mr Perr was chairman. The proceedings were harmonious and orderly. But there was one item on the agenda which might cause friction. The secretary of the Sympathizers of Russia – the signature was Jasmine's – had sent a letter proposing that the two organizations should hold a joint meeting to celebrate the anniversary of the November Revolution. Mr Perr spoke strongly against it. Four others, all members of the old discussion circle, were equally upset at the thought that Aid for Our Allies had anything to do with politics or revolutions. The majority of the committee – housewives, clergymen and so on – could see nothing against it. The heroism of Stalingrad made even the November Revolution respectable. Besides, it had happened a long time ago.

The two men in question were both silent until the end of the discussion, though Mr Perr repeatedly looked towards them, inviting them to speak. One was a Scotsman, a bulky bluff corporal with a broad sensible face and shrewd grey eyes; the other was Anton Hesse, a German refugee, a young man of about thirty, of middle height, very thin, very fair – he had that extreme Northern fairness, hair so blond it was almost white, very keen blue eyes of the kind which look as if there is white ice behind the iris. Anton Hesse had been on the committee since its formation. Andrew McGrew had been posted up from G — , a small southern town where he had served on the counterpart of this committee. His sensible, calm appearance inspired confidence; when he rose to speak, Mr Perr visibly relaxed.

He said that, speaking for himself, he could see no reason why the Help for Our Allies organization should not celebrate the revolution, which after all had contributed a great deal to the defenders of Stalingrad and Leningrad; on the other hand, the function of the committee was to raise money for medical supplies, and he was quite prepared to waive his personal feelings in the interests of harmony and good feeling. With this he sat down, crossed his legs, put his pipe back in his mouth and looked — as did everyone else — towards Mr Hesse.

Who rose, in his stiff deliberate way, and said he agreed with the last speaker. He would like to add, however, that in his personal opinion it would be better if a vote was not taken. It was clear from the discussion that the majority of the committee were in favour of joining in the celebrations; if a vote were taken it might embarrass Mr Perr and those members who felt so strongly about it. Such embarrassments should be avoided wherever possible. He then sat down, and lit a cigarette, giving his full attention to the process.

This caused a short silence. Mr Perr was agitated. Such was Mr Hesse's manner that it was impossible to know whether he was being accurate and helpful or airily offensive. Mr Perr looked uncomfortably around the table, and suggested they should pass to the next item on the agenda. Once again the unpolitical members of the committee had been made to feel that there were unpleasant undercurrents which they ought to be understanding. They all proceeded to discuss how best to produce a pamphlet, while Mr Hesse smoked in silence, satisfied with the barb that he had left to rankle.

It was noticeable that he and Corporal McGrew watched each other for the rest of the meeting; and that afterwards they left together, apparently fortuitously. At which Mr Perr said avidly to Mr Forester that that damned German got under his skin – he didn't trust him an inch.

The two men walked away in silence, each waiting for the other to speak. Then the Scotsman took the initiative by remarking, 'I met a friend of yours in G — . He met you in London in 1938. Barry, the name was.'

'I remember Barry – the Committee for Spain.'

Andrew took his pipe from his mouth and remarked, 'I was on the Northern Committee during that period.'

'You were?' This had a suggestion of stiff amusement.

The two pairs of eyes met frankly, and both men grinned. All the same there was a small hesitation before Andrew took the plunge: 'I take it you are in the Party?'

'Since 1933,' Anton said, and looked questioningly towards Andrew, who said, 'I've been in since 1930.'

There was a pause. Instinctively, the two men moved closer together as they walked down the pavement under the trees towards the business centre.

'I'm not quite clear as to the situation here,' observed Andrew. 'I only came last week.'

'There's nothing here – we're the only two members that I've discovered.'

'There are a couple of dozen in the camp. But as to the local situation, I would appreciate it if you would clarify my mind a little.'

They both stopped. It was at a street corner. The traffic fled past noisily in two streams.

Anton narrowed his eyes, concentrated, began to speak. He spoke for about ten minutes, while the other listened. He concluded, 'Taking these facts into consideration, I think it is correct to say that we have not the cadres for a party group.'

Andrew nodded, but added, 'I agree, more or less. But since I came I've been hearing nothing but rumours about a group. What is this group?'

'There is no group. There's a group of intellectuals – if you can call them that.'

'Some of them seem quite promising.'

Anton said, 'I am in contact with Jasmine Cohen. She knows I am in the Party. Through her I know about the rest. They all do a lot of talking, but that doesn't do any harm.'

'It's all very well,' said Andrew, annoyed. 'It does do harm.'

'Look,' said Anton. 'Let's analyse the position. There are about a dozen men in the Air Force who can address envelopes and make a speech occasionally, but they aren't allowed to take part in politics. There are a handful of aliens and refugees – such as myself.' He smiled with controlled bitterness. 'Politics are naturally not supposed to interest us. Then there are a handful of girls who want love affairs and a bit of excitement. This is not the basis for a Communist group. Besides,' he added, with finality, 'the working people of this country are black.'

Andrew nodded, but was thoughtful.

'What do you know about Sergeant Bolton?' went on Anton. 'He keeps getting up at Help for Our Allies meetings and shouting for a revolution. He'll split the thing if he isn't stopped.'

'Admittedly he's a bit – overenthusiastic.' Andrew added with apologetic humour, 'The feeling in the camps is rather less indirect than it is in town.'

But since Anton Hesse did not feel himself part of this town, he was able to say casually. 'It is bound to be.'

They began walking again under the trees, which still shed their purple rain.

'It looks to me like this,' observed Andrew at last. 'I agree there is no basis for a group in existing conditions. But one is going to come into existence for all that. If so, we should be in on it.'

Anton Hesse did not at once reply. The fair handsome face had a curious look of obstinacy, of reluctance. Andrew glanced sideways at him, but said nothing. He had heard that this man had worked in the underground against Hitler, done a spell in a concentration camp, survived torture, escaped; he respected him. But there is no law which says one Communist should like another, and he did not like him. His antipathy expressed itself thus: He's not the sort of chap I'd like to spend an evening in the pub with.

As for the German, he was conscious that his analysis of the situation had a factor in it that he ought to be ashamed of. He knew he did not want to take part in politics in this country. He had spent the last fifteen years in the political struggle in Europe, with the most sophisticated revolutionaries of his time. He had been a schoolboy when he first went to prison, and had been in and out of prison ever since. He had survived death when he had thought of himself as already dead. He had reached the backwater which he felt England to be, and had adjusted to it, only to be sent away from it to this country, where he had spent three years of such boredom and despair he had considered suicide. But Communists do not commit suicide. He loathed the empty, ill-educated, easygoing colonials; he despised the life of sundowners and good times. He hated everything down to the food and the drink. Above all, the political backwardness of the place depressed him. He dreamed of that moment when the war would be over and he would be free to go back home – to Germany. But that place in his soul, Germany, was an agonizing darkness where even his loyalties were shamed. His comrades were nearly all dead. His wife was dead. He had no romantic notions left about suffering and revolutions. He had had little sympathy with the revolutionaries – 'so called', as he invariably muttered to himself – of Britain, who seemed to him a pack of children. He shut himself up, shielding that raw place in himself by a shell of patience. He spent his time reading the Marxist classics and studying Russian. He was a man in cold storage for the future. To start work again here, in this half-baked country in the middle of this backward continent, and with a group of romantic amateurs – his pride revolted. There is such a thing as revolutionary snobbishness. But more than this, far deeper, was the reluctance to come out of his shell – to start *feeling* again. Yet, just as he had clung tight to that raft in the black sea of longing for death, the phrase 'Communists do not commit suicide', so now he said to himself, a Communist has the duty to work in whichever country he finds himself.

He did not know how long that silence lasted, while he walked, cold-faced and stiff, down the street beside Andrew, who strolled patiently beside him, waiting.

Then he said, 'Let's go to some quiet place and talk it over.'

'I've got to go to a meeting in half an hour,' said Andrew. 'Young William is addressing the schoolteachers on Hegel. I promised to go along and help him out.'

'William Brown – on Hegel!' Anton stopped dead. 'What does he know about Hegel?'

'More than the Zambesian Association of Schoolteachers, very likely,' said Andrew good-humouredly. 'Why don't you come along, too?'

There was a pause. 'I might as well. Yes. Hegel – the Zambesian schoolteachers!'

'There are some good people among them,' said Andrew with definite reproach.

The German coloured, and then said, admitting the reproof, 'You're quite right.' After a pause he said, 'I must find a telephone and ring up someone – I was going to dinner.'

'Oh, if you've got another engagement, we can meet tomorrow.'

Anton had been conducting a love affair for the last two years with an Austrian refugee, a charming woman of a silliness quite phenomenal – it was as if he took a perverse pleasure in the dullness of the relationship.

'It's not in the least important,' he said, as he went towards a telephone booth.

In the meantime, William had seen Jasmine. She informed him under a bond of secrecy that there were real Communists in the town – they could do nothing without their sanction. She was prepared, however, to meet Sergeant Bolton again; he had struck her as being a valuable person.

Chapter Three

About a week after these events, Mr Maynard, who was on his way to dispense justice in the Courts, heard his wife's voice calling him from the drawing room. He was in the passage outside. He turned his bulk around in a half-circle, took a step forward and was in the doorway.

Mrs Maynard was giving orders to the cook for the day's menus. She stood in front of the empty fireplace, feet planted wide, arms linked behind her back. The cook – white drill, red fez, white sandshoes – was making notes in a small book.

'. . . and French pancakes. I think that's all, Elijah.'

He said: 'Yes, madam,' and retired, begging Mr Maynard's pardon as he came past. Mr Maynard moved a couple of inches to one side to accommodate him.

Mrs Maynard stood silent, head slightly bent, separating her real interests from thoughts of eggs and butter.

She was wearing a greenish silk dress, loose about massive thighs and hips which, as Mr Maynard remembered, were always encased in heavy pink brocade from waist to knee. Above was prescribed no such repression: her full low bosom rocked just above the belt, and over green folds were suspended loops of pink coral. Mr Maynard remembered wondering what intricacies of conscience made her feel indecent without that corset even in a dressing gown, whereas to wear a brassière would have seemed to her even more indecent. Never had cloth, or even lace, confined those full, loose, empty breasts, which shook and rolled unchecked. The neat greying hair, the straight brows, seemed one with the lower half of her body – that tight mass of controlled flesh. But the upper femininity, so naïve-looking and exposed, seemed in harmony with certain moods of hers, when she was eager after an enthusiasm. Sometimes she looked almost girlish. Mr Maynard remembered a stubborn but charming girl.

This was one of the moods. She was flushed and animated. She raised her head, let her arms fall to her sides, and began abruptly, 'You remember my Coloured Committee.'

'You mentioned it.'

'Well . . .' She contracted her brows, and appeared to be summoning some point which she wished to present to him. For the first time she looked at him, twisting the coral around her fingers. 'It's going very well. A good response.'

'I congratulate you on its composition. You seem to have got all your black sheep harnessed satisfactorily.'

'I'm in a hurry,' she said impatiently – meaning that she was prepared to be teased at another time. 'Now, this is the point. I think some younger people would be a good thing. One might get some of the Left Group, Russian Sympathizers – whatever they call themselves.'

'I think they are fully occupied in raising money for Russia, my dear.'

'A good thing, too – those poor things obviously need medical supplies.' For she had taken away any unpleasantness there was in the thought of being allied to the Soviet Union by clasping the whole nation to her bosom as suitable objects for her charity. 'But if they are so enthusiastic about Russia, then they can spare some time for their own unfortunates.'

'I rather imagine they would ask you why you confine your sympathy to the half-castes and ignore the blacks.'

'I am in a hurry,' she said again. 'No, I've got Mrs Perr and Mrs Forester – quite reasonable women, really. But I feel one might go further.'

'What's your first step?'

'We are having a concert next week to raise money. In the Brazen Hall. By the children.'

He raised his brows. 'Coloured children play to white audiences?'

'It'll be a nice change for everybody. Besides, Bishop White is sponsoring it. And the Roman Catholics are being co-operative. For a change.'

'And having raised the money?'

'We'll see afterwards.'

'I feel that you are underestimating the idealistic enthusiasm abroad at the moment.'

'Well! Surely they ought to be glad to do something for those unfortunate people!' She was genuinely indignant. Mr Maynard was again enabled to see her as an enthusiastic girl – even as a rebel. For it is by no means an accident that people find themselves in the colonies. Mrs Maynard, as a girl, had infuriated her family by refusing to get married at the right time. Instead, she had become a crusader for better housing in Whitechapel. She had been prevented from marrying a penniless clergyman who was similarly devoted only by the greatest effort on the part of her relations. As a revenge she had married Mr Maynard; Africa had seemed to her both romantic and suitably exasperating to her family. She had seen herself ministering to grateful savages. And Mr Maynard had left England because he found it insular. They had both been rebels, of a kind. Perhaps the strongest strand in their relationship was the feeling that they were rebels against tradition – even now, when their first concern was to uphold it.

For that matter, there is no white person in the colonies who has not arrived there for some similar reason: they are crusaders against tyranny to a man. Which accounts for that shrill note of protest when the world suggests that it is both stupid and old-fashioned to suppress native populations: for when these same colonials are passionately engaged in fighting against a minimum wage of one pound a month, or advocating the sjambok as a means of guidance for the uncivilized, they are always, in the bottom of their hearts, quite convinced that this too is part of their character as rebels against the tyranny and conservatism of the mother country which they left as adventurers into a free world.

Mrs Maynard was quite genuine in her cry that these young people must feel with her in helping the unfortunate half-castes; that they should not, must kill her idea of herself as a fearless and progressive person.

Mr Maynard watched the flushed and agitated face and felt a pang of reminiscent affection. But to the matron who was his wife he remarked drily, 'Well, my dear, I'll do what I can, but if my information is correct you're wasting your time. Whom do you want, particularly?'

'There's the secretary – Cohen, I think. Jewish, of course.'

A brief pause while things were left unsaid.

'She seems rather efficient. And there's your friend Quest, Knowell, whatever her name is. And various girls of that kind. Also there's a batch of refugees. We should get hold of them. If I had my way they'd all be interned, anyway.'

'You can't intern refugees from Hitler – they're on our side, so to speak.'

She shrugged this off and said irritably, 'All the same, I hear that – but it might be rumour. But after the war they'll go back to wherever they came from, and the Air Force will go, and we've our own people to think of.'

'I'm late,' said Mr Maynard. 'Give me the details of this concert of yours.'

He left his wife in her pose before the fireplace, hands behind her back, rocking back and forth from heel to toe. The beautiful quiet room with its green-and-rose silks, its flowery carpet, was almost identical with the one in Chelsea from which he had plucked her thirty years before.

On his way downtown, he passed the Knowells' house and asked to see Martha. The cook said she was out. For some time he stood watching Caroline at play under the trees, allowing himself to dream of the daughter he had so badly wanted. Then he pulled himself away, and hurried off to the Courts. At the third attempt to find Martha, he met her on the pavement outside the house, files packed under her arm, hurrying past him. He had to catch her arm to make her see him. She was looking animated and eager. He knew the look.

Having put the proposition – briefly, since she was impatient of it from the first word – he waited rather ironically.

'Let's get this straight,' said Martha. 'You want Jasmine Cohen and myself and Boris and Betty Krueger to come and help your wife run a concert to raise money for the Coloureds?' She sounded fully as derisive as he had expected.

He instinctively made a mental note of the names for future use, and inquired, mildly, 'Why not?'

'It is not,' said Martha, 'the nineteenth century.'

'Ah.'

'Charity,' said Martha aggressively, 'has always been an expression of the guilty consciences of a ruling class.'

Thus confirmed in his diagnosis of intellectual influences not Zambesian, he inquired casually, 'You know a man called Hesse?'

She looked at him suspiciously. They were standing facing each other under the tree outside her gate. She was angry and earnest. That quality of sincere enthusiasm sanctioned his own youth, and he said suddenly, 'You know, my dear, I'm very fond of you.'

Martha's face softened; but she was looking at a kindly old gentleman, he could see that. For one reason and another, he abruptly set himself in motion away from her.

'I'll ask them,' she called after him; and he raised his hat to her with an elaborate irony that was altogether lost on her, for she had turned away before he concluded the gesture.

She mentioned to Jasmine and Anton later that day that that bunch of reactionaries wanted them to run a charity concert for the Coloured community. They smiled, briefly.

She forgot the concert. But two days later there arrived a letter from Douglas. She read it with disquiet – the letter was not from the Douglas she had been creating for herself. He was returning home in a few days. Why did she not write – And she had signed her last letter to him 'Yours sincerely, Martha Quest' – what did she think she was doing? As a postscript he said he was glad to hear that she was helping the Maynards with their Coloured children; it was just up her street, he thought.

The letter conveyed a peevish and rasping complaint. Guilt, unacknowledged, began its work. She rang up Mrs

Maynard to offer her services for the concert, and felt that this gesture would be enough to convince Douglas of her goodwill. She had not clearly considered what she must do when he came back, but she held long imaginary conversations with that image of him about the future. She would make certain adjustments, he others. Her sacrifice would consist in not leaving him altogether for the group – which was not yet in existence. She saw him as a calm, sensible, brotherly young man who would fully understand what she felt.

As for William, she knew herself to be in love with him. He had kissed her one night after a meeting. That kiss had called into being a Martha she had recently forgotten – it was chalked up against Douglas that she had been able to forget, except as a question of principle, the other Martha. In short, she clamoured with every impulse for a love affair with William. But it had been agreed that a sensible talk with Douglas was the minimum concession to decency. Besides, with meetings following one another, sometimes three and four a night, there was no time for love-making. They sat on opposite sides of a room, discussing the state of affairs in Uzbekistan, while their eyes met, and neither knew whether they loved each other or the revolution. In between one meeting and another, they stood on the veranda outside the office for a moment, hands touching, while they discussed if they might arrange matters to spend half an hour folding leaflets together tomorrow. Romance can be no keener than this. Happiness flooded through them at a touch or a glance.

In the meantime, Martha was reasoning thus: her marriage with Douglas was essentially sensible – which was her euphemism for the word 'modern', too old-fashioned to be used. It had always been understood that they did not believe in jealousy or even infidelity. Besides – and this secretly justified Martha far more than these reasonable arguments – she had heard through devious routes that he was having an affair with a girl in Y—. It was obvious, then, that he should be no more than interested in the news that she intended to have a love affair with William. Everything should be honest and above board – this above all. She loved William for understanding why they must wait until Douglas came back.

Two more letters came from Douglas. One complained that she had not written. But, being nothing if not dutiful, she had written twice a week since he left. The other was hysterical: Mrs Talbot had written saying something – she could not make out what – and she, Martha was clearly going mad. He had managed to arrange his affairs so as to be home by tomorrow morning.

Martha read these letters with fear; but instantly she revived that picture of a brotherly understanding Douglas, and looked forward to the moment when she would tell him everything. But she had torn up the letters in a panic need to get them out of sight and thought.

At seven in the morning she was standing on the long grey platform, waiting for the train to come in. She was light-hearted and confident. The train came, black and serpentine, across the veld; vanished behind factories; appeared, enormous and black, in a rush of filthy blue smoke. She stood peering along it for Douglas. Then she saw him getting out of the carriage. The image collapsed, and she stood staring at him in incredulity and horror. It was that moment again when he had returned from up north – but then he had been in uniform, another person; now he came smiling angrily towards her, a fat and ordinary young man in a thick grey suit striped with white. She remembered her father's 'commercial traveller' – that was the truth. She thought, while she looked at this stranger who was her husband, that while her father might despise clothes, he never despised them enough to wear clothes like these.

Her heart was pounding. She understood she was terrified. There was a gleam in the small blue eyes, a working of the lips, that literally terrified her. By now he had reached her, and was holding out his arms. She received his kiss on her cheek, and instantly moved away, saying, 'Let's get to the car. You must be ready for breakfast.'

A nervous glance showed him to be red and glaring. But they went to the car in silence. She got into the driver's seat;

she needed to be doing something. Usually she moved aside to let him drive. He was looking at her with a deadly black anger which made her feel faint. But she drove fast and straight up through Indian stores and kaffir-truck shops, through the shady avenues; parked the car neatly under the tree, and walked before him through the flower beds and shrubs to the veranda. He came after her with set shoulders, reddened eyes, and a look of pursuit.

They reached the bedroom. She sat on the edge of her bed as if it were her last place of refuge, and waited for him to speak. He, however, stood threateningly near her, glowering. Suddenly she let out a short and angry laugh; at once she was dismayed, because it was the first sound either had made since they had left the station.

'Don't be so damned silly, Douglas,' she said, trying to sound placatory, although her voice was embarrassed.

He shouted suddenly, his face swelling up, 'Why didn't you write to me?'

'But I did write to you.'

He came nearer and bent, his face working. 'Why did you sign yourself like that – "Yours sincerely"?'

His face, which was so genuinely puzzled and hurt, moved her. It was the last time she was to allow herself to feel moved. 'But, Douglas,' she said, almost humorously. 'It's not very important, is it? And I had just signed about a thousand circulars.'

'You signed it "Martha Quest"?'

'Yes.' Then she added, cold and angry, 'You are always talking about the danger to your career.'

He straightened himself and stood blinking at her. She could see that he was finding, and then discarding, one point of attack after another.

'What did Mrs Talbot write?' she inquired.

He turned his face aside; began to say something; changed his mind. Then: 'Why are you spending all your time with this ridiculous – outfit?'

She said contemptuously, 'So you're afraid of the left wing?'

At once he said in clumsy appeal, like a child, 'But, Matty, you know how it is with the Service. You know I can't do as I like.'

'When we got married you said you wouldn't stay in the Service,' she pointed out.

He looked wounded: he felt it very unfair of her to remember things he had said then. But if she was going to take that line, he thought, it was true that he always said he hated the Service, hated the life, hated this damned second-rate country. He jerked out, 'What's all this I hear about your having an affair with a corporal in the Air Force?'

'Well, what did Mrs Talbot say?' she asked satirically.

But he flushed up again, turned his eyes aside, and began in an indignantly sulky tone, 'And Caroline – haven't you any sense of responsibility towards her?'

She let out a peal of angry laughter. He watched her, fascinated.

'Where is Caroline?' he urged reproachfully. 'What have you done with her?'

'Caroline was playing in the garden three feet from you when you came in – as you must have seen, since you are so worried about her.'

He blinked again, moving his lips. Then he turned and began hanging things up in his wardrobe. She waited for him to attack again, while she noted with calm satisfaction the thick redness of his neck, which seemed a justification of her attitude.

He turned and said, 'Matty . . .' in a thick pleading voice. He came stumbling towards her, clutched her in his arms, tried to kiss her. Then, as he began fumbling with her breasts in a determined and aggressive way, she twisted herself free in a flash of such pure hate for him that her eyes went black for a moment. She allowed to raise themselves in her memory all the other times he had tried to rouse her physically when she was set against him in spirit. She moved to the dressing table, and brushed her hair, sitting with her back to him.

'What's got into you, Matty?' he shouted at last, on an aggrieved note which sounded so comically inadequate that she laughed again.

'What do you suppose can have got into me?' she inquired after a pause, calmly. She rose and faced him. She began speaking in a tone of final contempt. 'I am working for the Communist Party. Though there isn't one yet, but if there is I shall join it. Also, I am attracted by a "corporal in the Air Force". I should have told you about it myself, there was no need to spy on me through Mrs Talbot. And I propose to have a love affair with him. Since you've been having an affair with Mollie in Y—, I don't see why you should object.'

Again he stumbled across and tried to embrace her. 'Matty!' he brought out. 'Matty! We're all right, aren't we? We're all right?'

This echo of the rallying cry of the Club made her laugh again, though she had no intention of laughing. He fell back from her, and this time he was grinding his teeth and glaring.

'Your breakfast is on the table,' she remarked breathlessly into that glaring, working face. To her surprise, he turned and went blindly out of the room, slamming the door behind him.

She went back to the edge of her bed. She could not think. Her mind was dim, and confused, and she felt sick. For the last few weeks she had perhaps slept four hours a night; the group felt sleep to be a waste of being alive, and they had no time to eat proper meals. She felt tired, even indifferent. The ugliness of the scene seemed impossible – it was impossible that he should be so stupid and obtuse, and she so stridently self-righteous. In the space of the few minutes he was away eating breakfast, she had again succeeded in creating him as that friend with whom she could talk things over.

When he entered the room, it was cautiously, and apparently in command of himself, and she looked hopefully towards him. 'Now, listen, Douglas,' she began in a different voice, almost friendly, 'do let's stop all this – nonsense, and be sensible.'

His face was still rather swollen and red, but she was unable to make out what he was thinking. Encouraged, however, she said, 'I want to suggest that I should go away for a while – two or three weeks. Let me get over it.' This last phrase seemed to her as being nice to him – putting the blame for everything on herself.

'Where are you going?' he ground out.

'I don't know – anywhere.'

'*Where*, I said?'

It astounded her that he thought it mattered. 'I really haven't thought. Why?'

'Somewhere near an Air Force camp, I suppose.'

She flushed, but let it pass.

'Which camp is the corporal in?'

'Oh, I see!' She let out another peal of laughter, and he ground his teeth again.

'You needn't think I don't know,' he said. 'I know – you'd go away with him.'

'Well, of course,' she said, surprised. 'That's what I meant.' She added inevitably, 'You've just been in Y— with Mollie.'

He got up, and began prowling blindly about the room. He was beside himself with anger. 'Mollie's a sweet kid,' he said. 'She's not a whore – like you.'

'Oh, I don't doubt that she has preserved her virginity against all comers. But, for all that, you've been spending hours of every night in the backs of cars, doing everything but. As far as I'm concerned, it's the same thing.'

He suddenly picked her brushes and hand mirror off the table and flung them crashing against the wardrobe. She remained still. She was now bitterly regretting what she had just said – she was as bad as he was. And that wasn't the point at all! She looked steadily at him, and knew she was no longer afraid of him. She had been – very afraid. It was because – she saw this from an inward-looking gleam in the puffed eyes – he had slid over into that mood of self-controlled hysteria which she knew well. It was as if he were saying to invisible onlookers, 'Look how I'm treated! Look how I'm behaving!' It was with her nerves that she understood that it was not genuine. She waited for him to speak.

Then again he abruptly left the room. She watched him cross the lawn to where Caroline was playing. She was amazed to see him clutch the child to him. He was making a scene of being an anguished father, and for her benefit. The indecency of it appalled her. She turned away, took up some sewing, and was working at it when he came back. She saw he was furious because she had not been watching him.

'I think you should leave Caroline out of it,' she said coldly.

He sat down again and watched her.

'Oughtn't you to go to the office?' she asked at last. He did not reply. 'Because I said I'd go downtown to the Aid offices to do some work – I could drop you if you like.'

'I won't let you use the car.'

'Oh, well, then, I'll walk.' She put away her sewing and got up, while he watched her with a steady, hysterical gaze.

'I'll be back for lunch,' she said.

She was walking down the garden path, when she heard him pounding up behind her. Her nerves shrank apprehensively; then steadied again. One glance at him reassured her. She did not understand this controlled hysteria, so self-conscious and displaying, but she did know that in proportion to the degree he succumbed to it, she became cold and impervious.

At the gate she turned, and was about to walk off down under the trees, when he said sentimentally, 'Why don't you get into the car with me?'

She shrugged as if he were a madman, and climbed in beside him. She expected him to park the car outside his office, but he said, 'Where do you want to go?'

She gave the address. He parked the car and got out with her. She understood he was coming in with her to see whether William would be there. She wanted to laugh again, with that fatal upwelling of pure contempt. She said lightly, 'You know, William will be working at the camp at this hour of the morning.'

He did not reply. They went together up the stairs of a big block of offices, and entered the door of the Help for Our Allies Committee. Jasmine was typing under the window. She nodded at Martha, smiled at Douglas, and went on with her work. Douglas stood watching while Martha collected papers and arranged another typewriter for herself. Then he said, in a perfectly normal voice, for Jasmine's benefit, 'Well, I'll leave you to it. See you at lunchtime.' He went out again.

For a while the two women typed in silence. Then Jasmine inquired casually, 'Well, how's it going?'

'Awful,' said Martha briefly. Then: 'Men are really quite extraordinary.' She fitted paper into the machine and began on a new letter.

'Does he mind about you doing this work?'

Martha paused, thinking. She did not know what it was he really minded. For she did not believe in his jealousy for William – she had not felt jealousy herself, so she did not believe in it. More, she did not believe that Douglas *really* loved her, as she put it; really loving, now, meant the exquisite fragile relationship with William. Finally, she thought, Anyway, there's Mollie – he's got no right to be jealous. But under all these was the abiding thought, I don't see how he can complain that I am what I always said I was. For at this moment she forgot the years of feminine compliance, of charm, of conformity to what he wanted. They had all been a lie against her real nature and therefore they had not existed.

At last she said, 'I've no idea at all what he's really angry about. All I know is, he's not angry about what he thinks he's angry about.' She went on with her typing, forgetting Douglas entirely in the fascination of the work.

Before they parted for lunch, Jasmine gave a small intimate grimace, and squeezed Martha's arm. 'Well, good luck with the battle. All that's wrong with him,' she pronounced in her maidenly and demure way, 'is that his property instinct is outraged.' The night before, they had been discussing the freeing of women from male tyranny in the eastern parts of the Soviet Union.

'Oh, well – obviously,' agreed Martha at once.

She walked home. Douglas was not there. Her suspicion as to where he might be was confirmed when Mrs Talbot rang her up and suggested in a murmuring, intimate voice that she might like to come and visit an old woman tomorrow morning. Martha agreed. She was again in that mood in which a woman says silently to a man, Very well, then, I will behave as you want me to – that'll put you to shame!

But it was now, as she put down the receiver, that she said for the first time, I must leave him; it's all useless. For she had a very clear picture of Douglas, who was now engaged in going from person to person to enlist sympathy. Yet she shrank from the finality of it. No, when he came back, he'd be sensible again and they could discuss it all . . .

She spent the afternoon reading and making notes – she was to give a lecture that night.

Douglas came in rather late. One glance showed him to be in the same mood. She mentioned that Mrs Talbot had rung her up; she expected him to be embarrassed, but he said in that sentimental voice, 'Yes, Matty, do go and see her – she'll help you.'

'I suppose I must expect telephone calls from – who else?'

'Oh, Matty,' he murmured like a lover, while he stared at her with swollen and hate-filled eyes, 'you must listen to reason, you know.'

But by now he seemed to her like a madman. She finished her dinner quickly, and said, 'Why don't you come with me to the meeting? There'll be at least half a dozen civil servants there, it's really quite respectable,' she could not prevent herself adding.

He simply kept the glare of his eyes fixed on her. But it was a blind glare, for he was seeing himself, the object of pity and sympathy for Mrs Talbot and – but she did not know who were the others.

'Why not come? It's very interesting, after all.'

He kept silence, so she got her things and left him as he settled on a chair on the veranda with the look of a watchdog settling for the night, head on paws.

'My mother's coming in to stay,' he remarked as she left. She did not reply. This did frighten her. She drove down to the meeting in a state of pure terror. It was not of Douglas, but of society. She could see her mother-in-law, her own mother, Mrs Talbot, the Maynards, massed behind him. They were all much stronger than she was. But as soon as she walked into the room where Jasmine nodded at her with a look of understanding, and William smiled over at her in calm support, as soon as she felt herself surrounded by people to whom 'personal problems' were the unimportant background to their real responsibilities, her fear vanished.

There were about forty people in the room. This was a meeting of a subsection of the Sympathizers of Russia.

She was already reading her paper, which was about education in the Soviet Union, when she saw that Joss was seated in a corner. He was in uniform. He was on leave from up north. And in another corner sat Solly, also in uniform. She felt confused at delivering a paper in front of those young men who had been her mentors in childhood. But she kept her voice steady, and continued, not looking at either of them.

During the discussion that followed, neither of these men spoke at all. Anton Hesse controlled it, in that calm, correct way of his, which − as she saw with dismay − caused Sergeant Bolton to smile with sarcastic forbearance. It upset her that there could be personal antagonisms inside the group itself. But she was already familiar with this atmosphere where everyone in a room was in willing respectful submission to Anton, who was able to answer any problem with two paragraphs at least (one always felt he was reading from an invisible book) of clear and grammatical prose, while they were held in sympathy with Sergeant Bolton, who leaned forward intently, holding their eyes with his, one after another, and spoke with a sort of gentle intimate persuasion. It was extraordinary, this contrast between the open sarcastic antagonism of his attitude towards Hesse and McGrew and that intimate current of sympathy he established with the neophytes. There was an intellectual pole and an emotional one.

When the meeting was over, about half the people left. The rest stood about, looking at each other. It had been decided there must be a meeting to 'settle things once and for all'. They were all waiting for it to start. In the meantime, no one seemed ready to take the lead. Sergeant Bolton sat lounging on his part of the bench, from time to time exchanging smiles with whoever looked his way; while Hesse and McGrew sat silent in their corner, one smoking a pipe, the other a cigarette.

Martha wondered why they did not start at once. Then she saw that people were looking towards Solly, who stood by himself against the wall, with a sarcastic smile on his face. She heard Jasmine whisper, 'Damned Trotskyite', and it hurt her that Solly should be thus cast out.

She protested to Jasmine, 'Oh nonsense, he's perfectly all right.'

Jasmine merely smiled. She nodded towards Solly so that Martha might see what was going forward. Solly and Joss were now isolated against one wall. They were exchanging a long stare. Both were rather pale, but smiled steadily, tight-lipped. The resemblance between them was striking at that moment, though they were so dissimilar. Solly was still a tall, lanky, unco-ordinated-looking youth. Joss was more solid, squat, and stronger in his khaki than he had been out of it. But both faces showed a keen, hard intelligence, a grim antagonism. Then Martha saw, with a suddenly pounding heart, how Solly let his eyes waver away from Joss's stare. He looked for a moment under his brows at the others. He was still smiling, and very pale.

'Well, good luck to your – decisions,' he said, blurting it out. To Martha it sounded like an appeal. Then he turned and slammed hastily out of the room.

Immediately the people in the room seemed to flow together in a long sigh of relief. It was only then that Martha understood that his staying there had been a demonstration, and it struck her as both childish and offensive. She looked towards Joss, who still remained against the wall, with an odd twisted smile, looking after his brother. Then he too sighed and looked around. At once several people went up, and one after another took him by the arm and spoke in low voices. Martha thought, I'll ask him what to do, too. But she had to wait until the others had finished. Joss nodded and listened and smiled, but seemed not altogether happy in this position.

When she at last was able to go up to him, he first smiled,

remembering their childhood, and then stiffened when she began to speak. She clumsily tumbled out her problem; then she saw he was embarrassed. 'I don't see why everyone comes and expects me to sort out problems,' he said with an unwilling smile. 'I've been back on leave two days, and every person in this room without exception has been to ask my advice.'

She said, 'It's the price you have to pay for being the big man from the Party down south.'

He grinned, but said finally, 'In the first place it's all nonsense. I have no – authority. And secondly, I've been in the Army for two years.' She looked so disappointed that he said, 'You should think it all out carefully, and then do what you decide to be best.' He added, 'It's not a small thing, breaking up a marriage.'

She was indignant that Joss should offer so conventional a viewpoint.

'But if you can't stick it, then leave, of course.'

She went on hastily, offering him a confused picture of quarrelling and misunderstanding – she bickered with her mother, her husband was forbidding her to work in politics: it was as if they were back in the district, and she was bringing him her problems as usual. But she saw that he was looking past her, and she turned to see that everyone was seated and engaged in making conversation so as not to hear what she was saying. She retreated in confusion to a chair, and Joss crossed the room and sat beside Hesse and McGrew. The three men sitting there inspired the deepest respect in them all. They represented the Party itself. They also inspired resentment. For everyone clamoured to start a group, and these three argued steadily against it. It was understood now that Joss, who could take an outside view of affairs, would finally decide it.

Anton Hesse glanced around, saw that everyone was looking towards him, turned to Joss, and said, 'You know what the situation is. I propose to analyse the position as I see it. Afterwards the others can argue against me.'

He spoke for about half an hour. For most of the people in the room, it was the first time they had heard a Marxist explaining the world. It was right over their heads. He was in fact speaking to Andrew McGrew, Boris Krueger, Joss Cohen, Sergeant Bolton. For the others, such was their innocence that they were realizing that a vague enthusiasm for the Soviet Union was not Marxism – they had imagined they were already initiates when in fact they knew nothing. They listened, watching the four intent men, with an awed respect, while Anton Hesse analysed the world situation, considered the British Empire, dealt with the colony in which he now found himself; its class forces were thus, its potentialities so, and the stage of development it had reached was ... The conclusion was ten minutes of facts, figures, quotations from white and blue papers, which were all neatly ranged in his head, for he had no notes.

His final sentence was, 'While everyone in this room would undoubtedly agree that a Communist Party is necessary and desirable, I submit that it would be inadvisable to start one with the existing cadres.'

He stopped speaking, and looked at Andrew McGrew, who took the pipe from his mouth and said, 'I agree entirely. May I point out that of the twenty people in this room, fifteen will have left the colony within a few months of the end of the war?'

The six who would remain were Jasmine, Martha, Betty, her husband, Boris, and a young girl who had drifted in to join them, a delightful eager creature of about twenty, a schoolteacher recently arrived from England. These five looked towards Joss. They felt that he, one of them, brought up in the colony, would understand them, whereas these cold-minded logicians would not, for if every word Anton Hesse had said was true – and they were too ill-informed to know whether it was or not – he completely ignored the passion for service which filled them all.

But Joss said, 'I would like to hear what the others have to say.'

Sergeant Bolton at once began to speak. Immediately the atmosphere changed. He said that Comrades Hesse and McGrew were probably right – theoretically. But he did not set himself to be a theoretician. All he knew was, the masses of the people in the country were suffering under a yoke of oppression, and if he could set them free, that was enough theory for him. There were more people in this room than there had been, very likely and for all he knew, when Lenin met for the first time with his comrades. If they started a Communist Party, they would soon have all the decent people in the colony with them. Comrades Hesse and McGrew were defeatists and – he felt he ought to say – unable to feel the atmosphere of the time. It was the psychologically correct moment to start a Communist Party . . .

He was speaking, not to comrades Hesse, McGrew and Cohen, but to them, the beginners. He would turn those intense burning black eyes on theirs, hold them for a moment, then on the next person; he was leaning forward, passionate, dedicated, inspiring. He had an extraordinary power to rouse them. They would have risen at a word from him and gone into the streets to die. And yet, the very moment those potent black eyes had moved on, each felt a faint uneasiness and glanced as if for help towards the three men who sat silently watching in the corner.

When Sergeant Bolton stopped speaking – on the cry, 'We should go out into the streets, we should go into the locations, we should go among the suffering masses of the country!' – something unexpected happened. For Boris Krueger began to speak. It was only then that they realized he had been very quiet, not only this evening but during any other such discussions.

He too was very pale. He was upset and angry. He said in a dead silence that he agreed entirely with Comrades Hesse and McGrew. This colony was extremely backward. (This aroused the most violent resentment in the breasts of the colonials, even though they all agreed with him.) It was correct and appropriate to further the most advanced forms of organization already in existence – such as the Sympathizers of Russia, the Help for Our Allies, and the Social Democratic Party. Also, they had the duty to educate themselves. He would like to say here and now that they were in danger of splitting what organizations there were. Sergeant

Bolton's fondness for appealing for immediate revolution at committee meetings of the Help for Our Allies would succeed only in losing all their respectable sponsors – without whom no money could be collected.

At this there was a soundless heave of mirth from Sergeant Bolton, and a spontaneous groan of sympathy for him and his viewpoint from everybody but the three members of the Party. For those same respectable sponsors aroused a quite remarkable degree of contempt in Sergeant Bolton.

Anton Hesse said quietly that Boris was quite right. No one but an amateur would use the Help for Our Allies as a platform for revolution.

Sergeant Bolton turned to Anton Hesse with a sudden violent movement, and was opening his mouth for a torrent of words, when Boris intervened with a long statement which amounted to a complete denial of Sergeant Bolton's bona fides.

All the time Boris was speaking, Sergeant Bolton shook with silent derisive laughter, and he interrupted before Boris had finished. He might not be a formal member of the Party himself, he said, but he had spent the last fifteen years of his life with the real people, the real working class, and that was more, he thought, than Boris could say.

To which Boris replied stiffly that in Poland he had been a member of the Party for five years, and he thought it was correct to say there was very little he did not know about agitation and underground methods of work. But there was a time and a place for fomenting revolution, as Sergeant Bolton would know if he had not such a contempt for theory. He wanted to know why Sergeant Bolton insisted on being so conspiratorial in a country where there was no need for it –

But here Sergeant Bolton exploded in a puff of laughter and the word 'Democracy!'

Boris lost his temper and said angrily that there were degrees of democracy – he did not consider it was anti-revolutionary to say so.

To Martha, Jasmine, and the others, this was extremely painful. They longed only to hurl themselves 'for once and

406

for all' into complete self-abnegation; and if they were asked to spend the rest of their lives in prison, so much the better. To hear Sergeant Bolton, who aroused them in flaming sympathy, attack the Party, which was how they thought of Hesse, McGrew and Joss, checked them in their feelings – they wanted a complete unanimity, a fused purpose 'for once and for all'.

But all this time Anton Hesse and Andrew McGrew and Joss sat watching the dogfight between the two men, and saying nothing.

At last Boris turned direct to them, with a clear reproach that they had been silent, and appealed, 'I would like to know what Joss thinks.'

Everybody looked at Joss. Boris insisted, 'I suggest he sum up – let's give him the final word.'

There was a cry of agreement. After a quick look around at his disciples, Sergeant Bolton also nodded.

Joss shifted his legs uncomfortably, smiled, and said, 'I'm prepared to give my opinion. I have no responsibility for anything else. I'm a rank-and-file member of the Party down south, and that's all.' He paused and said, 'I agree with Boris. I think you should run the existing organizations, and start a discussion group on Marxist lines. You should also do a great deal of self-education. Perhaps that's of more importance than anything else.' With a small smile he added, 'I do not agree with Comrade Bolton that theory does not matter.' A dispirited silence followed. He said quietly, 'Do I have to remind you that every face in this room is white?'

'That seems to me sectarianism,' said Sergeant Bolton. 'We can easily recruit the Africans. There is no problem.'

'Perhaps. Perhaps not.'

This cautious, almost flippant remark caused Sergeant Bolton to reap a harvest of support from the eyes of the disciples. He at once cried out, 'Let's take a vote on it.'

Boris said angrily, 'You suggest a vote on whether or not we start a Communist Party? That isn't the way to do things.'

'Why not? It's the democratic method,' said Sergeant Bolton.

'Listen,' said Boris, with heated calm. 'The Communist Party is a world organization. You have no right to start little groups here and there as you like. You should at least inquire from a superior body – the Party down south, for instance.'

'We should start one, and then inform them. You don't suppose they'd be sorry?'

At this everyone laughed, even Hesse, McGrew, and Joss.

There was a shout of 'Let's take a vote.' Hands shot up everywhere. They remained in the air for a very long time. Andrew McGrew's hand went up, then Anton Hesse's.

'It's decided,' said Sergeant Bolton, quiet with triumph. He looked coldly towards Boris and said, 'The majority is against you.'

'I do not consider myself bound by such a vote,' said Boris quietly. He was dead white. There was sweat on his forehead. 'It's irresponsible and amateurish.' He looked at Anton Hesse and Andrew McGrew and said angrily, 'I'm surprised you should vote for it.'

Andrew said, 'Well, let's see how things work out.' Anton said nothing.

Boris asked Joss, 'Why didn't you vote? Does it mean you don't think there should be a party, or you don't think it's your affair?'

'I'll be back in the Army inside a week,' said Joss. He looked embarrassed, however. 'I've said what I think.'

Sergeant Bolton said pointedly, 'Half the people in the room are in uniform – not everybody finds that an excuse.' But he did not pursue it; what filled him with contempt in Boris was allowed to pass in Joss.

Boris stood up, smiling a steady unhappy smile. The others were shocked to see that his eyes were filled with tears. 'You can count on me with anything to do with Help for Our Allies, or the Sympathizers or that sort of thing.'

'You're simply scared of losing your job,' said Sergeant Bolton, with his sarcastic smile.

There was a deep indrawn breath around the room – they were all shocked.

Boris said, 'I am not afraid of losing my job. I'm not even a British national yet. But if I were I would take the same line.' He looked down at the bench where his wife was still sitting. Betty was flushed; the delicate small face was wet with tears. She was unconsciously wringing her hands.

She rose suddenly, put her hand in Boris's arm, and said indignantly, 'You're a lot of – children!'

Sergeant Bolton smiled steadily.

Boris again said, 'I'm surprised that Comrade Hesse and Comrade McGrew should take this line – I'm surprised . . .'

These two men, in their turn, were looking uncomfortable. But before they could say anything, Boris had gone out, supporting his wife. They could hear her crying as she went down the corridor.

'And now,' said Sergeant Bolton, 'let's get cracking.'

Joss rose and said, 'I've got to get home now.'

There were cries of protest, but he simply shook his head, smiled, said, 'Good night,' and went out. He left behind him an impression of criticism. Authority had gone with him. They all looked towards Anton and Andrew to supply it.

'Now we've got rid of those saboteurs,' said Sergeant Bolton, 'let's start work.'

But Andrew remarked, with humorous protest, 'I want to make it quite clear that while I think Boris should have considered himself bound to stay, he's a good chap and quite sound.'

There was a vote taken – a majority vote decided there should be a Communist Party. As an old Communist, he was bound to join it.

Anton said, 'I agree that he should have stayed. But I would like to protest against the word "saboteur".'

Sergeant Bolton let out his shoulders in his heaving silent laugh. Andrew interrupted it by saying, 'We should elect a committee.'

Sergeant Bolton shrugged impatiently. 'A committee with a group like this?'

'Yes,' said Anton, quiet but firm. 'A committee.'

Sergeant Bolton looked towards William, then Jasmine,

then Martha. It was not until then that she realized he considered them his supporters.

At Sergeant Bolton's look Jasmine said, 'I vote for Comrade Bolton.' His eyes met hers and held them in a long intimate look. She blushed.

Martha hesitated, and said, 'I suggest Comrade Anton.' She did not look at Anton, but involuntarily at Sergeant Bolton. He was smiling with tolerant sarcasm. It was really remarkable how the man could suggest he was being betrayed. But why? One could scarcely have a committee of one. But voting at once for Anton, instead of confirming Jasmine's vote for himself, was a blow against him, those reproachful black eyes said; but he understood the world – and women too, for that matter!

She smiled apologetically; the alliances in the group were, in short, being formed even then.

There was a longish pause, which was ended by Anton's casual 'I would like to suggest Comrade Andrew.'

Sergeant Bolton immediately countered with 'And I suggest William and Jasmine.'

'Too big,' said Anton Hesse immediately.

'Jasmine,' insisted Sergeant Bolton.

Jasmine, whose loyalties were almost equally balanced between Anton Hesse and the sergeant, looked for confirmation towards Anton, and saw that the watchful eyes said neither one thing nor the other. 'I'm not experienced enough,' she said confusedly.

The young schoolteacher cried out, 'I protest – why aren't there any women on the committee?'

At this all the tensions dissolved in a roar of laughter. Jasmine automatically became a member of the committee.

As the laughter subsided, Anton said, 'I suggest this meeting be now closed. It's very late. The committee will discuss things and call a meeting of the whole group shortly.'

They all rose. Sergeant Bolton went, smiling, over to Anton and Andrew, taking Jasmine with him. These four shortly announced they would hold a committee meeting there and then. The others had better get home to bed.

They all walked down the dark stairway in silence. There was no need to say anything. They were together, dedicated and promised, and on the pavement they wrung each other's hands, smiling at each other without speaking.

Then William came up to Martha, and said, 'Is everything all right, Matty?'

She had to think before she remembered what he meant.

'Oh, yes – I expect it will sort itself out,' she said hurriedly. Her mind was still on what had happened. 'I don't think we should have let Boris go like that,' she said.

'Oh, Jackie knows what he's doing.' He was speaking out of the service loyalty, she could see. 'You should see him with the lads on the camp – he's marvellous,' he added.

She could imagine it. She saw Jackie Bolton, persuasive, understanding, almost tender – she had felt the spell herself.

He said too casually, 'He thinks quite a lot of you.'

At first she was pleased, then she saw he was jealous because of that evening the sergeant had spent with her. She resented it.

'Shall I come up and have a talk with the old man?' he asked.

'I wish you wouldn't call him the old man,' she said irritably.

'Now, don't be cross,' he said persuasively, taking her hand. They were together in sympathy again. 'After all – if you don't love him, that's all there is to it. You should simply tell him so. And that's that.'

She laughed a little. 'That isn't at all that.' And now he again seemed young and inexperienced.

'Why don't you get yourself a room in town and simply leave him?'

'Oh – I don't want to hurry things.'

'What's the good of dragging it out?'

'I'd better get back home quickly – it's after twelve.'

She was thinking again, He really is such a baby. And he was thinking, She doesn't want to leave that comfortable life, that's all.

They parted, without even a kiss. But as she reached the car he came after her, and took her in his arms. They clung together in contrition because they were on edge with each other.

'Why don't you simply come with me to the hotel? Then you'll have burned your boats.'

'But it's so unpleasant that way.'

'It's so unpleasant that you have to leave him. Not how you leave him.'

She was silent. He said, 'Are you afraid of his divorcing you or something like that?'

'You don't understand him. He wouldn't do anything *ugly* – not really. He's just in a bad mood. He's very sensible and straightforward . . .' But here she tailed off in a sigh.

A single stroke from the bell in the church across the park fell through the air, and she said, 'I really must get back.'

She drove home, parked the car quietly, and then saw that the house was filled with light. On the veranda Douglas was sitting where she had left him.

'Why haven't you gone to bed?' she inquired lightly.

'Where have you been – why are you so late?'

'There were two meetings.'

He ground out, 'Was *he* there?'

'Well, of course,' she said, on that false light note.

She went through into the bedroom, and he followed. He was grinding his teeth – she could hear the ugly sound just behind her.

'Did you sleep with him?'

She looked at him, astounded, 'Of course not.'

He grabbed her wrist and twisted it. 'Tell me the truth.'

Her wrist hurt, but pride forbade her to cry out. He dropped it, and stood looking at her with a swollen glare.

She flung her clothes off, flung on her nightgown, got into bed. 'I'm going to sleep.'

He stood for a moment, then abruptly went to her cupboard, and began a frantic search among her things.

She sat up. 'What on earth are you doing?' She was herself dismayed by the light inappropriate tone she could not help using. But both of them were playing roles, she felt. None of this behaviour was genuine, either hers or his. She felt that something would slip into place and they would become themselves.

In the meantime he was flinging her clothes out behind him like a digging terrier. He found what he was looking for, the little box that held the contraceptives. He ground his teeth again, looking at it. Then he swiftly crossed the room and put it into a drawer of his own. 'You aren't going to have it,' he said.

'But I don't want it,' she said, helplessly laughing.

It infuriated him. He locked the drawer and stood thinking. She could see that he was about to propel himself off into another course. Then, abruptly, he left the room. She leaned on her elbow, listening, while lights crashed on in one room after another through the dark empty house. He came back carrying Caroline, who was half awake, blinking in a sleepy smile.

Douglas aggressively presented her the child, holding her out on his two forearms. Like a tray, she thought involuntarily. He said, in the sentimental voice, 'Look, Matty, look at this.'

She snapped out, in extreme embarrassment, 'Oh, don't be revolting, Douglas.'

The disgust in her voice startled him out of his own picture of himself. He stood there holding out the child who was asleep again, on his two extended forearms, blinking at her in comical bewilderment. Then he went red with shame, and rapidly retreated again back through the rooms. She saw the lights switch out methodically as he came back, and thought, He's not at all out of control. He might imagine that he is, but he wouldn't forget to switch the lights out if the skies were falling. It might put up the electricity bill by tuppence.

He began to undress.

Now what's going to happen next? she wondered, out of her sense of improbability – it was not possible that this was really happening.

As he was getting into his own bed, he suddenly changed direction and flumped over on to hers. He ground her shoulders, so that she felt the balls of his thumbs deep under the collarbone, and said viciously, 'I'll give you another baby – that'll put an end to this nonsense.'

'Oh no, you don't,' she remarked breathlessly. But it all seemed so much more vulgar than was probable that she looked at him with embarrassment. 'You're hurting my shoulders,' she pointed out reasonably. He gripped her tighter for a moment, and pushed her shoulders back. She felt an instinct to struggle, then let herself go limp and said, 'It's no good trying to rape me, you know. You can't rape women unless they want to be.'

The word seemed to check him. He let her go, and stood up, thinking, blinking at her. Then he went to his own bed. She put out her hand and switched out the lights. She lay in the dark, trying to breathe silently, but her heart was beating like a mine stamp.

She could hear him breathing heavily and irregularly across the space of darkness. Then she was asleep. She awoke with difficulty, hearing his voice, slow, persistent, as if he had already said it many times: 'It's no use pretending to be asleep. Wake up, Matty. Tell me, Matty – did you sleep with him, did you?'

'No, I didn't.'

He repeated it; she repeated it. She fell off to sleep again. Again she woke in the dark, to hear that persistent voice, this time repeating, 'Did you sleep with Hesse?'

She laughed. 'No, don't be absurd.'

He went through a list of names – it occurred to her after a while that he had memorized a list of the names on the Help for Our Allies Committee. She preserved silence for a while; she was only half awake; tiredness kept dragging her into sleep, and then she would be awake with the pain of fingers digging into her shoulder.

She knew quite well that he knew she had not slept with William or anyone else. What, then, was this all about? He's enjoying it, flashed into her mind; and the truth of this startled her completely awake. He was thoroughly enjoying the whole thing, and particularly the idea that she might have slept with twenty men. She lay in the dark, pondering: she was being confronted for the first time in her life with that phenomenon, male jealousy when it is self-conscious, with one eye on the invisible observer, enjoyable jealousy. But she fell asleep again, and again was woken by the pain of those jabbing fingers, which pride forbade her to protest against.

Finally, towards dawn, when she was sick and dizzy with exhaustion, she said calmly, 'Yes, I've slept with William, and with Anton Hesse.' She then repeated, one after another, the list of the men on the committee. At once his fingers relaxed, and she heard him breathing deeply and regularly. She was wondering what he was thinking about now, when she realized he was asleep. It seemed that whatever he wanted had been given to him. She fell asleep again.

She woke to find him dressing. She looked with curiosity at this sturdy and apparently sane young man, and remarked, 'Well, and how does it strike you this morning?'

But he ignored this, saying in that other voice, sentimental and pleading, 'Now, don't forget you must go and see Mrs Talbot, Matty.' With this he left the room to get his breakfast.

She thought that she must immediately collect her clothes and leave him. Then she thought, No, I'll see Mrs Talbot first.

Before he left for the office he came back, apparently normal, but with a wandering look in his eyes which told her that he was still in the grip of that hysteria. He pronounced rapidly, 'I forbid you ever to see William again.'

'Don't be silly,' she said promptly.

This, it seemed, was what he had expected, even what he had come for, for he ground his teeth again, gazed at her in self-consciously shocked astonishment, and went out.

Chapter Four

The door was opened by Mrs Talbot herself. The door to Mr Talbot's study was shut, and Elaine was nowhere to be seen. Mrs Talbot was fully dressed – stiff grey silk, with white bands at throat and wrists.

Martha followed her into the drawing room and sat down. Mrs Talbot remained standing. Her eyes were filled with tears.

'Oh, Matty,' she cried out, 'it can't be true, it can't. You can't be leaving such a nice boy as Douglas for that other – of course I don't know him, but . . .'

'I'm not leaving Douglas for anyone,' said Martha after a pause, during which she examined this new view of the position. The words 'I am leaving him to live differently' came to her tongue; she did not say them, because they sounded absurd – they should be said flippantly, in this house. Then she saw Anton Hesse in her mind's eye and brought out aggressively, 'I'm going to live differently.'

But Mrs Talbot's look at her was very shrewd. 'We all feel like this, you know, Matty dear.'

Martha thought, She means, everyone falls in love with someone else and wants to leave their husband. But Mrs Talbot was going on: 'I remember when I was young – I was a pacifist – I quarrelled with my *fiancé* over the war . . . But Matty, it's all such nonsense.'

This depressed Martha; but she summoned the memory of Anton Hesse again, and recovered her sense of purpose.

'You don't understand,' she began. But what was she to explain to Mrs Talbot? She was unable to go on.

'Oh, I do, I do!' Mrs Talbot positively wrung her hands. 'Oh, I was so happy thinking of you making Douggie so happy. If Elaine could be properly married, I think my last wish would be granted, and I'd die happy. How can you break it all up like this, Matty?' Now she was crying, and patting her eyes delicately with a fragment of silk.

'But, Mrs Talbot, I'm not properly married. I'm bored, bored, bored, you can't imagine. I can't bear it. I haven't anything in common with Douglas, and I've been unhappy all the time.' For this now seemed to her the simple truth.

Mrs Talbot said in the murmuring voice. 'But Matty, dear, you are such a well-suited couple, we could all see it. And he's so proud of you – and you are such a good cook, and everything like that.'

Martha smiled; and Mrs Talbot said hurriedly, 'No, don't do that.'

'I can't say what I mean, let me think.' She even turned her back for a moment, and looked out of the shaded windows. She appeared very beautiful to Martha then; and that was more persuasive than anything she had said. This elegant elderly woman in her pretty room had such a look of completeness, of harmony, that once again that group of people seemed absurd and graceless; everything they were, or said, rang false for a moment, beside Mrs Talbot.

She said, 'There's that nice house, you've got such a settled future, and that lovely little girl.'

Martha flushed angrily. Mrs Talbot saw it and cried out, 'But he's good to you, isn't he, Matty?'

'I think he's mad,' said Martha. 'I hate him. I hate everything about him!' she added violently.

Another quick look from the shrewd eyes. 'He's only jealous, Matty,' she said placatingly.

'But there's nothing for him to be jealous about. I've always been quite faithful to him – I suppose that's what you mean. And what he means, too. And he certainly hasn't been to me,' she added with the feeling that all this was irrelevant.

'Oh, Matty! They aren't like us, they really aren't, you know.'

Martha interrupted with 'I don't see why we should treat them like so many children.' She resented having to use that

417

'we', associating herself with Mrs Talbot's division of humanity.

Mrs Talbot was silent for a while. 'Look, Matty,' she said in a different voice, brisk and practical, 'you simply must realize that everyone feels like this. Everyone.'

But Martha had mechanically risen to her feet, repudiating this argument. She was picking up her handbag, about to leave.

'No, don't go yet, Matty. If you'd only tell me what you have against him?'

'But I haven't anything against him!' said Martha, laughing angrily. 'I'm leaving, that's all.' She looked straight at Mrs Talbot, laughing. Suddenly, she observed, without knowing she had been going to, 'Besides, we don't get on sexually.' She blushed, and was angry with herself.

And now Mrs Talbot had coloured up, too, and had become animated. She turned on Martha as if this had been what she was waiting for. 'Oh, Matty,' she cried, 'I *knew* it.'

This surprised both her and Martha into silence. They turned away from each other, embarrassed. As for Martha, what she had said, the use of those words then, had had the power to set her at a distance from what everyone in their circle called their love life. Hers with Douglas slid backwards into the past, and seemed wholly abhorrent. It was finished. She had never felt anything but repulsion for him. The idea that he might ever touch her again made her shrink. Love with William shimmered ahead, a pervasive radiance which coloured the whole of life.

Mrs Talbot was weeping again. 'Oh, Matty, dear,' she sobbed gently. 'Oh, how I loathe this sex business!'

Martha looked at her in astonishment. She thought of the room next to this one, the large bed, and those dark suave pyjamas tumbled by Mrs Talbot's pillow. What on earth did she mean?

She inquired, 'Do you mean you don't like making love?'

At this, Mrs Talbot gasped, and the frail enamel of her face was pink. 'I can't talk about it – I'm not like you young things, you can say anything. And all your books and ideas . . .'

'Well, that isn't the point, anyway,' said Martha flatly.

'But, Matty . . .' Mrs Talbot had come quite close, and had grasped her arm; it was stiff, so she dropped it again.

'Matty, let me tell you this. The man I really loved, the one that was killed – well, sex had nothing to do with it. Nothing!'

Martha was regarding her with discomfort. Mrs Talbot was being dishonest, she thought. 'Do you mean,' she asked seriously, 'that sex has nothing to do with love?'

'Oh, how I hate it all!' cried out Mrs Talbot.

She collected herself, and said quickly in a low voice, 'Matty, you are making a great mistake. All that's got nothing to do with marriage – nothing at all! It never did have. If you want to have love affairs, if you feel like that – well . . . I never talk about it, *never*. But, Matty, you can have love affairs if you want – oh!' And here she finally broke down, and leaned against the back of her chair, weeping.

'Well,' remarked Martha, conscientiously pointing out to herself that what Mrs Talbot found ugly was not the fact but the talking about it. 'Well, I think it's all revolting. I don't think I really understand what you're saying.' Mrs Talbot, head collapsed back against the chair, was now regarding her with an unhappy but acute gaze. 'If you're in love with a man, you sleep with him. If you're not – you don't. And I'm not going to stay married to Douglas and call him a dear boy and treat him like an idiot.'

'Well, I don't know,' said Mrs Talbot helplessly, 'I really don't. It's all so easy, really, Matty. Everything can be arranged – if you want. There's no need for all this. And you'll only be unhappy.'

'I think I'd better be going,' said Martha. She went towards the door.

Mrs Talbot came after her. 'Matty,' she said appealingly, 'but what are you going to do? Of course, you'll probably get married, and you're quite attractive.' Here she blushed, at this unintended exposure of her real assessment of Martha's charm. 'But, Matty, I'm sure that boy hasn't any money. He's not even an officer, is he? Of course, I know that quite nice people are in the ranks these days.'

'Look,' said Martha awkwardly, 'I don't think you really understand any of this, you know.'

'Go and see your mother and talk it over, do, Matty.'

Martha stopped. It had never entered her head to do so. But it occurred to her as strange that she had not, until this moment, wondered what her parents knew.

'They're so unhappy,' urged Mrs Talbot.

'They know?' asked Martha hopelessly.

'Oh, Matty, Matty!' cried Mrs Talbot in despair. 'How could they *not* know?'

Martha kissed Mrs Talbot's cheek, automatically inclined forward for that purpose, and offered her a hurried unhappy smile. Then she escaped.

No sooner had she reached home than there was a telephone call from Mrs Brodeshaw, reminding her that she had promised to help with the concert that night. Would she take the car down to the Coloured area, and bring certain children to the hall at seven o'clock?

Martha said that she would. Afterwards she realized that she had committed herself to stay in the house for another day. But lethargy was setting in again. She was thinking that tonight she would have a really sensible discussion with Douglas, when the telephone rang. It was Douglas; and she listened to his sentimentally urgent voice saying that he was so glad she had stuck to her promise to help with the concert. 'That's the ticket, Matty,' he said. 'That's the stuff.'

The telephone went silent while she was still thinking of appropriate things to say. For what was this sentimental appeal about? He would surely feel about the concert exactly as she did; yet he was making it a personal triumph for himself that she should go. But if he was indulging in unreal emotions, what was she doing? One thing answered another, always: she looked from outside, for one shocked moment, at that frozen obstinacy she called pride, and hastily averted her eyes from it. For if she ceased to maintain it, even for a moment, she would be lost; she could positively feel, rising inside her, a satisfied self-pity – which was the emotion that would well up from the cracked surface of that 'pride'. But she would not let it crack. She must behave like this, there was nothing else she could do. She would go to that concert, and then – wait and see. Something would happen, something she did not understand was working itself out.

She was very tired – she had not slept; she was hungry – she could not remember when she had eaten properly. She hurriedly ate some stale cake she found in the pantry, and set off for the offices downtown. They were empty. She spent the rest of her day addressing piles of envelopes in solitude. She did not leave the offices until it was time to fetch the children for the concert. She walked home to get the car; Douglas had left it there for this purpose, and gone off somewhere on his own.

She drove off downtown. She felt, as usual, that she was entering a new world when she turned into the squalid little street she was looking for. Extreme poverty lay a hundred yards from wealth – as, indeed, it tends to do, but in this case it coincided with a physical ghetto. Five parallel streets, each about half a mile long, held the Coloured community. This was still the nineteenth century. She, Martha, could expect to live to a ripe old age; and if she bore a child it did not enter her head it might not live. Here people would die in early middle age, and babies died like flies in their first year. She, Martha, had never had anything more urgent to worry about than whether her emotional life was or was not satisfactory. Here were debt and anxiety and dirt and an atmosphere of a doom which might strike at any moment through illness or death. This was the other world – or rather, how nine-tenths of the people of the world lived – and all she could feel about it was that everything that could be said about poverty had already been said; poverty was boring; there was no need for it to exist, and therefore she felt as if it already did not exist. It had, as Anton might say, been by-passed by history. But Anton would certainly not approve of this feeling of almost exasperated boredom: it occurred to her that joining the Communist Party did not make one a Communist. She was feeling, as she drove through these squalid streets, exactly as she always did: she had not been issued, as she had vaguely expected, with a completely new set of emotions.

She left the car in the street, while the usual swarm of ragged urchins gathered about it. She entered the building where she would find the children she must drive to the hall. It was built in three sides around a courtyard. A gutter ran dirty water down the middle, washing flapped over her head. All around the veranda which opened off the court stood dark-skinned men and women and children, watching her curiously. She felt like an intruder. She asked to be directed, and found a door standing open in a corner. It was a small room. Evidently a family lived here, for it had two large broken-down beds, a wooden table on which lay a loaf of bread in a bit of newspaper, some wooden chairs, and a wood stove. It seemed full of people. Two little girls detached themselves from the mass, and came shyly forward, while a large fat Coloured woman chivvied at them to be good with the kind lady.

It was all false and unpleasant, the high subservient voice of the woman, the thin little girls with their dirty hair and their ragged frocks, the smell of poverty, sharp and sour. The only honest thing in the place was a young man lounging against a wall, lounging of set purpose, radiating a calculated insolence and resentment. But no one else seemed to resent her. She went rapidly from room to room, and assembled another five little girls, all as ragged and as dirty as the first two. As she left, a whole group of women stood calling admonishments and threats after their children, in order to impress her with their respectability and their willingness to oblige.

She took the children to the car, and helped them in. None of them had been in a car before, she realized. The little girl sitting next to her was trembling and shrinking away. Martha understood she was afraid of her and asked her name. A small high voice piped, 'Flora!'

At once the others offered their names – a chorus of Sandra, Marie and Anne. Then they began a high nervous giggle which upset Martha. She understood that the firm kind patronage of a Mrs Maynard would at once set these

422

children at their ease. She asked shyly what they were to do at the concert, and they burst out singing, 'Three little girls from school are we . . .'

'No, Sandra, not girls, Miss Pattern sez maids.'

'Meds,' corrected the small sharp-eyed imp who was Sandra. And they began again cheerfully, 'Three little meds from school are we . . .'

They kept it up until they reached the hall, where Martha parked the car and helped them out. They stood uncertainly, hands devoutly folded in front of them in a way which suggested the influence of the Church, and watched her with bright curious eyes. She led them to a room at the back of the hall, and ushered them into a scene of crowded confusion.

Mrs Maynard, in a black lace dinner frock, was helping Mrs Anderson strip half a dozen brown infants naked and clothe them in neat white dresses. Martha saw that among the white women were Stella, Stella's mother, Mrs Talbot, Mrs Lowe-Island, and Mrs Brodeshaw. A rotund priest stood beaming in one corner.

She retired to the hall itself. It was a barn of a place, with a plain board floor, and walls stained a sad mustard colour, but strings of little coloured bulbs were festooned everywhere, and someone had tied bunches of red balloons over the doors. The place was full, since it was the first time people of colour had entertained a white audience. The *News* had made a point of it that morning. There was a feeling of expectant curiosity, made benevolent by those names on the programme: Mrs Maynard, Mrs Player, Mrs Brodeshaw.

After a long wait, the curtain, a heavy piece of dark-green serge, jerked slowly to one side on its brass hooks, and there stood Miss Pattern, a representative for this occasion of the Roman Catholic Church. She was wearing thick linen of electric blue, over which a faded little face peered with a mixture of encouragement and apology. She raised her hand nervously, silence fell, and she began to speak.

She had been asked by the committee — of which she was proud to be a member — to introduce this concert, which, she felt sure everyone would agree, was a novel and enterprising attempt to introduce one section of the community to another. Perhaps some people might feel that it was not altogether – how should she put it? – advisable to let our less fortunate brothers, to whom we stood in the position of parents and guides, start running before they could walk, but children have to begin sometime, don't they? And many people, among whom she was happy to say were some of great prestige and influence, felt that art was the greatest of the barrier-breakers, and she was sure that everyone present would be proud to attend at the first occasion when people of colour, or, as they preferred to be called (she emphasized this), the Coloured community, entertained a white audience. It was a landmark in the cultural life of their city. A happy event. (Here she blushed, stopped, then courageously continued.) She would like to make a few more points, if the distinguished audience would indulge her. The more enlightened members of the community, among whom she felt sure were all the members of this audience, could feel that a new wind was blowing. Times were changing. Ideas were abroad. It was natural that their fellow citizens . . . (she paused, looked at them firmly, and repeated) fellow citizens should want to be in the stream of change. It was much better that such movements, or perhaps she should say tendencies, should be guided and encouraged by people of experience and common sense, than left to be prey of those agitators and trouble-makers who unfortunately were always ready to exploit discontent.

She paused again, seemed about to go on, then leafed through her notes, shifting one piece of paper behind another. 'I think that's all I have to say, ladies and gentlemen.' She bowed forward from her waist, with a nervous smile, and retired backstage.

There was some perfunctory applause. Then, since it was observed that Mrs Player and Mrs Brodeshaw and Mrs Maynard were clapping loud and firm from the front seats, the audience took it up again. The sound died in a ragged volley as a small girl smiling a stretched, fixed smile appeared where Miss Pattern had stood. Martha recognized her with difficulty as one of those she had brought from the slum. She was now shiningly clean; her pigtails stood stiffly out to each side of her head, tied with large pink bows; her dress was starched white. She stood for some moments stretching her head hopefully to one side, as if listening, before they realized she had forgotten her lines. Then she proceeded to repeat, phrase for phrase, in a high tense shriek, a speech whispered to her from behind a fold of green serge. Unfortunately, it was impossible to understand a word of it. She retired, in confusion, to a storm of clapping, and shouts of 'Shame!' from some rowdies at the back, who had come under the impression that the concert was the work of the Sympathizers of Russia – apparently Miss Pattern's speech had confirmed their worst suspicions. But they were hushed sternly by the loyalists.

A gramophone began playing very loudly. 'The Blue Danube.' About fifty children flocked on to the stage, jigging and prancing, every face stretched in a prescribed smile. There was no attempt to follow the rhythm. After five minutes or so, the gramophone abruptly stopped again. Some continued to jig wildly, others stopped. Confusion. The gramophone set off in the middle of a bar, and then the green serge folds on either side shook violently. The music stopped finally with a loud squawk, and the children dived in all directions off the stage.

There was loud derisive laughter from the back. But Mrs Maynard turned and delivered a frowning stare at them.

There followed a short sketch between a little girl in a poke bonnet and crinolines and a little boy in blue knee pants. Neither wore shoes. It was a proposal of marriage, which evoked cries of 'How sweet!' from the front rows, and more raucous insinuating laughter from the back. After a pause, during which the stage remained empty, the same two walked down the stage as a bride and bridegroom – white butter muslin and black casement cloth – while all the other children flung confetti at them.

Then came three little girls against a bevy of other little girls: 'Three Little Maids From School Are We'; but, as

Martha had hoped, they had forgotten 'maids', and sang 'girls'.

Then a long, long pause. The audience fidgeted, and the stage remained empty. A hitch, obviously. Miss Pattern emerged and, smiling with complicity towards the audience, proceeded to play some Chopin waltzes. Her eyes were fixed anxiously on some point off stage. Suddenly she sharpened her pace, brought the waltz to a galloping end, and rose, hastily gathering her music. She almost ran off, as a little boy of about twelve was propelled on by an invisible push from someone. He was wearing a child's Red Indian head-dress, white shirt, white shorts, no shoes. He came very slowly and reluctantly to the front of the stage, sweating with terror, and, with wandering eyes and long intervals of silence, proceeded to recite selected portions from *Hiawatha*. Suddenly he stopped in the middle of a line; his mouth remained open for a while, then he bolted off the stage. Tumultuous applause.

And now it was the interval.

Martha worked her way to the back, and was delighted to find that groups of earnest and enraged Zambesians were forming a committee to protest to 'the Prime Minister himself if need be' because of this insult to white civilization.

She returned to her seat, hoping for the worst.

It appeared that protests had already been received during the interval, for the second half of the programme began with a speech by Mrs Maynard herself. She delivered it with great firmness, eyes and rings flashing, her black lace swaying, looking at the back rows. They must move with the times, she informed them decisively. Did they realize that the Coloured community lived in conditions which would disgrace pigs? (Ironical cheers from the back.) The whole area was a breeding ground for disease, which, as anybody with a ha'p'orth of sense would realize, was no respecter of persons or colour bars. If this concert did nothing else, it might make the white community realize what a danger spot it tolerated in its midst.

There were a couple more cheers, rather enfeebled, apparently by the processes of thought. Mrs Maynard stood, subduing them all by her presence, for a few silent moments, then retired to her seat.

The programme resumed without incident. The Southern Sambos did an Irish jig with great spirit. A chorus sang 'Tipperary'. There was a vivacious rendering of that inevitable song 'Hold Him Down, the Zulu Warrior'. Then another pause. It was prolonged. The barrackers at the back plucked up courage and began booing. Mrs Maynard stood up in the front row, and glared at them over the intervening rows. Then something unexpected happened. Towards the middle of the hall a solid mass of grey-blue indicated the presence of the Air Force; half a hundred aircraftsmen, tired of the cinema, had come in search of entertainment. Now they began shouting, 'Up with Uncle Joe!' and 'Progress, that's what we want!' One yelled, 'Down with the colour bar!'

Some of the more solid citizens were observed leaving their seats and slipping out of the side doors.

Then Miss Pattern came slowly on to the stage. She was very nervous. She apologized for the delay, but the committee had been wondering whether to allow the next item in view of the – response of the audience. She had to make quite clear that the committee took no responsiblity for the next item. The leaders of the Coloured community had suggested it. It had been agreed to because ... She hesitated some moments, and then remarked firmly, 'Anyway, it shows the sort of thing we've got to contend with. The sketch was written by a Coloured boy, a South African Cape Coloured, now in England.' Another pause. 'There is talent among them – real talent. It should be directed. It *must* be directed,' she cried out, on the verge of tears, and ran off the stage.

And now the audience leaned forward intently. The stage was completely dark.

Then a white patch gleamed in the darkness and a high, shrill voice said, 'I am Asia. I am the teeming millions of Asia. I am ...' There was a sudden chorus of boos from the back.

Another white patch appeared, and a second voice

427

shouted desperately, 'I am India . . .' But the rest of this was lost in tumult.

The white patches were agitatedly swaying in the darkness on the stage, and shrill isolated voices could be heard: Hunger, Poverty, Misery.

The audience was standing up. Someone was singing 'The Red Flag'. The lights came on to show three small urchins draped in white sheets, shouting above the din from the hall. 'I am Africa,' yelled one determinedly. Miss Pattern appeared on the edge of the stage, waving her hands. Africa, India and Asia rushed off the stage, tripping over their sheets, while Miss Pattern smiled appealingly at the audience. The back rows were now singing 'Sarie Marais', while the delighted aircraftsmen in the middle were sitting with arms linked, swaying from side to side, and singing, 'The people's flag is deepest red . . .'

Mrs Maynard rose to her feet, climbed up the wooden steps that led to the stage, and stood waiting for silence. At last she got it. She said it was a disgraceful exhibition and she was appalled at their irresponsibility.

The khaki rows at the back hissed; and were at once answered from the Air Force blue with satirical cheers.

'You will kindly have the goodness to stand up for the last item,' Mrs Maynard said, and stood aside while the stage filled with the children waving Union Jacks. She lifted her hand – the rings flashed and glittered – and brought it down on the first chord of the National Anthem. The audience sang it boisterously through to the end, with undercurrents of 'Sarie Marais' and 'The Red Flag'.

Afterwards, the place seethed as if stirred by a vast stick. People hastily left; isolated groups of Air Force and the khaki-clad – some uniforms, some not – looked at each other and meditated whether it was worth while to fight. A couple of half-hearted dogfights were developing as Martha squeezed out, and saw Douglas waiting for her, smiling mistily, as if from emotion.

'Wait,' she said, 'wait.' She ran around to the back door, while he followed. She wanted to know what was going on behind the scenes. She found a dozen matrons energetically divesting the children of their stage clothes, while they congratulated each other on their courage: 'It's time they woke up.' 'Yes, I think we've broken the ice.'

But it was not a united committee any longer. Mrs Lowe-Island, upright and sturdy in mauve chiffon, was whispering to Mrs Anderson that the Communists had introduced that disgraceful last item on to the programme, the whole town was full of Communists, they were everywhere. Miss Pattern leaned against a wall, half laughing and half crying, while Mrs Maynard gruffly urged her to pull herself together and the fat priest hovered by, making sympathetic tut-tutting noises.

And now arrived six of the other committee, all fine open-necked sunburnt young Zambesians, all angry, but earnestly reproachful. Martha heard the note she had heard so often recently from Douglas, and looked at him involuntarily to see if he recognized it. It was that sentimental appeal, the note of goodness betrayed.

Mrs Maynard confronted them, calm and majestic, and proceeded to point out that the art of good government was to make use of dissatisfaction for social ends. This being too abstract – it was countered with an indignant 'But we can't have the kaffirs doing as they like!' – she translated it thus: 'My dear young men, they will get out of hand unless you give them rope.'

They looked at each other rather doubtfully, and Mrs Lowe-Island came in to support. With her hands on her hips, eyes burning, she said that people like them encouraged the Communists. Of course Communist influence had caused the last item on the programme, but why did they behave like that, the way to treat Communists was to take no notice of them, all they wanted to do was to make trouble . . .

Mrs Lowe-Island's speech and personality being more understandable to them, violent discussion continued, while Mrs Maynard stood on one side, watching thoughtfully, with no more than the faintest smile on her face. Finally, when her lieutenant ran out of breath, she stepped forward and invited all six of them up to her house for a discussion next afternoon 'at six o'clock, mind, because I have to be at Government House for dinner.'

They retired, prepared to control their indignation until they had heard the other side, like true democrats. Only then did Mrs Maynard allow herself to look exasperated. 'And I'm so busy!' she was heard to exclaim. Unfortunately nine-tenths of the time of any political leader must be spent not on defeating his opponents, but on manipulating the stupidities of his own side.

Martha's charges were soon delivered into her hands, in their faded rags and bare feet. She was thanked profusely by Mrs Brodeshaw for her kind co-operation, while Douglas grinned a bashful boy's smile just behind her.

She took the children to the car. Douglas came with her.

'Well, Matty?' he inquired eagerly. It really seemed that he expected her to show enthusiasm.

'Everything that happens in this place is like a caricature – it simply isn't possible that it should happen at all.'

She heard his breathing change. She said hastily, 'Were you there? Did you see it?'

'I saw the last part. But, Matty – it's a beginning. It would have been impossible to have Coloured people entertaining the whites even a year ago.'

'The beginning of what?' she inquired reasonably. She noted with dismay how amusement and indignation, any emotion she might have been feeling, vanished instantly under the calm cold anger that rose in her the moment she heard him begin to breathe deep, saw his face redden and swell. 'Don't let's start again until we've dropped the children,' she said quickly.

The house in the slum was in darkness. Martha shepherded the children over the rough court, under the bits of washing. A slit of yellow showed under a door. It opened slowly. From the light of a stub of candle stuck in a bottle, she saw a room full of sleeping breathing bodies. The large woman, still dressed, came forward and received the children, who began bolting along the veranda this way and that like so many rabbits into their doors. The woman began curtsying and bobbing, while she took her child to her skirts. 'Thenk-you, missus, thenk-you, missus.'

Martha said good night, and went back to the car.

Douglas said: 'My mother's come.'

'Oh – well, that's good,' she said flatly.

'Now, do let her talk to you, Matty,' he implored in that lover's tone.

Mrs Knowell was sitting in the drawing room, reading. She rose at the sight of Martha, smiling uncertainly. Martha also hesitated. Then she realized they were both bothered by a problem of etiquette: Was it suitable for a young woman on the verge of leaving her husband to kiss that husband's mother? She went forward and kissed Mrs Knowell on the cheek. The older woman grasped Martha to her in a quick anxious embrace, and then released her.

'Matty,' she said urgently, 'Matty . . .'

They looked around. Douglas had gone into the next room, leaving the door open. He called out in a loud, hearty voice, 'You two girls would like to have a nice chat!'

Martha glanced towards Mrs Knowell, embarrassed. That lady, as tired, bony and yellow as ever, looked indignant, and then involuntarily smiled and sighed. Both women flushed guiltily, and became solemn, conscious that they were disliking each other.

'I've come to stay a few days,' began Mrs Knowell quickly. 'I hope you don't mind, Matty.' She glanced towards the open door.

'Of course not,' said Martha politely. She smiled again; she realized that she wanted to burst into hysterical laughter. She noted that upwelling of hysteria with terror. She controlled herself and said coldly, 'Well, this is a mix-up, isn't it?'

'Oh, it is, Matty – it is. Awful,' agreed the elder lady sullenly. She was about to say something else; then Martha could see that she was thinking, I must not interfere. She settled back in her chair, and said, 'You must be tired.'

Martha at once said she was. She looked nervously away; she wanted to escape.

Then Mrs Knowell scrambled up, came close, and said in a low, angry voice, 'Matty – must you? Must you, Matty?'

'Yes, I must,' said Martha at once.

Mrs Knowell's face twitched, then she smiled a cold, disapproving appeal, and said, 'You must do what you think is best.'

Martha was deeply touched. She impulsively embraced the old lady again, suppressing the distaste she felt at touching the emaciated body. The skin felt cold and clammy. And Mrs Knowell was trembling with emotion. Martha could not stand the emotion. She gave the elder lady a quick apologetic smile and went to the bedroom.

Douglas immediately followed. 'I think you might have spared her a little more time,' he began.

'Douglas,' she suddenly wailed, 'do for God's sake shut up.'

She saw a look of satisfaction come on to his face at that despairing wail. He began firmly, 'Matty, I must talk to you.' His eyes were stern and calm, his voice steady. This, in fact, was that sensible and brotherly young man. 'We must get this thing sorted out. Tonight.'

She felt fear rising in her. 'You don't think we should have a jury of Mrs Talbot and your mother and my mother?' she asked sarcastically.

The moment was over – his eyes reddened, his lips shook.

'I'm going to bed to sleep,' she said. She was in bed in a few moments. She turned away from him and thought, I must sleep, I'll go mad if I don't sleep. She was drifting off when – as she put it – it began again.

That night was a repetition of the last. Again he worked himself up into a rage of misery, cross-questioning her about every man she might have casually met during the last four years. And again she was astounded and appalled – it was like listening to a madman talking. Towards dawn she did what she had done the night before. She recited a list of about forty names, enthusiastically admitting guilt with all of them. And at once he was satisfied and went to sleep.

It was all impossible – but it was happening.

Several days went by. She went to meetings, worked at

the office, spent as little time as possible in the house. She returned at night to sleep broken every five minutes by a tug at the elbow and that stupid, maudlin questioning.

But why did she not leave? All she had to do was to take a suitcase, put a few clothes into it, and go. But she could not. She still felt that something must happen: someone would say something, and she would be released.

She was now in a condition of tense, heightened exhaustion. Her brain ticked over steadily, with a clear, cold analysis. She was watching the situation from outside, as if she were not implicated in it, and even with absorbed fascination.

She was considering such questions as, What did the state of self-displaying hysteria Douglas was in have in common with the shrill, maudlin self-pity of a leader in the *Zambesia News* when it was complaining that the outside world did not understand the sacrifices the white population made in developing the blacks? For there was a connection, she felt. Not in her own experience, nor in any book, had she found the state Douglas was now in. Yet precisely that same note was struck in every issue of the local newspapers – goodness betrayed, self-righteousness on exhibition, heartless enemies discovered everywhere.

But *she* was being heartless; she was as cold as a stone; and had to be.

She would even begin making such dispassionate comparisons to her mother-in-law, who would watch her, disquieted and disapproving, and murmur, 'But, Matty, men are like this, you know.'

'Nonsense.'

'All you young people,' she cried, in her sad yellow voice, 'you have such awful ideas.' And then: 'Life is so terrible, Matty, it's so sad, and you make it worse.'

'It isn't,' snapped Martha, frightened.

She made resolutions not to talk thus to the old lady. It was cruel and stupid. But at the bottom of it, she knew, was a vengeance against Douglas: You drag your mother into this, so that I can talk to her – well, then, I shall! She was playing that female role to its limit.

And all the time it was as if it were happening to somebody else.

She was surprised that all the women of the set had come to her, one after another, in secret, to say that they admired her courage, and wished they could do the same. They saw it simply as escaping from an unsatisfactory marriage: the political side of it did not exist. They were not political, and besides, at this particular point in history, Communism was respectable. All of them, however, began telling stories of their intimate lives which she had never suspected as possible. With what low-voiced and eager relish did they divulge these secrets! Then it occurred to her that what unpleasant things had not happened it was necessary to invent – precisely because they wanted her, Martha, to share with them the enjoyable crises that were taking place in her life.

She made one discovery. It was this. That her feeling that she was being moved along a process which had its own laws was justified. When a woman left her husband, or threatened to leave him – that is, a woman of her type, who insisted on her rights to behave as a man would – then the husband went through certain actions like an automaton, beginning with confiscating the contraceptives, threatening to make her forcibly pregnant, accusing her of multifarious infidelities, and ending in self-abasing weeping appeals that she should change her mind and stay. The thought that Douglas might weep and appeal horrified Martha. She felt she could not withstand it. But even more frightening, because it was so humiliating, was the idea that what she did and what Douglas did was inevitable, they were involved in a pattern of behaviour which they could not alter.

To Mrs Knowell she remarked: 'I'm beginning to see how the whole thing works. When a woman leaves her husband she is forgiven on one condition: that she complain shrilly about how badly he treats her. Then certain women will champion her. They are the women who themselves would like to leave and don't. It is these women who will re-establish her, provided she marries another suitable man.

But it all depends on whether she complains and arouses sympathy. They won't forgive me, because I have no intention of complaining. It's disgusting,' she said firmly and shrilly. Then she hated herself for that shrillness. For that group of women, in their secret interviews with her, were such a bunch of self-righteous and outraged feminists – and there was nothing she hated more!

'Oh, but, Matty,' said the old lady apprehensively, 'surely my Douggie doesn't ill-treat you.'

'No, of course he doesn't,' said Martha angrily. Then she felt overwhelmed with guilt because she was making the old woman so unhappy.

If only Martha would weep! If only she would drop her voice and nervously complain of small unhappinesses! With what delicacy and kindness would the old lady then comfort, and approach Douglas; how gently she would have brought the young couple together again; and then, having fulfilled her function as an old lady who was allowed no other, with what pride and tact would she have effaced herself! But, instead, here was this set-faced, cold-eyed, satirical young woman who never, not for a moment, allowed herself to weep or to soften.

The old lady lay awake at night, thinking of her life, and particularly of those children she had borne and lost. Inside her, even now, there were spaces of dark pain because of those children; even now her arms ached with emptiness when she remembered them. Whatever loneliness and disappointment she had felt had flowed long ago into those small lives, cut off so soon. She had never allowed herself to say, I was lonely, I am unhappy. She wept for the dead children who ought now to be a group of tall and strong young men and women around her. Small Caroline was so like the daughter who had died of malaria that swampy hot rainy season. And Martha was prepared to leave Caroline, leave everything – for what? Mrs Knowell lay awake night after night, looking into the darkness, crying steadily, tears soaking down a set, unmoving face; she felt betrayed by Martha. Her own life was made to look null and meaningless because Martha would not submit to what women always had submitted to. She longed for that moment when Martha would fling herself into her arms and cry out that Douglas could not understand her, but she would stay with him, that she was unhappy, but would make the best of it.

As for Martha, it had occurred to her that this compulsive process of analysis and comparison was nothing but an excuse for doing nothing. She was retiring to that bed each night for the sheer fascination of seeing what would follow, and because she was able to think contemptuously of Douglas, Aren't you ashamed to behave like a self-pitying child – look at yourself!

She was so disturbed by this thought that she set off to see Jasmine, having first made an appointment, since she would otherwise be at a meeting.

Until this moment Jasmine had appeared only in her public guise – a secretary on a platform, a girl never without files and papers. She was now revealed to be the daughter of a prosperous Jewish family. It was a large house, very comfortable, and secluded from the street in a well-kept garden. Inside this house Jasmine had a suite of rooms, filled with books, files and typewriters.

She was calm and sympathetic. She listened without comment while Martha made a long self-critical speech about how intellectuals were doomed to futility because they always thought about things instead of doing them. For one of the advantages of living in the suburbs of the world is that commonplaces which are too tedious for repetition anywhere else come as overwhelming discoveries. From the fact that the working people are destined to deliver the world follow certain other conclusions as night follows the day. Martha had discovered, rather to her surprise, that she must be an intellectual. Therefore: Was it, then, the case, she inquired, that intellectuals were bound to be useless to the revolution because their behaviour would always inspire such disgust in the onlookers that no one would take them seriously? She was developing this with all the fervour of someone on the track of a completely new idea, when she saw that there was a look of patient irony on the small, sedate face.

'Now, Matty,' said Jasmine reproachfully, 'why don't you just leave him and be done with it?'

Martha was checked.

'We simply can't understand,' said Jasmine firmly, 'why you don't just leave. You really look awful, Matty.'

'Well, I don't get much sleep,' admitted Martha.

'Naturally not. And it's not doing you any good. You're quite useless at meetings – you talk the most dreadful nonsense, you know. We are all very sympathetic, but we do wish you'd get it over with.' And then, the calm, demure little face changing not at all: 'Besides, there might be a revolutionary situation at any moment – and here you are wasting time on personal matters!'

Martha promised that she would take herself in hand at once. She went downtown and engaged a room, told the landlady that she would move in tomorrow, and then returned home.

She was now bound to leave tomorrow. She still felt like a fly caught in the web of her incapacity to move. She set off to see her parents.

She came near the house and saw her father in his chair under the tree. A newspaper was slanted up over his face, half concealing it. She stopped. He was surely looking at her? She waved, and hurried in through the flowering bushes of the crowded garden. By the time she had reached him the paper had slid over his face, and his hands were folded over his chest. She stood looking around. The house was warmly glowing off sunlight from its red brick, the leaves glittered, across the street the acres of the park stretched in lawns and ordered flower beds and calm unmoving trees. There was no wind. A servant was chopping wood at the back of the house. There was no sign of Mrs Quest. She pulled up a chair and sat close to him, waiting. She could see his closed eyes just over the edge of the paper. The sun shone warm over the lines and creases of his face. A little mesh of lines at the corner of his eye quivered. This time, she thought, I'll stay here till you wake. You aren't going to escape from it.

A couple of birds dropped from a tree into the bird bath,

and dipped and swooped over it in flashes of yellow and black. They fought in a ball of flying feathers, bounced apart, and then, with a flurry of chitterings, rose together into the tree. Mr Quest opened his eyes cautiously in the direction of the noise. Seeing his daughter in the corner of his vision, he let out a groan, and let his head fall back again.

'Daddy!' said Martha indignantly.

He remained with his eyes shut for a few moments, then opened them, and slowly woke up, blinking. He coughed, and inquired as if he had just seen her, 'Well, old chap?' But his eyes were evasive. 'Lord, that was a deep sleep,' he observed. 'Those birds are making a row.' They were fighting again; drops of water flew sparkling from the bird bath as they skimmed shrilly over it.

'Oh, very well,' said Martha crossly, getting up.

'Just going in to see your mother?' inquired Mr Quest hopefully. 'Well, that's a good thing. I'm not feeling very well this morning.' He pulled his paper upright and began to read.

Perhaps he didn't see me after all? she wondered. Then she saw in his eyes that sly, triumphant gleam she knew so well. She smiled, intending that he should see it. But he would not look. She walked off dispiritedly to the house.

Mrs Quest was cutting out on the back veranda. Piles of white material lay everywhere.

Martha had been planning a quiet, reasonable discussion with her mother, who would first be upset, and then understand her point of view. This consoling fantasy had even included a warm embrace, and tears shed together. It was only when she actually arrived in her mother's presence that she understood this was absurd.

'Oh, is that you, Matty?' Mrs Quest said, and went on cutting. She had a look of withdrawn, sullen disapproval. Martha thought that her mother was rather like Douglas just then, there was that swollen reddened look about the face, the accusing eyes. But she went straight into battle, with the abrupt announcement, heart pounding, knees trembling: 'Mother, I am going to leave Douglas.'

Mrs Quest went on cutting for a moment, the big scissors

flashing. Her hands were shaking. The scissors fumbled and slipped. She turned on Martha, hands lifted in fists. 'Mrs Talbot told me. I always knew you'd come to this,' she cried dramatically.

Martha had not expected the torrent of abuse that then followed. She realized that all the arguments she had come armed with were irrelevant. She must listen to this until its end, crossing off one after another, as it were, the threats and accusations which were supplied to Mrs Quest – by what? She sounded like a vituperative kitchenmaid. Martha had no idea that this elderly and proper matron knew such language. Mrs Quest said that Martha was killing her father; Martha said briskly, 'Nonsense.' Mrs Quest said she was ruining Caroline; to which Martha replied that she could not see, even at the very worst, that Caroline would turn out any worse or more neurotic than the children of ordinary marriages. Mrs Quest said she would never speak to Martha again, and that she must immediately marry that corporal, or whatever he was, and go to England to save her, Mrs Quest, from this disgrace. Finally, she wrung her hands and said it was a woman's role to sacrifice herself, as she had done for the sake of her children.

Martha reflected that Mrs Quest did not really believe in any of this, she was simply playing a role laid down for her.

Just as, in early middle age, she had written letters to be opened after her death, which she felt was imminent, to her husband choosing his future wife, to her children exhorting them to forget her immediately and not to wear mourning – behaviour which, as Martha had discovered from inquiries among her friends, was common to all their mothers at a certain stage in life – so now did she feel she must refuse ever to see Martha again, must exclaim over and over again that Martha was killing her father.

But at last she cried out in complete despair, from the heart, 'And what will people say?' For this was the kernel of the matter.

Martha went home with the feeling that she had accomplished another stage in that curious process which would set her free.

And now it was that the thought of parting with Caroline became real. She took the child into the garden. Caroline played with her toys on a rug, while Martha talked to her. She felt as if the child understood perfectly what she was saying – more, that there was only one person who really understood her, and that was Caroline. She felt a deep bond between them, of sympathy and understanding. When Caroline lifted her arms to be picked up, Martha took her on her lap, and for the last time touched the small round knees, the perfect dimpled arms, and was pleased because Caroline would never stay quiet in her arms: she was at once striving to be up, twisting herself to reach over her mother's shoulder for some leaves, or bending for a feathery head of grass. Martha held the energetic and vibrant little creature tight for a moment, and whispered in a flush of pure tenderness, 'You'll be perfectly free, Caroline. I'm setting you free.'

Then she gave the child to Mrs Knowell, and went indoors. She packed her clothes and her books. These belonged to her. She would not touch any of the things that she had brought into the ménage: nothing that had been given to the marriage, rather than to herself. She left the wardrobe empty, save for her mother's coats and wraps.

Then she waited for Douglas to come. He did not until very late that night. He had been with Mrs Quest.

He looked savagely at her and said, 'I'm going to make you have another baby.' He did not believe it, but he said it, gripping her shoulders and twisting them. The door was open into the next room, where Mrs Knowell sat knitting.

'You ought to shut the door first, at least,' said Martha with a grunt of nervous laughter.

He started back, looked vaguely around, and went to shut it. She wondered what was coming next. He took a few steps towards her, then turned and went to a cupboard and pulled out a revolver. It was the revolver he had insisted on leaving with her when he went up north with the Army.

'I shall shoot you and Caroline,' he said to her. He started rummaging for bullets. He stood up, fitting in the greasy plugs of steel. He was crying, she saw with discomfort. The tears were springing from under his swollen lids and splashing on to his shirt. She thought, Well, he might shoot us. But she was unable to believe in it.

He finished arranging the revolver, and stood pointing it vaguely in her direction, his face working. He thought for a while, then said in a voice choked but full of satisfaction, 'I shall shoot Caroline first and you afterwards.' He went into the nursery. Martha followed him to the door, her heart pounding with fear. He was bending over the cot, shaking with sobs, the hand holding the revolver hanging loose at his side. But his eyes were rolling around in her direction to see if she was watching him.

She went into the drawing room and said to his mother, 'Douglas says he's going to shoot Caroline and me.' She laughed, and again noted the hysteria in her voice. She steadied herself and said in a flat steady voice, 'I don't think for a moment that he will, but he says so.'

Mrs Knowell did not look at Martha. She laid aside her knitting, with tight sad lips, and came into the bedroom. Now Douglas was standing in the middle of the room, the revolver dangling loose from his hand. He was saying, 'I shall shoot myself. I have nothing to live for.'

His mother went to him and took him in her arms, and murmured, 'There, there, my baby. She won't leave you, she won't.'

Martha said nothing. Douglas staggered a few steps, and collapsed, heaving with sobs, on the bed. Mrs Knowell was saying, 'It's all right, dear. She couldn't leave you – could you, Matty?' Now she looked with peremptory anger at Martha, the yellowing eyes exhausted, but not frightened. Martha obeyed her. She came and sat down on the other side of Douglas, but was unable to touch him. She saw that what his mother wanted was for her to put her arms around Douglas and promise in a maternal murmur that she would not leave him. This was what Douglas was waiting for.

She saw the revolver still dangling limp in his fingers. She took it from him, rose, and went to the dressing table. With her back to the couple sitting on the edge of the bed, she clumsily slid the chamber around and let the bullets fall out. She had never handled the thing before.

Then she stood looking helplessly at them. Mrs Knowell was still murmuring in that dry tired voice: 'It's all right, it's all right.' And Douglas was seated, his thighs apart, looking at her with insistent reddened eyes.

Suddenly she lifted the empty revolver and handed it to him – she did not know why. He took it, then bounced up, letting out a yell of affronted rage. 'Matty!' he yelled. 'Matty!'

Mrs Knowell rose, and said drily, 'I think you'd both better get to bed and have some sleep.' She went out.

Douglas stood, his face working, doubtful of what he would do next. Then he said, 'I shall go out and shoot myself.' He repeated it, waiting for her to appeal to him.

'Oh, do stop it, Douglas,' she said, exasperated.

He held his shoulders straight, then whirled around and marched out with the revolver into the moonlight. There was a bright moon that night.

She sat for a while thinking, Perhaps I ought to go after him. Then, in a small flush of panic: Perhaps he managed to put a bullet in the chamber after all. But she knew he had not.

After all, she thought, people do shoot themselves. They do it constantly, she added, unable to stop herself salting in the humour. It was no good: not for a moment was she able to believe he would shoot himself. She rolled over on the bed and was asleep immediately.

When she woke, everything was very quiet, and Douglas was standing at the foot of the bed looking at her with his steady reproach. 'You've been asleep,' he ground out.

'You haven't let me have half an hour's consecutive sleep in weeks,' she pointed out.

He carefully put the revolver away in his drawer, collected the bullets from the dressing table, and fitted them into their box. Then he turned towards her. His face was quite different, set and murderous. She thought, Those women said there was a point where they started knocking you about. She remembered the satisfaction in their voices and thought, Oh, no, not for me. She quickly stood up beside the bed, warily facing him, every sense alert. He was leaning forward now, about to spring.

'Douglas!' she cried out. But it was too late. He jumped, brought her down, and began pulling out handfuls of her hair. She thought, I simply will not – I won't! She struggled a little, then, as he was shifting his hands for a better grip, rolled free sideways along the floor and got to her feet. He was coming after her. She walked straight out of the room, into the garden, and out into the street. Moonlight was pouring down. It was long after midnight; the houses were all dark.

She was going to her mother. I'll stay with her until morning, she thought, and then come and get my things.

She walked steadily down the middle of the street, which glared white with the moon, banked by the heavy dark trees. He was following her. It was about ten minutes' walk to the other house. She was numb, her knees shook, but she made herself walk quietly, although she could feel fear crinking up and down her back in cold waves at the thought that he was coming after her. But as soon as she glanced over her shoulder and saw him, she was not afraid. He came striding along, head down, like someone training for a walking match, she thought disgustedly.

It seemed a very long way. She had time to think of many things: she had forgotten to pack her sponge; she must tell Alice about Caroline's lunch tomorrow – Caroline did not like carrots, it was absurd that Alice kept cooking them, children should not be made to eat what they did not like; she must remember to tell the cook to whip the ice cream in good time . . .

As she neared the gate, which gleamed dead white, she heard him running. She began to run, in an impulse of pure panic. They reached the veranda together. He reached out to grab her shoulder; she twisted it under his hand and fled to a window, where she banged hard on the glass.

Now he stood behind her, breathing heavily.

The window opened inwards; her mother stood there, blinking with sleep.

'I want to speak to you,' said Martha quickly.

'Wait a minute,' said Mrs Quest nervously.

She vanished, and Martha ran to the door off the veranda. Douglas followed. Mrs Quest stood in the doorway, and Martha said, 'Mother, I want to come in.'

Mrs Quest looked at Martha and at Douglas with a sullen disapproving face.

'Mother,' said Martha desperately, 'I must come in, let me in.'

Douglas had gripped both her arms from behind and was wrenching them methodically.

'Mother!' she yelled out.

Mrs Quest looked away and said evasively, 'But it's late, what are you doing here?'

'Mother!' wailed Martha. Her arms were almost being wrenched out of their sockets. It had never entered her head that her mother would not let her in. Now she saw that it was obvious she would not. Mrs Quest observed them furtively, and on to her face came a look of satisfaction and pleasure.

'He's hurting me,' said Martha, keeping her voice steady now, out of pride.

'Be quiet, you'll wake your father, he's not well.'

'Mother, you aren't going to let him bully me?'

'Well, you deserve it,' said Mrs Quest. 'He's quite right. Now go back to bed,' she added quickly, in a vaguely admonishing way.

Douglas, apparently as surprised as Martha, had let go her arms. She stood rubbing them, looking at her mother. Then she shrugged and laughed. For Mrs Quest was retreating hurriedly indoors.

'Go back to him,' she was saying, 'it serves you right.' The door shut in Martha's face.

That cold dark door shut in her face made Martha go sick inside for a moment. Then she said in a bright angry voice, 'Well, so much for that.' She turned to Douglas and said, 'And now let's go home.' She set off walking, not caring whether he followed or not. She no longer cared about him one way or the other.

He came up level with her. 'Lord, what a performance,'

she remarked, laughing angrily. 'What's it all about? You don't believe in it, I don't believe in it – what do we do it for, then?'

'I suppose you arranged that so as to have a witness?' he asked suddenly.

'What do you mean?' She had no idea what he was talking about.

They walked the distance in silence. She was not at all afraid of him now. He was not there, for her.

When they reached the bedroom, she said at once, 'And now I'm going to sleep.' She fell on the bed fully dressed, and added casually, 'I shall leave you tomorrow morning.'

She saw a look of satisfied misery on his face. He let out a calculated groan, collapsed on the bed face down. But he was asleep at once.

In the morning he was quite changed. He looked almost obsequious. 'I'll help you to pack,' he said.

'I think that's taking it too far,' she said. 'Besides, I am packed.'

'Well, you'd better take the car for your things.'

'Oh – I don't need it.'

'I suppose *he* will come and fetch them.'

The truth was that she had almost forgotten William.

'I'll tell you one thing,' he said, in a firm agonizing voice, 'I shan't give you a divorce.'

'I haven't asked for one,' she pointed out. Then she added spitefully, 'I suppose it hasn't entered your head that I could divorce you for what happened in Y—?'

His face changed. Far from not having thought of it, she saw, he had worked it all out, and had already probably taken legal advice. He had a crafty considering look, and was blinking his eyes, framing a noncommittal answer which would not give him away, when she said with a sort of gay contempt, 'My poor Douglas, my poor, poor Douglas.'

She picked up her suitcase and looked about. She had forgotten nothing.

'Do take the car, Matty,' he pleaded sentimentally.

'Oh, well, I give up,' she said. 'Good, I'll be delighted to use it. I'll bring it back in half an hour.'

He carried her case to the car. When they reached it, they saw Mrs Talbot and Elaine coming towards them under the trees, which were lit with early-morning sunlight. They wore pale summer dresses and large straw hats. It was about nine in the morning.

Martha thought. What can have happened to get Mrs Talbot out of bed so early? Then Douglas went forward to welcome them. He had slumped into a pose of weary suffering. His smile at Mrs Talbot was the quivering smile of a child. He shook Elaine's hand wordlessly. Martha stood dumb. An idea had come into her mind: Obviously Elaine would marry Douglas. Nothing could be more satisfactory. All the same, she felt a pang at the thought of Elaine in her place, Elaine with Caroline. Almost, almost, she gave in and went back.

The three of them, Mrs Talbot, Elaine and Douglas, were standing in a group beside the car, waiting for her to get in.

Suddenly Douglas's face worked again. 'Matty, you haven't said goodbye to Caroline – surely you'll see her before you go?'

That was for the benefit of Mrs Talbot and Elaine. She saw them exchange the briefest of shocked, comprehending smiles.

She got into the car, which was filled with books at the back. Her two suitcases were beside her. Her eyes were half blinded with tears. But she blinked them clear, and drove away.

As she reached the corner of the street she saw Mr Maynard come strolling down under the trees on his way to the Courts. He raised his hand, and she stopped.

'Deserting?' he inquired.

'Quite so.'

'You look extraordinarily pleased about it.' It was true, she was now so elated she felt as light as an air bubble. 'Well, what are you going to do now?'

She misunderstood him and said, 'I'm going to drop my things in my room, look for a job, and then – there are five hundred envelopes to be addressed before tomorrow morning.' She said it as if describing the height of human bliss.

'Well, well, well,' he commented.

She slowly let out the clutch.

'I suppose with the French Revolution for a father and the Russian Revolution for a mother, you can very well dispense with a family,' he observed. She pushed in the clutch again and looked at him from behind that veil which was between her and the rest of the world. After a while she conceded, 'That is really a very intelligent remark.'

'Not at all.'

'I really am in a hurry, Mr Maynard.'

'So I can see. I'm not going to forgive you for leaving my goddaughter,' he said, smiling painfully.

'I haven't asked you to,' she said coldly, wincing. She shrugged herself up in the driver's seat as if chilly, and her face looked pinched and bleak.

'Well, good luck, at any rate,' he said suddenly, rather gruff.

Her smile at him was painful. She was going to cry, he could see. He hastily raised his hat, and walked off in one direction, while the car slid off in another.

Printed by RR Donnelley at Glasgow, UK